W9-BYA-549

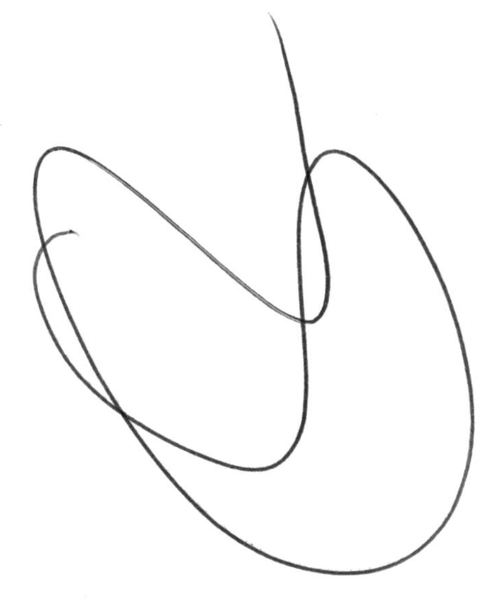

CAMERON KELLY ROSENBLUM

Quill Tree Books
An Imprint of HarperCollinsPublishers

Dedicated with love and laughter to TFB,
an indelible spirit

Quill Tree Books is an imprint of HarperCollins Publishers.

The Stepping Off Place
 For information address HarperCollins Children's Books, a division of HarperCollins Publishers, 195 Broadway, New York, NY 10007.
www.epicreads.com
Library of Congress Control Number: 2019957880
ISBN 978-0-06-293207-5
Typography by Catherine San Juan
20 21 22 23 24 PC/LSCH 10 9 8 7 6 5 4 3 2 1
❖
First Edition

I USED TO THINK OUR MEMORIES BELONG TO US. Now I don't think they're that cooperative. They interrupt when they please, and leave right when you want to hold them in your hands and arrange them on a shelf, so they tell the story you think they should. They haunt you or comfort you at will. But when memories are all you have left of a person, you'll take them thin as the tail of a cloud or so thick you're lost in them for hours. Just don't ever assume you have memories; your memories definitely have you.

In my mind's eye, I watch the one of me leaving my Scofield Dinner Theater job that day in August right before the start of senior year, worrying about things that didn't matter for shit, completely oblivious to the way my world was about to detonate. Shouldn't I want to be that version of me again? Obviously the correct answer is yes. The weird thing is, I don't think I do.

PART ONE

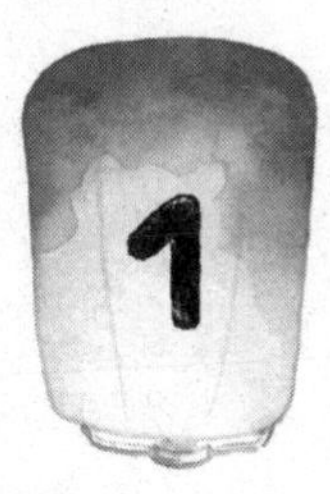

August 27

I didn't know this was the day I would stop breathing.

It was rush hour in my hometown of Scofield, Connecticut, and I was heading home from my matinee hostess shift at the dinner theater. Unfortunately, I'd forgotten my running clothes and still wore my compulsory hostess uniform: a polyester "girl tux" with a skirt instead of pants, too-thick panty hose, and black loafers. God help me. I just hoped nobody spotted me. I crept along with the other cars jammed on the Post Road. It was the kind of traffic where you should pay attention so you don't rear-end someone, but the sky was so captivating I couldn't take my eyes from it.

The clouds were equal-sized puffs arranged as though a pastry chef had carefully decorated the endless sweep of peacock-feather blue. It was so impossible and so much like this Georgia O'Keeffe print Hattie had hanging in her bedroom called *Sky above Clouds IV*, it bordered on freaky. Hattie and I texted each other when we spotted one or two O'Keeffe clouds—perfectly oval ones—but this was like Georgia herself had stopped in Scofield and painted the sky. I wanted to FaceTime Hattie. She would love it.

That this would be illegal while driving wasn't the reason I didn't. I didn't FaceTime Hattie because it was August, which meant she was still at her summerhouse on The Thimble, an island off the Maine coast. The Thimble, by the way, is a six-hour drive from southern Connecticut.

Six.

Hours.

Cell service on The Thimble ranges from patchy to nonexistent, and Mr. Darrow won't get Wi-Fi up there. He prefers his islands rustic. So, not only does Hattie desert me every summer for eight solid weeks, but we can only communicate via snail mail. And she sucks at writing letters. Care packages? She rocks them. But no letters. No words. It was the Hattie Way to arrive right before school started each year. This was our last spin on the Scofield High merry-go-round. We were finally seniors.

It's hard to pinpoint when Hattie Darrow became my social oxygen. It didn't start out that way, and I don't think she meant it to happen any more than I did. We'd been best friends for almost six years, and it must have been gradual, like how our bones grew longer and our faces lost their baby plump. We didn't notice that, either.

Right now, I couldn't drag my eyes from these clouds. They seemed alive, the way they moved as one. A driver behind me beeped and I jerked my attention back to the road. That's when I saw, four cars ahead, Hattie driving her '85 VW Rabbit convertible. The top was down and she had her blond hair in a ponytail. Her shoulders were tan and I recognized the white straps of the shirt we picked out the day before she left in June.

"*Snowcap!*" I cried shamelessly. Her car is black with a white top, like the movie candy. "You're home!" I nosed up on the SUV ahead of me, but nobody was moving.

I watched Hattie's head dip to a beat, so I knew she had music on, which meant she was singing. Badly. I turned up the radio to see if her beat matched whatever songs played on our stations, but there were only commercials. Why was she back already?

We rolled past Mighty Bean, the café that may as well be part of Scofield High School.

Normally, I would hunker down so nobody could recognize me, but I reached for my phone instead, thinking

I could at least call. I saw a cop car in my rearview mirror and practically heard Hattie say, "Watch it. Johnny Law's on the case." A laugh bubbled out of me.

My need to be out of the suffocating panty hose became unbearable. Hattie wouldn't have been caught dead in them. They were a crime against the natural world, those hose. I wondered if I could slip out of them while driving, but the used Ford Fiesta I shared with my older brother Scott was a stick shift, requiring a foot on the clutch. Besides, the knot of cars scuttled forward. This was my chance.

Hattie zipped ahead, under the commuter rail bridge. I lost her. Johnny Law hooked a right toward the train station, so I buzzed around a pickup and under the bridge. I passed the Sport Shop. A mannequin clad in pastel golf clothes pointed his club toward Snowcap, cheering me on in the kind of Scofield style Hattie would have found hilarious.

I gained on her. Only a silver Jaguar separated us, driven by a coiffed matriarch I vaguely recognized as a friend of my parents. She wasn't my concern, but I tapped the horn, hoping to get Hattie's attention without seeming obnoxious.

Hattie's head remained stubbornly focused on the road ahead. The light turned green, and we were off again, down the big hill beside the graveyard. We passed the library, then the police station. At the next light, I leaned my head out the window.

"Hattie!"

Jaguar lady cast an uneasy glance in her rearview. I smiled weakly. Hattie remained oblivious, engaged in pulling the elastic from her hair, smoothing a new ponytail, and retwisting the elastic, a habit she claimed was unconscious. Though I couldn't see her face, I knew she held the elastic in her teeth.

"Hattie!" I yelled, louder. Nothing.

"*Hey, Harriet!*" I bellowed. Jaguar lady's eyebrows disappeared under her puffy gray bangs. Hattie's head maintained its metronomic dance. *Is she ignoring me?* a pathetic part of me wondered for a breath. I recognized the familiar anxiety swooping over me like a huge bird ready to land. All it needed was the opportunity, and it would roost. *No*, I told myself. Hattie wouldn't ignore me. Of course not.

But the light turned green and she sped off, alpha wolf of the traffic pack. The gap between her and the Jaguar widened. I pressed the gas and passed the Jaguar, thankful for the lack of Johnny Law. She topped Three Church Hill and was out of sight again. I smiled when I crested it and saw the red light at the next intersection. "Gotcha," I whispered.

But when I got to the line at the light, Snowcap was nowhere. I lifted my sunglasses, squinting into the horizon and its endless field of confection clouds. No Hattie.

On three of the four corners were churches. On the fourth was Pickle Barrel Deli. The choice was obvious, given her obsession with Pickle Barrel deviled eggs. They grossed me out, but I always brought her a half dozen packed on ice for my annual July Thimble visit.

I turned into the deli driveway and rolled behind the building to its small parking area. No Snowcap. I turned off the car. My lips tingled, like I'd had a shot of novocaine. I got out and stood on the concrete. My thighs were sweating under the asphyxiating hose. I tried to ignore a ripple of light-headedness.

I peeked through the deli's screen door and when she wasn't inside, I checked behind the big smelly dumpster, like maybe she'd hidden, which was stupid and of course she hadn't.

I stood motionless, between the dumpster and my car. Hattie had achieved the truly impossible. She'd vanished.

I glanced at the sky. The clouds were marching into the distance, like a passing parade. Like they'd ushered her off.

I spent the ride home trying to convince myself I must have been mistaken. I called her, Johnny be damned, but it went straight to voicemail. I imagined telling the story to Hammy. "Maybe I had a premonition," I pictured myself saying to him, "and she *was* coming home early." And Hammy would laugh, because a) he'd be as psyched as me if that were true and b) we both knew I was way too practical for premonitions.

But here's the thing. When you have to reconcile something that doesn't make sense with something your emotions say is true, your emotions win. Try to convince yourself all you want; deep down you'll know you're lying. Hattie was there. Then she wasn't. It happened.

I made my way home and tried calling her again from our driveway. Straight to voicemail again. Instead of leaving a message, which I'd long ago learned she wouldn't listen to, I texted her. *What happened to you? I saw you, then you disappeared! wtf, are you now magic?* I waited a few seconds. Nothing. I tried to shake it off. My after-work run would uncoil me, I thought. It always did. Hattie had convinced me to join the cross-country team last year, and this year we were co-captains. I totally did *not* deserve this honor, but Hattie and I were the only seniors, and I think Coach Smitty didn't want me to feel like a total loser, so she made us both captains. I'd spent all summer trying to get my 5K faster than the younger girls, and I'd become kind of accidentally addicted.

Our house was dark and quiet when I got inside, the hum of the refrigerator the only sound. Boomer, our fat black Lab mix, lifted one eyelid and rearranged himself on his bed before sighing. My little brother, Spencer, age ten and deep on the autism spectrum, is never quiet, so he must have been out with his caregiver, Linda. It's against MacGregory code to discuss it, but the only time our house is like this is when Spencer is out of it. We all love him so much. But when he's gone, we can stop checking to see if he's okay. We can let five minutes in a row pass without looking up from our books or our show or our absolutely anything.

So, yes, he was gone, and Dad of course wasn't home from NYC yet. Scott was painting houses on Martha's Vineyard with his fraternity brothers this summer and planned to go straight back to Colgate from there. Mom was probably upstairs in the office planning for her big autism charity gala in October. She had been honored by the American Autism Coalition three years in a row for her massive fund-raising success. She's a classic over-achiever, and had met her match in raising money for autism research; there is no end of need, and Laura Mac-Gregory has no end of energy to devote to it. Autism and Mom make a symbiotic perpetual motion machine. At the moment, I did not want to get recruited to stuff more envelopes. That may sound cold, but I'd stuffed in sets of fifty for weeks. I crept to the kitchen.

I stood in the light of the refrigerator, staring at milk and mayonnaise and whatnot, and wondered again if I was so desperate that I dreamed Hattie up. God, that was needy. I thought I'd made some strides this summer with Hammy, I really did.

I poured an iced tea and leaned on the kitchen table, sliding out of the loafers and peeling off the offending hose at last. They kept the shape of my feet and calves and looked something like a decomposing body on the floor tiles. I rustled them with my foot and rechecked my phone.

The stairs squeaked. My mom appeared, in her robe. It was nearly dinner. She's the kind of person who comes to breakfast dressed. More alarming, her eyes were red and puffy. "Sit down, honey," she said softly.

I had seen her cry once in my life, when our cat Leopold died. I was seven. That's it. Either she cried in private or she was superhuman. I had yet to figure out which. My neck pulsed. "Will you sit?" she repeated. "Please?" I obeyed.

"What?" My lips tingled again. "Where's Spencer?" In a flash of sickening clarity I saw our family without him, floundering like fish on a hot dock. Who would we even be? My breathing sped up.

Mom shook her head. "Spencer's fine." Her voice was strangled. She covered my hands with her cool ones. "It's Hattie," she whispered. "Something terrible has happened."

Her words bounced off my face. "I just saw her."

My mom squared her shoulders. The room vibrated with the fridge. She closed her eyes and kept them closed. I watched tears travel the newly charted path on her cheeks. It was chaos. Blackness leaked over my peripheral vision. "I'm so sorry, Reid," she was saying, "but Hattie drowned last night in Maine."

"No she didn't," my voice said, but a hole started to tear open deep inside me. I saw her in my mind, passing the Jaguar just a few minutes ago. Didn't I?

She looked up at me from her chair. Her lips vanished she squeezed them so tight. She nodded and nodded, her nostrils red and trembling.

"Stop doing that!" I wanted to slap her away, this weird version of my mother. "She did not!"

My mother was a crumbling statue, dropping her head. Her shoulders convulsed. Twice. She inhaled and leveled her eyes with mine. "Reid, it's true. Her uncle Baxter called an hour ago. I spoke to him myself. She . . . Hattie . . ." Her tears ran in rivulets, but her eyes had mine in a choke hold. "They're investigating it as a suicide."

I heard myself laugh through a sob. "That's fucking ridiculous." I couldn't look at her and took my glass to the sink. The air had dissolved into buzzing molecules swimming around me.

"It's still unclear," she whispered. "But—"

"*Shut up!*" I threw the glass down. I never talked to her like this, and it was empowering and disgusting. The glass didn't break and I whirled to yell at her more, but her face was red and twisted in a silent cry.

"Oh God," I croaked, nauseous. Rubber legs carried me to the back door. Boomer heard the screen slide open and rushed to my side. We bumped into each other and I stumbled onto the flagstone patio to the edge of the pool, searching the sky. No more evenly spaced confections. The clouds had dissolved into tatters, ripped sails that betrayed me.

Our O'Keeffe sky was gone.

I couldn't breathe. I never would again.

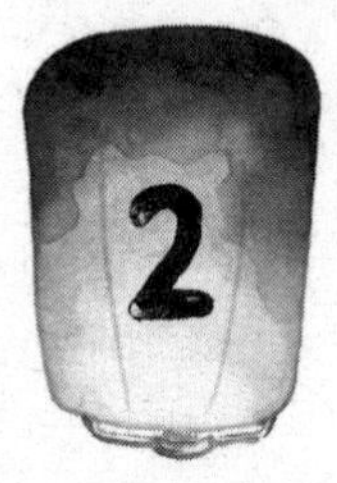

THEN

June 18 ~ Two Months Earlier

Hattie and I drifted around the pool on our floats like lily pads. We hadn't said or moved much in the last hour, soaking in the end of a long afternoon of sun. We had officially become Scofield seniors today at 12:35 p.m., Eastern Standard Time, after the final exam. It was Hattie's last night in Scofield, and thank God, because a kinda bitchy girl who just graduated, Sabrina Bradley, was having a huge summer send-off party and I would never go alone. Tomorrow, Hattie would leave for The Thimble.

When I first heard of the summerhouse on an island

named The Thimble, I pictured a quaint cottage with brightly painted lobster buoys hanging on the front door. Wrong. The Thimble was a private island the Darrows had owned for three generations, by my count. The house had six bedrooms and was part of a family compound, complete with a stable, a dock, and a boathouse. Mr. Darrow loved sailing.

I was gazing at a group of clouds that resembled a school of fish, debating whether they were worth mentioning, when Hattie said, "I'm going to lose it tonight at Bradley's." Hattie's the kind of person who calls a junior-snubbing senior like Sabrina by her last name—to her face—which is so brazen it impresses the senior and earns Hattie acceptance. Fondness, even.

"Huh?" I responded lazily. My fingers played across the top of the warm water trapped in the raft with me.

"I just decided." Hattie's voice is sort of low and a little raspy, which can make it seem like she's letting you in on a joke. Which a lot of times she is. Now she lay on her belly, eyes closed, which we both knew was her way of prompting me to question her.

Always game, I said, "Care to elaborate?"

"I'm getting this whole virginity thing over with," she replied. "Tonight."

I rose to my elbows. Cold water spilled into the raft. "What?"

She still didn't move. "I don't want to be a virgin anymore. Think about it. It's a burden."

"A burden?"

"Yeah. You keep waiting for the right guy, and all that is just bullshit. There is no *right guy* in Scofield. Which means I go through senior year a virgin, and the next thing you know I'm in college, and nobody in college wants to sleep with a virgin."

"Seriously?" I cocked one eyebrow.

"Yeah. Nobody worth sleeping with, anyway. I'm not going to be the inexperienced one. You can spot inexperience a mile away."

I couldn't suppress my laughter. "Oh my God. You think you can tell who's a virgin by looking at them?"

"Can't you? Compare Fiona Mejos to Emma Rose."

"You're ridiculous." But picturing Fiona's clear eyes and uncomplicated smile, I had to admit Hattie might be right. As for Emma Rose, she'd probably hit on my dad if she had the chance. What did my eyes give away? I held my breath and rolled into the water.

"You should consider doing it too, Reddi-wip," she said when I surfaced next to her float. During a seventh-grade ice-cream-sundae-making session, she contorted my name, *Reid*, into *Reddi-wip* when she discovered you only had to flip two letters and double the *d*. "That's you, Reddi for Action!" she'd said. It used to be ironic. As far as she knew, it still was.

My cheeks flushed and I splashed water on them in what I hoped was a nonchalant way. Hattie didn't know I'd lost my virginity already, with Jay Seavers at the junior-senior prom about a month earlier. I felt guilty not telling her all this time. We both knew he was an ass. How could I explain it to her? I couldn't even explain it to myself. When Jay looked at me with his way-too-hot-for-me eyes, I threw caution and my awesome green prom dress to the wind. And we did it. On the sixteenth hole of Howebrook Country Club golf course. He wasn't even my date.

It was reckless, and I was never reckless—of my own accord, that is. Admittedly, this was a pretty big exception. And I was surprised by how exhilarating it was. Not the sex itself. I mean being so un-*me*. The sex was, well, uncomfortable if not painful. But the kissing part? The gateway drug to my fast, hard fall.

At first, I couldn't wait to tell Hattie. But she slept all Sunday after the prom and bagged school on Monday *and* Tuesday—which she had done a lot this year. I don't know how she talked her mom into so many excused days. Twelve times since September. That's three more than Ferris Bueller, and he's *from a movie about skipping school.* As it turned out, I was glad she wasn't with me in the cafeteria that Monday, for what I now know was the most humiliating moment of my life thus far. Here's the thing: when Captain Dickhead saw me smiling at him from my lunch table, he averted his gaze and walked right past me. Like I didn't exist. I feel sick even recounting it in my head. It was so mean, and made him an even bigger asshole than I already knew him to be, yet clearly

I was the one feeling like a loser. How had I done this to myself? I tried not to think about it, let alone talk about it. But it snuck up on me at weird moments and gutted me anew, this feeling that I was an embarrassment. With Hattie, I could get my bearings again and know it was him, not me. Most of the time.

"You might surprise yourself," Hattie was saying, "and find you're a real tiger in the sack." She added a growl.

We laughed and I tried to flip over her raft, but she paddled water at me.

I pulled myself to sit on the pool edge. "Meanwhile, let me push your thinking here."

"Go ahead, but my mind's made up." She rolled over and looked into the sky. "Hey, a school of fish," she said.

"Focus!" I said, hiding my awe at our synchronized imaginations. "First off, there's trouble with your reasoning. I completely agree that there are no Mr. Rights in Scofield—besides Gib Soule maybe—but this party is in Scofield, and is, therefore, bound to be populated by only Scofield guys."

"And your point?"

I didn't know what my point was, so I changed tack. "Why don't you wait till you're in Maine and fulfill your destiny with Santi?"

"That's incestuous."

Lie. The Family Herrera shared The Thimble with the Family Darrow. The Darrows came from Boston. The Herreras came from Valparaíso, Chile. Mr. Herrera and Mr. Darrow rowed crew together at Princeton or prep school or maybe both. Santiago was our age and definitely *not* a relative of Hattie's.

"I call BS."

"Gross," she said flatly.

It was pointless to argue—she'd never cave—so I said, "Wait, you're just going to pick up someone random?"

"Probably," she said, as if not having all the kinks worked out of her scheme was perfectly okay. "I leave tomorrow, so it's not like I have to face him anytime soon." She paused. "I'll aim for someone I kind of like."

"Someone like who?" I asked.

Just then my brother Scott came out from the house. Scott played lacrosse at Colgate. He got the lion's share of MacGregory athletic genes.

"Reid, where'd you put the keys?" he said, then noticed Hattie. "Hey, Darrow. Where's it at, puddy tat?"

"On the fly, porkie pie."

"Don't I know it, GI Joe-it."

They laughed. They'd done variations of this routine since forever.

"GI Joe-it?" I repeated.

"Some day you'll be a hepcat, too, Reid," Scott said.

"She's a closet hepcat. It's in there somewhere, right, Reddi-wip?" Hattie said, climbing the pool ladder. Scott was unable to resist a full visual sweep of her body. She was getting really beautiful in a way that made me feel happy and left behind at the same time.

I squinted at Scott. "Busted," I whispered.

In middle school, Hattie and I had been the last girls to hit puberty. Boys noticed her for her hijinks and because she won every damn sport she played, but they didn't crush on her. We did eventually catch up, sort of, but it was this year that Hattie emerged from the pasty winter months like one of those iridescent-blue rain forest butterflies. Suddenly, we were included at all the parties, and not because of me. I was jealous at first, but I hated that shallow part of me and willed it away.

Scott rolled his eyes. "Keys?" he said too loudly.

"Dining room table."

"Catch ya on the flip side," he called, disappearing into the house.

"Jim jam in the double-wide," Hattie replied. She wrapped the towel under her armpits, grinning.

I stared at her.

"What?" Sometimes she laughs *while* she's talking, like her words and her laughter are competing for air time. It's contagious. Usually.

"You were going to tell me *who* the lucky guy is tonight." My voice was sharp, for me, and I wasn't sure why her plan irritated me so much. Because I had blown my chance to lose my virginity in such a power move? Or because I'd never have the guts?

"I'll decide at the party," she said.

"What if people find out?" I said. I'd worried the same about me and Captain D. A lot. My pulse thudded in my neck and I brought my hand up to smooth the skin.

She made a "duh" face.

I stared again.

She shook her head. "Reid, you can choose not to give a shit."

I didn't know how to respond. How was that a choice?

She patted my shoulder on her way to the screen door. "You want to go on a run before dinner?"

It was eight o'clock when we left for Sabrina Bradley's, and the June sky had only just begun to turn pearly. Besides the Post Road, Scofield's roads are residential, winding and thick with trees—all-around intoxicating to drive on with the windows down to the first party of summer, even in a bomber like the Fiesta. "How about Shunsuke, your crew buddy? He seems undemanding," I offered. Since I couldn't conjure a good reason, any reason, why Hattie's little operation was a flawed plan—and I tried during our run and then again while we got ready for tonight—I jumped on board. It was fun, actually, since it was ridiculous and I risked nothing. In her mind, neither did she.

"Shunsuke, yes. I do like his shoulders," she said, just as that obnoxious Cake Pops song came on the radio. "Oh my God!" she squawked, cranking the volume. She rocked out from the waist up. "I can have it!" A raspy voice is pure gold for many singers—from Etta James to Adele. Not so much for Hattie. She sounds like a bagpiper's warm-up: off-key and desperate. In middle school chorus, the music teacher's aide privately asked her to lip sync during the concert. It's the only time I've seen Hattie wounded by someone's opinion. Probably because it's the only thing she truly sucks at. Now she considers it hilarious and uses her singing to torture me.

"My ears are bleeding," I said.

She chuckled and turned it down, still humming. Even that was off tune.

"So Shunsuke's an option," I said. "Or you could pick a guy who just graduated. Then he'd be gone next year." It was like shopping for a new outfit, one that would look better on Hattie than on me, which was more or less every outfit.

"Good idea."

"Or Hammy. He's always loved you." I waited. She'd ramped up the dancing for Cake Pops' final chorus. I realized I was avoiding looking at her, which in general is a good thing while driving, but my motives were more mysterious. I felt strangely protective of Hammy—officially named Sam Stanwich, but dubbed Ham Sandwich, the Sandwich, or Hammy in fourth grade.

"Nah," she said. "I thought about it at the prom, but Hammy knows me too well." We rolled to a four-way stop. "Plus, he's so skinny."

True, Hammy'd had a recent growth spurt. He was six feet and virtually invisible when he turned sideways. Think Flat Stanley. Still, I'd witnessed the thinly veiled, unrequited crush he had on her, and it kind of made me love him. *For her.* Not for me. Which is really sad—developing a vicarious crush on someone because you like the way he likes your best friend? I guess I just wished she was nicer to him.

I shook my head, secretly talking to both of us when I said, "This is complicated."

"Not really," she said. "I'm just not into him. Padiddle!" She tried to thump me on the arm—protocol when you see a car with one headlight—but I beat her to it.

"Ow." She rubbed the spot.

"That's my third win," I said. "I'm posing a challenge to the Padiddle Queen."

"Never," she said.

I snickered. "You are so competitive."

I slowed when we got to Maywood Road, turning onto the street. The homes, like most in Scofield, were large and very expensive, landscaped to perfection. It's pretty easy to hide a big party like this here. Cops would either have to be alerted or stumble upon it.

Sabrina herself was on the very edge of the ruling clique of seniors who'd just graduated. She'd been the kind of senior who flirted with the junior boys and made the junior girls, Hattie aside, feel like they owed her a favor for being alive. Word was her parents flew to a wedding in California and left her older sister, Eve, in charge. Eve was "taking a year off" from Boston University and really shouldn't have been in charge of anything, let alone a house on two acres and Sabrina, but the cluelessness of some parents knows no bounds. In any case, I had to wedge the Fiesta between two willow trees to park.

"Well, *this* is the place to be," Hattie said as we squeezed out our doors. She started across the moonlit lawn. It stretched around the immense house like a moat. People clustered on the terrace, bathed in yellow light. "What's that quote about moths and whispers and champagne in *The Great Gatsby*?" I asked. I was stalling, suddenly overwhelmed by the energy it would require for me to appear like I belonged here.

"I didn't read it," she said. She glanced at me standing there and stopped walking. Hattie belonged. Naturally. I only belonged by virtue of her. "It'll be fun," she said quietly, coaxing me with her eyes.

"I know," I lied. The summer ahead already felt like an eternity. Ever since the ill-fated golf course sex romp, I'd been having waves of the kind of social anxiety I had back in fourth and fifth grade, pre-Hattie. The humiliation had a life of its own in my imagination sometimes. Like now.

"You sell yourself short, Reddi MacGregory," she said, reading my mind without knowing it. "PS, I'm not going in without you." She linked her arm through mine, humming the Disney movie *Brave* theme song. This was a long-standing joke based on the fact that I do resemble the main character more than a little—especially after we frizzed my wet hair by twisting it into dozens of braids and then unbraiding it. Hattie broke into the lyrics with an attempted Scottish brogue as she twirled me around by the elbow.

I laughed. "Your voice is so bad!" But she got me over the hump, and we ran to the hedge shadows to spy.

"Damn," she marveled.

Holding the keg nozzle: Gib Soule. I could actually see his perfect white teeth from here. Dark hair swept across his forehead as if to say, "Behold! The masterpiece of Gibson Soule's blue eyes." Smoking hot, this boy. He could have had any girl at SHS, probably repeatedly, but he kept one girlfriend at a time for months on end, loyal as my dog Boomer. This made hearts everywhere stir all the more fervently, of course.

Until his dad died in fifth grade, Gib lived in my neighborhood, and we'd played in the same games of flashlight tag. In those days I full-on loved him, in spite of the fact I never raised the nerve to say more than "Not it!" to him. Eventually I recognized my futility and moved on. Now he lived downtown with his mom and her new wife. Next to Gib stood Max Silverman and Hammy. The usual suspects populated the rest of the patio, mixed with older friends of Sabrina's sister, Eve, the supposed babysitter here.

"What about Max?" I whispered with fake innocence. As if on cue, Max punctuated some story he was telling by commencing a weird hip-thrusting dance. Gib and Hammy cracked up.

She laugh-said, “No thanks! The arm hair—he’s like Chewbacca.”

“It’s settled, then,” I said. “Gib’s your man.”

“Yep,” she said. “I guess I have no choice.”

“I’ll tell him.” I rushed ahead, but she passed me and broke into the pool of light as if stepping into her scene onstage. I watched all the faces turn, then followed.

“Hey, look.” Max nodded to us. “Batman and Robin.” He threw his head back, laughing at his own joke.

“Shut up,” Hattie said, slugging his arm.

“And it’s Gumby and Pokey,” I said, meaning Max and Hammy, but there were three of them standing there, so it didn’t really make sense and I felt myself blush. Thankfully, everyone chuckled.

“Hi, Gib,” Hattie said. I echoed her, sounding stupid.

“Ladies,” he said, casually flashing the smile that stopped a thousand hearts. Deep down, he must have known he was hot, but he never let on.

“Beer?” Max held up two cups, showcasing the Chewie arms. Hattie and I laughed with our eyes. I had to look at my sandals.

“Sure,” Hattie said. “How much do we owe?”

“Gratis for you, Harriet,” he said. “Of course.”

I shifted my weight.

“And you, too, Reid,” Hammy added. Sweet Hammy. “Max keeps telling the girls their beer is free, like he’s all generous, but Eva’s frat boy friends donated it.”

Max grinned. “Cheers.”

We clacked cups. I wasn't a big drinker, but I appreciated the social lubricant a beer provided in moments like these. I wiped foam from my lip. "Where's Charlie?" I asked. Charlie Bishop had been my own platonic prom date. I should've stuck with him instead of Captain Dickhead.

"He's here somewhere, with"—Hammy twirled his hands with a flourish—"*Alesha*."

"Ohhhhhh!" Hattie and I said at the same time. "*Aleeeeeesha!*"

"They're back together and the world is right again," Gib said.

We laughed. Charlie obsessed about Alesha, and everyone gave him crap about it. I found it kind of endearing.

Just then, Gib's recent ex-girlfriend, Priya Patel-Smith, came through the French doors from the kitchen. Priya had sleek black hair and moved like the world was her personal catwalk. She'd edited the school paper for three years and was off to Yale in the fall. It was unusual for a girl of her caliber to date a junior, but who wouldn't break the rules for Gib Soule? So nobody was surprised when she dumped him, but for the Braeburn hockey goalie? It was excessively cruel, since Braeburn is Scofield's biggest rival in all sports, *especially* hockey, and Gib was the star junior this year. Plus she had apparently been flinging with the guy for weeks, but waited until the day after prom to break up with Gib, just so she could go.

Gib turned toward her before he possibly could have seen her, as if he sensed her presence intuitively. His face softened immediately and for a flash, all Gib's vulnerabilities passed across his eyes. He demi-smiled. Priya nodded. Gib's face tightened and he turned back toward us *just* in time to catch me watching him.

Crap! Such a voyeur! I glued my sight line on Max and took an extra-long pull off my beer, hiding behind the cup.

Max finished whatever story he was telling now and the three boys burst out laughing, Gib heartiest of all. *That's the spirit, Gib.*

A bunch of kids approached the keg, putting Max and the Sandwich to work. Hattie pointed over my shoulder. A small crowd had gathered around a pool table in the family room, including Shunsuke. She looked at me slyly. "Reid, may I challenge you to a game of billiards?"

"You may," I replied. We left the boys by the keg.

On the way through the French doors, Sabrina collided with me, then muttered something like, "Whoamph." Looking at me in a bleary-eyed, vaguely Quasimodo way, she straightened her jade miniskirt, flashing us a pretty sizable boob in the process.

"Sor-ry, Reid." Then she spotted Hattie. "Hey! *Haaaattie!*" She threw her arms around Hattie's neck. "You're here! That's so . . . happy! You shoulda come early. Beer pong started at ten o'clock . . . or one. Whatever!"

She kept hugging Hattie, or maybe using her for balance.

I glanced around, hoping nobody saw the way Sabrina blew me off. She'd pretty much illustrated the Scofield pecking order right there in living color. And this feeling? This was what me without Hattie felt like. I crossed my arms in front of my chest, surprised by the sting of tears.

Hattie smiled at me, and I forced a grin back. She patted Sabrina's back. "Great," she said. "Beer pong."

Sabrina straightened, a thick strand of brown hair stuck to her lip gloss. "I told'm you'd be heeere."

Hattie tilted her head. "What?"

But Sabrina moved on.

Hattie didn't mention Sabrina's complete dis of me, though of course she saw it. To mention it would be to validate it, and Hattie wouldn't grant Sabrina Bradley's opinions of me (or lack thereof) any power. She had my back that way; it was our unspoken code. She was silently coaching me in the Art of Cool. We also let Sabrina's comment, "I told'm you'd be heeere," slide. Did she mean *them*? *Him?* Hattie was becoming the *It* girl right before my eyes. The fact that nobody at SHS had less interest in being *It* than her exemplified a kind of irony that would bring tears of joy to the eyes of our English teacher, Mrs. Langhouser.

Once in the family room, we played a cutthroat round of pool with a couple of the football guys. While I'm no match for Hattie, I can get surprisingly competitive in these situations. Nonetheless, my focus remained on assessing our opponents' virginity-taking worthiness. Mostly, my intentions were uncomplicated, but I'd be lying if I didn't admit a small part of me wanted Hattie to lose it so I wasn't alone. Maybe it would make it easier for me to confess the truth.

I scanned her prospects. Shunsuke, poor guy, unknowingly squandered his chance and left the room. Sean Wolcott was cute, in a Neanderthal kind of way. We were each other's designated spin the bottle kiss at Max's bar mitzvah in seventh grade. I looked at his beefy hands on the pool cue. He just wasn't right for Hattie, even for this sort of thing. *Especially* for this sort of thing?

I was halfway through my third beer (my limit before I'd slide into the Sabrina zone). Hattie'd had nearly five. Before I could process how out of character that was for her, Captain Dickhead strolled through the family room door. Panic flitted through my chest. We hadn't been this close since the prom.

"I play winner," he announced, assuming full command of the room while still managing to ignore me.

Oh, how I loathe you, Jay Fucking Seavers.

Hattie sidled next to me and gave me a nudge. She cast a side glance at him and then back at me. A slurry smile spread across her face. "Whoop, there it is," she whispered.

God no.

"You don't like him," I said, almost too quickly, pulse popping in my wrists, sober as the eight ball. She shrugged. Her eyes weren't quite connecting with mine. "Crap," I muttered. "You're drunk."

Her laugh was throaty. "He's such a man whore he's probably not bad," she said, adding, "I stole a condom from my brother's room."

I shuddered at the invading memory of his hands everywhere at once and spun toward the wall, pretending to fiddle with one of those blue chalky cubes used on pool cues. I couldn't bear it if he slept with her *and* me. It was gross. *He* was gross. And not gross. There were so many objections colliding in my head, I couldn't make sense of a single one.

"Look at you, Reid, with the Master chalk," Neanderthal Sean said, perhaps remembering the smooch we'd shared in a broom closet those many moons ago. I could not care and smiled tightly at him.

Jay brushed past me to close the space between Hattie and himself, resting his hands on the pool table and leaning in to appraise her best shot. His tiny, muscular ass presented itself like a trophy. I thought about spitting on it. He was posing, but straightened up in time for plausible deniability.

"Six ball in the left corner pocket," he said to Hattie with a saucy gaze. Right in front of me. "*That's* your shot."

I set my jaw and glared at him. She *knows* her shot. And could kick your ass. How 'bout we shoot *your* balls in the fucking corner pocket, Dickhead?

It didn't matter. I was invisible to him in Hattie's glow. This was the heartbreaking truth of the sidekick: in the big moments, it's all about the superhero. I wanted to scream. Instead, I yanked her arm.

"Wait!" I pretended to point out another shot but hissed in her ear. "Real friends don't let friends sleep with dickheads."

She broke a smile and nodded. "Riiiiiiight," she whispered, all sly. "Here." She tossed Jay her cue with perfect accuracy. "You give it a go." He smiled, but blinked like he'd been stung by a bee.

I swept Hattie outside.

"You're right," Hattie said. "He's a wanker. I lost my focus."

"You would have regretted that," I said over the music. "He doesn't deserve you." My thoughts swam from the beer and the close call. I couldn't even figure out where I fit into the scenario. If I'd told her the truth from the beginning, she wouldn't have entertained the idea at all, drunk or not.

On the patio, it was the point in the party when kids danced, and a compact mob throbbed.

I spied Matt Stedman, band geek turned hipster and drummer for Vanilla Yeti, a rock band composed of high schoolers. Stedman and I had been in the same Spanish class for three years. "I've got it! Stedman!" I said. I counted his virtues on my fingers. "Not needy. Cute. Leaving for college. . . ." I struggled. "That might be enough."

She narrowed her eyes, spotting him. "Ooh, very good."

"Plus, he has rhythm." I was talking to myself at that point. Hammy had appeared from nowhere and dragged Hattie to dance. Of course he had. I glanced at my phone. Ten forty-two. I supposedly had an eleven thirty curfew.

"Hey, Reid," Emma Rose said, touching my arm. "Love your skirt. Abercrombie?"

I found myself next to the Bobbleheads. Why is it so easy to dislike perfect-looking rich girls? Have we been brainwashed by movies? Exhibit A: Emma Rose Burnham. Long, straightened blond hair. Large, liquid brown eyes. Size two. Dressed like a Polo ad. Greta and Mimi, royal attendants, each imitated Emma Rose in her own way. The hairstyle. Touching people while talking to them. The shallow compliments that flowed like water in a brainless, babbling brook. Maybe it was the other way around: girls like Emma Rose were brainwashed to think this was how you act if you're born pretty and rich.

"Thanks," I said. I couldn't bring myself to wade into the shopping chatter while scouting, so I said, "No dancing?"

"Meh," she said. "In a beer or two. These jeans are pretty low-cut. Don't want to get caught flashing my bum."

"And if you wait two beers?" I asked.

"I won't mind flashing it."

Okay, she could be funny, occasionally. I nodded.

"If I had that butt, I'd be flashing it all over the damn place," Mimi said.

I did my best to sigh silently. God, summer was going to suck.

"Where's Hattie?" Emma Rose asked.

"With the Sandwich," I said, nodding toward them.

"Oh yeah," she said.

The song changed. Hattie danced with Matt Stedman now. I smiled.

Emma Rose's eyes narrowed. "Look at Priya dancing with that Braeburn hockey player." We turned simultaneously. Please, God, don't let me become a Bobble.

"That's not even the one she dumped Gib for," Greta said. "Sabrina said that guy's a Rockefeller cousin. Total trust funder." The guy, clean-cut and tan, was grinding with a hand on each of Priya's hips.

"Ew," I said.

"God, Priya's a bitch. Gib has *got* to move on," Emma Rose said, like she had been counseling him through the breakup. Like she didn't want to jump him herself. "Who could blame him if he did beat the crap out of that guy. Or the other hockey player."

"Right?" chimed Greta.

"Come on, that's a rumor," I said. After Priya dumped

him, it got around that Gib broke into the Braeburn kid's car at the ice rink, hid in the back seat, then jumped him and supposedly busted his nose. It was so violent and cowardly and *un*-Gib that Hattie and I never believed it. Hammy said it was bullshit, too, and he would know. Listening to the goddesses of gossip here take it as truth annoyed me. I mumbled, "Bye," and stepped into the shadows of the lawn.

The grass felt dewy and cool, so I took off my sandals, carrying them in one hand while I ran my free hand along the groomed hedges ringing the house. Accidentally, sort of, I looked in each window I passed. In a den, Eve and her college friends laughed, lounging on leather furniture. In the living room, Charlie and Alesha made out on the couch. I blushed and looked away. Why was I always the observer and never the observed?

"Reid."

I jumped—a reflex, I guess, since I recognized Hammy's voice. I squinted toward his lanky figure under a tree. He was like Scarecrow in *The Wizard of Oz* when all his straw is missing.

"What are you doing?" I asked, then noticed the orange glow of his joint. "Ah. Hammy the Stoner tonight, eh?"

"Reid the Peeping Tom tonight, eh?" he said.

"I didn't mean to peep," I said, walking to him. "But yay, Charlie!"

"His persistence paid off at last." He sucked the joint and held his breath, offering me a hit.

I shook my head. "Makes me stupid."

"Me too," he said.

"You and Hattie had the moves like Jagger on the dance floor," I said. His eyebrows folded in on his eyes. So fun to tease, the Sandwich. "You know I know you love her, right?"

He looked like he might deny it at first, but broke into a smile.

"I knew it!" I said. "Don't worry, it's not obvious to everyone. Just me. I have a sixth sense for who likes Hattie."

"Okay, but, is *not obvious* a good thing?" He leaned against the tree.

I considered telling him she was on a mission to sleep with someone tonight. My role was scout, after all, and they'd make a great couple. But I couldn't bear to think of him rejected. I patted his sinewy shoulder and leaned against the wide tree trunk beside him. "Tomorrow she goes."

"Thanks for reminding me." We studied the patterns the leaves made against the night sky for a while.

"You're not the only person it sucks for," I said. "I've got eight weeks of zero fun girls to hang with. There's a disturbingly real possibility I will morph into a Bobblehead."

He abruptly turned toward the tree and banged his

fists against it. "She's so perfect!" he wailed. "Life is not fair, Reid." He slumped to the ground, sitting crisscross applesauce, like in third grade.

"No shit, Sherlock," I said, sitting beside him. "At least you have *friends*."

He popped to his knees, grabbing my shoulders. "I've got it!" he said. For a second, I thought he'd go all desperate romantic guy and kiss me, but he didn't and then I felt stupid for even suspecting it. "Let's make a pact," he said. "It will be the Summer of Reid and Sam."

I chuckled, both at his idea and at him calling himself by his actual name. He was so *Hammy*, anything else seemed ridiculous.

"I'm serious!" he went on. "We'll force each other to go out so we don't become hermits."

"Ummm. I think you're toasted. A toasted Hammy Sandwich." It was an awkward joke, but he rallied.

"Yes, I am. But that's irrelevant. I'm tired of this scene. Hattie's the only thing that makes these stupid-ass parties worthwhile."

"Your flattery is stunning." In truth, I was terrified to come to one of these stupid-ass parties without her. "You know you'll go out anyway, Hammy. You're at every party."

"Not anymore. I'm sick of it. And what then? Are we just going to sit home and play Xbox all summer? We're *seventeen*, for chrissakes."

"I don't have an Xbox."

"Come on. You know what I mean! We're supposed to be living the dream. Groping people on a daily basis."

"Right," I said. We watched a couple of fireflies blink over the lawn. "I was planning to work a lot and bank some serious college money."

Hammy threw his hands up, like he was fending off a smelly dog. "Don't! You're killing me. *My* idea is so much better. The Summer of Sam and Reid."

"You don't need me, Hammy."

"But I do." He stuck out his hand for a shake.

I forced a laugh. "What are we going to do? Hunt for buried treasure? Build a tree fort?"

"Anything but stay home alone," he said. He grinned his goofy crooked grin. Why was I stalling? His attention, and the promise of it all summer, was a game changer for me. It was also terrifying. *Do you want to play it safe or have an actual social life of your own?*

"Can we get a groovy van and solve mysteries with Scooby?" I said.

"Abso-fucking-lutely. I'll be Fred."

He was a bit more Shaggy, but I couldn't say that. I mean, obviously I was Velma.

He wagged his hand for the shake. I took it. "You're on, Stoner Boy. I'll get you a red cravat like Fred's."

"Righteous!" he said. I admit it felt like he'd pulled me into a lifeboat from the *Titanic.* "I'll call you tomorrow after work," he said, getting up and walking backward toward the pulsing crowd on the patio.

"Excellent," I called. And I smiled for much longer than the Art of Cool dictates.

I made my way back inside through the garage, where beer pong wreckage lay scattered and forlorn. In the kitchen, I slid into my sandals and searched the fridge for something nonalcoholic. Here's the weird thing about Scofield parties: I barely knew Sabrina Bradley, and yet I somehow felt perfectly comfortable pushing aside a carton of almond milk and a container of wilted greens in her refrigerator to snag a can of sparkling water. I swung the door shut to find myself face-to-face with Hattie.

"Where'd you come from?" I said.

"We were playing pool." She smiled.

"We?" I peered over her shoulder. When I saw Gib, I actually had to grab the counter. Wasn't she just dancing with Stedman? How long had I been with Hammy?

I tried to sound composed. "Who won?"

"Me," Gib said, patting his chest, all self-satisfied.

"He cheats," she said. Her eyes twinkled.

"How do you cheat at pool?" he said, flinging his arms wide. Flirting. He was flirting with Hattie. Gib flipping Soule. I scanned the patio for Priya and spotted her with Rockefeller by the keg. *He's moving on!*

"I don't know, you tell me," Hattie said. She held her Solo cup under the ice maker in the freezer door.

"Hattie, I have to get home. . . ." I said.

"I'll drop her off," Gib said. "It's on my way," he added,

as if we didn't all three know the subtext here.

My eyes snapped to Hattie's. We had an instant silent conversation.

Me (eyebrows up): *Holy shit, are you kidding me?*

Hattie: *No! I am not! Put down your eyebrows and* go*!*

It took all I had. "Uh, yeah, okay."

She flicked her eyes to the door. I backed toward it. "Be quiet when you come in. My mom's, like, CIA." What was I saying? This wasn't true. My mom reserved all parental energy for her war on autism.

Hattie gave me a funny look. "Right."

I waved in an embarrassing toodle-oo action and slipped out the front door, rushing onto the soft grass. "Oh my God," I whisper-screamed to the stars. Unable to stop smiling, I crossed the soft grass, murmuring a few awestruck swears, and plunked into the Fiesta.

I looked at her empty seat and sighed.

August 27

I stood on our patio, searching the sky until the clouds darkened to the color of the flagstone beneath my bare feet. My mother was behind me, her hands on my shoulders. “Reid,” she repeated my name over and over again, like a quiet, mournful birdcall. At some point my dad arrived, wrapping his arms around me. I pressed my face into his collar and inhaled his city smell, a smell of the world beyond Scofield. He led me to the living room sofa. We never used the living room.

The two of them sat across from me, mouths moving.

All-night search.

Pulpit Head.

Rocks.

Their words floated above us. I pictured the individual letters somersaulting through the ceiling and the second floor, through the attic and out the roof, into the evening sky, kite tails on her clouds.

Heavy fog.

Riptides.

My eye caught a gnat spiraling around the table lamp, bouncing between the shade and the bulb. I let myself stare at the light until my vision grew fuzzy. I couldn't make myself blink.

"Reid," my mother said, shaking my knees gently. I only saw her silhouette until my eyes readjusted. She and my father looked at each other.

"This is hard, baby," my dad said, holding my hand. The skin under his eyes looked papery and gray, riddled with crosshatchings in pen and ink. I wanted to reach out and smooth it with my thumb.

"Reid," Mom said. "Do you understand?" Her chin quivered with dimples, like pebbles splashing in a puddle. Who was this woman who cried?

"It's a mistake," I said, staring at the floor now. Hattie would come home and we'd start our senior year next week.

"The police think it's . . ." my dad said. He rubbed his neck, inhaled deeply. "Not an accident. Hattie's uncle Baxter said they're still investigating. But the Coast

Guard found her. For now, she drowned while night swimming. But," he said, his gaze direct. Hot. "It's not a mistake."

I glared, staring into an eclipse. "Yes, it is."

The sob that came from my mother was so alien I put my hands to my ears. The numbness protecting me erupted into a roar, rolling up my throat. I bolted for the bathroom.

I closed the door and curled onto the floor, but it was not solid. It was cold and shifting like water.

"Reid?" my mom said with a knock.

"Do you need help, baby?" Dad said.

"*I can't*," I wanted to tell them. Closing my eyes, I let the words in my head take shape silently. My scalp tingled and the plea escaped into the room, an SOS drifting through the small window, out into the sky.

Please cut the shit, Hattie. I can't. Please.

Over and over the words cartwheeled, waves spinning, fish swimming. A school of fish.

"Look, Reid, a school of fish."

Please. I'm serious, I told Hattie. *I'm so serious.* Tears were hot on my face.

"Reid!"

My eyes popped open. I stood on Pulpit Head, the rocky cliff on The Thimble that looked out to sea. I recognized the Maine sky and water, bound together and stretching out forever, sparkling and endless in a way that was both awesome and terrifying. A rolling swell lifted her up before sloshing into the rocks, speckling my skin with spray. When the wave receded, there she was, a grinning seal. Hattie. I blinked at my bathing suit, the one with the big white flowers. I'd outgrown it years ago. I remembered this day, when she first got me to jump. The summer of seventh grade.

"Hattie?" Happy tears sprang to my eyes.

"Dang it!" she yelled, and I knew we were somehow back in that day. "That one was perfect!"

"All right," I heard myself say, just like I did back then. I spoke without hesitation, like I was a puppet, some keeper of memories operated from behind a billowy white cloud. "I'll go on the next one," I called, fairly certain I was lying. I couldn't unsee the image of the surf on rowdier days, exploding against these same rocks with volcanic force.

"If you go when I say, you'll be fine! The tide's perfect!"

She watched the incoming waves. To me, they all looked the same. Hattie saw jumpers and duds. My fears were like an alien language to her.

"Okay!" She pointed. "This one!"

"Which one?" I yelled, shifting my weight.

"Ready?"

One wave did seem larger than the others.

"Set . . ."

I bent my knees, turning off my brain.

"GO!"

I shut my eyes and launched. The drop felt forever. I screamed. I'm pretty sure I peed a little.

Splash!

I flailed against the water, bubbling and swirling around me. My body swished one way, then back. I kicked toward the sunlight, popped through the surface, and sucked in a breath.

"Woo-hoo! You were awesome!" She beamed with happiness for me. Or maybe for her, having coerced me into doing something roughly fourteen miles outside my comfort zone.

"That was terrifying," I said breathlessly.

"Let's do it again," she said, paddling for shore.

I paddled behind her, privately so proud. She showed me how to feel that feeling, *I thought.* She makes me better.

Yes, again, I thought. *Again.* But when I looked for her, I found I was a shell, cold and hollow, washed up on the hard bathroom floor.

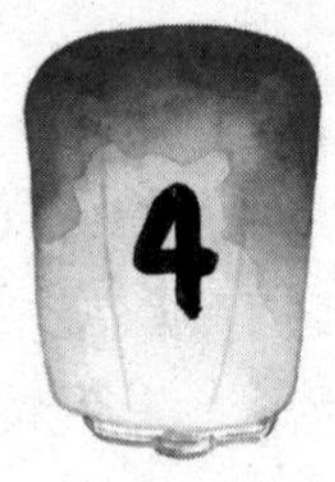

THEN

June 19

Tap tap tap.

I stirred in my sheets.

Tap tap tap.

My eyelids unpeeled from my eyes. Hattie and I routinely snuck in and out of my bedroom window via the bushy pear tree, so a looming figure separated by a flimsy screen didn't alarm me.

"Reid, wake up."

I glanced at my clock: 4:11. Then I remembered. Gib. Hattie. Losing it. Next, Hammy, more or less inviting me to be his partner in crime this summer. The enormity of everything brought me to full consciousness.

I flipped the light to its low setting, unhinged the screen, and waited while Hattie rolled onto the bed next to me. While I reaffixed the screen, I wondered if I should tell her about the Summer of Reid and Hammy. It didn't really fit into our code, and it might be an unfair outing of Hammy's love for her. Anyway, per usual, her story was sure to be far more interesting. Also, per usual, my story was derivative; if it weren't for Hattie, there would be no pact between the Sandwich and me.

"Well?" I said.

"What?" She plucked a twig from her hair, then broke into a big smile.

"Uh, Gib Soule, that's what! I cannot *wait* to hear this," I said. "Hang on."

I stumbled to the bathroom. When I returned, she was in her sleeping bag on the floor, eyes shut.

"Oh no you don't. You don't get to go all cat-swallowed-the-canary on this one, Hattie. Don't even try to fake sleep."

She snored and we cracked up.

"I'm serious."

She rose on one elbow. "What do you want to know?"

"Everything. Where did you go?" I crawled under my covers.

"Siwanoy Beach. It was closed, but he knew a hole in the fence, so we got in and went to the pier."

I pictured them walking in the moonlight to the end of the long dock of the town beach.

She didn't say more, so I waved my hands. "And?"

"We talked."

"About?"

"I don't know." She rolled to face the ceiling. "He told me about a time he and Max snuck into Siwanoy. They thought they saw a dead body floating off the pier. Max barfed before they realized it was a huge jellyfish."

I grimaced. "I hope this gets better."

"I don't remember."

"Bull," I said.

She rolled her eyes. "I dared him to jump off the pier. He said only if I did. So, we jumped."

I squinted at her, noticing for the first time that her hair looked damp and she'd put it in a ponytail. "What were you wearing?"

She stayed quiet.

I sat up. "Hold the phone, you skinny-dipped? With Gibson Soule?"

She chuckled.

"Oh my God." I shook my head.

"Don't be such a prude. It was dark, mostly, and who cares? You're forgetting my endgame."

"You," I said, "are unbelievable. Keep going. So you're swimming, *nekid*, with Gib Soule, also *nekid*, off the dock at Siwanoy, and . . ."

"Seriously?"

"Oh yes, seriously. I wish I had popcorn."

"We raced to the beach."

"And . . ."

"I won."

"Of course you won. Duh. That's not the part I need clarified. Unless . . . he didn't get freaked out by your girl power, did he? That would ruin everything."

"No. He laughed it off. But we realized our clothes were still on the dock, and I made him get them since he lost."

"Sweet Jesus, you saw him running, *nude*, in the moonlight across the sand, like some kind of *Greek Olympian*?"

She tapped her temple with a forefinger. "Always thinkin'."

"Okay," I said, trying to amp up my processing speed. Already she had the story of a lifetime and we hadn't even gotten to holding hands. I steadied my breath. "Keep going."

"Can we get some food? I'm starving."

"Don't make me kill you. He came back with the clothes, right?"

"Yeah. A few cookies, maybe?"

"Come on!"

"Reid, get me some food or I stop talking."

"You're infuriating," I said, heaving my sheets aside. I crept down the back stairs and returned a few moments later with Mint Milanos and a glass of milk. "Now bring it."

"Ahh. Thank you." She dipped a cookie into the milk, pausing for proper absorption time.

I growled.

"So, Gib comes back with our clothes and we"—she took a bite and looked at the ceiling contemplatively—"don't put them back on."

"That's it? You didn't—" I don't know what I thought they should have done. "You just went at it? On the sand?"

"Okay, we had towels from his car and you're creeping me out now." She ate another cookie.

"Sorry." I rolled onto my back. "On the beach." I blinked. "Like a movie." *Infinitely more romantic than on a golf course surrounded by duck shit.* Still, I had a not-unpleasant flash of the kissing that happened on the well-manicured turf. If only Captain Dickhead wasn't such a . . . dickhead. I shook my story out of my head. Hattie had Gib to flash to for the rest of her life. "Wow."

She gulped her milk and set it on the bedside table, then curled up like a caterpillar in her sleeping bag. "'Night."

"That's it?"

"Reid."

"Okay. Fine." I flipped off the light. Her breathing lolled into the unmistakable pattern of sleep.

"You are so . . ." I almost said *lucky*, but caught myself. Luck had nothing to do with it. Not a single thing. It was *her*. Hattie's energy luminesced around her, but you couldn't see it. You felt it. From the moment I met her, in our first middle school PE class, I recognized it without even realizing it. Something deep in my twelve-year-old bones knew being Hattie Darrow's friend would make me better.

The day we met went like this: I emerged from the locker room with the rest of the girls in a parade of powder-blue gym suits, sneakers squeaking. The smell of floor wax in the school gymnasium almost overwhelmed the stench of sweat and sixth-grade nerves. Almost. Our gym suits were one piece with stretchy necks you stepped through, designed to look like a striped tee and shorts. For rounder people, it looked like a Humpty Dumpty costume. Coach Collins, a towering and frightening woman, directed us to the bleachers.

Meanwhile Coach Jenkins, a short, barrel-chested guy with hair like a black football helmet, filed the boys to the opposite end of the gym with a couple of curt, echoey commands. People said he and Collins were a couple, but it looked like she could take him out. In any case, the two of them made quick work of unfolding a partition wall, splitting the gym in half.

"Thank *God* the boys are separate from us." Emma Rose perched next to me on the middle bleacher bench, a gaggle filling in around her. "Can you believe these uniforms? *Heinous.*" She loved this word, *heinous*, and when I tried it out at home, Dad said, "That's a word you use to describe war crimes, not spinach on your pizza." This allowed me to feel slightly more worldly in the current context, but of course I'd never say anything. It was more salient at the moment that Emma Rose's comment insulted half the girls in the class, since Emma Rose alone rocked the gym suit. I was still shaped like a skinny third grader.

"Be glad you don't have boobs yet, Reid," Emma Rose continued. "The horizontal stripes make mine look *huge*."

I smiled awkwardly, trying to feel good that Emma Rose had anointed me her sidekick. In gym, anyway. Because really, in elementary school, I was a kid people didn't tend to notice. In life, come to think of it. I'd made an art form of going unnoticed in public settings with Spencer. He rarely failed to raise eyebrows or cause eyes to flicker away awkwardly, and he'd embarrassed me during so many playdates, I'd stopped inviting friends over in fourth grade. Meanwhile, Scott managed to steal the spotlight effortlessly by way of his athletic prowess and social ease. My dad seemed almost starstruck by Scott, and my mom would flat-out say things like, "Reid, can I count on you to help with Spencer while I ______?" I wasn't the type to answer, "No." So, even if I didn't like Emma Rose that much, being noticed by her felt pretty good.

Coach Collins positioned two Little Tikes basketball hoops on the floor and hauled a dumpster-sized cart full of scooter boards in front of us. She pulled a pink rubber ball covered with nubs from a barrel in the corner. Spencer had one of these—they were extra easy to catch.

"What game is this?" asked Sabrina Bradley.

"Nippleball?" someone said. The class burst into laughter.

A person I didn't recognize a couple rows back said it. She had blond curly hair and was little, like me, but her skin was suntanned instead of pale and freckled. She looked directly forward, a smile playing at her lips.

Collins, expression unreadable, stood in a half straddle and dribbled the ball three times. If there's such a thing as aggressive dribbling, she was doing it. We shut up.

"Okay, ladies, listen up! We're starting off the year with a game of scooter basketball. First, let's get to know each other. I'm Coach Collins. Say your name when I pass you the ball, then pass it back to me."

So it went, and when we got to the lone, funny girl, I learned her name was Hattie Darrow. We ended up on the same team. Emma Rose, too.

Collins demonstrated how you sit on the scooter and use hands or feet to motor yourself around, then explained the rules of passing.

"I am not playing basketball on this thing," Emma Rose said, shoving her scooter away with her foot. "We look like idiots." She glanced toward the open door. The boys were playing dodgeball. Gib Soule, sixth-grade hottie, dashed past. Emma Rose spun a lock of hair around her finger.

Hattie propelled herself backward on her scooter. "Look, I'm a squid!" she called. She and I raced across the gym, cracking up, and practiced passing with our teammates. Scooter basketball was freaking fun.

Emma Rose mostly rolled in small circles in a corner with her underlings, hidden from the view of any curious boys. Named Gib. Who as far as I could tell hadn't even noticed our class existed. I probably could have motored over to Emma Rose and scooted my way right into becoming her full-time sidekick. But I didn't.

And I am awash in gratitude every day for my incredible judgment, even though I had no idea how brilliant it was at the time.

Hattie snored softly on the floor, bringing me back to the present. I stared at the moonlight coming through my white curtains. Damn, I wished we could be together all summer this year. Our future seemed bright and I didn't want to wait until September for it to begin. Closing my eyes, I thought of Hammy by the tree.

It's the Summer of Sam and Reid, he'd said. The idea made me anxious and happy at the same time. Maybe he would follow through. Maybe not. If he did, would I even be able to survive a social life without Hattie to lean on? *Try*, a voice somewhere within me said. *Just try.* It was probably the same daring little voice that told me to play scooter basketball.

I took a shaky breath, nodding to the darkness, and let myself fall asleep.

* * *

When I woke, Hattie's sleeping bag was empty.

Hattie often got up to make everyone breakfast. My family loved it. I found her standing at the stove, freshly showered.

"I didn't hear you get up," I said.

"I'm stealthy." She nudged a couple of sausages with a spatula. "I wanted to make a farewell breakfast for everyone."

"Hmm. Perky for someone out so late. But I'd have a skip in my step too, if I were you," I said, leaning against the doorway.

"And you *could* be skipping." She pointed the spatula at me. "You definitely could."

"Ha," I said. "Not Gib-Soule-nekid-in-the-moonlight skipping."

"How would you know if you haven't tried?" She flipped a pancake.

Her faith in me was both ridiculous and heartening. "And now you'll disappear to The Thimble like nothing happened?"

"That's the plan," she said.

"Man." I shook my head and stole a sausage from a plate near her elbow. "No regrets?"

"Nope," she said, adding a pancake to the stack on another plate.

"No guilt?"

She laughed. "What, like Hester Prynne? Would you ask a *guy* that question?"

"Good point."

"It's not a big deal, Reid. I told you. I wanted to get it over with and now it is." She held my gaze for a second. I thought her eyes hardened, but she smiled, so I must've been mistaken. "Now it's your turn."

My neck prickled and I spun to gather utensils from the silverware drawer, allowing the clatter to fill the space between us. I piled forks and knives on the table. "Don't you feel the slightest bit curious about where it could go?"

"Where what could go?" She ladled batter onto the griddle.

"*You and Gib.*"

"Nah." She pushed a sausage link with the spatula. "It wasn't like that. Besides, Reid, the whole boyfriend thing is overrated. Too many demands."

I waited for her to flash me a grin, show me a sign that even the mighty Harriet Darrow could fall for Gibson Soule. Nothing. I clucked my tongue. "I'd say, 'Demand on, Gib.' You, Hattie, are made of some kind of crazy shit."

Her eyes were *definitely* hard.

"What?" I asked uneasily.

She stared over my shoulder, somewhere else momentarily, then blinked when Spencer, wearing underwear only, buzzed in carrying his Clifford the Dog stuffy in one hand and a red sock in the other. "Cazy shit!"

"Spencer," Hattie laugh-said. "Your sister is a bad influence."

"Oh, good one, Man-Eater," I said.

"Cazy shit," Spencer repeated, rolling on tiptoes.

"Spencer, don't say that to your speech therapist, okay?" I chuckled.

Hattie inspected him, her face brightening. She opened the cabinet and pulled out a set of red plastic measuring cups on a ring. "Hey, Spence. I have something for you."

Spencer stared, captivated, then took them from her outstretched hand. He bounced to the family room.

"What's that about?" I asked.

"He's on a red kick. You can't tell? Clifford, the red sock, and the red plaid boxers," she said.

Spencer went through spells of gathering objects that matched—the round kick, the vehicles-with-wheels kick—like a crow collecting shiny things. The objects' attribute changed every few months.

"He *is* pretty cute, isn't he?" This was a continuation of a conversation that stretched years. Seeing Spencer through Hattie's eyes helped me feel proud instead of embarrassed. The way she was curious about what made Spencer tick, and loved trying to teach him something new, and laughed when he was weird. "He's the best," she said, on her way to the bottom of the front hall stairs. "Mr. and Mrs. MacGregory! Scott? Breakfast is ready!"

"I'm pretty sure they love you more than me," I joked.

She laughed. "Right. That's how my family is about you. We should swap."

"It would make a good movie," I said, pouring orange juice into glasses. "Like *Freaky Friday*." But I knew her family didn't love me the way mine loved her. We both did.

She got Spencer to help set the table. He's really good at things with repetitive steps. "Fork, moon, knife, spoon," she said, laying the silver and plates in order.

Spencer said, "Fowk, mooon, knife, spooon."

My dad appeared in his robe and pajamas. "Hey, good job setting the table, Spence," he said, patting his shoulder. Spencer made a happy sound. "Mmmm, smells delicious, girls."

I pointed both barrels at Hattie. "All her, not me."

Mom, fully dressed for the day, joined us, then Scott. He looked like he'd been caught in a buffalo stampede—hair in six directions, eyes bleary.

"I thought I'd make you breakfast one last time before I leave for the summer," Hattie said.

"Excellent plan," Dad said.

"Definitely an excellent plan," Scott said.

"Exceyent," said Spencer. Hattie high-fived him.

"What happened to you?" I asked Scott quietly, though I was pretty sure he went to a Colgate party in Greenwich.

"What? Nothing," he said innocently, fixing me with his shut-up stare. I smirked and sat down. I would miss him this summer, too. He left in a few days for the Vineyard. They were both going to islands, and I was the one who felt deserted. I sighed into the fridge, getting syrup.

"Hattie, where will we be without you all summer?" Mom said, pouring coffee for her and Dad.

"I feel the same way," Hattie said. She wasn't lying, really, but she couldn't feel the same way. From the beginning, Hattie brought a breath of normalcy into our house that had been absent my whole life. She allowed us to relax in our own home. Of course nobody said it out loud. If we did, then we'd have to acknowledge how hard it could be the rest of the time. And that would be defeatist, which is no way to survive Spencer's kind of autism. Just ask my mom—the annoyingly relentless autism warrior.

"To Hattie," Mom said, lifting her mug. "May your summer be bright and fun!"

We clinked juice glasses and coffee mugs, and I felt a pang of something like homesickness, which didn't make any sense, until I realized it kind of did.

In my room, Hattie zipped her duffel. Her sister Helen would arrive to whisk her away from me any time now.

She stood slowly. "Ooch. A little sore in the nether regions."

I snorted, remembering the same sensation after prom. *Confess, now!* I thought. But I couldn't bear her knowing what a fool I'd been. I'd let myself be *taken advantage of*, an old-fashioned phrase reeking of weakness, but perfectly fitting. Jay Seavers took advantage of my naivete, of my hunger for attention, and to do that he must have spotted it, which means I exposed it. I didn't even have the wits to hide it. No, I couldn't confess. I told myself it could be like that tree falling in a forest thing. If nobody heard about it, it didn't happen. I changed the subject. "You do realize you're deserting me, right? Because you don't look sad."

She squinted, but she was busted. And why *would* she be sad? She had sailing and tennis and cousins with tales of surfing off the horn of Africa. Her parents even transported their three horses up to The Thimble so she could ride all summer. Most of all, she had Santi, the guy she wouldn't admit she *truly* loved. She checked her phone. "Eleven eleven," she said, no stranger to the art of distraction herself. "The magic time." This was in reference to a fortune-telling game we'd played at sleepovers since forever. It's called Sea of Life and involves a Nordic gnome, a bowl of water, and a walnut shell boat. I smiled, turning the table on her.

"Mr. Tomten?" I asked the air. "Did Hattie sleep with Gib Soule in preparation for unleashing her lifetime of repressed lust for Santi Herrera?"

"Oh God!" She laughed.

"Mr. Tomten says YES!"

"Mr. Tomten?" Hattie said, looking up. "Will Reid be burden-free by the time she crosses the bridge into Maine in two weeks?"

"Please," I said, carefully avoiding eye contact. "And it's two and a half weeks."

She hoisted her duffel bag onto her shoulder and I did the same with her second one. We walked downstairs and outside, and sat on them on the driveway. It was already hot and muggy.

"What's that, Mr. Tomten?" Hattie continued. "She'll be a sexual warrior by the end of the summer?"

I chuckled. "Okay, let's leave poor Mr. Tomten out of this. He only answers yes/no questions anyway."

She put on her Ray-Bans, pulled her hair elastic out, and redid her ponytail. "Don't let his little red cap fool you. Mr. Tomten is also a tiger in the sack."

I snorted.

Near my bare toes, an ant carried a flower petal three times its size across the pavement. It didn't matter about trees falling in forests. Sooner or later Hattie would find out about Jay and I'd have to explain why I'd kept it from her. I sucked in a breath—the MacGregory reverse sigh. "About the burden thing," I began, watching the ant disappear into the grass.

"Don't give me any of your self-deprecating crap. This is nonnegotiable. Remember when you wouldn't dive off your own diving board?" She thumbed over her shoulder toward our backyard. "Now you jump off Pulpit Head. And you like it."

"I don't like it."

"You *do too*."

I gave her a look.

"By August, this is you." She hopped to her feet and

snapped an imaginary whip while making a *whi-chaaa* sound. "Hey, Max? Lemme wax your back." Then she laugh-said, "How 'bout those butt cheeks? *Whi-chaaa!*" She doubled over at her own joke, and I couldn't help giggling. Just like that, I let myself off the hook for hiding the truth.

"Promise me you'll only watch those crap romance movies one night a week," she said. "And you'll swim with Spencer. And take him bowling."

I nodded dismissively. "I'm going to work on my 5K for cross-country."

"Admirable," she said. "But also, go out, Reid!"

I almost told her about my pact with Hammy then, but if he didn't follow through, then I'd have to tell her that. I couldn't bear it.

Helen buzzed up the driveway in Mrs. Darrow's bright red Mini. She got out and hugged me. "Look at you, all grown up!" Helen, an international relations student at Brown, had just finished her junior year in some remote part of India. She was a flawless version of Hattie. Blond ringlets bounced around her shoulders in perfect disarray. Her smile was glamorous and friendly at the same time. And she always had these unbelievably hot, star-athlete boyfriends. "When are you coming to The Thimble?" she asked.

"July eighth," I said.

"Hattie's psyched for that." She squeezed Hattie's shoulders.

Hattie busied herself loading her luggage.

"Don't let her fool you," Helen said softly. "She misses you a *ton*." Her eyes stayed on me an unnervingly long time. I smiled stupidly.

Hattie slammed the trunk. I wanted to cry.

We hugged and she climbed in the car. "Two weeks," she said. "There better be some news."

Helen backed down the driveway. Hattie yelled, "Whi-chaaaa!" And she was gone.

In my room, I got ready for my first matinee shift at the dinner theater. The initial zip of my girl tux skirt made an audible mockery of the pathetic summer I had in store. Scofield Dinner Theater was the local landmark that time forgot, the one you drive by all the time and never notice. It mixed live musical theater with bland dining. Jasper Chang, my chemistry lab partner, was the one who told me the Scofield Dinner Theater was hiring in April. He'd bussed tables there for two years and talked me into applying, eyes buggy through his safety goggles. "It's so campy," he'd said, noting that the geometric orange carpet is the same one as in that horror movie *The Shining*—the one the kid rides his Big Wheel on and where he finds the terrifying sisters (Hattie had gotten me to watch it three times).

Faye, the floor manager, greeted me by the hostess stand. The air inside the place was tomblike, which made the fact that the patrons were bussed in from senior centers either hilarious or tragic, depending on your mood. Faye was raven haired, late thirties, with a bit of alcohol puff to her face and a lot of eye makeup. "We're sold out for two weeks," she said, blowing out her cheeks. "God, these old folks love *Man of La Mancha*."

"What's it about?"

"You know, 'To dream the impossible dream'? Chasing windmills? Don Quixote and Sancho Panza?"

I stared at her.

"It's old." Her phone buzzed. "Like them." She looked at it and sucked in a rattly breath. Faye's persistent stress, coupled with her frequent hushed phone calls, led to much conjecture among the staff about a possible second, less legal job. Jasper said drug dealer. The prep cook thought mob. I didn't doubt it. Faye handed me a stack of papers. "Tri-fold these? I need a smoke." She hustled toward the loading dock as I opened the program.

THE MAN OF LA MANCHA

BASED ON THE 1605 SPANISH LITERARY CLASSIC

THE INGENIOUS NOBLEMAN SIR QUIXOTE OF LA MANCHA

BY MIGUEL DE CERVANTES

And then the memory hit me. In eighth grade, Hattie and I had made an iMovie for Spanish class based on *Don Quixote*. Hattie played the starring role—suave, tall, thin dreamer Don Quixote. I played the squat sidekick,

Sancho Panza, faithful squire. We drew mustaches and beards on ourselves and recited ridiculous lines, like, "*Don Quixote es guapo y muy muy alto*," and, "*Sancho Panza es gordo.*" Hattie rode her horse, Lyra, and I rode old Barnaby. Back then, Hattie wasn't tall or suave, but it was an alternate version of our reality, which made it comic genius. The class loved it.

And I realized that I'm still Hattie's Sancho Panza; it's who I'm meant to be.

I dropped the programs on the hostess stand with a thud and texted a picture of one to Hattie.

Me: Remember our Spanish movie in 8th grade?

Jasper rolled his cart into the lobby. "Reid MacGregory, thank GOD! I've had four straight shifts with Bitter Barb."

Bitter Barb worked the day shifts all winter. If I were sixty-two and a hostess at the Scofield Dinner Theater, I'd probably be bitter, too.

"One more story about her ungrateful daughter-in-law," Jasper said, "and I might have had to stab her in the kitchen."

"Geez, that's a little drastic," I said, though I smiled.

He made his Bitter Barb face and launched the whiny voice. "'Jasper, why does she feed my son such *terrible* food? Now he's *FAT.* My Billy was never *fat*. My husband Hal was never *fat*.'" He implored the sky, still in character. "'*Make some salads already!*'" He shook his head, steering his bussing cart toward the kitchen and backing through the cushioned doors. "Bitter Barb," he grumbled.

Jasper Chang hung with the drama rat pack at school. He took the leads in *Once Upon a Mattress* and *Grease* and taught me jazz hands and pas de bourrées during our downtimes. Hattie and I didn't spend time with the theater kids. Hattie barely knew who Jasper was, and having a friend she didn't know was a foray into uncharted land for me. I wasn't sure how I felt about that. But he's the kind of guy who gets you to spill a lot of info without realizing you're doing it.

After we'd seated the house and shut the doors for Act One, he said, "Why so blue, MacGroo?"

"I'm not blue."

Jasper squinted at me. His hair, black and shiny like patent leather, swept his forehead.

"I hate Scofield in the summer," I said.

"What? Are you on something?" he said, with a dramatic eye squint.

"It's so boring!" I said. "I'm doing this"—I waved my arm in front of my uniform—"by choice." I sighed. "It's unnatural."

"True," he said. "Hattie left, didn't she." It was a statement, not a question.

"I know I'm pathetic."

"You aren't pathetic. You just need to widen your circle. Step outside your comfort zone."

"You sound like Oprah," I said.

He considered this. "I'm okay with Oprah."

I organized menus in a basket. Jasper was right, but the problem was, as evidenced last night at the party, I generally needed a Hattie to push me out of my comfort zone (save the disastrous Dickhead incident). "Well, I *might* be stepping out a little bit." My voice went quiet. "With Sam Stanwich."

He cocked his head.

"You know, *Hammy*."

His eyebrows jumped. "The Sandwich?" Jasper wagged a finger at me. "You sly honey badger."

I laughed. "It's not like that. We just understand each other, kind of." I'm not quite sure that covered the Summer of Hammy and Reid, but it was the best I could do on short notice.

"Understand schmunderstand. Surely you know boys and girls can't be just friends," he said. "Except in cases such as ours, that is."

"He probably already forgot he suggested it," I said, hoping I was wrong but starting to brace myself in case I wasn't.

"Unlikely. He's secretly into you. Or you're secretly into him. Either way, someone's hormones are an inferno. Two weeks and you're on each other like horned-up snow monkeys." He snapped.

I shook my head. "Snow monkeys?"

"YouTube it—*Our Amazing Planet*, episode sixty-three.

There's a reason their faces are so red."

"Ew." I tossed today's seating chart into the trash. "Hammy's in love with someone else."

"Pshaw."

"He is! Hattie."

"Uh-huh," he said. "Right. And while Hattie's gone, he's celibate? Methinks not. Take it from me, a guy will only wait around so long." He rolled away.

I hadn't let my mind entertain the possibility of Hammy and me—and I wasn't about to. I'd let myself hope about Captain Dickhead, and it almost killed me inside. Hammy Stanwich was all about Hattie Darrow. And I was Sancho Panza. That's just who I'm meant to be.

For the rest of the shift I kept flashing back to the prom. Captain Dickhead had wormed into my head again, even as I led elderly couples to their tables. The prom was at Howebrook Country Club, one of Scofield's fanciest, and because Charlie was a member, a waiter he knew let a bunch of us sneak out to the golf course—Charlie and me, Hammy and Hattie, and Emma Rose and her date, Captain Dickhead. We took turns joyriding in a golf cart way out by a duck pond. There were vodka drinks involved, and somehow Dickhead and I drove off together, leaving the others to practice putting on the fourteenth green.

As we puttered uphill, around a stand of trees, my bare shoulder jostled against his tuxedo jacket. The intimacy of it was oddly intoxicating. He smelled like one of those cologne ads in my mom's *Vanity Fair* magazine. Sophisticated. Out of my league.

"Let's see what this baby can do," he said, gunning it. I grabbed the edge of the seat cushion to keep from rolling into his lap. We hit a stump or something and both popped into the air. I lost my grip on the cushion, but landed on the seat. Jay bounced right out of the cart.

"Oh my God!" I cried. The cart kept its forward momentum. It must've been knocked into neutral. I grabbed the wheel, headed for the duck pond. "Help!"

"Push the brake!" Jay yelled.

I couldn't respond in my panic. My sandals were back on the green and I worked my toes, chimp-like, until I clamped onto the pedal and pushed. The cart went faster.

"Ahhh!"

"That's the gas!"

"No shit!" I resisted the urge to abandon ship and slammed the ball of my foot onto the second pedal. Too hard. The cart lurched to a halt. I slammed into the dashboard with a grunt. I kept my toes curled around the brake pedal and reached for the gear shift. Finally, all was still.

A duck quacked somewhere to our right.

Jay ran to me. "Holy crap! Are you okay?"

I lifted my head. Jay Seavers was frightened. For me.

I paused, blinking. A surge of Hattie's and my witchiness from the Headless Horseman night last October coursed through me. "From here out," I said, casting a teasing gaze his way, "I drive."

He turned away, breaking a smile. "Jesus, I thought you were dead for sure." He put his hand on the small of my back as I stepped onto the grass. I fluffed my skirt. His hand remained, rubbing slowly. It was awkward and not awkward at once. An ungainly laugh bubbled out of me, somehow passing as confident.

"Did you hear a duck?" His laugh was throaty. He pulled me against him, gently. Expertly. I heard Hattie in my head. *Seavers is busting a move!* My brain vibrated.

"Yes, somewhere over here . . ." I broke away—testing him, maybe. He stuck close, like Boomer.

Five paces more and a frenzy of quacking erupted. I jumped and Jay grabbed my hand. We watched in silence as three ducks rose out of the darkness and settled onto the middle of the glittery pond, bobbing as if nothing had happened.

He twined his fingers between mine. I felt completely unprepared for this moment. He turned my face toward him.

"Hey," he said softly. His eyes bored into mine. Brown. Lit with flecks of night sky. He pulled me closer. "You look beautiful."

I couldn't think. The vodka. The flecks. Feeling wanted. His mouth covered mine. I didn't kiss back at first, but his warm hands cupped the nape of my neck and I felt myself melt into him, so needy for this and the softness of his lips, his Vanity Fair scent filling my head.

Jay Seavers knew what he was doing. I heard a zipping sound and a few heartbeats later, my Mardi Gras green dress slipped from my torso. I clutched it, but heard Hattie. *You have a pretty smokin' hot bod these days, Reddi.*

"Hey," I said in the absolute fakest protest ever. I didn't know who I was. Certainly not my overthinking, neurotic self. I dropped my dress.

"Whoops," he replied with equal fakeness that he somehow pulled off.

Next thing I knew, we were lying in the grass and his breath was on my cheek and his hands were everywhere at once. He murmured embarrassing things in my ear and I couldn't get ahold of myself. His glossy eyes hovered over mine. I watched a vein pulse in his temple. Thump. Thump. Thump. Were we going to be a couple? Me and Jay Seavers?

"You want to?" he asked. I had no idea. "Don't worry, I have a condom." That was actually not at the top of my worry list, but I couldn't think. Thump. Thump. Thump. He smiled and I closed my eyes.

Somewhere in the midst of replaying all these memories, I finished my shift at the dinner theater. I found myself sitting in our driveway with the engine running, staring at my dad's rosebushes. I shook my head like that would clear Captain Dickhead out once and for all. Not that simple. "I need to go for a run," I said aloud, and got out of the car.

As I changed, I told myself it didn't matter if Hammy forgot the Summer of Hammy and Reid, or changed his mind. He was pretty high when he asked me, after all. So if he didn't call, I wouldn't blame him. I'd be bummed, but I had the running goals for cross-country, and the third season of *Outlander* awaited me after my shower and dinner.

I swung one foot up onto a bookshelf in the family room and stretched my hamstrings. "I'm taking Boomer for a run," I announced to Mom, Linda, and Spencer, who were jigsaw puzzling at the kitchen table.

"Good job puzzle!" Spencer said. He wore his red Spider-Man cape. Clifford, the red sock, the measuring cups, and some red Legos lay in a heap beside him. Hattie was right—he was going through a red phase.

"He's up to a hundred and fifty pieces," Linda said.

"Good job puzzle!" Spencer repeated. He wanted someone to tell him he was awesome.

"Reid," Mom said, "isn't Spencer doing *a good job*?"

"Oh, Spencer, nice job! Look at that puzzle. All those red parrots!"

"Wed pawwots," he said, clapping his hands. Sometimes I envied how simply he could be made happy. But then I'd remember how simply he could be upset.

"Reid, can you help me stuff envelopes later?" Mom asked. "I'm behind."

"I thought the fund-raiser isn't until October," I said.

"It's five hundred people, the biggest ever. I'm so far behind," she said. She said this every year. "Can you help?"

"Yep," I said, yanking the leash off its hook with more force than necessary. Boomer sprang from his dog bed when he saw it, toenails tapping on the kitchen floor.

The doorbell rang. I craned to see who stood on the stoop. The hydrangeas hid all but a pair of legs from the knees down—hairy and wearing madras shorts. My stomach did the wave, like the fans at a Yankee game. Hammy didn't blow me off!

"Who is it?" Mom asked.

"Hammy."

"You should stop calling him that, Reid. It's not nice," Mom said. She picked the oddest things to take issue with.

The hairy legs shifted weight. I gathered my nerves and rounded the corner, smiling. I froze for what I hoped to be an imperceptible fraction of a second. Gib Soule watched me through the screen. "Hey," he said.

Gib flipping Soule! I thought about hiding, but I was too late for escape.

Boomer glanced from me to Gib and back. Even my dog was puzzled. "Hey, Gib," I said finally. "Um, what's up?"

He looked at the hydrangea for a second. "You going to walk your dog?"

Boomer happy danced.

I contemplated saying I wanted to go on a much-needed run but snapped myself out of it. "Yes. Umm . . . you want—" My voice sounded absurdly high. I coughed. "You want to come?" I could actually *see* my chest beating in my peripheral vision.

"Sure," he said.

"We do Tuttle Trail, around the pond." I opened the screen door and stepped out. *Channel Hattie, Reid.* A vision of him running across the sand naked in the moonlight flashed into my head and I worked hard not to burst into nervous laughter.

"I would have texted you before just showing up here, but I don't have your number," he said.

No kidding. "It's okay," I said, finding my cool and casual voice. I reminded myself he was interested in my best friend, not me. While it was yet another example of me being on the outside looking in, at this moment it cooled some anxiety. Still, from the driveway to the trailhead, his flip-flops smacking his heels made the only sound.

"So," I said as we turned onto the dirt path. I tried to pretend I was talking to my brother Scott. "You and Hattie made it home okay last night."

I felt him look at me, so I stooped to unhitch Boomer's leash.

"Are you giving me shit?" he asked.

He's just a guy. Like Scott. "Yes. Yes, I am." I let myself grin, standing.

He smirked. A vision to behold. I scratched my neck to distract myself.

"Is she really gone until Labor Day?" he asked.

"Yep," I said with a sigh.

"That sucks."

"Tell me about it."

Boomer dashed ahead, trotting a serpentine path through trees.

"Have you been to the Thumb?"

I raised my eyebrows and smothered my smile. "You mean The Thimble? Yeah, I go every year."

"Hattie *never* comes back during the summer?"

My God, I thought. *He's hooked.* "You looking for a rematch?" He stared at me. "In the swimming competition?" I added.

He dropped his head and I heard a low chuckle.

"She kicks butt in swimming," I said.

"I'd had a lot to drink," he said.

We faced each other and I narrowed my eyes. "You do know she let you win at pool, right?"

He tilted his head from side to side. "Hmm. *Maybe.*"

I felt emboldened. "Sucker. Anyway, no. She doesn't come back."

"Where is their house in Maine?"

"Midcoast. It's a six-hour drive, pure hell, but worth

it. I'm going the weekend after the Fourth. Want to hide in my suitcase?"

He smiled, which did have an arresting effect on my breathing, but I managed to chuck Boomer's tennis ball to diffuse my awkwardness.

We kept walking.

"Hattie's more fun than Priya," he said, like he'd just thought it.

"Boomer is more fun than Priya," I said.

"Oof," he said, pretending I'd hit him in the gut.

"Oh, come on. Priya leaves for college soon anyway. You've moved on. It's official."

"Yeah," he said.

"Hattie can be good in such situations."

"I'm thinking that, too." Boomer faced off with us, dropping his tennis ball and sticking his butt in the air. Gib took a turn, throwing it twice as far as I had. He looked not unlike that famous Greek sculpture of a discus thrower. He had the shoulder and arm muscles of a grown man, not a high schooler. "Maybe you could let her know I'm wondering about her." He watched me.

First, I thought what a sweet word *wondering* was for him to choose. Not *asking* about her, not *thinking* about her, or if my suspicions were correct, *lusting after* her. *Wondering.* Like Hattie was some great puzzle. Which she was. Then I thought, *You're Gib freaking Soule.* You *tell her!* But his shyness made me pause, and I remembered we weren't talking about the average SHS girl. We were talking about Hattie I-don't-need-that Darrow. Gib's only chance with her was to keep cool.

"I'm thinking," I said, "it's better not to talk about it."

"Why?" He made a face of such intense dissatisfaction, I thought he was pissed at me, but it disappeared and I thought I imagined it and carried on, tapping my chin.

"How do I explain? She's more a girl of action than a girl of words." I stopped, rolling my eyes. "That didn't sound right . . ." He chuckled. "What I mean is, she likes spontaneity."

He considered this and I caught a small upturn to his lips. "I see that."

I bet. "No drama allowed," I added.

"Man, that's the opposite of Priya."

"Hattie's a unique individual. And I feel compelled to tell you she's not in the market for a boyfriend." I felt like her publicity agent, but he didn't notice.

"I knew it!" He raked his hands through his hair. "I *knew* she'd have some guy up there."

"It's not that." I mean, there was Santi, but I was the only living person willing to admit she loved him.

Gib stopped walking and faced me. "Then what is it?" he said.

His impatience made me scramble for an answer, and I searched for words to explain what I'd probably been trying to articulate for years. "She's"—I kicked Boomer's ball a few feet—"a bit of a lone wolf." I realized then that I'd accepted this simple fact early in our friendship. I was closer to Hattie than anyone, but she still kept things to herself. "It's not a bad thing," I told the two of us. "It's part of what I love about her. It's her . . ." Clouds ambled high above the treetops, and I saw one that looked like a bear. "Her strength and her weakness."

He nodded thoughtfully, his brow relaxing, then threw another killer for Boomer. *Discobolus.* That's the sculpture. I suddenly remembered it from art history last semester.

"So, I don't do anything?" He squinted at me.

"Ill-advised at this time," I said. "Besides, the cell service sucks up there, so it's almost impossible. Maybe in the fall." I couldn't imagine Hattie giving in, but I wanted to leave the door open in case I could convince her that she was out of her ever-loving mind. Maybe something could happen with me and one of Gib's friends and we could hang out, two couples, all senior year. I almost didn't care who the friend would be, I loved the idea so much. Maybe Jasper was right and Hammy and I could be a thing.

"That's not what I wanted to hear."

"Sorry about that." I patted his arm. I. Patted. Gib's. Arm. "You'll learn to cope," I added, speaking from experience.

"Ha."

We were back to the road, and just when I thought he'd used me for intel purposes only, he said, "What are you up to tonight?"

My stomach did another wave. Thankfully, I could say

without lying, "The Sandwich and I had plans to hang out." I almost did Boomer's happy dance after I said it.

"Cool. There's a really small thing at the Maleshefskis' pool."

"What, a party?"

"No, not a party. Just a few people."

I squinted. "The Maleshefskis don't have any kids."

"True. But Max is dog-sitting and has the keys. Seriously, don't tell anyone. But come. Bring the Sandwich. He probably knows about it already."

It seemed so incongruous that Max, of Sasquatch arms and loud mouth, could offer entrée into the legendary Maleshefski pool. It was supposedly modeled after some natural waterfall.

"Okay." And I nodded, unable to come up with anything else.

"Oh, and what's your phone number?" In a true out-of-body moment, I exchanged numbers with Gibson Soule while we stood in front of his Corolla parked in my driveway. "Catch ya," he said, opening the door. He looked at me steadily. I couldn't move. "And we don't mention this"—he pointed at me and him—"to Hattie?"

"Nope." It would take all I had, but he didn't have a chance if I told her.

He smiled and said, "Thanks, Reid," thus creating one of the best moments of my entire life so far.

Then the garage door cranked open, revealing Spencer, like he was onstage for his curtain call—red cape, red shorts, red socks, no shirt, and no shoes. He galloped toward us in his ungainly but surprisingly speedy way.

"Not now," I groaned under my breath. "Bye, Gib!" I said, hoping he'd get gone before Spencer could do something horrifying.

"Is this your brother?" Gib asked amiably when Spencer stopped next to him and made his happy sound.

Too late. I nodded, reverse sighing. When I was younger and Spencer pulled this kind of thing in front of a friend, I'd yell at him. Then my mother would snap at me. And the friend would ask to go home. I'd end up crying eventually, in my room, alone. But now, I knew it appeared mean of me to be short-tempered with my brother. Even though other people have *no* idea what living with Spencer is like, and that I do all manner of kind things for him all the time. That I probably tied his shoes a half hour before, or sung him "I Love Trash" to distract him during a meltdown, or mopped up a gallon of milk he'd accidentally emptied on the floor just before I was about to pour it on my breakfast cereal. How about the simple fact that I've let him take priority in our house since before I can remember and *never* made my mother feel guilty for putting me second. Or third. I didn't like to count.

Of course nobody gets all that. Gib was being accepting and open-minded. I straightened my shoulders and bucked up.

"Yes, this is Spencer," I said. "He has autism."

"Hey, bud," Gib said.

Spencer's eyes flitted to Gib's face, then away. He flapped his arms a few times and pointed to Gib. "Friend," he said, ever searching to label people, like in his picture dictionaries.

"Yes. This is Gib."

"Frieeend," Spencer repeated, slowly and quietly, looking for my approval.

I shifted. "Yes, Gib is my friend." *God, I should have said* "a *friend,*" *not* "my *friend.*" Gib didn't flinch, I noticed. My shoulders unclenched.

"Friend!" Spencer rocked excitedly back and forth on his toes.

Anything could happen next, so I struggled for damage control. "Spence, what do you say?"

Spencer grinned wide. "I am fine how are you!" His first speech therapist taught him greetings in a script format, and he'd memorized the words without ever really understanding them.

"I'm good," said Gib, clearly charmed. "Thanks, man. High five?" Spencer packed a surprising wallop of a high five, but I didn't have time to warn Gib. Not that he needed it.

Thank God Linda appeared from the garage while things were still okay. She waved to Gib and me, her expression apologetic. "Spencer! We have to finish your puzzle."

"Puzzle!" Spencer skipped sideways toward Linda.

"Bye! Gib!" he said, followed by happy humming.

Gib smiled and made a face like: *All righty then!* But he didn't say more; people rarely do. I think they don't know what to say, because it's strange to all of a sudden learn how challenging someone's life might be, when a moment before you had no idea. I grimaced inside. I hated feeling exposed.

"Don't forget about the Maleshefskis," Gib said, getting in his car. Then he flashed me an open-hand wave and I remembered how awesome it was that Gib Frigging *Discobolus* Soule was backing down my driveway. That he came to see *me*. That I'd managed not to make an idiot out of myself, and that Spencer held steady.

I patted Boomer's head. "Even when Hattie's not here, she sets me up for coolness, Boom." He lolled his tongue to one side and wagged his tail.

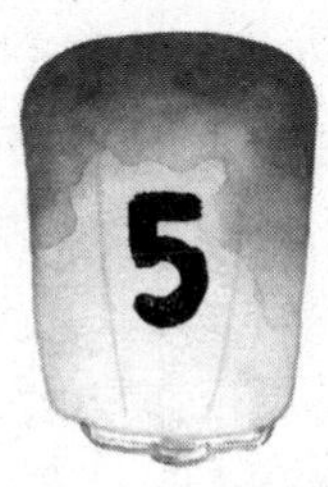

August 27

I knelt on the bathroom floor, forehead pressed to the cool tiles. My mother's knocks sounded distant, at the other end of a long tunnel separating me from her. They mixed with my pulse—throbbing through my neck, behind my eyes—until I didn't know which was which. I'd retched myself hollow. My ribs ached.

You can get up, *Reddi*, Hattie said.

I opened my lids, hot and dry.

I've seen you rally.

"Reid?" Mom said through the door. "Let me help you."

I stayed silent, hardly breathing, listening. "Where are you?" I whispered. My throat burned.

Nothing.

My mother tapped again.

"Just a sec," I said. Hauling myself up, I faced the mirror. My cheekbones seemed like the only thing supporting my face, my skull perfectly defined under the pale skin. For a second, I saw my own skeleton. I snapped my eyes away and ran the water, lifting palmfuls of it and slurping it in. I grabbed the washcloth and pushed against my eyes until I saw red and black blotches. In the spaces between, Hattie appeared on her horse Lyra, dressed in the Headless Horseman costume we used in our prank last Halloween. She signaled me toward her.

Come on, Ichabod! she laugh-said. Lyra danced sideways, raring to run.

"You're not gone," I said.

She didn't answer. Typical. I felt tired. Beaten. I returned to the floor, curling like a potato bug.

"What, Reid? I can't hear you." Mom grew more insistent. How odd, I thought, to have so much of her attention. She wasn't used to me being the problem.

The doorknob rattled. "Reid?" my dad said, cautiously opening the door. I was both embarrassed and immobile.

"What's she doing?" Mom asked.

"It's okay," he said. His dress shoes and trouser cuffs landed next to me as he wedged himself against the wall.

He squatted, his hand on my head. I was little, so little, again.

"Can you bring her out?" Mom said.

He didn't answer. "Are you going to be sick again, baby?"

I made an effort, such as it was in this pose, to shake my head.

"Okay then. Let's get you to bed." He raised me up and guided me to the hall.

Mom said, "Thank God," barely audibly. I looked at her face and she searched mine, expressionless, like she was trying to figure out who I was. She turned toward the kitchen. "I'll call Dr. Dankin. She needs valium."

In my room, Dad pulled back the bedcovers. "You wanna get out of that?" I'd forgotten about the girl tux work uniform. I nodded and he left.

Mom showed up again and my room filled with the smell of the lavender tea she gives me when I'm sick. I stared at the flowers on my wallpaper until they became swirly whirlpools of peach.

"You're okay, Reid, you're all right," she repeated over and over, rubbing my back. Her breath stuttered. I thought, *What the hell are you talking about? I am not!* I don't say things like that to my mother, though. Not true things about me.

It was easier to go see Hattie. Going to see Hattie was always easier, always better than staying home.

"Just go to sleep," Mom whispered.

I let my mind travel away from her voice. I wanted to relive my favorite memory, our most epic of pranks, last October. Before Gib, before prom. Before she was *It*. Maybe, I thought now, it was the beginning of her metamorphosis into a butterfly. I remembered, like a pinprick, how the week of the Headless Horseman didn't start out well, which is part of what made the fact that we pulled it off even sweeter.

It was October, and like every school day, I had come to pick her up. I waited in the Fiesta in her driveway. From the second Hattie waved from her window, I knew she wouldn't be coming to school. I shot her a look, but she disappeared behind her curtain. A text from her blinked onto my phone.

H: Take good notes in Am Lit.

"Again?" I said aloud. She'd missed a bunch of days already this year, with very iffy excuses. She knew it bugged the hell out of me, too.

Me: Why?

H: I need to work on my history paper.

Me: You'll just miss more work.

H: Maybe after lunch.

Me: Bull.

H: Take good notes? Please?

I blew my bangs out of my face.

Me: Fine.

We didn't talk that night. On Tuesday morning, I called. She didn't pick up. Her text came a minute later.

H: Now I'm sick.

Me: Come on.

H: I ate bad takeout last night. You know when they don't clean out that line of poop in the shrimp? 💩🤢

I growled. Another day of feeling like a leech stuck on Hammy and Charlie and Alesha.

Wednesday, while I idled in her driveway, hoping to guilt her into coming, she texted.

H: Sorry, thought I was better. Just barfed.

I squinted toward her bedroom window and saw a pathetic hand wave. I sighed, not sure if I should be pissed at her for faking or at myself for not believing her in the first place. It was easier to be mad at myself.

Me: Feel better.

After American Lit, I texted her.

Me: Langhouser threatened a pop quiz Friday on Legend of Sleepy Hollow.

No reply.

Me: Hope you're recovering. Shared the notes in Google.

After cross-country, I resisted checking my phone. Why kill a good runner's high? In the end, I only made it to our driveway. She'd texted an hour before.

H: Just finished the Johnny Depp movie of Sleepy

Hollow. We are totally reenacting this scene to scare the crap out of the boys' soccer team at their cookout Friday. Come over after practice.

Me: So you're better now?

Crickets.

"Seriously?" I said to Boomer, who followed me inside.

Me: You weren't sick. Just admit it.

But I deleted that and tapped her YouTube link, sinking into the family room sofa.

Scene: A dark and misty night, 1800s in Sleepy Hollow, New York. Geeky Ichabod Crane (Johnny Depp) walks his decrepit horse through a quaint covered bridge. A horse whinnies behind him. Lo, the dreaded Headless Horseman, wielding an evil jack-o'-lantern, on the hunt for a head! Ichabod freaks. The chase begins.

I laughed, amused. And relieved. And amazed.

Me: I'll come over after dinner.

Unlike our house, the Darrows' was always completely chill. A rambling antique farmhouse with the horse barn and acres of fields, it was a private country to me. There may be five Darrow kids, but only Hattie lived at home full-time. Walt and Ben were the oldest, both out of college and living in Boston. I'd met them a few times on The Thimble, but had trouble remembering them without a photo. Hattie loved Ben and talked about him often. Camilla, the artist, lived in San Francisco, and Helen was still at Brown. Mr. and Mrs. Darrow had raised four smashing successes already, and had no reason to assume Hattie wouldn't follow suit. So, we frequently had the run of the place while they went to art openings and operas in New York City. Even when they were home, they let us feel like they weren't. Hattie stood before her bedroom mirror, arms overhead, decked in black. I wound duct tape around her torso, mummy-style. It secured our masterpiece—the half broomstick and wooden hanger contraption that would hold her jacket high enough to give the illusion of headlessness.

I ripped the tape and patted it flat, standing back to admire my handiwork. "Too tight?"

She twisted gingerly, as if stretching for a tennis match. "Nope."

As Ichabod, I wore a long-tail tux jacket over all black with a white scarf tucked into the collar and my hair slicked into a colonial ponytail. We'd raided the Darrows' attic and found all we needed.

I handed her the black ski mask, followed by her riding helmet. We draped her dad's old suit jacket on the hanger. She buttoned it to her chin.

"Well?" she said, voice muffled.

"This," I said, Velcro-taping her cape to the helmet, "is freaking brilliant!"

I turned her toward the mirror. We spontaneously struck a pose, then lost it.

Outside, leaves crackled under our boots. I carried our jack-o'-lantern and Hattie gripped my elbow as we made our way to the Darrows' barn, which was across the lawn past some apple trees. Their property was a giant rectangle with a typical lawn near the house and barn, but then a pasture where the horses grazed down at the other end. It abutted woods, which they owned, too, and eventually those woods became the town's nine-mile recreational Green Belt trail. All these details fit in our plan.

The brisk air seemed trigger-happy and the sky stretched over us, gaping and purple. Lyra, Hattie's black mare, whinnied from her stall. Hattie called, "It's just me!"

Per usual, I'd be riding Barnaby, the old, bulgy-sided horse Hattie rode as a child. I was a decent rider on patient horses. Barnaby was not patient. He and I came to an agreement some time ago, though. I pretended he didn't scare me; in return, he would not kill me. We both knew I was full of shit, but I was his ticket out of the barn, so there it was.

I rooted around saddle blankets and leather harnesses in search of the flashlight Hattie kept there. "This is going to kick so much ass," I muttered like a mad scientist.

Hattie led the horses to the lawn. I gave her a leg up and handed her the pumpkin. She clicked on the flashlight so its fang-filled grin glowed.

"I literally have chills," I said, rubbing my arms. "You're terrifying."

"We're evil geniuses, Reddi. Evil. Geniuses." She spun Lyra around. "Come on!"

Barnaby's girth set my legs wide. "I see you haven't been

dieting as we discussed," I said to him. His ears flickered. "Just kidding." I patted his neck.

Hattie knew how to navigate to Halsted Park via the Green Belt trail, so we'd never go on the road. Halsted served as the town's venue for everything from fancy weddings to cross-country tournaments—and tonight, a pre-championship soccer cookout. Halsted Mansion had a huge patio, outdoor fireplace, and a wide lawn surrounded by acres of public trails available to people, dogs, and horses. Perfect cover.

Barnaby stuck close to Lyra as we entered the woods, moving faster than requested. The steady rhythm of hooves thudding against dirt, kicking up leaves, made a kind of music. I wondered if riding like this, through decaying foliage on a moonless night, was what gave Washington Irving his Headless Horseman idea in the first place.

Eventually light flickered through the trees ahead. Hattie signaled to me from the woods' edge. Side by side, we spied on the scene, lit dull orange by lampposts and firelight. Players and coaches clustered in small bunches. We had practiced our ride in daylight yesterday, and like an athlete on the field, I visualized my route around the party to another section of woods, just beyond the mansion.

The horses stomped in anticipation. Hattie pulled Lyra back. "Ready, Reddi?"

"I am"—I tipped my head nobly—"Reddi."

Leaning forward, I tapped Barnaby with my heel and we flew into the open. A laugh floated out of me as, cluster by cluster, the boys turned toward me. Barnaby was surprisingly fast and I could only see blurs of gape-mouthed faces. I reminded myself to say the lines before it was too late. "He's coming! Run for your lives!"

I heard someone say, "What the hell?" followed by lots of shouting, but before I knew it, I'd made it. I slowed Barnaby and slipped back into the woods. "Good boy," I whispered, breathlessly, straining to see the tree I knew to hide behind so I could watch Hattie.

A player crashed through branches behind me. "Is that you, Anderson? You asshole!"

I jumped down and pulled Barnaby to the tree, swallowing laughter. He grew closer and in the moonlight I saw Jay Seavers, the good-looking junior with too much swagger.

"I know that's you, Anderson." He stalked the path, scanning the shadows. Barnaby snorted. Jay froze. He squinted, eyes shiny, but somehow didn't see us. "Anderson?" he called hoarsely. I heard fear in his voice.

This. Was. Awesome.

Even in the heat of it, I knew moments of power like this were rare as Willy Wonka Golden Tickets for people like me.

I cupped my mouth and dug for my deepest baritone. "Beware the Headless Horseman!"

"Who is that?" He stumbled backward. Scrumptious as this was, I had to hurry for the second part of our play. I heaved myself into the saddle and spurred Barnaby. We exploded from hiding. Jay yelped and leaped sideways. I searched the wide *field I'd just crossed. The boys started to hoot and I squinted to see past the lampposts. I pulled the reins tight. Barnaby stomped sideways.*

At first, only the pumpkin's devilish face soared high above the ground in the darkness. Then, like a phantom, Hattie took shape, galloping toward us.

"What the fuck?" Jay Seavers whispered behind me.

She loomed ten feet above her captive audience and with the billowing cape, she was truly colossal. The boys gaped as she rode a huge and easy loop around them. With cinematic timing, Hattie pulled Lyra into a rear and the horse paddled her hooves over them.

"Please whinny, please whinny," I chanted quietly.

Whe-he-he-he-he!

I squealed with joy. She galloped toward me.

My cue.

I barely prompted Barnaby and clamped on, hunkering into his mane. We hurtled past the boys and I sucked in their bewildered, slack-jawed stares like the last of a glorious milkshake. Some chuckled, some were scared witless.

The faces turned away from me as one. I glanced over my shoulder. The vision of the Headless Horseman close on my tail sent panic rippling through me, even knowing it was Hattie. I forgot my lines and instead gave a wordless shriek into the night. It was genuine, but she'd never know.

Barnaby slowed to enter the wooded path. Lyra and Hattie hammered behind. I expected her to slow, but she raced past.

"They're chasing us!"

Male voices hooted and a mass of figures broke into the woods.

Barnaby didn't wait. We bolted through the tight tunnel of leaves and branches, my arms wrapped around his neck. I prayed—silently, out loud, who knew? My left boot slipped from the stirrup, then my right. My thighs burned, squeezing to stay on. My muscles gave out and my ass started bouncing off the saddle. "Shit, Barnaby!" I yelled, but my voice was lost in the clatter. Clinging with everything I had, I shut my eyes.

Just then, Lyra slowed and Barnaby followed the leader, bouncing to a trot and finally a walk.

"Thank GOD!" I said. Tears from the wind trickled down my cheek.

Hattie guffawed through her costume. She'd just done that hell ride with impaired vision. And she was still holding the dang pumpkin.

We rode in silence until we emerged on the Darrows' open field. She ripped off her helmet and ski mask and her eyes gleamed from a light deep inside her. "That," she said breathlessly, "was fucking incredible."

"Their faces!" I said.

She rubbed Lyra's neck. "Let's do it again!"

We laughed ourselves sore while the horses, drunk with self-satisfaction, swayed across the dry autumn grass to the paddock. Above, the October sky turned from violet to black. Silver clouds grazed the pale moon. The horses exhaled plumes of breath that swirled into the dark, dancing with our voices. I drank it all into my lungs and let it cascade through me. We were witches, Hattie and me. The moon, clouds, stars, and the limitless spirit of the universe knew it, too.

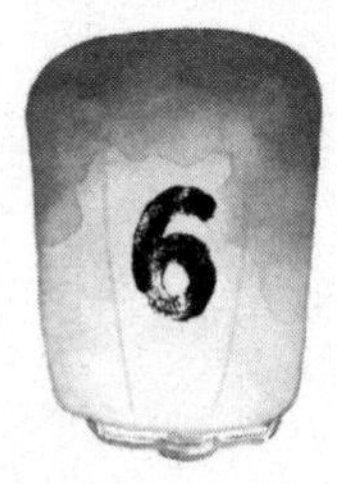

THEN

June 19

I leaned back in my kitchen chair, peering out the window for the third time since dinner started, just in case Hammy would magically appear without texting me first. The Summer of Reid and Hammy needed to start with a bang, did it not?

"What's wrong with you?" Scott asked, which spurred a flurry of hand flapping from Spencer. We three often ate dinner together before my dad got home from work.

"Huh?" I prayed Hammy would come through. Gib Soule had invited me to the secret not-party or whatever, but not *with* him; I couldn't go alone. I stabbed a piece of rigatoni and it skittered off the table. Spencer laughed as Boomer snarfed it up.

"Quit bouncing your knee," Scott said. "And pass the butter."

My phone vibrated on the counter. In a complete lapse of dignity, I sprang for it, my fork nearly catching Scott's eye.

"Watch it!"

Sandwich: Max is dog-sitting at the Maleshefskis'.

I grinned.

"Hot date?" Scott said.

"Shut it," I said. "And no."

I almost typed, *I know*, but decided not to mention Gib. It would lead to questions, which would lead me to reveal that Hattie scooped Gib in a *very* big way last night. If Hammy knew that, he might lose interest in the Summer of Hammy and Reid. Then I'd be back to the plan of college money, which after my in-person visit from *Discobolus* himself seemed seriously, seriously sad.

Sandwich: I'll get you @ 7. Bring a swimsuit.

I did a little dance.

"Reid is happy," said Spencer.

"Reid is whacked," said Scott.

"I get to go to a clandestine party at the Maleshefskis' pool," I sang.

"They don't have kids," Scott said.

"Max Silverman is dog-sitting." I had the inside scoop. *Me!*

"Not bad," Scott conceded. "You're quite the party girl these days. Aren't you going to miss the season opener for some BBC romance about vicars and scullery maids or something?"

"Ha ha."

"Just giving you shit, Reid. That's my job," he said while chewing. "You"—he pointed at me with his fork—"getting out there"—he swallowed—"is a good thing."

"Yes," I said. "Yes, it is." My dishes clattered in the sink. I felt like I'd cracked the code to the inner sanctum of the cool guy network, all thanks to Hattie, and she wasn't even here. I grabbed my phone and texted her.

Hammy AND Gib invited me to a party at the Maleshef-skis'!

Before sending it, I deleted *AND Gib*, following my own advice to him. But I really hoped Hattie saw this text before I got to Maine on July eighth.

I changed clothes six times before settling with the basic jean skirt and white peasant blouse. I'd go casual, like it was no biggie for me to be there. Unable to decide between a one- or two-piece swimsuit, I threw both in my bag. My stomach wouldn't stop fluttering. What would I say to people? Who would I talk to? What if the dickhead was there? I sat on the counter near the kitchen sink, uncontrollably tapping my feet as I watched the driveway. When Hammy drove up in his forest-green

Subaru wagon, I darted outside before he could come to the door. Scott would tease me, Spencer would embarrass me, and my parents, who were country club friends with the Stanwiches, would start an inquisition.

I plunked myself into the passenger seat. "Hey," I said in a passable attempt at calm.

He grinned, nodding his head. "The Summer of Sam and Reid," he said quietly, holding his fist up for a bump.

I raised my eyebrows, thankful for the release my smile allowed. "That's *Hammy* and Reid."

"Have it your way, MacGregory." He held his fist steady. I gave him a look. "Wait, are you rejecting my fist bump?" he asked. "That's bad luck. It's like—" He tilted his head. "That's like not blowing out the candles on your birthday cake. Or not wishing on a falling star. Or when you see a leprechaun. Are you telling me, Reid, you're the kind of girl who ignores a fucking leprechaun?"

"Um, no?" I said.

"Thank God." I bumped it and he did the fireworks fingers thing. He closed his eyes solemnly. "Let the games begin." He put the Subaru in reverse and yelled, "*Ad victorium!*"

"What the heck does that mean?" I asked.

"To victory!" he said. "It's a battle cry in Latin." He'd taken two years of Latin, telling us he'd be ahead of the curve when applying to law school someday. "In other words, Reid," and he rolled down his window. "ROCK AND ROLL!"

Hammy would make a great substitute for Hattie, I decided right then. And he had a better singing voice, which he demonstrated on the ride across Scofield.

Max and his next-door neighbors the Maleshefskis lived in Ledge Haven, the wealthiest section of Scofield, which, let's be real, has a lot of wealthy sections. The tangle of dangerously narrow and serpentine roads hugged the waterfront. Inlets and streams eddied between the elegant homes, under stone footbridges and out to the Long Island Sound. Besides its own yacht club, Ledge Haven was the only neighborhood with its own security detail. Hiding cars for even a pool *non-party* here was impossible, and Hammy explained to me that Max wanted everyone to park in town and walk.

"It's a mile from town," I said.

"No pain no gain," Hammy said. He really was perfect for Hattie. If the Gib thing didn't happen senior year, I would get to work on opening her dang eyes to this fact. "But don't worry," he continued. "I've got us covered. Seavers is letting us park at his house."

My stomach dropped. "What?"

"Jay," Hammy said. "Seavers? He lives four houses from the Maleshefskis. His dad's girlfriend is like twenty-two, and she told Jay she'll cover for us."

I am not sure if I whimpered out loud. I know I considered launching myself through the window into the bushes. Cafeteria Jay walked through my head, his expression aggressively blank, dropping my gaze like a hot potato.

Suddenly winding roads rolled my stomach. I opened my window all the way. "Are we speeding?" I croaked.

I felt Hammy glance at me, and the Subaru slowed. "Are you okay?"

My heart thudded and I remembered watching the vein pulsing at Jay's temple when our heads were close together. "I—I get a little carsick sometimes," I said.

"No worries, we're here."

He turned into a gravel driveway, past its round grassy island of flowering bushes. It was a magazine-beautiful chateau, almost too perfect to be real, much like the ass who lived there, I thought. Hammy parked and considered my face. "Need a minute?" he said.

I wobbled my head in something between a yes and no.

He started to chuckle but held it in and waved me off. "I'll get Seavers. Maybe stand up and take some deep breaths." He crunched off toward the house.

My mind raced for an escape. How had I thought I could do this without Hattie? How could I think Dickhead would NOT be at this thing tonight? God, I was stupid. I paced in front of an ivy-covered stone wall, gulping air. Maybe I could fake sick and Scott could get me. Or just frigging run. I dreaded seeing Jay up close, where he couldn't avoid me without raising Hammy's curiosity. And then, since he wouldn't want Hammy to know something happened between us—because apparently I'm *that* regrettable of a hookup—he'd have to be at least cordial, and so would I. And all this would take place on the driveway of his probably five-million-dollar house. I couldn't feel smaller if I were one of the Japanese beetles scuttling around the yellow rosebushes.

Hearing Hammy's voice made me peer over the roof of the car. He conversed with a blond woman at the front door. My God, she really *was* about twenty-two, barely older than Scott. Hattie had two brothers and a sister older than Jay's father's girlfriend! The door shut. Hammy jogged toward me. I leaned my face toward the bushes, trying to look ill.

"Seavers isn't coming." His words floated to my ears. "He's with his dad in New Jersey playing golf." I popped upright. "You look much better," he said.

I nodded, fanning my face for cover.

"You good?" he asked.

"I think so," I said.

"Are you sure? We can wait. Want me to see if she has Tums or something in the house?" he said, which touched my heart and horrified me both.

"No, no! I'm better, really," I said, forcing my voice strong. "Let's go." I couldn't wait to get off this property.

"I know the shortcut."

I followed him onto the lawn and into the wood that weaved between yards. *Breathe*, I told myself. *You'll be fine.*

We threaded through the trees, past four or five

impressive mansions. The daylight had mostly faded and warm yellow light glowed from the homes. I couldn't shake the feeling that Dickhead could pop out from behind a tree at any moment. New Jersey was too far for that to happen, really, but he was like one of those horror movie psycho killers who defied the laws of time and place. In my mind, anyway.

"Listen!" Hammy said in a stage whisper, stopping suddenly. "The waterfall!" I smiled, hearing the hushed gurgling. "It's the sound of Zen."

We broke through a line of trees and the pool appeared like a mirage. Water cascaded over boulders, spilling into the curvy pool. It luminesced from within and cast aquamarine streamers across the golden boys of Scofield, who languished on various pieces of lawn furniture. Behind them, the Maleshefskis' house sprang from a rocky ledge, a series of lines and angles interrupted by walls of glass. All at once, everything that had seemed untouchable to me became within my reach. Hammy opened the gate and just like that, we were in.

Matt Stedman and the rest of Vanilla Yeti surrounded a glass-top table, while Gib and the Burke twins sat in chaises, legs stretched before them. The twins, Ross and Artie, attended some elite ski school in the Colorado Rockies. They'd always reminded me of a pair of snow leopards—stunning and elusive, only appearing in Scofield a few weeks out of the year. Plus, I couldn't tell one from the other.

I followed Hammy across the patio. Gib flashed me a klieg light smile that made my heart stutter, and Stedman gave me a casual two-finger salute. The rest seemed completely unimpressed that I'd infiltrated their company, or that I was the only girl present.

Max appeared and rumbled out the word "Sandwich" like he was introducing a World Wide Wrestling champion. He nodded to me, then handed us each a beer. Everyone listened to one of the Burkes recount a near-death experience he'd had heli-skiing in Wyoming. His magnetism was undeniable: bright eyes, moppy hair, confident drawl, and words that fell like little jewels for the other boys to snap up.

Gradually more people drifted through the gate or emerged from what I guessed was the garage. I knew them all, but didn't know them. Gib gave me a second beer and I took it to sit on the pool's edge, dipping my bare feet in. My mind wandered. Hattie would have *done* something by now. They weren't even swimming. Still, they were undeniably cool. I tried to figure out what made that so—how they regarded themselves, or how the rest of us regarded them? I found myself watching the only person I didn't know, a guy with the band. He was obviously a friend of Stedman's and, like me, seemed bored by the snow leopards. His smooth, dark face glowed in the light of his phone and when he smiled at something, a startling pair of dimples appeared from nowhere. I love dimples. All at once I saw he was beautiful. I must have thought it really loudly, because he looked straight into my eyes.

"Hey." Hammy tapped my shoulder. "Let's swim."

"Yeah, okay." Rescued, I let him pull me up. We walked toward the pool house just as the Bobbles arrived: Emma Rose and her handmaidens Mimi and Greta. Emma Rose intercepted me.

"Hey, Reid," she said, putting her hand on my arm. (*Translation: I didn't think you'd be here.*) "I'm glad there are some other girls here." (*I'm lying.*) "Where's Hattie?" Her eyes meandered around the patio furniture.

"She's gone."

"Oh, right. Maine." She paused and I could see the wheels of her brain cranking into high gear. "So, you're here . . . by yourself?" (*So*, who *invited you?*)

A really low part of me loved the feel of these words rolling off my tongue: "I'm with Hammy. And Gib." A bit of a stretch, but I couldn't resist.

Her head tilted, and she made a face as if she were surprisingly impressed by the taste of, say, fried crickets. "Hmm." (*I did not see that coming.*)

"I'm going to change," I said, tipping my shoulder toward the pool house.

She swept her hair over her shoulder. "Cool. I'd never be the first one in my bathing suit here." Her fingers brushed my arm again, her eyes round. "You go, girl."

She spun away. "I will, girl," I said under my breath.

The pool house looked exactly like a family room,

including a bar and big screen TV. Trophies and framed photos lined the bookshelves, which I examined absently while Hammy occupied the changing room.

"We're going into the Maleshefskis' pool, Reid," he said, emerging in his swim trunks with a towel thrown over his bony shoulder.

Once he left and I was shut in the changing room, I had to admit Emma Rose's comments got in my head. I took out my bathing suits and agonized over the bikini (too Bobblehead-y?) or the one-piece (too Laura Ingalls Wilder?). Suddenly, the pool house door opened and I heard guys' voices.

"Check out this picture. He's shaking hands with George Bush. H. W. Bush, the cool one."

Captain.

Dickhead.

How? How did he get here from New Jersey? He *was* an evil psycho killer!

"That's my father's wet dream," the other guy, a Burke, said. They laughed.

My stomach rolled.

I yanked on the bikini, like they had X-ray vision and would see me naked if I didn't. *Shit shit shit*, I mouthed.

It was quiet for a few minutes, and I guessed they were looking at the trophies and other evidence of greatness. I pulled my phone out and texted my brother.

Scott! Come get me! Immediately! Please!

"Dude, I'm getting a beer," said a Burke.

"Bring me one," Jay said.

The pool house door swung open and shut.

I was alone with Jay Seavers, the only thing separating us a dressing room door. Scott didn't reply. My eyes filled with tears. I wondered how long I could reasonably hide in here. I crouched helplessly. My phone lit up, and I prayed it would be Scott, but it was Hattie.

I fumbled to get the message open. She'd sent a photo looking out to sea from Pulpit Head on The Thimble.

Look! O'Keeffe clouds! Miss you! xoxo

Five perfect oval clouds hung in the deep blue Maine sky, pink-tinged in the setting sun.

I took a steadying breath. If Hattie were here, she'd say, *Reid, what the hell are you worried about?* I glanced at my body, never too keen on what I saw in the mirror. *You have a pretty smokin' hot bod these days, Reddi.* "Fuck it," I whispered. I wrapped the towel around my hips and opened the door. Jay blinked twice. "Oh, look," he said, "It's the golf cart driving champ."

His expression was inscrutable. I didn't know what that was supposed to mean, but it sounded like a dig. I walked toward the door, shooting him a tight, unfriendly smile. On the way, I caught the *Vanity Fair* scent and my hair prickled. How sickening to recognize his smell.

"Maleshefski played soccer," he said, in a segue that would have been awkward on anyone else.

I paused. Was he trying to stop me? My skin tingled, like my whole body was blushing. I forced myself to face him.

"UPenn goalie," he continued. Almost imperceptibly, he moved closer to me.

I reached for the door handle behind my back, then I dared myself to stay. I didn't want to look like I was running away. "What do you play?" I said.

"Goalie. You didn't know that?" He looked shocked, but pleased we were discussing him.

I shrugged and said, "Why would I know that?" I didn't intend it as a slam, but it hit the spot.

His laugh held a hint of nervousness and his gaze rested on my chest. "Nice bathing suit," he said unapologetically. Like my breasts were his to approve of, or not. His voice was husky when he said, "You ever think about prom?" He reached for the curve of my hipbone, tugging the towel so I moved in front of him. "Man," he said, and I recognized the pulse on his temple.

Part of me felt like vomiting and the other part felt victorious. Jay Seavers was attracted to me, even if he didn't want to admit it. I grasped for clever words while he stared, mesmerized by my skin, apparently.

The door rattled. With a quickness he must have learned on the field, Jay jumped over the back of the couch—away from me. "I'll find you later," he said, one side of his lip curled up, before ducking into the changing room.

The pool house door opened. Hastily, I brushed past a Burke into the humid night air.

I'll find you later, he'd said. My head swirled.

I saw the Sandwich in the pool near the waterfall. I slid in, letting water slip over me, and the world became silent. In the pool lights, pairs of legs moved in surreal slow motion, legs attached to the Scofield elite. I was invisible, like a shark. A surge of my own power came over me. Jay Seavers was attracted to me, I thought again. Unimaginable! I propelled myself until my lungs burned, and popped up next to Hammy.

"Jesus, you scared me. What are you, Seal Team Six?"

I laughed, releasing my nerves, but watched the pool house door until Jay appeared. He strode across the patio, lots of muscle, no bulk. He didn't see me at first and I watched him scan the area. Our eyes connected. My insides locked, waiting for him to look away, but he held my gaze. Someone called him from the table, breaking the spell.

More kids jumped into the pool and Hammy and I tried the slide. There were Max's predictable cannonballs, and one of the twins threw the other one in fully dressed. All the while, I remained aware of Jay's location, like a spy. He joined everyone in the pool, and we caught eyes across the water. But Mimi, the Bobble, grabbed him by the shoulders. He twirled around and laughed, then scooped her by the waist and threw her. She screamed in a disgustingly girlie way.

Hammy asked me something about Jell-O shots.

"Yeah." I barely knew what I was saying, the sick feeling returning to my stomach. Mimi straddled Jay in the shadows so his back pressed against the pool ledge. They were making out. "Jesus!"

"What?" He followed my gaze and I quickly turned my back toward the spectacle. "Oh. Typical Seavers. Get a room, dude."

I felt my eyes fill again. What was I doing here? *You can choose not to give a shit*, *Reid*, Hattie seemed to tell me from afar.

Greta came by with a tray of Jell-O shots like a flight attendant or something. Hammy gobbled down four in about two minutes.

"Apparently I'm driving home," I said in a flat voice.

"Thanks," he said, smiling sloppily.

I clamped my jaw. I needed out. Immediately. I couldn't do this without Hattie. I wasn't at the same level as these people. I waited for a moment when Hammy was distracted (aka, every moment), and changed back into my clothes. Scott finally texted me back and agreed to get me. Waiting, I fumed to myself and the Maleshefskis' giant black poodle, who should have been the guest of honor but cowered in the shadows with me. Scott texted when he arrived.

We were out of Ledge Haven when Scott broke the silence. "So, are you just going to stew in silence?"

I sighed. Scott would not be hearing about Jay Seavers, but there was plenty more to be pissed about. "Hammy got all-out *tanked.* Greta Hayes hung all over him, but he didn't even notice—because Hammy loves someone three states away right now. He's not gonna fall for any pair of boobs that came his way. Unlike a certain dickhead I know!"

Scott snorted. "Don't let the bastards get you down, Reid."

"Hammy doesn't even know I left!"

"You like him?"

"No!"

"Oh, you like the dickhead who fell for someone else's boobs."

"HELL NO!"

"Does Hattie like Hammy?"

I groaned. "No."

"Does anybody like anybody?"

In spite of myself, I giggled. "Just Hammy loving Hattie."

"Huh," said Scott, nodding professorially. His lips quivered.

We laughed for a bit, but reality settled back in. "I thought I was going to have fun this summer, passing time with Hammy until Hattie gets back."

"Yeah, well, that can still happen. It's only June."

I made a growly sound.

"Don't worry, Reid. You and Hattie will have a blast senior year. You'll see."

"I hope so."

Later, in bed, I thought of the night before, when Hattie rolled through the window and told her story. I took my phone from the bedside and brought up her text from earlier, with the O'Keeffe clouds. She must have been off island to send that. It made me happy knowing she went to the effort. "It's only June," I said to the photo. I tried to frame my night in a Hattie point of view. She wouldn't let Jay get to her. Somehow she'd flip the tables on him. That should be one of my summer goals, up there with improving my 5K and college money. I texted Hattie back.

Those are amazing. Can't wait to be in Maine. xo

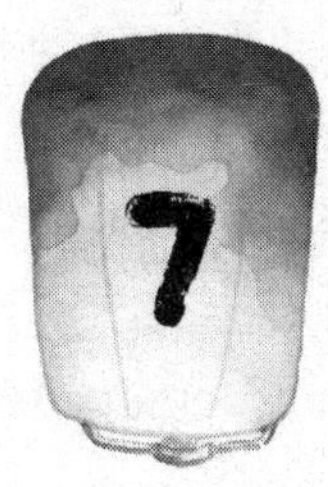

August 28

I smelled strawberries and Cheerios.

I heard breathing.

Spencer inhabited my personal space, staring at me. I knew this without opening my eyes. He'd eaten the same breakfast every day since he was four. It took longer to realize I'd slept in my desk chair. I started to remember the awfulness of Hattie. I just couldn't make it sink in. My skull felt wrapped in plasma. I'd seen her in Snowcap yesterday. I knew I had. Every inch of me hurt. In the quiet, Spencer began to hum.

I wiped spittle from my cheek.

"Reid is awake," he said.

I straightened up from my human question mark position. Pale sunlight spilled into the room. "Good morning, Spencer." He stood in his swim trunks, cradling Elmo, a red Wii remote, and the rubber lobster Hattie sent a few weeks ago.

"Reid is sad." He was like a ten-year-old anthropologist.

"Uh-huh."

He then cruised the room, pausing behind me. "Hattie."

"What?" I snapped around. He gazed at the prom picture on my bulletin board. I untacked it. Mrs. Darrow had taken it on the terrace when Charlie and Hammy arrived for dinner. Hattie goosed Hammy in it and he had this surprised expression while the rest of us laughed. Mrs. Darrow had given us each a copy.

"Hattie comes home Gus twenny-eight," Spencer said. I blinked twice. It was fucking August twenty-eighth.

He awaited my confirmation, eyes trained on my every facial muscle. We'd had this exchange many times this summer. When it was true. My heart broke again, knowing he wouldn't comprehend. Knowing I couldn't give him what he needed.

"Hattie comes home Gus twenny-eight," he repeated, his posture stiffening. He dropped his red things. This was Spencer about to blow.

"Umm . . ." I smoothed my hair, buying time. An ice pick lodged behind my eye.

"HATTIE COMES HOME GUS TWENNY-EIGHT!" He jumped, landing loudly.

I squeezed my eyes shut.

He yelled it again, getting closer to me. I knew he wanted me to say it, just to confirm the plan he'd counted on since she left in June. Again, he yelled, "HATTIE COMES HOME—"

"Okay!" I yelled, then calmed my voice like Spencer's therapists trained us to do long ago. I couldn't bald-faced lie to Spencer, so I hedged. "It's okay," I choked, adding, *All done talking about it* in sign language.

His pupils were giant with adrenaline. His neck flushed. I couldn't fool him. He saw my tears. "Reid is sad!" he said, voice pitched high. He bounced from foot to foot and whispered, "Hattie comes home . . ." letting his voice trail off in hopes that I'd finish his sentence. For Spencer, schedules tethered him to earth like the ropes on a Macy's parade balloon, made orderly a world he couldn't understand. "It's okay," I repeated. "Let's pick up your stuff."

Spencer let it rip. His emotions ran purer than anyone's I knew, especially mine. The screams seared me; my headache throbbed. "Please, Spence, please . . ." I sank to the floor and hid my head in my hands, like he was beating me. For a moment, our wails mingled, filling the room.

Linda, Spencer's aide, appeared. "Spencer!" She put her hands on his shoulders in a Reiki healing gesture.

I wished she could heal me. He quieted. “Reid needs to rest,” she said finally. “Do you want to swim?” Distraction.

“Swim,” he said, stooping to gather today’s red collection. Hattie and I taught Spencer to swim with a noodle. Hattie got him to jump in, and she taught him to hold his breath underwater. My parents never thought he’d learn those things and were way too scared to teach him themselves.

“Reid . . .” Linda blinked back her own tears. “I’m so sorry.”

I couldn’t speak.

She led him away. I flopped across my bed and lay still, listening to my heart’s tinny beat, staring at the ceiling.

The house phone rang. A little while later, my dad peered through the open crack of my door. “Can I come in?” Mom appeared behind him.

“That was Hattie’s uncle Baxter,” Dad said quietly. My pulse rang in my ears.

He sat on the bed. My mother locked eyes with him. He dropped her gaze and took my hand. “They’ve confirmed—” He cleared his throat. “She . . . it was suicide.”

Mom gasped, grabbing on to his shoulder. “Oh, Rob.”

“We’re asked to keep it private,” he said, hoarse. “Baxter thought Reid should know—” He drew a thick breath. “But it won’t be made public.” He hugged me, but I couldn’t sink into it like I always did. “Hattie loved you.

You know that, baby." His voice broke and Mom hugged both of us. I couldn't. I pulled away and blankly stared at my parents crying into each other's shoulders.

They were wrong.

They were *wrong.*

At some point, I found I was alone. I did not cry and I did not sleep. I watched the red digits on my clock change for an hour. My cell phone rang again and again, and part of me realized news was spreading, but mostly I thought about where she must be, really be, because I'd seen Hattie driving Snowcap earlier. I had.

The clock flipped to 11:11, the Sea of Life game time, and I remembered the first time we played in sixth grade. I squeezed my eyes closed and drifted in my head, skipping across the clouds of time, until I saw myself, age twelve, lying on my stomach reading *Calvin and Hobbes* on her bedroom floor.

"Think fast!" said Hattie, standing in her doorway. A small UFO hurtled toward me.

I have decent reflexes for all my other athletic failings, and my hand darted out in time for the incoming to land in my palm with a satisfying smack.

It was a whole walnut.

I raised an eyebrow. She handed me a small, sharp knife. "Make sure you split the shell along the crack. Take out the nut. Then we'll have two tiny boats, one for me and one for you."

As if that explained everything, she disappeared again and I set to it, carefully wedging the blade tip into the shell's seam. It was our first sleepover. Her parents were out to dinner in New York City, and none of her four siblings lived at home at the moment—boarding school, college, and so on. We'd had pizza, watched an old movie with popcorn, and changed into pajamas.

Before Hattie, I never had a best friend. She was the kind of kid who always had a game plan, and I was often surprised she found me a worthy companion. So I rarely questioned her ideas. What began as a fear of losing her interest evolved into the natural order of us.

Hattie returned, gingerly carrying a pottery bowl. By then, I'd cleaned out the two walnut halves. She laid the bowl between us on the floor, and I saw it was nearly filled with water. She checked her bedside clock: 11:04.

"Perfect," she said. "We start at eleven eleven."

"And we will be starting . . ."

"Fortune-telling," she said. She pulled a little forest gnome off her dresser, the kind with the red cone hat. "My grandmother sent me this last week, for this game called Sea of Life she used to play in Sweden when she was our age. We ask the tomten questions, set our boats in the water, and he answers us."

"I don't get it," I said.

She rifled through a desk drawer and pulled out a greeting card. "She says, 'If your boat sails across the water and touches the other side, the answer to your question is yes. If your boat stops in the middle, the answer is no. If it goes backward or sideways, the answer is maybe. If it sinks, the answer is unknowable.'"

"Ooh, this sounds fun," I said. Hattie made everything fun and I loved our times at her house. When you have a brother with the level of autism Spencer has, you don't invite friends over much. Let me be clear. I'd take on wild boars to protect him—the ones with tusks. But it had been two years since the Margot Poole incident, and I'd managed to have all my playdates off-site since then. Spencer, not a fan of clothes, had opened our bathroom door on Margot Poole peeing while he was naked. Even though Margot smiled and said it was fine, she told the entire fourth grade that Reid's brother showed her his penis. I hated Margot Poole. She'd since moved. Still.

"We have to start at eleven eleven, the magic time," she said, wiggling her fingers and waggling her eyebrows. "It only happens twice a day. We have three minutes."

We sat, watching the clock.

"What are you gonna ask?" I said.

"Hmm." She tapped her chin, then startled. "I forgot candles!" She scrambled out the door.

I propped the gnome on a small pillow from Hattie's bed. "Comfy, Mr. Tomten?" I asked as Hattie came in with two candlesticks and matches.

"I love that! Mr. Tomten. That's his new name. Can you get the light?"

In a moment, we sat in an orb of candlelight, which twinkled off the Sea of Life. Mr. Tomten watched over us from his perch. Hattie redid her ponytail, eyes glued to her bedside clock. The minute changed.

"The magic time!" she blurted. My stomach jumped. I don't know why. "Want to go first?"

I shook my head.

"Okay, I'll go. Mr. Tomten, will we get another horse this year?" She took her walnut and gently shoved it into the Sea of Life. I was afraid to look at Mr. Tomten, like he would come to life and start pacing the pillow or something. The boat drifted toward the other side of the bowl. "Keep going, come on," Hattie coaxed, her face golden and hopeful. Hattie's next older sister, Helen, had a horse that had been put to sleep last spring, before I knew Hattie. Each time the subject came up, all the Darrows seemed sad.

Tap. The boat touched the edge of the bowl.

"Yay!" Hattie threw her arms up and kissed Mr. Tomten. "Your turn," she said, resettling him on the pillow.

"Hmm." I turned the walnut shell in my fingers. "Am I going to grow"—really, I wanted to ask if I'd ever get decent boobs, but chickened out—"tall, like my dad's side of the family?"

Hattie looked confused. "I thought you were going to say 'big boobs'!"

I giggled. How did she know? "What if he said no?"

"Good point," she said, gazing at the gnome. "Some things better left unknown, eh, Mr. Tomten?" His solemn, wrinkly expression struck us as hilarious and we rolled on the floor.

"So," I sighed at last. "Will I be tall, Mr. Tomten?" I set my boat on the water. I pushed too hard, and it loop-the-looped. "Maybe," I said, my shoulders drooping.

"Maybe isn't no, Reid. There's a lot of promise in maybe," Hattie said, smiling. "Maybe's not bad at all."

"Reid." A gentle shaking on my shoulder startled me. Dad stood over me. "Sam's downstairs."

"No," I said. "I can't."

"It might help," he said. "He's a good friend, Reid."

An ache that had a backward echo in my earliest memories chased itself in my chest, like dry leaves in a whirl. "I know. Just—" I didn't even know what I wanted. "Later. Maybe."

I stared at the wall. Hot tears rolled sideways toward my ears. The funny thing was, I didn't know I was crying.

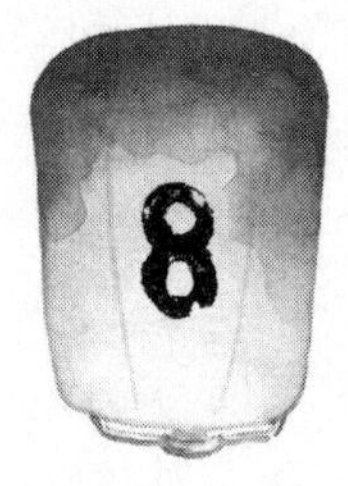

THEN

June 20

The candy-colored lobby of Pediatric Occupational Therapy tried so hard to be cheery that it was depressing. Folded into the corner of the pleather sofa, still annoyed about the previous night, I scrolled Instagram on my phone. One more smiling face and I might barf.

Earlier, my mother had asked me to take Spencer to his weekly occupational therapy session. She asked it like this was an unusual request, when in reality I ended up here practically every Saturday, amid plastic Barneys and Power Rangers and a couple of exhausted moms vying for the latest issue of *People*. Basically, my mother didn't like being here. Its vibe ran contrary to her "Autism knocked on the wrong door" attitude, a mantra I imagined she said to keep from locking herself in her room forever. Every kid who filed through here must have needed some kind of OT treatment, but they all had more language than Spencer. And they were all younger. Spencer hadn't outgrown treatment. Spencer would never outgrow treatment. This truth tugged at my heart in a way I'd learned to ignore long ago. I had to if I would survive the sadness of it all. It was maybe the single way I was tougher than Mom. So, I piled Spencer in the car each week and handed him off to Larissa, the twentysomething therapist, when she greeted us at the door. He'd disappear into her office for fifty minutes to work on tying his shoes or something and I'd hang here—sparing Mom.

File it under *Things MacGregorys Don't Say Aloud.* Talking about the painful truth is a slippery slope to Mom finally coming unglued. At least that was the unspoken threat Dad, Scott, and I lived under.

A pale little boy swerved inappropriately close to me on the sofa, singing, when my phone vibrated. My jaw clenched. I knew it wouldn't be Hattie from The Thimble, which meant Hammy, the Jell-O Shot Warrior. The phone buzzed again. I flipped it over. Yep. Hammy. "Fine," I muttered.

Hammy: Tongue is sandpaper. Head in vise.

I wanted to write, *I'm glad you are suffering.*

Me: Sorry to hear it.

Hammy: Thanks for

I waited.

Hammy: driving me home?

Me: Thank Scott.

Scott went back to retrieve Hammy after dropping me at home. I think he just wanted to impress Hammy's sister, but win-win, right?

Hammy: Shit. Does he think I'm an idiot?

Me: Does Scott or do I? I deleted this before I hit the send button.

The kid drove a toy car right onto my shoulder without looking at me at all. He stopped at my elbow and did a U-turn back up to my shoulder, making burbling sounds like a motor. I glanced at his mom, hiding in her magazine.

I'm not sure why, but I almost cried just then.

I shook myself, sitting straighter. The kid rolled the car back onto the couch.

Me: Don't worry about it.

Hammy: I'm sorry I failed at being a Scooby friend. The rest of the summer will be better.

Me: Are you suggesting we go out again?

Hammy: Hell to the yes, we are going out again! It's a pact, Reid. A pact.

I began to compose a rejection based on his failure to live up to the pact on Night One, but the fact was, Hammy was my only chance for any life at all this summer. Could I really face Hattie in two weeks without anything to talk about but the latest season of *Sherlock*?

Hammy: Please don't give up on me. I promise I won't do that again. The Mystery Machine will rock your driveway at 7.

I pulled my feet onto the couch and pressed the thumbs-up icon. I got a memory flash of Jay leering at my chest in the pool house. *I* was the idiot.

"You shouldn't chew your nails," the boy said, watching me. My cheeks flushed, which was frigging ridiculous. "Right, Mommy?" he said. His mom shot me an apologetic smile.

"You're right," I said for her, effectively sparing his mom, too.

On the way home, we needed to stop for Spencer's meds at Greenway's. Spencer in public places was an exercise in humility. He might start uncontrollably laughing in the grocery store line for no apparent reason. Pass horrific gas in an elevator. Touch a stranger on the arm. The possibilities were endless. My mother said things like, "Spencer works so hard to fit into our world, people can make a small effort to accept him." Yeah, right. Anyway, she'd given me the credit card and I fully planned on buying some new makeup to pay myself for the trouble.

I tested blusher colors on the back of my hand, aware of Spencer's humming half an aisle's length from me. When I got my driver's license last year, I'd crafted a deal with myself for community outings with Spencer (that's what the social workers called them). It went like this: I'd let Spencer stray a little ways from me, but never so that I couldn't a) see him or b) hear him. Option a) was preferred, so that I could preempt any perilous encounters with strangers, but sometimes I risked b) so I could, for instance, try out that third blusher like a normal girl would do.

I guess more time passed than I realized, because I heard Spencer say, "I am good how are you!" in his super loud happy voice. I dropped the blushers and hurried to the end of the aisle. When I saw him with a teenage guy, I was relieved—kids are always more tolerant—until I heard: "Hey, back off, little dude."

Jay. Freaking. Seavers. *Again?* Was I cursed?

I stumbled slightly. "Spencer!" I snapped.

Their two heads jerked to face me. Jay's eyes bugged momentarily, but he didn't skip a beat. "Reid." He tipped his chin without smiling.

I nodded in return, unable to make more than a flicker of eye contact. I thought my heart would blast out of my chest and land between us on the floor. "My little brother gets away from me once in a while." I took

Spencer's hand. "We don't talk to strangers," I said to Spencer in a voice spookily like my mom's.

"Don't talk to strangers," Spencer repeated, wearing a big grin. "Don't smell other people!"

Dear God. "Did he—?" Sniffing people's arms was another of Spencer's quirky things.

Jay shrugged, like he should act humble for handling the situation so well. "It's cool. Now that I know who he is." Jay patted Spencer's shoulder stiffly. "He took me off guard is all." He kept his eyes on Spencer.

"He has that effect on a lot of people," I said, now repeating my dad's go-to line. But I thought, *I can smell you from here, Mr.* Vanity Fair. *No wonder he's sniffing you.*

"Sucks for you," he said.

I have never wanted so desperately to kick a person in the crotch. All I could muster was, "I'm used to him." I wrapped my arm around Spencer's shoulders.

Jay combed his hand through his hair and stretched. Because apparently, we were that boring. "Yeah," he said, fake yawning. Then he looked directly at my boobs and said, "Hey, maybe I'll see you tonight somewhere."

I reflexively grunted, then turned it into a cough and said quickly, "Yeah," with a fake grin. "Come on, Spencer." I guided him in the opposite direction.

"Bye, friend!" said Spencer cheerfully. "Have a good weekend!"

Hattie would have said, "Have a good weekend" back,

even if it was Monday. But Jay said nothing. It was like Scott always said: “A great thing about Spencer is he gives you a fast track to knowing someone’s true nature by the way they react to him.”

Dickishness confirmed.

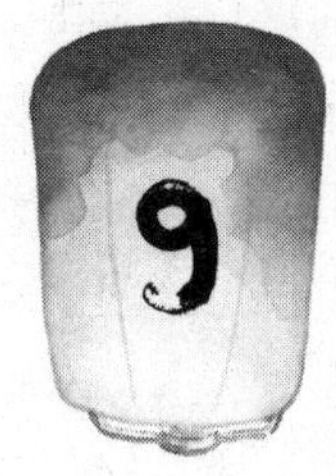

August 28

I sat wrapped in my blanket, perched on the sofa in front of our living room picture window watching chickadees land on branches. Mom floated in and out, oddly attentive. Tea. Toast. Soup. I must have eaten something or I'd have passed out by now. The setting sun hovered behind the trees and its bony fingers of light jabbed my face.

My thoughts wandered around my dad's words: *confirmed*, *suicide*. Around and around until they were an absurd jumble of sounds. Suicide? No.

I'd *seen* Hattie.

I chewed my thumb. Did I really think I'd seen a ghost on the middle of the Post Road? Sunlight danced in patches across the polished wood floor, little fish poking their heads out of the water, hypnotizing my fears so I could think. Here's the thing nobody understood like me: Hattie could be playing a prank. It *was* entirely possible that I saw the living Harriet Matsson Darrow driving through Scofield and that she was fine. Maybe.

There's a lot of promise in maybe, Hattie said. *Maybe isn't no.*

"I know, right?" I said.

"What's that, Reid?" Mom called from the kitchen.

This prank wouldn't be her smartest move, which I would have told her, if she'd run it by me. Which is why she didn't, obviously. Like she didn't run the idea of sailing into a fog bank by any of us this summer. Probably, she didn't realize how badly she'd freak everyone out. Maybe she didn't plan on the people-thinking-she-was-dead part. And the whole Coast Guard recovery could just be a ploy by Mr. Darrow to show he wouldn't be out-pranked by his daughter. That's why they wanted it secret. It wasn't true! Mr. Darrow was the original badass, and Hattie hated admitting she was like him, but once you saw them interact, it was impossible to ignore. In the Turkey Trot 5K every Thanksgiving, they ran like they were the only two competing.

So really, she could be fine. The little fish on the floor

faded. I sat straighter, pushing my hair from my face. *Fine.* A renaissance began in my chest. I wriggled free of the blanket and padded upstairs ready to get dressed and go find her.

I stared at my open clothes drawer, trying to remember what I was doing. *She could be fine.* Yes, she could be! My eyes leaked with hope, and, overwhelmed, I lay on my bed. I just needed energy.

Footsteps sounded on the back stairs and Dad stood in the doorway. The slump of his shoulders cinched my throat. *She may be fine.*

"Mind if I come in?"

She's pranking.

I wiped my eyes with my elbow and squeezed a corner of my pillow. "No."

She could be fine.

He held my phone out. "This thing has been buzzing like crazy," he said. "Maybe you should check in with your friends."

It's her, I thought, *she's calling me.* But a frightened, reedy voice in the middle of my heart whispered, *What if it's not?* My hand wouldn't reach for the phone.

"Hammy's called a bunch." He waited, then set it down and sat. "Think you're up to a little dinner? It would make Mom feel better." He put his arm around me and pulled me into his chest.

I tried not to be mad that we were focusing on Mom's

feelings. Instead, I said, "It can't be true." My words were sheets blowing on a clothesline, but he would understand.

"I know." His face crinkled up. "It seems impossible." He wasn't my dad for a second. Just a person, confused. I had a weird impulse to shoot out of the bed and run somewhere. Anywhere. I rubbed my thumb against my finger. *Swit. Swit.*

"Hattie's fine. I'm pretty positive."

He pulled back. "What do you mean?"

My eyelids fluttered under his stare. *Swit. Swit. Swit.* "I saw her, yesterday, in Scofield. Driving Snowcap. She's okay." *Swit swit swit.*

The tension in his jaw fell slack. "Reid." He put his hands over mine.

"Really. She's probably at home by herself right here in Scofield."

He looked at me sideways. "It couldn't be Hattie you saw, honey. You must've dreamed that. Remember?"

My words raced ahead of me. "No, I did see her. I bet she wanted to piss off her dad. He gets all psycho about their sailing races and the big one was the day after she disappeared and she probably—"

"Reid."

I pulled my hands away from his. "Nobody knows her like me. She'd do this; a prank." I couldn't stand his confused face, so I stood up. "She knew I'd tell. That's why she didn't tell me herself. Yet."

His gaze settled on my phone.

I walked in a circle and grabbed my bathrobe. "She's being an idiot, really. I'm going over there. I don't know why I haven't already. I'll take a shower and go," I said, whisking past him.

"A shower is probably good," I heard him say in a deflated voice, after I'd already left the room.

Under the steam, I planned my speech to her. "You know, you scared the fuck out of everyone. You could have told me, at least. Sent me a sign," I said. I thought about the O'Keeffe clouds on the way home yesterday. But she couldn't really do that, could she?

I thumped down the back stairs, hair still wet. My parents sat in quiet conversation at the kitchen table, Mom's eyes wide and owly. "Reid?" she said.

"Uh-huh," I said. I stepped into the walk-in pantry and I pulled a protein bar from the shelf. My lightheadedness was not entirely unpleasant, but Mom would insist I eat something and stop me from leaving if I didn't. This oatmeal log would fend her off.

"Are you feeling better?" she said.

"Yeah, I'm going to Hattie's," I said through a sloppy bite, a sentence I'd surely said seven thousand times. I grabbed a bottled espresso frappé from the fridge.

"Reid," she repeated. "Shouldn't you—"

"*Just*," I barked. I inhaled. "It's okay. Just let me do this." I whisked to the door. Boomer, my only ally in the place, trotted behind me.

"Wait!" Dad stumbled out the door, trying to pull his

shoes on. "Let me go with you," he called, his voice thin, like he had a square of wax paper over his mouth. Like a cheap kazoo.

I opened the car door. Boomer jumped in. "Dad! No. You'll see. It's okay, I'll be back."

Mom showed up and touched his arm. She said something and they turned toward the house.

I didn't speed on the winding roads to Hattie's, which showed outstanding restraint if you ask me, especially since my ears buzzed from caffeine. Of course Hattie was pranking. It was my job to snap her out of it. I was the calm one. The reasonable one. Twilight made the sky pearly and the thick leaves almost black. Boomer hung his head out his window, doggy smiling. He knew, too.

I rolled onto the Darrows' quiet road. Each familiar fence post and shrub comforted me. Past the Caldwells' well, past the apple trees. I pulled to the side of the driveway. She'd probably hidden Snowcap in the garage.

Across the field, the barn window glowed in the fading light. "She's feeding the horses," I told Boomer. "She's here." We got out and started walking, hopping the stone wall. As we tramped through overgrown grass, I wondered how she got the horses home from The Thimble already. Usually the horse transport was a week later than she was in getting home. I swatted the question away and unlatched the barn door. The reassuring smells of warm leather and undisturbed hay rolled over me. Below, the wood planks groaned. Above, a fluorescent bulb buzzed.

My breath fluttered like a light-boned bird in my chest. I felt her. She stirred the molecules around me. She was in the atoms.

Boomer snuffled around. I checked the feed room and the tack room, where the saddles, bridles, and such hung.

"Hattie?" I called. The emptiness sucked something out of my voice, like it was alive and thirsty.

Boomer returned to my side, ears down.

"She must be in the house," I whispered, closing the barn.

We padded toward it. Windows to two rooms glowed in the graying evening: the living room and Hattie's bedroom above.

"I knew it!" I hurried onto the brick patio where only a few months earlier, Mrs. Darrow had snapped our prom pictures. At the French doors, I dialed the alarm code, memorized years ago. The latch clicked. I began to sweat. The bird in my chest circled rapidly. "Stay, Boomer." He obediently lay down.

I felt a little like a burglar, sneaking into the house, but I heard her, rummaging upstairs. My huge smile prickled my cheeks. I left my sneakers by the door and crossed the Persian rug to the stairs. I passed two blue duffel bags. They weren't hers. She'd probably snagged anything she could find in her rush to escape The Thimble.

The steps squeaked in a familiar way I'd forgotten I knew. I moved to the less trod-upon edges and tried like hell to be silent, to not squeal with joy.

In the hall, creeping past the bathroom, I strained my ears. She was definitely in her bedroom, the door to which stood half-open. I slipped among some jackets hanging on the wood pegs outside her room. I recognized the blue zipper hoodie she'd worn in Maine just a few weeks ago. *I knew it!* A laugh bubbled up and I hid my face in the fabric, smelling the perfume she bought in Telluride last winter. I steadied myself and peered around the corner.

Through the wall mirror, I saw her curly blond ponytail in the open closet. She slid hangers across the rod. On a whim, I decided to camouflage myself with the hoodie and sneak up on her. She totally deserved a good scare. Removing it gently from the hook, I draped the hoodie over my head, so I could only peek out. I inched around the door and next to the closet, where I flattened myself against the wall. I watched her through the mirror, busily piling clothes. I heard her breathing.

I muffled another laugh. *Ready . . . (ha ha!) . . . Set . . . GO!*

I spun in midair and whipped the hoodie aside. "Surprise!"

She shrieked. Wild-eyed, she clutched her chest.

My heart thumped three full counts as we stared at each other.

And then I deflated. As in, all air left my lungs and with it, some ineffable lightness that I knew would never return.

Because the face I looked at was not Hattie's at all, but her sister Helen's—a distorted, blotchy version of it. I heard my eyelids blinking, slapping the truth into my head.

Helen crumpled into Hattie's clothes on the floor and cried.

I backed away. The bird burst through my chest, flapping past the O'Keeffe poster and shattering through the window, wailing into the night.

I don't know how long I stood frozen. Helen, perfect Helen, quivering facedown on a mound of Hattie's sweaters.

I stuttered toward her, dropping to my knees, resting my hand on her damp back. The scarf I'd given Hattie last Christmas lay rumpled atop the pile. Turquoise, to match her eyes. My lungs squeezed shut.

As if Helen sensed this through my fingertips, her shoulder muscles tugged together like knots. Inhaling deeply, she stood, looking down on me. This was the Helen I knew. Superior to me in every way. Her brow furrowed, trying to make sense of me.

"I'm sorry. I thought—" I managed. "I didn't know—if she was playing a trick. On your dad. Because she would definitely do that."

Helen blinked like I'd shot her with a dart, and my theory became so childish and hollow, like the lie a fifth grader tells herself to keep believing in Santa. I rose, shamed.

"She's not," Helen said. "I tried calling—"

A seismic rumble shook the mountains of denial in my chest. "But I saw her," I managed.

Confusion swept Helen's face. She closed her eyes. "It's real, Reid. Hattie's gone."

Her words floated like feathers, falling into Hattie's shoes lined up along the closet floor—into her cowboy boots and high-tops. The outlines of her toes showed on the sandals, and I remembered just how she looked on prom night. I saw her in my mind. Helen's feathery words drifted around Hattie in her prom dress. I shook my head, trying to focus.

I don't know what I said to Helen. I hurried down the stairs, onto the brick terrace. I'd stolen the hoodie, by accident or not I don't know. It felt oddly heavy, like her spirit was in there. I balled it up and clutched it like a quarterback. Boomer charged beside me—through the grass, over the stone wall, back to the car.

I lurched out the driveway, not caring that I nearly shot Boomer into the back seat. I ignored the fasten seat belt alarm and rolled down the windows. For at least a half mile I forgot to turn on the headlights.

"I tried to call—" Helen had said. "You were her anchor," she might have said.

The humid summer air clung to me, and the blurry walls of green leaves closed in like a gauntlet. Faster and faster, I drove from Helen and her swollen face.

Hattie's gone.

I pressed the gas harder. Boomer crawled onto the passenger-side floor. The odometer needle trembled on fifty. I pressed harder still.

An oncoming car swerved away from me.

"Fucking right," I said. "I'll take you *out*."

I zoomed past my turn for home, toward backcountry Scofield. The needle shimmied at sixty. I took an S curve like a NASCAR pro, my fingers wrapped around the steering wheel. Straightaway. Seventy.

I'll drive to Maine. I'll find her. But that was a lie.

I screamed. Took a breath. Screamed again. Seventy-three.

Boomer whimpered from the floor.

"Shut the fuck up, Boomer!" My words were bile smacking the air and flying back at my face.

A shadow flickered ahead. A fawn in the road. It didn't move. I swerved. Slammed the brakes. Rubber squealed. The car bounced.

I stopped with a jolt in the grass, headlights aimed at the woods. I sat for a moment, stunned and dizzy. I turned and craned to see if I'd hit the baby deer.

It stumbled a few steps, then fell motionless across the double yellow lines. "Shit," I mumbled. Tears blurred my vision as I leaped from the car. I ran three steps, stopped, tiptoed closer and knelt. Gravel dug into my knees. The fawn's ribs rose and fell, rose and fell. Relieved, I cried. "I'm so sorry."

She blinked but remained still. Slowly, I reached to touch her. She let me stroke her face, smooth and warm. I could have killed her and she let me pet her. Sobs twisted my stomach. "Be okay," I heard myself say, not sure if I meant the fawn or Hattie or myself. "Be okay." Her nostrils flared and closed, misting the back of my hand. I laid my wet cheek on her trembling chest and listened to her rapid heartbeat.

Her round black eyes looked into mine and saw right to my heart, I knew. All that is wild and wise lived in her ancient deer soul. "Please. Save me," I whispered.

She surged into motion, all scattered knees and sliding hooves. I wrapped my arms around her body, but she burst free. Light poured over us and we both looked at the oncoming headlights. She bolted into the woods.

The car stopped, and I stood, wiping my face and using my forearm to block the brightness. The driver leaned out the window, silhouetted.

"You okay?" he called out. He sounded old. "Should I call for help?"

I was the deer, paralyzed.

His hazards began to blink and the car door opened. Wisps of white hair floated around his head. "Miss, are you okay?"

Exploding from the bushes came one, two more fawns and a big doe. They sprang across the space between the man and me, disappearing like my fawn before them. The man and I stared at each other.

"I'll be damned," he said. "Blasted things are dangerous as hell." He shook his head. "You hit one?"

"Almost," I said.

"That can scare the bejesus out of anybody. You okay to drive?"

He came closer, squinting at me. He reminded me of my grandfather. I realized I might look crazy.

"I'm fine," I said, looking at my car angled perversely on the grass. "Thanks." I backed toward it. "For stopping."

He gave a small wave and turned to go. I fumbled for the door handle.

Boomer drew his ears down, resembling a frightened seal. I patted the seat to lure him out of hiding. "I'm sorry," I said, hugging him and dissolving into tears again.

I hung on to him, listening to the unsettled chirring of crickets and cicadas, a wall of sound that obscured the enormous truths looming. "I think she's really gone, Boomer," I whispered after a while, the words scraping along my raw throat.

I thought of the O'Keeffe clouds yesterday and they felt like a sign. A bridge between me and Hattie that I could almost walk across. Wasn't that what she always said about them?

I squeezed my eyes and squeezed my memory, thinking back to when she first got *Sky above Clouds IV* from her sister Camilla, the art student.

"Hey," said Pete, Camilla's boyfriend, wiping a rogue noodle from his beard. Pete wore a fisherman's cap and sort of smelled, but he was nice. "Did Camilla mention I saw a ghost last night?"

Hattie's eyes got huge. "What? No. Camilla! Where?" Camilla was babysitting for the weekend, sort of, and we were eating Thai takeout at the Darrows' kitchen table.

He pointed out the window toward the yard across their private road.

"At the Caldwells'?" Hattie jumped from her chair.

I looked at Camilla. Unlike Helen and Hattie, she resembled Mr. Darrow, with dark eyes and angular features. Camilla winced apologetically.

"Yep." He lay his napkin on the table. "I was standing at Camilla's bedroom window at about midnight, the one right above this one." He went to the window. "And I saw this woman in a white dress, dancing across the lawn." His voice was dreamy. "She wore a super long braid and she was, like, twirling through the grass. Her dress spun out. She looked like a big white moonflower—"

Camilla shook her head again. "Pete," she said. "Tell them how much pot you smoked."

"Nuh-uh! This is so cool!" Hattie said. She joined Pete at the window, following his pointing finger. "Isn't it, Reid?"

I only said, "Couldn't it have been Mrs. Caldwell?"

"Mrs. Caldwell?" Hattie said. "They're away. I'm getting their mail for them." She squinted, scanning the Caldwells' fields. "Plus she's definitely not the lawn-dancing-moonflower type. What happened next, Pete?"

My mouth felt sandy.

"He claims she just"—Camilla waved her fork—"disappeared. I think he's full of crap."

"I'm not." Pete smiled, but not in a faking way. In a wonderment way, which made him disturbingly believable. "That house was built in 1770, right before the Revolutionary War," Pete said. "What if the people who lived there got murdered by Redcoats?"

Camilla laughed. "Come on, Pete!"

Hattie pointed at me, both barrels. "Reid. Stakeout! Tonight."

"No way."

"Pete and Camilla will come with us," she said.

I felt queasy.

"Sorry," Camilla said. "We're going to a show at Toad's."

Hattie made prayer hands. "Pretty please?"

"No way, no way, and—" I raised my milk glass like a shield. "No way."

"Rats," Hattie said, sitting again.

Were we really going to be alone until well past bedtime? Still, I couldn't break our sleepover streak. We only skipped if one of us was away or sick. Those were the rules.

"You don't have to believe in ghosts, Reid," Camilla said, putting her hand on my shoulder.

"What? That's crazy," said Hattie. "Sure, don't believe. But that doesn't mean they aren't real."

Pete chuckled, fist-bumping Hattie over the takeout boxes.

"I don't believe," said Camilla, her eyes holding mine while she shrugged. Then, "Back it down, Ghostbusters."

Hattie grunted good-naturedly.

When Pete and Camilla left, we watched a movie. To her credit, Hattie dropped the stakeout idea. After brushing our teeth, Hattie showed me the new poster from Camilla on her bedroom wall. I read the caption. "'Georgia O'Keeffe, Sky above Clouds IV, 1965.'"

"Camilla says Georgia O'Keeffe was the coolest American artist. Cooler than the men."

"I love the colors," I said. Intense blues, a fading pink sunset, and neatly arranged rows of bright white, blobby clouds disappearing into the horizon.

"Camilla read that Georgia O'Keeffe painted this after she saw clouds from an airplane and felt like she could step onto them. Wouldn't that be awesome?"

I nodded.

"I bet that's what ghosts do," she said. "I'm gonna, when I'm a ghost."

"Hattie," I said threateningly, for me.

"Sorry." She shook herself and checked her clock. "Five minutes."

We played Sea of Life with Mr. Tomten, and then went to bed.

I drifted to sleep seeing Hattie and me, hopping across the sky. I'm not sure if I dreamed this, but once in the night I rolled to find her perched by the window, gauzy in the moonlight. Her eyes were soft, sleepily traversing the blue lawns below, driven by the promise of maybe.

THEN

June 20

“Sam Stanwich is here,” Dad said loudly on his way past my bathroom. I turned off the hair dryer.

“Oh no,” I said, watching my eyes widen in the mirror. “At the door?” He was early, wrecking my plan of meeting him in the driveway. I scrambled to stuff my feet into my sandals.

I was too late; Spencer and Mom beat me to the door and Hammy stood in the family room. Whenever a guest arrived, Mom saw an opportunity for Spencer to practice “greetings.” Hammy flashed me a smile as I joined them.

"What do we say, Spencer?" Mom quizzed him.

"Hi I am good how are you!" Spencer said, rolling onto his tiptoes.

Hammy stood patiently, his damp hair jutting in multiple directions. I reveled in the fact he was here just for me, romantically or not. I telegraphed a thank-you to Hattie.

"I'm great, Spence. High five?" Spencer walloped Hammy's hand. "His speech sounds much clearer, Mrs. MacGregory."

Mom beamed. "Then our efforts are paying off. Right, Reid?" She barely looked my way, confident I'd respond as expected.

"Teamwork," I said, not one to disappoint. "Bye, Mom." I swung the screen door open.

"I'd like to know where you're headed," she said.

"The beach," Hammy said. "People are cooking out."

"Okay," she said. "Eleven thirty, Reid."

"I know."

We got into the Subaru. "Who's cooking out?"

He shrugged, backing down our driveway. "We may not know them, but someone will be."

"Why do adults think you're so innocent, Hammy?"

"Because I am." He grinned.

We turned onto the busy main road.

"Are we even going to the beach?" I asked.

"When in doubt . . ." he said, as if I'd know the default choice on a boring Saturday night was Siwanoy, the location of Hattie and Gib's interlude a mere two nights prior.

As if on cue, my phone erupted—an unprecedented gush of Thimble-to-Scofield communication from Hattie. I casually shielded the screen.

Hattie: I'm at Twin Island Lobster.

Great reception!

Guess who DM'd me the whole ride up here yesterday.

Me: Gib!

Hattie: No. God. What do you know about Jay Seavers these days?

I popped upright. I knew *a lot* about Jay Seavers. His smell, his lips, his pulse point, the firmness of his lower back muscles. The way he looked when he pretended not to see you.

Me: Jay Seavers DM'd you?

Hattie: He didn't know I left for the summer.

Blood steamed up my neck. Seriously, Dickhead? My best friend?

My finger hovered. I glanced at Hammy.

Me: You know he's a wanker.

Hattie: Right.

I waited.

Hattie: I think he was asking me out.

And there it was.

Are.

You.

FUCKING KIDDING ME?

Hattie: Gotta go. Phil's on to me. Seventeen days, baby! Whi-chaaa!

I slammed the phone onto the seat by my thigh. I should have told her about Mimi and him making out in the Maleshefskis' pool last night.

Hammy startled. "What?"

I reverse sighed, closing my eyes. "Long story." So, Jay's whole act last night—first with me, then Mimi—happened *after* spending the day text-flirting with Hattie? And why did he intrigue Hattie *at all*?

Hammy eyed me intermittently. "Are you going to tell me?"

I shook my head. He did not want to know this.

We rolled past the Siwanoy tennis courts toward the picnic area. Charlie and Alesha, along with Bobbles Mimi, Greta, and of course Emma Rose clustered around a table. I groaned, then quickly scanned for the Dickhead, but he wasn't around. Hammy cut the engine.

"I hope you know I'm well outside my comfort zone," I said, a little embarrassed by the edge in my voice.

"See? The Summer of Sam and Reid is *already* bringing you personal growth," he said as we rose from the car. He raised his fist for me to bump.

"The Summer of Hammy and Reid," I grumbled, tapping his knuckles.

"Righteous." He grinned. One of his front teeth crossed just the slightest bit over the other, evidence of his retainer rebellion. I smiled back.

"We're so dorky," I said quietly, aware of the assembled group watching us approach.

"We're fucking swaggy, Reid," he replied. "Swaggy." I thumped his ass with my foot, like maybe I thought it looked cool, but I hit him too hard.

"Ouch," he said.

The Vanilla Yeti band members occupied another table. Stedman flashed me a peace sign. I didn't have time to react before Emma Rose said, "Reid! Three nights in a row."

"I'm on a roll," I said. Her interest in me was disarming.

"Nice." She guided me away from the others. Could it be she, too, found Mimi and Greta boring as bricks?

"Are you and the Sandwich a thing?"

"What?" I actually snorted. "No."

"Because he's getting kinda hot these days. Still skinny, but the shoulders are coming in," she added.

"Yeah, well," I said, "we're friends."

"We'll see. We should hang out, Reid, with Hattie gone all summer." I felt like we were back in the middle school gym. In a parallel universe, she might be my best friend instead of Hattie. It was funny that of anyone we knew, Emma Rose was the only person Hattie openly disliked. I wasn't ever sure why, exactly, beyond the obvious Bobble-i-ness. I guess they were just so different; Hattie's cool, Emma Rose is warm, even in her fake way. She was in everyone's business all the time, while Hattie couldn't be bothered with most gossip.

All I said in response to Emma Rose was, "Yeah, we should." And I sounded as fake as her. Yuck.

I managed to get myself back to Hammy, Charlie, and Alesha, sitting on a picnic table. Hammy captivated Charlie with talk of a classic BMW he'd seen for sale in town. When he wandered off to the Yeti group, I felt stupid trailing behind him, so I stood silently critiquing my DIY pedicure. Charlie leaned toward me. "You making it with the Sandwich?"

"Nope." *But let's see how many times we can remind me of* that.

"You'd be cute together," said Alesha.

"Friends," I repeated, hands up.

Like that, the novelty of my presence wore off and the talk moved on.

I so did not fit here. What if Hattie and Gib—or someone else—became a thing this year? I wouldn't survive without a boyfriend of my own. Hammy and Vanilla Yeti stood in an amoeba-shaped ring. Sitting at the picnic table nearby was that gorgeous dimpled guy from the pool party, strumming a guitar.

Go, Hattie would direct me from the wings.

I suddenly recognized the song he played.

"Hey, that's 'You Do You,'" I said, approaching him without thinking.

"You know this song?" A slow smile crossed his lips.

"From the first Dissidents album. I love it," I said.

He kept playing and I watched his fingers dance over the strings. Then he stopped.

"I'm Noah." He stuck out his hand.

"I'm Reid," I said. "Did you just move here?" I managed.

"I live in Sammis Point," he said. A little beach community in the town next to Scofield. "Stedman was my next-door neighbor. We played Jedi Warriors together—" he said loudly, nodding toward the boys with a grin. "Until he moved to Swanky Town in second grade." Stedman looked over and flipped him off.

"Don't listen, Reid," Stedman called. "Noah's full of shit."

"Yeah," Noah chuckled. "You always had to have the cooler lightsaber."

I laughed along with them.

"Good thing your bass playing kicks ass," Stedman said, returning to his conversation. I realized I just stood there. Noah saved me by playing more "You Do You." Yes, he kicked ass.

"Wait," I said. "That's not a bass." Even I knew an acoustic guitar when I saw one.

"Yeah, I prefer lead guitar, but Stedman said they needed a bassist this summer, so I've been teaching myself."

I raised my eyebrows. "Jeez, I took piano lessons for four years and I still suck."

"I'm actually not that good, but if you ever want to be

in a band, learn bass." He played a new melody, plucking the strings in rapid succession. "My old guitar teacher told me that. Everyone wants to play lead and sing lead vocals," Noah said. "But if you're willing to be backup, you'll get more gigs than any of them."

Did Noah realize who he was talking to? Reid MacGregory, sidekick extraordinaire? Sancho Panza? I listened to him play, wondering how his theory applied to my social life, but Dave Keller, Yeti's lead vocalist, interrupted.

"It's time. Let's blow."

"We're playing a bar mitzvah," Noah said by way of explanation.

"Oh," I said, sorry the first person I'd been able to find with something interesting to say was already leaving. At least I'd managed to strike up a conversation with a stranger. *Baby steps, Reid,* I teased myself. *Baby steps.*

"*Hasta luego, señorita,*" Stedman said, waving to me. And the band left.

A little later, Charlie and Alesha left. The Bobbles mobilized, too. "We're going to Jay's," Mimi said, tossing her long hair over her shoulder. "Want me to ask if you can come?"

My spine zipped into a rod, but before I could say anything, Hammy said, "No thanks. Yeti's got a thing we're gonna catch."

Emma Rose squinted at him, then me. Maybe she knew about the bar mitzvah. Or maybe she was still trying to figure out Hammy and me. Maybe she simply couldn't bear another night with Mimi and Greta.

When we got back to the car and Hammy started the engine, I said without thinking, "I'm so glad we're not going with them." I hoped he didn't ask me why.

"Yeah." He didn't say more, so neither did I. Maybe something had happened with him and Greta after I left the Maleshefskis' a few nights ago, that he didn't feel like revisiting. I was surprised to find I hoped that wasn't the case. It wasn't that I was jealous for me, or even for Hattie (which would have been weird in a whole lot of ways). His puppy crush on Hattie was just so . . . endearing. And while Greta had relentlessly thrown her bikini-clad self at him after feeding him Jell-O shots, I liked to think of Hammy as too honorable to give in to the temptation of an easy hookup. I chided myself, remembering Hattie wasn't even interested in him.

"So, where to now?" he asked, interrupting my musings at the Post Road stoplight.

"You're asking me?" I said, watching the Pickle Barrel Deli man turning out the lights in the window across the street. "How do you feel about *Sherlock*?"

"Sherlock Holmes? The book?"

"The fabulous BBC show," I said. "With Benedict Cumberbatch?"

He laughed, then pinched the big eyebrows together. "Wait. That's a joke, right?"

My cheeks got hot.

"We are not going home on the second night. It's barely dark yet. I won't have it," he said primly. The light turned green. He paused, growling and thumping the steering wheel.

I could think of nothing. "We need a Scooby mystery to solve," I said. "Seen any mummies lately?"

His face lit up, a surprisingly enthusiastic reaction, until I realized he hadn't really heard me. "Bowl-O-Rama."

"Yes. Bowl-O-Rama." Hattie and I took Spencer there a lot. I smiled. This, I could do.

Turned out it was League Night. Hammy and I got the only free lane, and were surrounded by people with matching team jackets and personalized bowling ball bags.

"Which team would you want to be on?" Hammy asked, resting his foot on the bench to tie his bowling shoe. "I'm thinking the Bowling Stones are my people." He nodded to the team, whose members wore black leather jackets with the Rolling Stones tongue and lip logo in a wreath of bowling pins.

"Yes. I told you you have the moves like Jagger," I said. "I'm more of a Split Happens kinda girl, I think."

"I see that. But don't rule out Ball Busters," he said. "Because you have that side to you."

I rolled my eyes, but inside thought Captain Dickhead would heartily disagree.

Hammy did a really sad tap dance in his shoes and

said, "Nothing says hot guy like these. I can't imagine why Hattie doesn't jump my bones."

"Me neither," I said, discovering I could flirt without flirting with Hammy.

Friends.

Later when he pulled into our driveway and I was about to get out, he said, "That was better than *Sherlock*. Once we put up the gutter guard, I mean."

I laughed. "Spencer and I live by the gutter guard. And you're right," I said. "It was better." For a moment I felt sad we weren't a couple. This was so close to perfect and yet missing a key ingredient. I swallowed a sigh and said, "When Hattie comes back, we can all go."

Hammy grinned. "Great idea. Maybe I can impress her if I get a personalized bowling bag."

I laughed. "Maybe," I said, opening my door. "Don't forget the matching jacket." I said goodbye and rounded the car when he rolled down his window.

"Wait," he said. He put his fist up. "Bump it."

I rolled my eyes and bumped it.

"The Summer of Sam and Reid continues," he said like a wrestling announcer.

"Hammy and Reid," I said.

"Whatever it takes. Thanks, Reid," he said earnestly, driving away.

I watched him take off down the road. "You're a fool, Darrow," I said to the clouds skittering over the moon.

Inside, an express mail package from Hattie sat on

my bed waiting for me. “That was fast,” I whispered. I ripped it open and dumped the contents. A black mound landed on the bedspread with a notecard.

Go get 'em, Reddi-the-Whipper! Whi-chaaa!

Love, H

I picked up the mound and a pair of black fishnet stockings unfurled like a pirate flag. I texted her, knowing full well she'd never see it.

Me: Very funny. Not.

But of course it was witty as hell. I felt sad I still hadn't told her about Jay. I would, eventually. In Maine maybe. I looked at the prom picture on my bulletin board and the look on Hammy's face while Hattie goosed him cheered me up. The summer could, *maybe*, be better than I thought. Maybe.

“Maybe's not all bad,” I said aloud.

THEN

July 3

June slid into July. The Thimble countdown kept me looking ahead rather than living in the moment, but the Summer of Hammy and Reid, while uneventful in terms of actual parties, did make the waiting fun. We drove around a lot, bowled ironically, drank coffee at the Mighty Bean, and caught multiple Vanilla Yeti rehearsals in Matt Stedman's basement. I mean, I actually felt like I might be a little . . . cool. If Hattie were here too, we'd be having the summer of our lives. Well, she probably was anyway. In any case, I'd also banked three hundred dollars from working with Jasper at the dinner theater, and maintained my running goals. *Maybe* I wouldn't end up an embarrassment of a cross-country co-captain after all. I still couldn't compete with Hattie's times, but I would at least be a better version of me.

Today, as Boomer and I rounded the final corner of our run, I sprinted for our mailbox like always. The mail truck was leaving as we approached. I leaned against the mailbox, catching my breath before retrieving the mail. A big brown envelope with Hattie's handwriting on it took up most of our oversized mailbox. "Yay!" I said, and then I looked up and saw Hammy's Subaru in the driveway. The familiar unease of having a friend encounter Spencer in his natural habitat swept me. But it went away when I observed them playing catch on the lawn. Hammy waved.

Besides Hattie, Hammy was the first friend I'd really trusted. Of course a big reason for this was the open acknowledgment of his infatuation with Hattie. I didn't have to worry about impressing him or wonder if he liked me. Simple friends. *So there, Jasper*, I said to myself. "I'll be out in a few minutes," I called, slipping into the house.

I started opening Hattie's care package at the kitchen table. Mom appeared, putting her second sparkly earring in. "Hi, honey," she said. "Listen, this is short notice, but I need you to watch Spencer while Dad and I go out."

I reverse sighed and made a face.

"You know I hate asking you, Reid." She applied lipstick in front of the hall mirror.

"Hammy and I are going out," I said, though we hadn't decided that yet.

"Sam is fine with it. Look at them!" She nodded toward the window. Hammy was chasing a very overstimulated laughing boy in red around a tree.

"Mom, did you *ask* him to babysit Spencer with me?" I grimaced.

"He practically *offered*," she said.

"What's he supposed to say when you, *the mom of the autistic kid*, ask him?"

"Oh, come on, Reid," she said, giving her hair a final fluff in the mirror. "It's not like that."

It's exactly like that.

"We're taking Dad's new client and her husband to the club. It could mean a lot of new business, Reid. And she's got a nephew with autism, so she may help with fund-raising."

You had to admire my mother's ambition. "It's already done, so you don't really need me to say yes." I slid the contents out of Hattie's envelope. Her note read:

To Sancho Panza, xoxo Don Quixote—PS There best be some whi-chaaaing going on in Scofield! Seavers called twice.

My stomach bobbed, but I looked at the framed print under the note. It was a Picasso pen-and-ink of the famous duo on horseback. I recognized it from my art history book. Sancho looked up to Don Quixote. I smiled. It was oddly sentimental for Hattie, which made me love it all the more. "Aw," I said.

Mom absently pulled her keys from her purse and said, "Thank you, Reid. I'll make it up to you."

I made a grumbly noise. Spencer got diagnosed when he was two and I was nine, so I had about eight years of makeups due from her. She kissed my forehead and whisked to the door. "I'm late. Love you!"

The door shut. "Love you, too," I muttered. Once she disappeared, I called out to Hammy. "I'm so sorry!"

"It'll be great," he said with a grin. "I told Spence we could go to the nature center and see the turtles."

"Tuw-dles!" said Spencer, then cracked up.

"The Summer of Hammy and Reid is always an adventure," he said. I made a face, but I could tell he meant it. Deep in my chest, something fluttered.

I need my own Hammy, I thought.

The Scofield Nature Center had foot trails with signs for parents to read to their children about the salamanders and frogs and rabbits that lived in the woods. The pond had frogs and turtles and lots of dragonflies. A funky shingled building that looked very 1970s housed a tiny shop to buy birdseed and nature books and honey, and a children's room where you could touch shedded snake-skins and observe a live beehive behind glass.

"I'm having a total flashback to day camp," Hammy

said, holding a shellacked turtle shell. "Did you go here?"

"Yep," I said. "Remember the guitar yurt?"

"Loved the guitar yurt. I had a crush on my hippie counselor. She taught us to drum 'Land of the Silver Birch' on oatmeal containers."

"I just remember a rain stick," I said, watching the bees. "I wonder if we were here at the same time."

Spencer did the chipmunk puzzle in seconds flat, and then wandered into the bathroom to flush the toilets repeatedly. I dragged him back to the children's room.

"Oh, remember this room here?" Hammy was saying, opening a door I hadn't noticed. A plaque read "The John J. Geller Wildlife Study Room."

I didn't and peered in. "Yikes!" Shelves were filled with stuffed animals. Like, taxidermy stuffed. Porcupines, skunks, squirrels. A little fox, a couple owls. Some cased in glass, others not.

"I loved this!" Hammy said.

"Creepy," I said. We stood side by side by side, observing the various woodland creatures with their little marble eyes. "Do you think they died naturally?"

"Letz go Ottuh's Island!" Spencer said.

"Yeah, Spence," I said. "He loves that show," I told Hammy. "He quotes lines from it at random times."

"Ottuh's Island," he repeated gleefully.

"Yep," I said. "Best to just acknowledge him and move on," I explained. "Look, Spence, a raccoon."

"Ottuh's Island," Spencer said.

"I think he's trying to tell you there's an otter in here," Hammy said, pointing to a stuffed sea otter. It lay in a fake pool of water holding a red sea star.

I laughed. "Spence! You're right! It's Otter!" Spencer beamed. He loved being right. The otter's fur was thick and silvery brown, its mouth set in an adorable upside-down V.

"Ottuh!" Spencer sang. He'd pulled it from its post off the fake water, holding the dead otter above his head and running around the room. "Letz go Ottuh's house!"

"Put that down!" We turned to find one of the employees—an older woman in a ranger uniform—staring at us in horror. "That's not even from our collection! He broke it!"

"Spencer!" I said. "Sorry, he has autism." I could name dozens of times I'd had to say that sentence, in grocery stores, trains, elevators, on beaches, where he unwittingly stepped on sandcastles and towels. A time-honored churning began in my stomach.

"He's got to put that down or you'll be paying for it and it isn't cheap!" she growled.

"Spencer!" I said again, but he was somewhere in autism land, rerunning an episode in his head. "He doesn't understand," I said.

"Give that here, young man," she snapped. "You shouldn't bring a kid like that in here."

My pulse banged in my wrists and throat. I gritted my teeth. “A kid like what? It’s just a dead animal!”

“Okay, okay,” Hammy said, nodding at me like I was armed and dangerous. “Hey, Spence, can I see Otter?” His voice was gentle.

“It’s a thousand-dollar dead animal, missy,” she said, eyes narrowed. “You entitled Scofield kids think that’s chump change.”

I narrowed mine right back, uncertain what exactly would come out of my mouth next. It had a lifetime of anger behind it.

Spencer skipped over to Hammy and placed the otter in his hands.

“Thank God,” I whispered.

Hammy set the otter back on its fake water. “Look, no harm done. Good as new. Okay?” He took Spencer’s arm and backed toward the door. I followed.

The old lady scowled at Hammy. She looked over her shoulder toward the shop. I realized she didn’t want anyone to know the very pricey guest otter had been broken on her watch. She grumbled something inaudible and then said, “*Stay out of this room.*” She slammed the door and marched back to her perch behind the shop desk.

Hammy made a whoops face and I had to hold back a laugh as we hurried outside.

“Sorry, Hammy,” I said. “This is why I don’t like—”

"Are you kidding? That was fucking awesome," Hammy said. We walked toward the pond on a path through tall grass. "Seriously, lady?" he said. "A ranger's uniform? At Scofield Nature Center?"

I felt like I should thank him or something, for just *getting it*, intuitively, but that seemed awkward. Finally I said, "I'm glad you were there so I didn't take an old lady out."

He laughed. "You are protective."

"I am."

Spencer loped onto the short wooden observation pier. "Fwog!" he called into the air. "Snake!"

I grimaced. "I hope he's wrong on that one."

Hammy chuckled.

Once we spotted the requisite turtle, we followed the path into the woods. Spencer lagged behind, humming.

"I wrote Hattie a letter," Hammy said, apropos of nothing.

"Oh?" I said, brushing soft leaves with my palm. "That's so sweet." Why didn't she see how sweet he was? And yet she entertained messages from Jay Fucking Seavers.

"I know she won't write back."

I wanted to shake him. "She might," I said tepidly.

He looked at me, hopeful and guarded. Was he blushing? My gaze dropped to the ground.

"Nah," he said. "She won't. But maybe when she's back, she'll remember."

I couldn't bring myself to lie out loud, so I just nodded.

We were crossing through a patch of tiger lilies when Hammy asked, "Who do you have your eye on, Reid?"

"Me?" I shrugged. "Nobody in particular."

"What about that guy Jasper you work with?"

"Jasper?" I said. "Jasper's gay."

"Oh," he said. We kept walking.

I turned to check on Spencer. The foliage was dense. I leaned back and forth, searching. "Come on, Spence!"

I stopped walking.

"Spencer?" I called. Hammy and I exchanged a worried look and jogged back to the field. Part of me wanted to sprint, but I was too afraid to panic. That pond. I swallowed.

We met a mom and little girl in orange Wellies. "Did you see a kid, about this tall, in a red shirt?" The mom nodded and pointed toward the sloping meadow. Relieved, I picked up speed.

"Phew!" Hammy said when we saw Spencer walking toward us from the store.

"How the hell did he get back there so fast?" I said. "Crap, what if the ranger lady saw him."

"Let's not find out," Hammy said breathlessly.

"I am not all done Ottuh," said Spencer when we got to him. His smile was huge.

I took his warm, sticky hand in mine. "Very funny, Spence. Come on, time to go home."

* * *

Later, after it had grown dark and we'd made dinner for three, Hammy talked me into watching one of the Spider-Man movies. Spencer played on his iPad, thrilled I hadn't put time limits on him. My parents came home in the middle of the movie, and I assured them it had been a wonderful afternoon and evening. They all went to bed, and when the movie ended, Hammy stood to go. He stretched that long, skinny body of his and said, "Hey, I think there might be something in your pool."

"What do you mean?" I said, joining him by the sliding door. I flipped the pool light on and sure enough, some kind of animal swam around in there. It was in silhouette, a black form in a blue sea.

"What is it?" I asked. "Shit, is that a big rat?"

We crept onto the patio like it might attack. It swam in a big circle, bouncing off the pool corners.

"Is it dead?" Hammy asked. He stood upright. "Holy shit." He grabbed the skimmer and moved toward it, no longer hesitant.

"Careful!" I said.

"I can't believe it!" He nudged it with the skimmer, but it didn't move.

"What?"

"Oh my God." Hammy scooped it out and dumped it on the stones. "Spencer stole the fucking otter."

I blinked. The otter, still holding the red sea star, was

smiling adorably up at the sky like he was in on the joke. We started to laugh, and then laugh harder.

"That's where he went!" Hammy said. "He must have smuggled it out in his backpack when he disappeared. Damn, he's fast!"

"And why he said, 'I am not all done otter!'" I squeaked.

When we finally regained our composure, Hammy said, "I totally get why Hattie loves Spencer."

"We have to give it back," I said. "The ranger lady is going to go postal."

"Do you think she knows?" Hammy said.

We paused. "She would definitely call the cops," Hammy said.

This started to be not funny. If the cops figured out it was Spencer—and they knew who he was, because my mother had done an awareness workshop with them years ago—they'd come for the otter and then my parents would know I'd lost Spencer on the job. And then I'd have to deal with my mother's disappointment and my dad's peacemaking diplomacy for days. Plus maybe paying to repair the otter.

"Crap," I said. I paced around, then brightened.

"Hours have passed. I don't think she knows." I explained my mom's autism workshop at the Scofield Police Department.

"I say we smuggle it back in." Hammy waggled his bushy eyebrows. "Tonight."

"What? We can't break in!"

He cocked his head. "Would you do it with Hattie?"

I started to object but stopped. My parents *were* asleep. I checked my phone for the time.

Eleven eleven.

"Let's go," I said, grinning.

In fact, we did not break in. A night custodian was vacuuming the store and the doors stood wide open. Disappointed we couldn't be as badass as we'd hoped, we attempted to sneak past him, but we were barely half-way to the dead animal room when the vacuum abruptly stopped. Hammy confessed the whole story, sweet talker that he is, and sure enough, he found a co-conspirator in our new friend Rick. Rick couldn't stand Ranger Pauline either. He got some Krazy Glue and, together with Hammy, affixed the otter to his stand.

By the time we drove home, it was almost one. My eyelids were heavy and I sighed contentedly.

"We are doing pretty damn well on our pact, seeing as how it's barely July, MacGregory," Hammy said.

Too tired to think of a reply, I smiled at him and put my hand on top of his on the gear shift. He blinked at me, puzzled, and I snapped upright in the seat, pulling it back in my lap. What was *that*? To cover, I said, "You're a kick-ass partner in crime, Stanwich," which sounded dorky as hell, but he was as happy for the embarrassing moment to pass as I was.

"Make sure you tell Hattie about it all," he said. I was leaving in two days for The Thimble.

"Of course," I said. "She'll love it."

And I turned to watch the stars until we were safely at my house.

August 30

The funeral was at noon. It was ten thirty. I pushed hangers from right to left in my closet. The sound took me back to Hattie's bedroom and my heart clutched again, seeing Helen on the floor.

"Nobody cares what you wear," Scott said from the doorway. He'd come home early from the Vineyard yesterday. A new flatness in his eyes broke my heart.

"Too bad you're not a guy," he said. "One outfit does it for all occasions. Khakis and a blue blazer. I'm surprised it's not one piece of material we step into, like my old Shazam costume."

His heroic attempt to cheer me up made me love him so much just then, but I couldn't get the words to my mouth.

"I should patent that idea, really," he said. "Make myself a shit ton of cash."

I crinkled my brow without turning. "I want to wear my green prom dress. She picked it out for me."

"Then fucking wear it." He put both hands on my shoulders. "She's your friend and you should do whatever you want."

I imagined making eye contact for the first time with Mrs. Darrow in the church, wearing the green dress, and suddenly I was crying into Scott's shoulder. Whenever I thought of Mrs. Darrow, I bawled. I felt her pain more acutely than my own. I hadn't cried for myself since the baby deer.

Scott wrapped me in his arms. "Mom?" he called quietly.

I cried through Mom helping me into her conservative blue dress, through Scott loading me into the car, shotgun seat, and through our family ride to St. Paul's. Mom shushed Spencer; I liked his babble.

Cars overflowed the lot, but Dad found a spot near the church entrance.

The MacGregorys exited the car, a handsome family scrubbed clean. Spencer held his red rubber lobster, a gift from Hattie's final care package, eleven days before it happened. Oblivious Spencer—half singing, rolling onto his toes. How I envied him.

My hands trembled. I couldn't get out.

Hammy and his parents and sister approached. Dad and I locked eyes. I dropped my head, slipping on my Ray-Bans. I heard Dad speak softly.

"Hey," Hammy said. He got in the driver's side.

I twisted the wadded tissue, my eyes burning.

"Come on. Don't make me go alone," he said.

I stayed quiet, afraid to speak.

"It's a way to say goodbye, Reid." He removed my sunglasses.

Finally, I dragged my gaze to him, and the wave broke. I sobbed into the padded shoulder of his blue blazer.

I sputtered, "I can't stop. It's embarrassing."

"Reid, it's a funeral. Everyone is sad."

I shook my head.

"We can do this."

"I can't say goodbye!" The snarl in my voice took us both by surprise.

He exhaled slowly, resting his hands on the steering wheel. "It might help."

I shook my head again.

"Think of the Darrows, then," he said. "Let's support them."

"It kills me to think of them." I threw the tissue on the floor. "Why aren't you sadder, Sandwich? Huh?

You're in love with her, right?"

Pain spilled into his eyes. I let out another sob, this one for being ashamed. "I'm sorry," I whispered. "I didn't mean that."

He blinked. "Honestly, I don't want to do this, either. We just . . . have to."

I nodded.

"Summer of Sam and Reid." His voice wobbled. He extended his knuckles for me to tap. I covered his fist with my fingers and squeezed. He got out of the car, came around, and opened my door. I couldn't budge. He raked his wayward hair with both hands. "Look, if you don't go in there, you'll regret it for the rest of your life."

"Okay, okay. Just . . . save me a seat."

He raised his eyebrows. "For *fuck's* sake! It will be over in an hour."

"I'll come." I had no idea if this was true.

He sighed, glancing at the steeple clock. "It starts in two minutes." He got out of the car and started walking.

Over in an hour. The finality of it, of *her*—this person who had shaped me into all I had become—being tossed into the past merely sixty minutes from now was unthinkable.

"Hattie! You're the one I need to get me in there." I tried to imagine what she would do if she were me, which was pretzel thinking and pointless.

A loud bump on the car roof made me jump. Scrabbling sounded above me, and a bunch of acorns rolled over the windshield. Before I could react, a squirrel slid headfirst down the glass, claws trying to stop, white belly pressed flat, until it came to a stop. Its unmistakable squirrel testicles stared me in the face.

I stared back, stunned, and while I did, the squirrel's hind paws began to let go, causing him to slide down the rest of the windshield with a tiny squeaking sound. It was like a cartoon. A laugh took shape in my stomach, imprisoned by sadness.

The squirrel landed and sat up on his haunches. His little squirrel anus thrust against the windshield, pointed directly at me.

Hattie hooted with laughter, next to me, doubled over, thumping the steering wheel with her palms. I froze. I wanted to touch her. To grab her arm and run with her into the church so her mother could see her. But I was afraid to lose her again. So, I let myself laugh with her instead. We laughed together, Hattie and Reid, Reid and Hattie, for the kajillionth, zillionth time. Through the laughter, I thought, *This is not a person who takes her own life.* The squirrel stuffed acorns into his mouth with miniature hand-paws and scampered away.

The church bells tolled, startling me again. She was gone. I flung open the door and stood, sucking in a long breath of summer air. The bells stopped. I had to go.

A guy in a beige suit and sunglasses greeted me at the doors, handing me a program. Like I do all the time to the old people at the dinner theater. I stepped into the vestry, filled with white lilies, and he closed the doors. No escape.

A poster-sized photo of Hattie on the family sailboat stood on an easel. I recognized it from a bookshelf in the Darrows' living room. It was from the summer before I met her, when she was eleven. Surrounded by blue sky and sun-bleached sailcloth, wind, and water, Hattie leveled her eyes at the camera—playful, challenging. To me, she was an element in and of herself.

I felt a touch on my elbow. "It's starting," whispered the guy in the beige suit. A Darrow cousin, but I was too tired to remember which one. He led me into the sanctuary, where a sea of heads young and old filled the pews. Santi and his family sat near the front. As if he sensed me, Santi turned and our eyes caught for a moment. Expressionless, he looked away. Across the aisle and a few rows back I saw Gib Soule, his beautiful face sallow and gray. I couldn't look at more pain and watched my feet, strangers to me in Mom's blue heels.

Hammy tipped two fingers toward us and I wedged myself between him and the pew's hard end. The organ stopped, leaving naked the eerie sound of many people gathered but none saying a word. Hammy held my hand.

On the altar, her urn.

My breath stopped. Lava slunk up my throat.

It was blown glass—pink, purple, and green flowers swaying against a blue sky. A piece of art, and I felt Mrs. Darrow's heart beating next to mine. She'd picked it, I knew, maybe with Camilla. I wanted to tell her she was so brave. I repeated it in my head, sending it to her through the air. So brave.

A door opened near the altar and the reverend led the line of Hattie's family like a frieze on a Greek temple. My stomach cramped and expanded. I was a helium balloon and Hammy's grasp was all that kept me from floating away.

Hattie's brothers, Walt and Ben, supported Mrs. Darrow at each side. She stepped like the ground billowed beneath her feet. Mr. Darrow followed, jaw set, skin ashen, holding Helen's hand behind him, and Camilla entwined her arm with Helen's other arm.

My eyes heated. I dug my nails into my palms. Hammy was wrong. I couldn't support the Darrows.

The reverend began. I heard nothing but followed the motions of those around me. We stood for a hymn. I watched Mrs. Darrow's shoulders, which started to shudder somewhere in the second stanza. She buckled over and Mr. Darrow helped her upright. My heart collapsed. I let out a cry. It was swallowed by the assembled chorus. At the end, the Darrows took their seats and she became marble.

Uncle Baxter and Walt read passages from the Bible, the reverend gave a eulogy entitled "An Angel Beckoned Home," and we sang three more hymns. But I didn't hear any of it. I'd left my shaky body there on the pew, with Hammy holding my hand. Hattie and I were galloping the horses through the woods at night. Through the fields with the vaulted blue sky alive with stars. The horses' breath plumed above as they ran, the hoofbeats ringing an ancient song.

We were weightless.

We were strong.

We were witches.

PART TWO

THEN

July Days ~ The Thimble

The day arrived at last. I'd purchased the requisite Pickle Barrel deviled eggs, packed them on ice, zipped my suitcase, and now watched for Mr. Darrow in the driveway. Not my ideal driver—usually one of Hattie's sisters brought me. Phillip S. Darrow III, graduate of Princeton and Wharton, lover of opera, pulled his Audi coupe into our driveway eighteen minutes early (but I'd been ready for an hour). He shook my dad's hand, threw my suitcase into the trunk, and our six-hour voyage commenced.

Phil wasn't much for small talk. Nor was I, but its absence made things even more awkward. And by things, I mean me, because he clearly didn't give a hoot. To his credit, he gave it a go around Stratford, pointing out historic bridges. I tried to sound halfway intelligent, dropping a few art history terms I'd learned last semester. That conversation died a merciful death in North Haven, where he turned up the opera and sang along in Italian. Loudly. You know, after a while I realized he (unlike Hattie) wasn't too bad.

Still.

Since I couldn't look at my phone without displeasing my driver, I found myself reviewing that embarrassing hand-holding event with Hammy on our drive back from the nature center. God, I think I did secretly like him. I closed my eyes and shuddered.

Truth: if you fake it long enough, you *will* fall asleep, even with someone belting *The Marriage of Figaro* next to you. I woke abruptly with wind whipping my hair. I blinked to discover all the car windows down. Phil's way of waking me up. We'd come to the causeway—a long wooden construction that carried us out to The Thimble.

Thud-duh-dunt, *thud-duh-dunt*, *thud-duh-dunt.* You didn't just hear the causeway, you felt it in your gut. In my earliest visits, I thought of it as the circus drumroll before the clown gets shot from the cannon or the elephant stands on its head. Okay, I still felt like that. And was it me, I wanted to ask Mr. Darrow, or did the way the waves popped up and down make them look downright happy to see us?

The tires rolled from the wood onto the gravel roadway, which fanned in two directions. He hung right, toward the Darrow side of The Thimble.

Before I'd arrived here for the first time in the summer of sixth grade, Hattie had never bothered to mention that the Darrows owned the private island themselves, and had for at least three generations by my count, until Mr. Darrow convinced Mr. Herrera to buy the eastern end. The Herreras owned Chile's oldest vineyards. Like his kids, Mr. Herrera was educated in America, where he rowed crew with Mr. Darrow. All jokes about free wine aside, Phil and Rafi were obviously the best of friends. Why not invite your best college buddy to buy part of your private island, so you can raise your beautiful alpha children together?

I didn't call Hattie on it until a year later. "What?" she said, staring at me. Her gaze darted away and she redid her ponytail, looking absently in the mirror. "Reid," she laugh-said, "we are *not* loaded."

The summerhouse seemed not to want to be rich either. Sun drenched and cedar shingled, it rambled in a bunch of different directions like unfinished thoughts. Maybe it was the antique telescope pointed toward the ocean that gave it away, or the 1920s photos filled with flapper dresses and old Fords. Rich is rich, and there's no hiding it, but it was a ridiculous point to argue because it didn't matter anyway.

We passed the barn and paddock. Barnaby and Lyra

grazed placidly. We drove through a field and as we approached the unkempt red clay tennis court, I saw Hattie's racquet connect with a ball. *Pop!* My world fell back into place.

Mr. Darrow had barely stopped before I jumped out.

I recognized Santi's wavy black hair from the back. He whacked his return so hard his shirt flew up, exposing his slim brown torso.

Hattie saw me and brightened, hitting Santi's shot into the net.

"Baah!" Mr. Darrow bellowed. "What was *that*, Hattie?" But she'd dropped her racquet and run to greet me.

"My game!" Santi called.

"Dream on," she said without looking. "Interference." She hugged me and spun us in a circle. She must have been wound up from the game, because her enthusiasm never matched mine in the reunion department. "We're going to have so much fun, Reddi!"

Mr. Darrow drove off. Santi wiped sweat from his brow and took a slug off his water bottle. "Hey, Reid," he said with a short hug. His eyes were brown and bottomless with thick black lashes, his skin a rose-toned almond.

"Reid, tell Hattie that point was mine," he said. When he smiled, the ends of his lips turned down, like he was physically incapable of surrendering his competitive edge.

"Don't even," Hattie warned.

"Switzerland," I said, both hands up. Neutrality was the move with these two.

She laughed and punched his arm.

"I need Mac," he said. "He's not biased."

"Right," said Hattie.

I pushed my hair behind one ear. "Mac's here?" Mac was Santi's roommate from Holderness, the prep school they attended. I met him the summer of eighth grade. Full disclosure: Mac Leonhirth was my first real kiss and I wrote his name with hearts around it for months. We hadn't visited The Thimble at the same time since, though. Twice he'd come right before school, after Hattie was already home.

"Due at six thirty," he said, gathering tennis balls in a bucket.

Hattie tapped my shoulder and mimed cracking a whip. "He's here the whole time you're here," she said full volume. She watched Santi. "And you're going to snag his ass," she whispered.

"Why didn't you tell me?" I couldn't hide my smile.

"Because you would've freaked out."

True.

Santi walked toward the footpath on the other side of the court. "We'll come by after dinner."

"Campfire?" Hattie called. "Our beach."

I rolled onto my toes to hold back a squeal. The kiss happened at the campfire on Hattie's beach.

He held his racquet up in acknowledgment and disappeared into the trees.

"*You* are having rocking sex with Mac Leonhirth this week," she said. "I mean, unless you have something to tell me." She eyed me sideways. "Work any magic in those fishnets I sent you?"

I examined the tops of the pine trees, pointing like arrows at the sky. "No." I *hadn't* worked magic in the fishnets. That part was true.

She grabbed my hand and tugged me toward the path. "So, it's official. Mac's totally happening."

"Maybe?" I said, unable to keep from smiling.

"There's a lot of promise in maybe," she said. "A lot of promise."

Before dinner, while she tended to the horses, I unpacked my clothes in her room. Seeing Mac on short notice had me all freaked out, and I daydreamed about when we had our little romance, in the summer of eighth grade. With the scent of the sea roses floating in Hattie's bedroom window, it was easy to take myself back.

July, eighth grade.

"Who's he?" I asked, swinging the telescope to Hattie so she could look. We often spied on Santi during downtimes from Mr. Darrow's second-floor study. It was the kind of place with model sailboats, constellation maps, and a giant freestanding globe with faded lettering and sea dragons poking out of the

oceans. At the moment, Santi was skimboarding with a moppy-haired kid on the Herreras' beach.

"Must be the new Holderness roommate." She pulled her eye from the lens and squinted out the window. "Santi said he might visit."

Santi would board for high school, like all the Darrow siblings besides Hattie did. I'd panicked last spring when I saw her parents leaving the middle school guidance office twice in the same week. Already two other kids in our grade announced their plans to leave. When I couldn't bear it any longer, I finally blurted, "Are you going away to school or not?"

"Nah," she said. "I don't want to go just because it's what Darrows do." This sounded like something she'd spat out in a fight with her parents, but she didn't look at me when she said it. Hattie code for Back off, Reid. *I was too happy to push my luck.*

Santi did a front flip off the skimboard. Hattie pulled her ponytail out and redid it. "He's such a show-off."

"You love it," I said.

She squeaked, "I do not!"

"Oh, um-hmm, right," I said. "Hattie and Santi sitting in a tree . . ." She swatted at me. "Or should I call you Hattiago?"

The roommate snuck up behind Santi with a pile of seaweed, hurling it in his face at the perfect moment. We laughed like we were there.

"This is gonna be a fun week," she said.

* * *

At dinner, we officially met Mac. Up close he was a bit pudgy and had dimples that made him look perpetually amused. His hair dried the color of summer sand and his white skin was a deep tan from all the hours in the sun. Over our eight-day visit, this much became clear. Mac was beta to Santi's alpha, just like I was beta to Hattie's. He brought a symmetry to The Thimble that made you wonder where he'd been.

On my last night, Santi, Mac, Hattie, and I slipped away from the Darrows' screened porch after a two-family dinner to build a fire on the Darrows' beach. After dousing ourselves in citronella spray, we followed the Alice in Wonderland *path through wild rosebushes and loped barefoot across the sand. Stars spread over us in a mesmerizing way I'd only ever seen in Maine. Mosquitoes triple the size of Connecticut ones wafted overhead, but the citronella worked and they never bit.*

The firepit was in a nook of dunes far enough from the house to feel secretive. We scavenged firewood under scraggly pines. Hattie and Santi stoked a crackling inferno in minutes, because they were alpha dogs and that's how alpha dogs roll. Four log benches surrounded the firepit, but we occupied two, in an L formation: Hattie with Santi, Mac with me. I didn't give it a second thought. I was fourteen and my only kiss had lasted seconds and happened in a broom closet at a bar mitzvah.

"Let's tell ghost stories," Hattie said, her face lit like a jack-o'-lantern.

"You look possessed," Mac said to Hattie.

"Maybe I am," she said with a grin.

"She definitely is," said Santi.

I leaned toward Mac. "This is when they try to freak us out. They do it to me every year."

Mac leaned toward me in return, his eyes bright. "I have three older brothers," he whispered. He turned toward them. "Bring it."

"Should we tell them what happened to your brother Walt last month?" Santi asked.

"What? Nothing happened to Walt last month," I said, mostly to bulk up my courage before the onslaught.

But Hattie and Santi shared a conspiratorial look before she said, "Sorry, Reid. I didn't tell you before because I know how you get."

"Come on," I moaned. "Can't I have a last night where we listen to the tide and name the constellations?"

"Knowing the truth is important," Hattie said, then cracked up with her squeaky laugh into Santi's shoulder.

"Don't mess with Ponytail, Hattie," Santi said. "We don't know where he is right now."

"Sorry." Hattie cleared her throat and straightened. "You start, Sant," she laugh-said.

"Ponytail?" Mac said, with a chuckle.

"Shh!" Hattie and Santi shushed him in perfect synchronicity. She smothered her laughter again, coughing into her fist. She waved her free hand at Santi to begin.

With a mock serious face that shouldn't have scared me but kind of did, Santi started. "So, in June, Hattie's brother Walt is beach camping with his girlfriend and another couple right over there." He pointed farther down the beach. "They've got the tents, the campfire, some beers."

"And it was a perfect night, exactly like this," Hattie chimed in. "Gentle waves and breeze. Not dark and stormy like most ghost stories. That's how you know we're not lying."

I snickered to Mac. He shrugged, his eyes playful.

Santi swung a piece of driftwood like a cane, pacing. "So, they're watching for shooting stars when Walt's friend—"

"Harrison," Hattie offered.

"Right," Santi said, "Harrison spots this old dude—all skinny and bent—hovering in the shadows. He's got a Grateful Dead shirt on and a gray ponytail down to his ass."

Mac chuckled again.

"Totally true," Hattie said, smiling.

Santi cupped his hand over his eyes, like he's Harrison. "The old guy doesn't react. He just stands there in the shadows, ten feet away, watching them."

We all looked into the shadows beyond the fire's glow. It was way too easy to imagine someone there. A log collapsed with a loud snap. I startled. "This isn't funny," I said. But Hattie wasn't laughing anymore. Her eyes were wide. I remembered that look, from a long time ago, when I woke to see her searching for the moonflower ghost out her window. She believed.

"Well, what happened?" Mac said.

"So, Walt asks, 'Can we help you?' And the guy goes, 'I lost

my dog, Shep. Have you seen him? Yea big, black and white, wearing a green bandanna?'" His voice is flatline. It's weird, because he's standing cadaver still, not looking for anything. Walt says sorry but no, and the guy says, 'I lost my dog, Shep. Have you seen him? Yea big, black and white, wearing a green bandanna?'"

Goose bumps rose on my sticky citronella arms. Mac rested his hand behind me on the log. My heart ticked in my ribs and I couldn't stop from leaning toward him, feeling his solid warmth.

"Maybe he was hurt," Mac said, pressing into me ever so slightly.

"Right?" Santi says. He sat on the log now, bronze in the firelight. "They thought maybe he had dementia and Walt and his girlfriend, Tina, go try to help him. But when Tina touches his arm, she pulls away real quick, her eyes all tweaked. She said he was cold as an ice block, and he smelled like wood smoke. The guy starts to go, and says, 'You see Shep, and you find me in town. Ask for Ponytail.' And he wanders into the darkness."

"But he walks toward Pulpit Head," Hattie said. "He can't get to the causeway from there."

"Holy shit!" I said. "You mean he could still be on the island?"

Hattie and Santi caught eyes. I saw her lips quiver. They simultaneously dissolved into peals of laughter.

"Oh my God," I said to Hattie. "You are so full of it!"

Mac pounced on Santi.

Hattie's eyes sparkled and she shook her head. "We only made up that it happened here! It happened to Walt! At Blue Point State Park. Which might even be scarier, but . . . we're here, so . . ." She held both hands out like she was weighing options.

I thumped her on the arm and Mac sat next to me again, leaning against my shoulder. Hattie's eyes flickered and she shot me a look. I turned away, cheeks hot. I wasn't sure what was happening.

Santi sat and leaned on the stick. "And I haven't even gotten to the most fucked up part," he said.

"Like we'd believe you," Mac said. We. I felt Hattie's eyes on me and I didn't dare look.

Santi almost whispered. "Next night, Walt and Maggie go to Scallywag's in town, and ask the bartender, Owen, if they've seen this old hippie guy looking for his dog. Owen's this big burly dude—he does not scare easily. But his face goes white. 'You saw freaking Ponytail? Ponytail's been dead since 1978.' Walt's all, 'What?' And Owen tells them, this sixties burnout known as Ponytail went rowing on the bay. While he was gone, his shack caught fire. He ran into the burning building to save his dog."

"Tina said he smelled like wood smoke!" Hattie said.

Santi nodded and said, "Both Ponytail and Shep died."

"Is that true?" I said.

"Scout's honor," Hattie said, holding up her palm.

"You're not a freaking Scout," I said.

"I swear," she said with an earnestness I found sincere and unsettling.

"People have seen him over the years. Always at night. Always asking the same thing," Santi said.

"And they've seen his silhouette, in his dory, rowing across the bay." Hattie pointed toward the water and we all four turned to look. The moonlight broke in a million slivers on the surface, and the waves picked up speed for a few beats, doing their best to add to the eeriness.

Satisfied, Santi and Hattie sat. More wood collapsed and sparks shot from the embers. Mac and I flinched. After a while, Mac said, "I'm thinking Ponytail is pretty harmless," in a way that made me think he was scared, too.

"So you're saying if you saw him over my shoulder right now, you'd be cool with that?" Santi said.

Mac tilted his head back and forth, his dimples starting to show. I shamelessly leaned into him, scanning the shadows.

"I swear to God, that is what happened," Hattie said. "I just couldn't resist seeing you flip out one more time before you leave, Reid." She sighed contentedly, throwing wood on the fire. "What should we tell next, Santi? The Shelf Island Lady in Black?"

"Shelf Island?" I said. "You never told me about any Shelf Island ghosts." Shelf Island separated The Thimble from the open sea. We watched its lighthouse blink in the distance from Pulpit Head sometimes. It was iconic Maine postcard stuff.

"You're ready now, Reid," she said, patting my shoulder. "Reddi MacGregory."

Santi picked up a rock and threw it. We watched it splash in the water, then he leveled his eyes at us. "It's the granddaddy of scary shit. Shelf Island is haunted as hell."

"I'm fine not knowing," I offered.

Mac stealthily clasped my hand. My heart thumped in my throat.

Hattie saw and shot me a gleeful look. "Santi," she said. "Help me get marshmallows." Santi looked confused. She nodded in a deliberate way that made me want to kill her, but I was also breathlessly excited to be alone with Mac. I felt so in the moment, so without time to double-think. She wanted me to feel this way, like she wanted me to jump off Pulpit Head.

"Yes, gotta have marshmallows. Leonhirth, stoke the fire," Santi said with a quiet chuckle. Mac blushed. And like that, the alphas disappeared.

"What?" I called after them. "Like I can't stoke the fire?"

"Can you?" Mac asked.

"No," I said. He laughed.

We made a pretense of foraging for wood, straying far from the firelight, Ponytail be damned. Mac put his hand on the small of my back and drew me toward him, which is pretty romantic when you've only just finished eighth grade. When he kissed me, I closed my eyes like I'd seen in movies. For a couple of minutes all was sweet and perfect until we heard Santi's voice. We jumped apart and scrambled back to the embarrassingly low fire. Santi got to work.

We settled in with our speared marshmallows, and Mac secretly wrapped his hand around my waist. The world was astounding. The alphas told of crazed, shipwrecked sailors washing up on Shelf Island, murdering the lighthouse keeper and his wife and baby. Cannibalism? Mysterious infant cries in the night? The wife's ghost still patrolling Shelf Island in her long black dress? What could I care.

Oh, I was going to miss The Thimble.

When I heard Hattie coming up the stairs, I reminded myself that eighth grade was a long time ago, which meant Mac probably wouldn't remember as clearly as me, so I should calm down. True, I was not the virgin Hattie thought I was. Nor was I beyond butterflies at the prospect of seeing Mac. Mac, who once liked me for real and not because I happened to crash a golf cart in a deserted part of Howebrook with him. While having boobs. Mac, who wrote me actual letters until Thanksgiving of ninth grade.

"Okay, Reddi-Wip," Hattie said, popping into her room. "The time is now!" She was possibly more excited than I was. We took a long time getting dressed. Or getting me dressed. She had me model outfits, ultimately picking the white scoop-neck gauzy top and a blue batik skirt we got at our last trip to Collective Eye.

Hattie looked over my shoulder into the mirror. "I almost get a tear in my eye," she said. "My little Reid, all growed up. Soon"—she laced her fingers and held her hands beneath her chin—"you'll be deflowered."

"Ew! Shut up!" We laughed.

She pulled Mr. Tomten off her bookshelf and looked him in the eye. "Mr. Tomten, will Reid have the best. Night. Ever?" She didn't have the Sea of Life bowl and it was only seven fifteen, but I loved it.

"What about you and Santi, huh? You know you want to!"

"That's such bull," she said, zipping her new blue hoodie. She sprayed her wrists and neck with the perfume she'd found in Telluride over winter vacation.

"Mmm," I said, then narrowed my eyes. "You cannot fool me, Harriet. Santi's the only boy on earth who challenges you."

She turned from me and for the first time in our history of times, I saw her blush. I'm 95 percent sure about that. First the Don Quixote print and now a blush? What was happening? I teased her and she teased me back and somehow I made it through dinner with Hattie's parents, grandparents, and cousin Marshall, who was twenty-seven.

Finally a knock made the screen door bounce. Without a pause, it opened and in walked Santi. He stood in the living room with a guy I didn't recognize behind him. I panicked. What happened to Mac?

Until.

The dimples.

Mac Leonhirth stood six two, taller than Santi. The

moppy hair I remembered had lost all its blond and was cropped close to his head. His shoulders were square and solid under a Holderness tee that hung loose around his once-pudgy belly. Don't get me started on the face itself. I almost cried out from the shock of it.

"Holy crow! Mac, you're huge!" said Hattie. "Santi!"

"What?" Santi said, hands at his sides, palms open.

"You didn't tell us he doubled in size!" Hattie said.

Santi looked at Mac like he was seeing him for the first time. "Well, yeah, he's bigger than last time. Jeez, Hattie."

Mac grinned, ever amused, while I tried to reconcile this vision before me with the one locked safely in my memory bank.

Hattie hugged him and I did, too. He didn't smell the same. I guess hormones change everything. Except the playful eyes. And the dimples.

Mrs. Darrow asked Mac about school and blah blah. Hattie and I had one of our silent conversations.

He's about ten thousand times cuter than he used to be! she said.

No shit! I replied.

You're loving it!

I nodded subtly, but my cheeks flamed.

When I reengaged in the actual out-loud conversation, I heard Mac saying, "I'll stay at Stephanie's dad's in Paris for two weeks."

The room melted around him. Stephanie?

Hattie swatted the air, like Stephanie was a Connecticut mosquito. Mrs. Darrow asked where she was from. Paris, of course. Stephanie was trilingual. Stephanie played soccer. Stephanie sailed, too, on the French Riviera. Stephanie's father was a foreign diplomat. Mac must have said *Stephanie* twenty times in the four-minute conversation.

The boys were heading outside, us following, when Hattie looked at me with sad eyes. She held her hand behind his butt and made a face like, *Oh, the waste!*

I pressed my lips into a tight frown.

Sorry, she mouthed.

I grabbed her hand to give them distance and leaned into her. "Please," I whispered. "I can't take the campfire where we made out in eighth grade."

She looked at me, processing my words, then nodded, pulling me out the screen door.

I wanted to turn around and go back inside. But we could hardly *not* hang out with the boys simply because of Stephanie. Besides, Hattie still loved Santi, even though she wouldn't admit it.

"To the beach?" Santi said as we passed around the citronella spray on the porch.

"I say Ouija Night," Hattie said. She squished up her nose while spraying. To the betas: "Santi and I set up the Bat Cave before you got here."

It was almost worse than the campfire option, but of course, not quite. Hattie flashed me a grin and nodded, like, *Relax!* I rolled my eyes, then tapped Mac's arm with the citronella bottle so he'd take it, and also look up from his phone. Stephanie's texts will not come through, dude.

"To the Bat Cave!" Santi tweedled the tune from *Batman* and I watched the three of them step into the grass.

"I hate Ouija Night," I said to the air.

"You love Ouija Night," Hattie called over her shoulder.

I moaned, catching up as they headed for the path through hedges long grown rogue. Mac waved me ahead of him. We walked in line, alphas up front, betas bringing up the rear. The bushy tunnel felt like a portal to a secret land, which made the Bat Cave—an eight-by-twelve mini cabin that Hattie's brothers, Walt and Ben, built with Mr. Darrow—all the cooler. Or scarier. Depending on whether or not it was a Ouija Night. It was the dream kid hideout: walls of exposed two-by-fours, two camp cots, and a precarious approach that kept adults uninterested in paying visits. Best of all—if you're a Darrow—every summer a family of bats roosted under the eaves. If you're a MacGregory, you try to forget that part. When Walt and Ben hit late teenage-dom, the Bat Cave transformed from a hideout to home of the Wall of Bongs, which it more or less remained to this day.

The moon lit the backsides of clouds so their edges glowed. It was an A-plus romantic situation. My insides squirmed wondering what Mac remembered about the summer of eighth grade. In desperation I just started talking, a device I'd discovered during the Summer of Reid and Hammy.

"I don't get the concept of 'summoning' dead people"—I put *summoning* in air quotes above my head so he could see them—"on purpose. *Why?*" He made a small sound of acknowledgment.

"Hattie swears she isn't moving the planchette thing. *I'm* not moving it. I tell myself it's crap and she probably *is* moving it. But—" We stopped behind Santi and Hattie, who fiddled with the Bat Cave doorknob. "What if she's not?" Our eyes met.

"Okaaay," he drawled, amused, like always.

The dimples.

Killing me. I turned away.

Hattie swung open the door. The hot, still air smelled of cedar and mildew and more than a hint of pot. Santi opened the windows over both cots. There was a *click* and Santi's face lit up. He held a flashlight under his chin and with half-lidded eyes and a stuffy British accent said, "Good evening. I'm Alfred Hitchcock."

"Not funny," I muttered, fumbling for the pull cord to the light bulb I knew hung in the middle of the room. We blinked in the relative brightness. Already the temperature dropped, ocean air sweeping into the cabin's crannies.

"Let's summon Ponytail," Hattie said, retrieving the Ouija box from a shelf. She sat cross-legged on the braided rug and set the board in front of her. "You all remember Ponytail, right? The guy with the—"

Mac dropped his voice. "'I lost my dog, Shep. Have you seen him? Yea big—' I've told it a hundred times at school."

"Oh, great, a convert," I said, then blushed because it sounded flirty. And why were we revisiting a ghost story from *the kissing night*? I tried to shoot an eye dart at Hattie, but her eyes glittered. She was unstoppable.

"I'm in," Santi said, dropping next to her. "We need candlelight."

I reverse sighed dramatically, playing it up to cover my awkwardness. Mac produced a lighter and lit a candle on a milk crate table. He cupped the flame and sat next to Hattie, setting the candle on the floor. He shrugged to me. "Sorry," he said, a glowing Adonis.

It occurred to me this might be an actual ring of hell. Again I tried to catch Hattie's attention. She wasn't having it.

Santi pulled a wine bottle and corkscrew from under the cot. "Courtesy of Herrera Vineyards." He uncorked it like a pro and handed out cups.

"There are perks to having him as a roommate," Mac said.

I sniffed the red liquid and stifled a shudder. "Desperate times call for desperate measures," I said, kind of not caring how they interpreted that. "Salud." I forced a swallow and sat between the boys.

"We begin with a moment of silence to honor those gone before us," Hattie said. "Close your eyes."

No way was I doing that, so I watched the others, pale in the flickering light. It got quiet enough to hear the surf's *shush, shush, shush.* Even Mac's dimples faded. The surf started sounding distressingly like an ax murderer mouth-breathing and I couldn't unhear it. I took another slug of wine.

Hattie blinked. "Hold hands."

Oh my God, are you trying to kill me? I said with a look. But her face was impervious.

Mac's hands were soft and warm and I could barely stand it.

"If there is a spirit in the room, thank you for visiting us tonight. We are looking for the spirit of a man known as Ponytail."

"And his dog, Shep," Santi added.

Hattie pulled her hand away and whacked his thigh with her knuckles. "I'm serious, Santi," she said.

"Jesus," Santi said with actual irritation.

"Come on." She laid her fingers on the planchette and Santi did the same.

Mac and I dropped hands at last.

"Is there a spirit in the room?" Hattie asked.

We waited, our eyes darting about.

"Spirit, can we have a sign?" She remained cadaver-still.

A sharp thump sounded.

"What was that?" Santi said, straightening up.

The thump again.

"He's here!" Hattie whispered, eyes glossy.

"Shit!" I whispered, scrambling onto the cot. "Mac, did you do that?" I held a pillow near my eyes. "Tell the truth."

He threw his hands up. "I am completely not doing anything."

Hattie smiled. "Ponytail?"

"Hey," Santi whispered, staring at their hands on the planchette.

It prowled along the Ouija Board, stopping at *Yes*. A shiver rolled over my shoulders.

Hattie continued. "Ponytail, are you the only ghost in our town?"

"Why do we want to know *that*?" I squeaked.

Hattie's concentration bordered on creepy. My God, I thought. She truly *wants* to communicate with a ghost. Santi looked pained. I couldn't tell if he was being ironic.

"Ponytail?" Hattie said.

The planchette slid toward the alphabet. No one breathed.

B-E-

"Shit! You're not pushing it?" Santi asked.

She gave her head a tiny shake.

W-A-R-E

Something crashed near the Wall of Bongs.

I screamed. Santi swore. I yanked the light's string. One of the bongs lay on the floor.

Hattie's eyes were wide.

"Ponytail's a stoner!" Mac said, cracking up.

"Get your damn hands back on there, you're releasing the spirit!" I said, which made Santi hoot with laughter.

"You *did* push it, didn't you!" Hattie said.

He nodded, rolling to the floor.

Hattie thumped his butt with her foot and I joined her. "God, I almost swallowed my tongue! Mac, did you knock the bong over?"

"I swear I didn't," he said. "I did do this." He revealed a baseball bat that had obviously been under the cot, and thumped it against the wall.

"It must've been the wind," Santi said, catching his breath.

We watched the curtains flutter every few seconds, like flies when you think they're dead but they're not. "How convincing," I said.

"Obviously, it was Ponytail," Hattie said.

"Seriously?" Mac said. "It was Santi."

"How would I knock down the bong from here?"

Nobody had an answer.

"We better say goodbye. It's Ouija law," Hattie said. "Always say goodbye to the spirits so they don't stay."

Mac sighed. "There was no spirit."

"Come on, Santi," Hattie said, her fingers on the planchette.

He sighed with a ridiculous giggle that would make anyone fall in love with him, then laid his fingers as directed. "Don't we have to turn the light back off?"

"No!" I said. Mac laughed.

"Goodbye, Ponytail," Hattie said. "Thank you."

The planchette zipped to *goodbye* on the board so fast Hattie actually gasped. She glared at Santi.

"That wasn't me," he said. "I swear to God."

She cocked her head suspiciously and got him in an eye-lock that dared him to come clean.

"I'm not lying," he said earnestly, meeting her eyes. They seemed frozen, and then her face softened, almost imperceptibly, yet in a way that made her unrecognizable to me. For a moment, it was like all seventeen years of Thimble summers—tumbling around beaches, learning to rig boats and build campfires and crack lobster claws—became real and palpable things that fueled the molecules in the space between them. Like maybe, right then, they realized they were destined to fall in love. Mac and I shared an awkward glance, confirming I hadn't imagined it. He shifted and the cot creaked.

Hattie ended the moment then. I could almost see her usual expression of invulnerability snap back into place, like a mask. Her face broke into a somewhere-else smile. "Ponytail was freaking here," she said, twisting to get the game box.

"Okay, time to go!" I said, tossing the pillow back on the bed.

"I don't know what you're so afraid of, Reid." Hattie replaced the board and closed the box.

"Let me think." I tapped my chin, standing to go. "Oh yes, dead people."

I led the way out of the Bat Cave into the big, freeing night sky. We teetered across the rocks like tightrope walkers.

"There were no dead people," Mac said.

"Dude, I didn't do that at the end," Santi said quietly. I don't think he'd recovered from whatever happened with that eye-lock in there.

"It was Hattie," Mac said.

"It was *not*," she said. "It was Ponytail. You guys are fools. When I'm a ghost, I'm definitely going to freak out kids who play with Ouija boards," Hattie said.

"God, Hattie. You're freaking me out *now*!" Santi said. "What's with you?"

"I'm just saying, it would be the best part of being dead, don't you think?"

"Um, I'm pretty sure there isn't any good part of being dead," Santi said. "Quit with the creepy shit."

"Baby," she said.

Mac shook his head to me, and I shook mine back with a shrug.

We made our way to the house and drove Snowcap to the Carousel Dairy Barn with the top down for ice cream. I was glad I got shotgun so I didn't need to sit two inches from Mac in the tiny back seat. Hattie got me on two padiddles on the way back to the island, slugging me a bit too hard. We parked back at Hattie's and the boys got ready to walk the cross-island path back to the Herreras'.

Again, Mac and I caught eyes. He looked away quickly. *Damn you, Stephanie!* I thought.

Later, Hattie and I shared the space at her bathroom sink. She mopped her face with a cotton ball while I brushed my teeth. "Okay, Reddi," she said. "I'll full-on admit that Stephanie is a *devastating* development."

"Yeah," I said, my voice garbled by toothpaste foam. I swished a cupful of water. "*Pluh*," I spat extra loud. We chuckled. She handed me the toner and I tipped it onto a fresh cotton ball. "Why is it so dang hard for me to find a boyfriend?"

Hattie made a face. "You don't need a boyfriend. Get over that bullshit."

"Need? No. *Want?*" I tossed the cotton in the wicker wastebasket. "Yes."

"Why?" She scrubbed her teeth.

"Easy for you to say, Miss I Randomly Decide I Want to Have Sex One Day and Sleep with the Hottest Guy on Earth the Same Night," I said, leaning against the doorjamb.

She paused without looking up, then spat. "Please."

"Oh, I'm not done." I poked the air with one finger.

"*While* I'm Pretending Hammy Doesn't Love Me *and* That I'm Not Playing Jay Asshat Seavers Like a Frigging Happy Meal Kazoo."

"Wow," she said, wiping her mouth. Her eyebrows hardened in a way I only saw when she was mad at her father, and I thought I saw her mist up. It completely unnerved me, since I couldn't think of a single time she'd cried in all our years. I told myself I imagined it.

"I'm kidding, Hattie," I lied, my own voice thick. "Sometimes you just don't know how good you have it."

She stared at me, not blinking for several seconds, then waved me out the door. "S'cuse me," she said, voice cool, and shut it.

I felt really alone suddenly, there in my nightgown. I retreated to her bedroom and sat on the bed, unsure how the conversation took this turn. Maybe because she was treading on my story with Jay—a sorry story, to be sure, but it was all I had. Hattie could have *twelve* stories if she wanted. The moon pierced the clouds, splattering light across the waves. It was so beautiful. I tried to pull strength from it.

The bathroom went dark, signaling her approach. I tidied the clothes left in my suitcase so I wasn't just standing there.

She strode in. "Look, Reid. Don't take Stephanie out on me."

"I'm not," I said, refolding my T-shirts. "I just—"

"*What?*"

"I just don't get you on this boyfriend thing." I tucked my shoes neatly under my bed. What was I even doing? I put my hands on my hips. "Forget Jay and Hammy and, yes, *Santi*—who we both know you'll marry—and let's just talk about Gibson Soule."

She made a face, then crawled into her bedding and leaned on her pillow. "What about him?"

"What about him? Okay, I wasn't going to tell you this. Gib Soule came by the afternoon you left for Maine—the day after your Olympic romp at Siwanoy—to interview *me* about *YOU*."

She sat up. "What?"

"Yep," I said. I watched her in the mirror. "He wants to be your boyfriend."

She blinked twice.

"*A lot.*"

I'd done the rare thing of surprising her. She ran her hand over her nubbly white bedspread. "I mean, he's a nice guy and all—"

"Are. You. *Insane?*" I yelled the last word, surprising us both.

"I don't want a damn boyfriend, Reid! Why is this so hard for you to comprehend?"

I had no answer, so I kept pressing. "Don't you want someone who cares about you like nobody else just because you're you? Isn't that what everybody wants? A *relationship*?"

She opened her Stephen King novel and looked at

the pages. "I have relationships," she grumbled. "I don't need all that other stuff."

"What?" I said, waving my hands. "What *stuff*?"

"It's too complicated." She laid the book flat. "Take Jay."

"Oh God," I said, rolling my eyes.

Her brow crinkled, but she continued. "Jay Seavers wants no attachment. Jay Seavers is not texting me because he wants to cuddle up and watch Netflix. Jay Seavers just wants to play the game."

I raised one eyebrow.

"Come on, Reid. It's a big freaking game. He wants *me* to want *him* and when I do, he'll be ready for the next challenge. It's a clean and simple competition to see who has more power."

I folded my jeans for the third time. How long did *I* resist Jay? Six seconds?

"If I keep him hanging on, he keeps following. He's dumb, thinking with hormones only, so I win."

I looked at the floor, the quilt, anything to avoid seeing my foolish self in the mirror. I was dull to him, I thought. Boring. Not worth the effort. It all fit together.

"I'm not hurting his feelings—not sure he has any anyway—so it's exactly like a game of tennis." She grinned. "And I can *kick his ass*."

I smiled, but some part of my soul wilted. We were erasing Jay and me—something I'd wished for since that Monday in the cafeteria. I'd never tell her about him now. I should've felt liberated. Instead, I felt like I was pretending something that was a pretty big—*very* big—deal didn't matter. I was letting *myself* not matter in the story of Reid and Hattie. Hattie's story was always better than mine. Always.

"But," I said. A breeze kicked up the white curtains.

"What?"

"I saw that look between you and Santi," I ventured.

She smirked and pulled her ponytail elastic out, setting it on her bedside. "Can you quit it with that, please?" she said.

A new theory popped into my head and I blurted, "*Why?* What is it about having someone close to you that scares you so much?"

Hattie's turquoise eyes turned gray. She was angry, at me, and I couldn't bear it. I wanted to reel my words back in, and even opened my mouth like I could.

She stared, half telling me to shut up and half daring me to continue.

For once, I dared, however meekly. "Why don't you want a friend who's into being with you just because you're . . . you?" *And worships you, like Hammy.* "So you can have sex that's . . . I don't know. Meaningful?"

"Oh my God," she said with an eye roll, pulling Stephen King up again. "Why would I want some guy nosing into my life like that? It's claustrophobic."

"Okay, forget Santi," I said diplomatically.

Her jaw relaxed the slightest bit.

"Gib Soule isn't *some guy*. He's a living, breathing person you've known since sixth grade—a really sweet guy who happens to look like one of the Greek statues we studied in art history. *And* he wants to spend his time"—I twirled my finger, then aimed it at her—"*with you.*"

"It's not happening." She rolled onto her side and flipped off her light, the lone wolf loping into her dark woods.

"Arghh," I growled playfully, trying to smooth the tension. Ever the beta. I sighed.

"Good night, Reid," she said.

And while she fell quickly asleep, I couldn't stop thinking about what she'd said regarding Jay. Of course she was right, and it made me sick all over again, knowing how little he thought of me.

I watched the yellow moon out the window, round and small, playing hide-and-seek through the clouds. Part of me, I thought, was up there with it, far, far away from the part of me here with Hattie. Sometimes we were so different it hurt.

THEN

More July Days ~ The Thimble

The next day Hattie and I took the horses trail riding across the island and for a gallop on the beach. The boys went fishing. After dinner, I talked them into mini-golf in town. Anything but more ghosts, the supernatural kind or the romantic memory kind.

At bedtime, I came in from brushing my teeth and Hattie sat propped against pillows, Stephen King in hand. "You know," she said, putting the book down. "I got the feeling on the ride back that Mac might have unresolved feelings for you."

"Right." I pulled the covers back and sank into the mattress. "Mac literally couldn't have checked his phone more." In town he got Wi-Fi, and composed maybe ten texts to Stephanie. Thankfully, she was on Paris time and didn't respond. We had to take a picture of him in front of the mini windmill when he got his hole in one.

"Maybe you throw yourself at him and see what happens," Hattie continued. "Picture it. You have a fling and then he's off to school. No repercussions."

"That's your gig, not mine," I said. She was bordering on rude with all this.

"It's lonely here in Non-Virgin Land, Reddi. Won't you join me?"

A switch flipped in my head. I couldn't take it anymore. "I've got to tell you something," I blurted.

Hattie raised her brow. "Yes?"

"It's kind of a . . . confession. I should've already told you." Sweat already gathered at my temples.

She grinned. "This sounds good."

There was no turning back. I played with a clay Cheshire cat she kept on the bedside. It had blue and turquoise stripes and a peach muzzle. "I—actually, I had sex. On prom night." It was like expelling a big fat hairball that had been lodged in my throat for months. It lay on the floor between Hattie and me, undisturbed, while my pulse throbbed in my ears.

She looked at me quizzically for several moments.

"You slept with Charlie?" She jumped a few times like she was on a pogo stick. "Freckle madness!"

"No! Not Charlie. Jeez," I said. "This very weird thing happened . . ."

"My God, Reddi! Out with it!"

Her expression matched the clay cat's and a smile crept across my lips, either a nervous reaction or some kind of contagion. "You're going to be shocked."

"Try me." She scuttled next to me on the bed.

I closed my eyes. "Jay Seavers."

No response. She was stock-still, like the figurine.

"What?" Her shoulders sank the tiniest bit.

"I should have told you," I said. "I'm so stupid!" My skin felt on fire. I threw off the covers.

"You slept with Jay Seavers?" she asked, barely loud enough for me to hear.

My eyes steamed. My chin wobbled. I nodded. The waves outside filled the space between us.

Rushhhhhh.

Rushhhhhh.

She looked away, brow furrowed, like she was calculating some puzzle in her head. She was rethinking her assessment of Jay Seavers. And of me.

"You slept with Seavers?" she said again, cocking her head.

"I like to call him Captain Dickhead, but yes."

Her eyes went big, then small, then big. "Wow."

I couldn't read how she felt about it beyond the surprise. Was I now her competitor? We'd never competed. Ever. I'd always thought it was because I wasn't worthy. And I'm pretty sure she thought that too, though she loved me anyway. Maybe it's why she loved me, I thought now. I started to panic. I hugged my knees, hiding my face.

"Where?" she whispered.

I peeked through my elbow. "Remember when he and I left on the golf cart?"

She squinted. "No."

"Well, we did."

Rushhhhhh.

Rushhhhhh.

Her pupils looked huge, though I'd never paid attention to them before, so I could've imagined it. *She's furious,* I thought. I lobbed words into the air. About hitting the stump, Captain Dickhead flying out of the driver's seat, my saving the cart. "He was worried at first and the next thing I knew we were making out and my dress was in the grass."

I stopped, sickened by the memory of how I'd let myself get taken advantage of so easily. No, not easily—*willingly.* I couldn't look at her.

"Reddi-Wip!"

I jumped.

She grabbed my arm. "You screwed Jay Seavers on the

golf course?" Her eyes flashed. "I knew you were a sexual ninja! *Whi-chaaa!*" She paced the room. "This is great!"

She didn't even ask why I hadn't told her. I couldn't fathom her thinking, but my muscles unclenched. "No, no," I said. "It's not like that. I mean, there was duck shit everywhere." That wasn't the important part. I shook my head. "And . . . it went downhill from there. Really bad."

Staring at the Cheshire cat's face, I told her about the cafeteria. I knew why I'd kept it secret. Humiliation was a language she didn't speak, and she didn't want me to speak it either. She protected me from it. Always. It was her way of sharing her superpowers with me. Her version of me was a little better than me in real life.

"What an ass," she said, moving to her own bed again. "We'll teach him. He doesn't deserve you, and he knows it."

I ran my thumb over the cat's smooth ears. "Mmm, I'm pretty sure he doesn't know that."

"Bullshit. We'll show him."

"What do you mean?"

She drummed her fingertips together, eyebrow cocked. "Revenge. What else?"

The next morning, Mrs. Darrow served her famous Maine blueberry French toast. She'd already been out running, and now moved between the kitchen and dining room like a purposeful butterfly. I loved her.

"This is amazing," I said. "Thank you."

She smiled. Hattie had her turquoise eyes, but only Camilla had her artist's breeziness. Where Hattie, Helen, Mr. Darrow, and the boys were intensely driven by who knew what, Mrs. Darrow and Camilla, I suspected, were secretly amused by their competitiveness. Mr. Darrow needed Mrs. Darrow to keep him from pursuing world domination.

"We love when you're here," Mrs. Darrow said. Hattie went into the kitchen and I heard Mrs. Darrow whisper, "Did you remember to take—"

"*Yes*, I took care of the horses," Hattie said loudly. It seemed aggressive.

Mrs. Darrow paused. "Oh, good." She disappeared into the laundry room.

"My dad wanted them fed early," Hattie said when she saw me eyeing her. I didn't believe that, exactly, but I didn't always get what went down between Hattie and her dad.

"You already fed them? This morning?" I said, adding syrup to my toast. "I didn't hear you."

"I'm half cat burglar."

"When do you sleep, for crying out loud?"

"Who can sleep when there's revenge to plot?" She carried her dishes to the kitchen. "What if, for instance, we got all the girls Seavers has screwed together and threw him a giant baby shower," she called. "We could say everyone's pregnant with his children." She returned, scooting her chair under the table.

I nearly spat out my food. "We are not doing that." I wiped my mouth. "But it would be hilarious."

"We could say you all have herpes," she said, nice and loud.

"Okay," I whispered. "Really?"

"Hattie? What are you talking about?" Mrs. Darrow called. I scowled at Hattie.

"Don't worry, Mom! Just trying to avenge this wanker who didn't treat Reid like the goddess she is."

"Oh," said Mrs. Darrow. "Well, she should be avenged."

"I am *not* saying I have herpes," I said softly—a sentence I never thought I'd utter in front of Mrs. Darrow.

"It might be worth it," Hattie replied. "Just saying."

Mrs. Darrow appeared in the doorway. "It might be." We laughed, and I wished I'd told Hattie the truth from the beginning.

After breakfast, we jogged down the sloping hill toward the dock for our sail. Mr. Darrow had just started letting Hattie skipper the *Aria*, the Darrows' twenty-eight-foot sloop, on her own. "We could get Charlie to steal all Jay's clothes when he's showering in the locker room."

"That's pretty good, but he'd probably enjoy running naked through school," I said.

"Good point."

The boys were already there.

"Great day for a sail!" Hattie called.

Santi shook his head. He lifted his sunglasses and squinted toward the horizon. "Did you see that?"

Comments such as these caught my attention. I looked over the water.

"It's fine," she said, taking the *Aria*'s stern line off a cleat on the dock. Rope is not rope if you're a sailor. It's line. I'd made progress in sailing terminology over the years. "The sky's blue," she said.

Technically, this was true. But I saw the same gray stripe out there that Santi did, and that gray stripe was a fog bank. I'd been to Maine enough to recognize one of those all by myself.

"For now," Santi said.

I followed Hattie and Mac on board.

"Can't we check some gauge?" I waved toward the dashboard of nautical gadgets.

Mac chuckled. I shrugged. "What?" He shook his head and it was official: Mac Leonhirth had turned alpha. I didn't even know that was possible.

"We've got at *least* an hour," Hattie said. She tugged on a sail line. "We can show them Shelf Island lighthouse and come right back."

"Does it matter that I am fine skipping the lighthouse?" I asked. It'd been easy to dismiss the story of crazed, cannibalistic sailors and the mother and baby ghosts when I was in la-la land with Mac, way back when. Before Stephanie.

"No," she answered, flashing a grin. "Mac's into it."

His dimples appeared. "Why not? Maybe we'll find some bones."

"Thanks," I said.

Santi came aboard but looked seaward. "We could go this afternoon, after it burns off."

"Santi, we'll be back in no time," Hattie said. "If you hurry up."

Santi and Hattie exchanged commands—jib, boom, transom. I hand-cranked the line around the winch near the stern. An important job. The sails ballooned and we were underway.

Shelf Island lay ahead in the distance, the only land left between us and the open sea. The top of the light was visible, blinking every twenty seconds or so, but the house was on the Atlantic side of the island, hidden by a craggy hill.

The on-deck flurry of activity settled. The water had some chop, but barely any swells. I liked to stretch my legs out on the bow and climbed up. Warm sun, clean air, sea spray—I understood how it all became addictive. We glided along, and I leaned on my elbows. Mac joined me.

The minutes ticked by and Shelf Island grew bigger, the light tower fatter. Hattie sat against a railing, the picture of confidence. She and her father raced together all the time, and on occasion he'd travel to race in Australia and South Africa. They'd qualified for a father-daughter championship race in Penobscot Bay, which was the reason she wouldn't be home until August twenty-eighth.

We were close enough to the island to make out individual spruce trees and see the corner of the keeper's house through the woods. And right then, white tufts rolled over the treetops like tumbleweeds from the sea.

Hattie and Santi caught eyes. He made an I-told-you-so face. "Relax," she said.

I scanned the blue sky. We were too close to land to tell where the actual wall of fog began on the other side of Shelf Island.

"We'll just loop the island so we can show them the house and head back," Hattie said.

Mac and I looked at each other. "Why do I have the feeling I'm going to be terrified at some point in the near future?" I asked.

"Because you are?" he said.

As if on cue, fog drifted around the corners of the island, a thin mist skimming the tops of the waves. The temperature dropped, and I wished I'd brought a jacket. Mac and I moved off the bow into the cockpit with Hattie and Santi.

Hattie and Santi took the *Aria* the length of the island.

To round the eastern side, we had to go out a ways and then tack back again. We sailed past the end of the island and did a U-turn to sail around the Atlantic side of it. By the time we came about, the island was veiled in thin fog.

"I think we've officially become a Stephen King novel," I said.

"Cue lighthouse keeper screams," Mac said.

"Not funny," I said.

"Darrow, we better keep moving," Santi said from the stern, a serious tone in his voice. "This is only the front edge of the fog bank. It's gonna get worse."

Hattie said, "Chill." She pointed to a piece of rocky beach. A faded dock reached out toward us. "That's where the crew cooked the people. Wanna tie up and check it out?"

I ignored her and pointed through the trees. "There's the keeper's house. Is someone home?"

"No, it's run remotely by the Coast Guard," Santi said.

"Why the light inside the house?" Mac asked.

"Dunno," said Santi.

"The ghosts, fools!" Hattie cackled.

"If we hear a baby, I'm going to lose it," I said. The light at the top of the tower blinked, as if responding to me.

In the minutes it took to reach the other end of the island, the fog had completely blotted out the sky. Dampness clung to my arms, my hair, my face. "It feels like it's eight o'clock at night," I said.

Past the dock, the island shot from the water in massive sheets of granite.

"Makes you wonder what kinda rocks are under us, doesn't it?" Mac said, his dimples showing.

Movement among the trees caught my eye.

"Hey! Did anyone see that?" Hattie said.

We all had.

"What the hell was it?" Mac said.

And *poof.* Shelf Island disappeared. A complete whiteout engulfed us.

"This was a really fucking stupid idea," said Santi, all swagger absent from his voice. "Hattie, bad choice. I don't know what's going on with you lately. You know fog—"

"We're *fine*," Hattie said sharply. She wouldn't look at him. "We can use the light as our landmark."

"I can barely *see* the light," I said. "Should we call your dad?"

"Don't be alarmist," said Hattie. "We're good."

We stared into the nothingness.

"I don't see the light," Mac said.

I strained my eyes, but the whiteness had this micro-motion that made me dizzy. Only the black water sloshing against the boat kept me from complete disorientation.

"Are we looking in the right direction?" Santi said.

"What if a face came out of the mist right now?" Hattie said.

"Hattie, kindly shut up," I said.

"The Thimble should be northwest. . . ." muttered Santi. He wiped moisture off the gauges by the wheel with his shirt.

"I know where it is," Hattie insisted, stepping next to him.

We waited. I tried to breathe evenly. An anemic glow lit off the stern. "There!" I cried. I pointed behind us.

"How'd it get back there?" Mac asked. "Are we headed out to sea?"

Hattie and Santi did something with the boom and the jib and we turned in a new direction. But the sails fell slack. Lines dinged against the mast like a toy xylophone.

"Great," said Santi, throwing his hands up. "Hattie, you're taking the blame on this. We should have waited out the fog, like I said."

"Can't we use the motor?" I asked. I kept my eye on the spot I'd last seen blinking.

"We'll just dock on Santi's side of The Thimble," Hattie said. "It's closer."

"What about the motor, *Skipper*?" Santi mad was a little scary, which didn't help matters.

"There isn't much gas," she said. "Besides, this is more fun."

I turned to Mac. "She's deranged." I couldn't hide my annoyance.

"This is fucking insane. She better know what she's doing," he said in a hushed voice.

Hattie told me and Mac to stay in the cockpit for ballast, which felt demeaning, but panic-stricken betas are good direction followers.

She threw commands at Santi.

He barked back.

Then the sails billowed with a glorious whooshing sound and we glided into motion. Spray prickled my face.

"Sweet life!" I said giddily, gripping Mac's forearm.

"Yeah," said Mac. "But do we know where we're going?"

True, we sailed through the middle of a cloud.

When I checked Hattie's concern level, I saw her near the stern, crouching on the outside of the safety railing, hanging on to it with both hands and leaning her head into the misty wind as far as she could without falling off. She let go of the railing with one hand and worked to balance herself so she could lift one foot off the edge. She looked like a flag.

I jumped to my feet. "Hattie!" She didn't hear me. "Does nothing scare her?" I said to Mac.

His expression didn't change. It gave me a chill. "Mac?"

He wagged his finger, signaling me to be quiet. His brow furrowed. "What's that sound?"

Somehow Hattie was back on deck, next to a still simmering Santi. They looked up. We listened.

I heard it. Low. Mechanical. *Whir-wuh whir-wuh whir-wuh.*

Santi said, "I really think this might be the stupidest fucking thing we've ever done."

"What is it?" I said. The whirring grew louder. "Oh my God. Is . . . is that a ship?"

"Where the hell *are* we?" Mac said, eyes dark. "Do you even know? How are we in the path of a *fucking ship*?"

Hattie didn't reply, waving her hand at him to keep quiet as she cocked her head toward the sound. I searched for Shelf Island Light. The disorientation was unbearable. She reached under the side seats and tossed me and Mac orange life jackets. My chest went numb.

"Can you see it?" Hattie called to Santi.

"No! Port, I think," he yelled over the noise. He held a clump of his own hair in his fist. "Mac, take the jib. We've gotta come about."

I buckled the life jacket with shaky fingers and huddled on the floor of the cockpit. "What should I do?"

Nobody answered.

"There's not enough wind!" Hattie yelled.

Santi's eyes were steel. "The motor."

Mac was on his feet. I couldn't just sit on the floor and stood, searching the whiteness. Red lights blinked to our left. They were so high I thought a Coast Guard helicopter had arrived. "Look!" I pointed.

"Holy shit!" said Santi. "Are we in the path of the *fucking Bluenose*?!"

Mac squinted, puzzled. This one I knew. "The high-speed ferry!" I said. "To Nova Scotia!"

Mac yanked the cord on the motor, once, twice; it wouldn't turn over. The *Bluenose*'s engine was deafening. My reptilian brain took charge. I fumbled through stuff tucked under the steering wheel until I found a flare and an air horn.

"Gimme the horn!" Hattie yelled, holding out her hands.

She caught it, jumped onto the port edge of the boat, and pressed the button. A screech ripped through the cold smokiness.

The engine kept coming. *Whir-wuh whir-wuh whir-wuh.* The deck rumbled under my feet. Santi shot the flare—a flaming arrow that vanished in seconds. "Get more," he said. I dove under the steering wheel. Hattie blew the horn again.

The *Bluenose* sound changed. *Whuh-uuuh-whuh-uuuh-whuh-uuuh.* It was like it had a voice and it was saying, "Hey, did you hear something?" Still, the red lights loomed closer.

Hattie blew the air horn a third time just as Mac got the engine started.

A deep blast bellowed through the fog, so loud it rattled my teeth. I slapped my hands to my ears.

Hattie and Santi dropped the sails. Santi took over the outboard.

"*GO!*" Hattie yelled. He gunned the engine and we banked right so hard I fell on my ass. The fog trapped the engine exhaust around us. I held my elbow over my mouth, scrambling to the seat.

Hattie took the steering wheel. Mac dropped into the seat next to me. We were silent while Santi and Hattie navigated for I don't know how long. Finally, the interlaced fingers of fog spread apart, exposing streaks of blue. The blue grew bigger, the fog lacier. Then the sunshine burst over us with an almost audible pop. I rubbed goose bumps on my arms. The Thimble was dead ahead.

Hattie bounded to the bow. "Well, look at that. And you guys doubted me." Nobody responded.

When she hopped onto the Darrows' dock minutes later and tied up the boat, she said, "Now you can say you've had a bona fide high seas adventure. You're pirates now. Don't tell me you guys didn't love that."

"Love is a strong word," Mac said.

Santi shook his head. "You're lucky you didn't kill us, Darrow." He said it quietly, without looking at her, and went back to de-rigging.

"Move," I said loudly. "I need to kiss the ground."

She swatted my ass and looked me square in the eye over her sunglasses. "Bullshit, Reddi. You crave adventure more than any of us—you just wait until no one is looking."

I brushed past, casting her a sideways smirk.

But for the rest of the day, I turned her words over in my head, wondering if she might be spot-on. She knew me better than I knew myself. I don't know why this comforted me, but it did.

THEN

August Days ~ Back in Scofield

I'd been home from my glorious Maine adventure for a few weeks and had begun to look back fondly on the fog bank day. It's funny how your mind can do that. Right before I left, Hattie made me vow to get revenge on Captain Dickhead, and suggested Hammy as a great boyfriend for me, if I must have one. My two tense bedtime conversations with her had exhausted me, so I didn't bother to explain the whole reason we hung out was to help him pass the time until she returned, when he hoped to make her his girlfriend. Instead, I told her about that

Vanilla Yeti guitarist, Noah, and she encouraged me to throw myself at him and worry about boyfriends later.

Still, once in Scofield, I'd carefully managed my hostess schedule at work so my nights were free to spend with Hammy. As friends, I told myself.

"What's the snow monkey status?" Jasper asked. The customers had left the matinee and we were cleaning the dining room. Jasper wiped the tables while I replaced sugar packets. "You must have hooked up with Hammy by now. Gotten a little red in the face with him like on that *Our Amazing Planet* episode?"

"Seriously?" I said, laughing. We moved to the next table.

"I was right, wasn't I?"

"Nope," I said, though not with much heart. "I told you, he loves Hattie."

I left out what Hattie had said. And the horrifying hand-holding incident after our otter caper. *And* that recently, driving to the beach or hanging at the Mighty Bean, I caught myself staring at Hammy's profile.

"I don't buy it," Jasper said. "He likes you. You've gone out every day for weeks."

"And nothing has happened. That's evidence he *doesn't* like me," I said. "PS, do we need to dwell the fact that I'm not recognized as girlfriend material?"

"Straight guys are fucked up," he said, squirting cleaner on the next table. "For what it's worth, I'd be all over you by now. If I were straight."

I made a face. "Thanks?"

The next day, I went for a run and returned as the mail truck drove up. The mailman handed me a stack of envelopes and a package from Hattie. "Hattie fix!" I said to Boomer.

Inside, Mom sat stuffing autism fund-raiser envelopes in the kitchen. With the event date approaching, her party perfectionist stress increased.

"Mail," I said, dropping the envelopes next to her. "I have a care package." I gulped down a glass of water and got a knife.

"Fun," she said, watching me open the box.

I pulled out some tissue and then a bright red rubber lobster. The gift tag on its claw said, *To Spencer, Love Hattie*, in red marker with lots of hearts. "Awww," I said.

Mom smiled, shaking her head. "That Hattie."

I tossed another layer of tissue aside and uncovered my gift. "Oh man."

"Is that a Ouija board?" Mom asked. "I haven't seen one of those since college."

"She knows I hate them." A slip of paper taped to the box said, *xo, Ponytail.* "Always messin' with me," I said with a low chuckle. In a separate box, she gave me a bracelet of ceramic beads with bright blue eyes painted on them. *To protect you from evil spirits. xo*, that note said. It was kind of creepy, but my mom interrupted my thoughts.

"Looks like you got something else," she said, handing me an envelope.

"Huh?" I examined the front and back. No return address, just *PR VI* hand printed in blue ink. "Who's that?"

"It looks like an invitation."

I had no idea what it could be. A preseason cross-country cookout? Gently I split the top with the knife and slid out a cream-colored card. I read it three times before it made sense.

THIS CARD SERVES AS A TICKET +1,
FOR YOU AND A FRIEND
PIG ROAST SIX
BY INVITE ONLY
AUGUST 14
IF YOU DON'T KNOW WHERE IT IS OR WHO HOSTS IT,
YOU'VE RECEIVED THIS BY MISTAKE.
ENTERTAINMENT: VANILLA YETI.
ENTRY FEE: $20

"Holy crap!" I said. "I got invited to the Burkes' Pig Roast." I reread the return address. "PR VI is Pig Roast Six!"

"What's that?"

I couldn't stop smiling. "Oh my God! It's tonight," I

whispered. That was how they kept it so secret. "It says plus one. I can bring a friend. How did this happen?!" I hopped in a ridiculous circle behind her chair, my running shoes squeaking on the tile.

"What pig roast?" she asked.

"I'll explain later." And I ran out.

The Burke twins, Ross and Artie, had two more brothers, aged up to twenty-six or so. Every summer, the Burkes threw an epic bash known simply as the Pig Roast. Nobody could see the party from the road, the Burke property was so massive. Generally, the uninvited didn't find out about the Pig Roast until after it happened. Being prep schoolers, the Burkes rarely mingled with Scofield high schoolers, but there was some Ledge Haven Yacht Club crossover. My brother Scott got to go once—lacrosse star cachet, I guess. He told me it was the best party of his life, college included.

On the patio, I called Hammy.

"Hey," he said. I heard him eating, which I'd realized weeks ago was his resting state. In a just world, he'd weigh three hundred pounds. "I'll be there at seven." We were scheduled to watch the two-hour season finale of *Foreign Intelligence*—my pick—tonight. "I have to admit, I'm curious to find out what happens to Portia and her kid," he said, chewing.

"I have news," I said.

"What if the president won't pay the ransom?"

"It's way bigger than Portia's ransom."

"Something bigger than Portia's ransom? Her kid is in the hands of a *terrorist cell*, Reid."

I ignored him. "The Burkes' Pig Roast—Pig Roast VI. We got invited. It's freaking tonight. It starts at four!"

"Wait, what?"

My cheeks stretched wider. "I know!" More ridiculous hopping. "I got the invite in today's mail. Go get your mail!"

"I—"

"Do you think I should invite that guy Noah from the band?" I blurted. I pictured him at the last Vanilla Yeti practice. "Get your mail!" I repeated

"Um. Who? Lemme call you back," Hammy said.

We hung up. What would I wear? I checked the time. Eleven forty. I had time to get to Collective Eye. I dreaded shopping sans Hattie. I was calculating driving time when my phone buzzed.

"I wasn't invited, but Max and Gib are. Are you, uh, going to ask that guitarist? Because I think he'll already be there with Yeti."

"Hold on. How could I be invited and not you? Max, and not you?!" I plopped onto a lawn chair in disbelief. Oddly, and without thinking, I heard myself saying what Hattie would say to me. "You're coming with me."

The phone stayed quiet. I felt like my entire social identity was pivoting right here and now.

My dad rolled the wheelbarrow out of the garage,

headed for his prized rosebushes. His earbuds were in. He gave me a wave. I waved back, but a creeping nausea gripped me as I waited for Hammy to respond. Did he think I was asking him as a *date* date?

"I'm going with Max," he said.

"Oh." He'd rejected me. My eyes stung. "I wish Hattie could get here in time." So much I wished this.

"We can go the three of us," Hammy said. "Max will drive."

"Yeah, okay." But I could have said, *Thank God.* Who else would I go with? Gib? "Hammy," I said, tugging the hem of my shorts, self-doubt washing over me. "Maybe I'm not supposed to be invited. Maybe it's a joke."

"Reid."

"What?" I squeezed the fabric in my fist.

"You're cute and cool. Why wouldn't you be invited?"

My face flamed. I couldn't tell if he was serious. I needed out of this call. "I gotta get ready," I said.

"We'll get you at four."

As promised, Max and Hammy arrived at four in Pigskin, Max's ancient brown, football-shaped Saab. A bass line vibrated over the gurgle of the engine. Hammy's head bobbed to the beat and Max drummed on the dashboard. I got in the back seat. Pigskin smelled like pot and Old Spice.

Max stretched his furry arm across the passenger seat and backed out the driveway. Hattie would be *dying* right now. I couldn't see his eyes through the aviator sunglasses, but he must have looked at me. "You're ravishing this afternoon," he said in the way only Max could—just sarcastic enough not to be taken seriously. It's not a bad MO, really. It allowed him to say whatever he wanted.

I didn't tell him the outfit was new and I was in love with it and it was what made me feel worthy of going to PR VI. He wouldn't get it. I'd gone to Collective Eye and the owner, Beatrix, a Londoner with the best accent, picked the sundress for me. "You're absolutely smashing," she'd said. "Own it, Reid. Own yourself!"

Hammy looked at me through the mirror again. "You look great," he said, sounding awkward. He probably did think I was asking him as a date before. My cheeks flamed again. I opened the window, but the air was hot and mossy. I was glad the music distracted them.

We entered Ledge Haven and the Burke property materialized: hilly green fields crisscrossed by bucolic stone walls and dotted with grazing sheep. Happy nervousness zipped through me. Max downshifted and we rolled through the white gates.

"Where is everyone?" I whispered. Besides the sheep, this place was deserted.

Hammy turned the radio down. "Are you sure this is the way in?"

"We might be trespassing," I said softly. Old-growth trees lined the long driveway.

“Why are we whispering?” asked Max. “They’re fucking sheep.” The car inched over a hill. The landscape leveled out, revealing an impromptu parking lot.

“Thank God,” I said.

Max parked. I got out, flattening my paisley dress over my stomach. My hands shook the tiniest bit. I couldn’t believe I was here without Hattie. How did I get here, even?

On cardboard, scribbled in marker, an arrow pointed toward a break in the stone wall. We followed a path until finally we came upon the party, spread below us across a wide lawn—groupings of people, Ultimate Frisbee, a stage for Vanilla Yeti, a smoking firepit with the pig spinning on a spit.

“It’s really a whole dead pig?” I said.

“Yeah,” Max said. “And it smells good!”

I grimaced.

“Just don’t look at it,” Hammy advised.

Beyond it all lay the Long Island Sound, dark and still, under the thick meringue sky. We walked down a stone staircase set into the hill, like the Druids put it there. A moose of a guy waited for us at the bottom with a sleeveless yellow shirt that said “STAFF” in block letters. “Twenty each.”

He winked at me when he handed me a cup. “Have fun, sweet thang.”

I grimaced. That was the kind of guy who dug Reid MacGregory. I could hear Hattie laughing at this. I might have to sneak a picture of him later to send.

"To the keg," Max said, like a Viking. Once we filled our cups, Max left Hammy and me by the Yeti tent. I could just make out Noah's legs and flip-flops beside his coiled bass cord.

A group of girls came down the stone steps. Two wore mid-thigh sundresses with cowboy boots, one wore short shorts, and the other two wore miniskirts. Their arrival was like that of a single exquisite spider, long-legged and bright-eyed, descending from above.

Those girls weren't Bobbleheads, though. *They* owned themselves.

I turned toward Hammy and drank my beer straight to the bottom.

"Whoa, chugger."

"Ready for another?" I asked, burping into my hand.

He met my eye and drained his cup. "Yep."

Things got a bit fuzzy after that, for a while anyway. I kept putting my cup down and losing it. Max brought Hammy and me another, and then another. Maybe. I think.

I hung out with any SHS kids I knew, and by the time the Burke twins started a game of croquet, I felt courageous enough to play. I didn't even care that Ross and Artie watched me intently, leaning on their mallets as I tapped my ball through not one but two wire wickets.

"Yeah, baby!" I exclaimed, jumping.

"You sure you haven't played this before?" Artie (I think) said.

"Beginn-her's luck!" Words were becoming difficult.

The band went on break and I saw Noah at the keg. "Think it's time for another beer?" I said, elbowing Hammy.

"You're barely halfway done," he said.

I emptied my cup into a bush. "It's now or never," I said, which made no sense.

He followed my gaze. "Oh, I get it. The guitarist. Go get him, Reid," Hammy said.

I set off, the way a newly hatched sea turtle weaves across the sand. *I love this dress*, I thought. *I own this dress.*

You rock this dress! I imagined Hattie saying. I straightened my shoulders.

Gib approached the keg, too. Gib, standing next to Noah. A few weeks ago this would have terrified me. Not anymore! I knew Gib Soule's kryptonite and she was my best friend. He'd confided in me, asked me for advice. *We're buds.* I waited for the klieg light smile. He barely nodded. I couldn't believe I was thinking this, but he looked sort of . . . not perfect. A little pale, maybe. I wondered if he'd been sick and I decided to ask him, but he slid into the crowd before I could.

Even through the beer haze, I knew this was awkward. My fuzzy smile fell away. I wanted to climb back to my turtle eggshell and unhatch.

I couldn't make my eyes look at Noah. *Channel Hattie channel Hattie channel Hattie.* "Hi." I paused for effect. "Noah?"

"Yeah." He smiled and every hormone in my body sprang to life. "You're Reid."

I nodded, then studied the tent ceiling. "You guys sound amazing."

"Thanks."

Noah's cup filled and he motioned the nozzle toward mine. I stuck it forward.

Silence.

"Quite a party," said Noah, surveying the crowd. "Have you come before?"

"No," I said. "I really don't know how I got invited."

"It helps to be in the band," Noah said.

I realized we were both outsiders in our way. I let myself look him squarely in the eye as I lifted the cup to my lips. I faked a sip, since I couldn't manage another ounce of beer. Noah's eyes didn't waver and it was like someone shook a blanket of champagne bubbles through my chest.

"Bro, Yeti is the balls tonight. That cover of 'Sandman' was un-fucking-believable."

I didn't need to turn. I could smell him. Jay Seavers clapped Noah's shoulder. "You guys are on, man." Then he noticed me. His eyes did their usual down-and-up. I folded my arms across my boobs, dripping beer on my hip. "Reid MacGregory," he said, the way my dad would say "Mold" if he found it on the shingles.

It didn't matter that Hattie and I had fourteen different plans for revenge. Here, now, I couldn't speak. I felt humiliated all over again. "See you later," I said, carefully keeping my balance as I turned. It was too abrupt and surely seemed weird, but I marched back to Hammy and slumped against him.

"What's with you?" Hammy said. He looked over my shoulder. "Oh. Seavers."

I slugged down some beer after all.

"Don't let the bastards get you down, Reid," he said.

"You sound like my brother," I said.

"Let's get some food," he said.

"I'm drunk." I laid my forehead on his shoulder.

"Yep," he said, patting my back.

"You got drunk on me at the Maleshefskis'." My pronunciation lacked vowel sounds. "Payback."

"It's all good," he said. "You need food."

I felt suddenly sentimental for his unflagging attention this summer. I hugged him. "Hattie's lucky."

"What?"

Uh-oh. Those feelings I'd squished down wanted out of the turtle shell. I leaned back. *Get a grip.* "You're kind of like a brother, Hammy." I told myself this as much as him.

"My sister tells me that," he said.

I puzzled over that and burst out laughing. "You're killing me, Sandwich," I sighed, righting myself. We ambled over to the firepit. I steeled myself for the pig viewing as we passed through a group of college kids. They parted for us, and there it spun in all its porcine glory.

"I told you, don't look at it," Hammy said.

"It looks sunburned." Its mouth hung a little open, like it had something to say. "Save me!" I squeaked, filling in an imaginary speech bubble.

"What?" Hammy said.

"Nothing," I said.

Hammy pushed me toward a row of warming tins. "Forget the pig."

Two of those spider girls towered over Gib. He leaned back in his folding chair like he was prey. I recited in my head, "'*Will you walk into my parlor?' said the spider to the fly . . .*" but my smile fell away when I saw another three spider girls chatting up Noah and Stedman. I'd never seen Stedman maintain a grin that long. Noah's laugh mingled with female laughter.

"And there went that hope," I said, grabbing some corn bread.

We sat with a few SHS kids and one of the twins, who told a story about a goat roast in Argentina. That inspired Max to brag about a roast cat he ate in Mexico. Nobody believed him, but it set off a string of disgusting food stories. Somewhere in the middle of it all, Captain Dickhead joined the table. He laughed with the rest of them, contributing a quick story about snake meat. I watched his face, unusually animated. His skin was smooth and tan, his hair perfectly cut, his brown eyes glittery and intense. How is someone handsome, yet not? As I wondered, his eyes locked with mine.

Crap!

I tried to fake that I'd been looking at something else, but my reflexes sucked. For a moment we stared at each other with all the banter swirling around us. A barely perceptible velveting came over his eyes. One corner of his mouth turned up.

Even in my haze, my heartbeat stuttered. Was he flirting or mocking? I pushed myself back in my chair and gripped Hammy's arm, positioning him between us.

"Ow," Hammy said.

"Sorry." I regained composure.

"Max," said Artie or Ross, "I dare you to eat that." Everyone followed his finger to a june bug the size of a chicken nugget perched on a folding chair.

Max grinned and raised one eyebrow. "What's it worth to you, Ross?" Max leaned toward the bug. It wobbled a few inches across the chair.

Ross checked his wallet. "Five bucks."

"Done." Max rose from his seat, growling low, and sprang into motion. "*Waaa-haaw!*" He crashed into the chair, reaching with both hands. He landed with a thud on the ground. People gasped. Our group exploded into laughter. Max popped to his feet and opened his hand, wherein toddled the beetle.

Ross chanted, "Silver-man! Silver-man!" Others joined in. I realized I was about to witness Max eating it for real. Because, he would.

I tugged Hammy's shirt. "I'm outta here."

He nodded, never taking his eyes off Max.

I set off for the porta potties, crossing through the line of tiki torches. The lines were unbearable. A ways off, I saw a white barn. The Burkes were known as serious equestrians, which made me think that barn might have a bathroom.

The dewy grass made my toes squeak against my sandals. It reminded me of sneaking across the golf course with Hattie and everyone at the prom, which reminded me of the Dickhead.

I wished I could be like Hattie and not care.

The familiar, universal smell of horse barns swept over me as I opened the door, and the lights flicked on automatically. A clean hallway lined with photos of winners led to the stalls. Halfway down it: a bathroom. "Score!" I said. A horse made that snuffling sound horses make. For perhaps the four billionth time, I wished Hattie were here.

After drying my hands on monogrammed towels,

I crept to peek at the horses. A sleek chestnut head emerged from the shadows of the first stall, appraising me with flickering ears. I read the brass name plate. "Hi, Posey," I cooed. She let me rub her nose. When the barn door swung open behind me, she stepped back with a snort.

I turned.

Jay Fucking Seavers.

I stared. "Fuck," I said, unfiltered as I was.

He moved closer. "Sounds good to me."

"You're a riot."

He stood beside me, overpowering the earthy barn smells—a criminal offense. He reached to touch the other side of Posey's head. "I knew you'd be waiting for me."

"Seriously?" My face pinched. "You *did* think I was hitting on you back there."

"You were," he said. The eyes, silken. "You are scorching hot in that dress."

"Stop doing that," I said. "It's so toady."

"What, I'm not supposed to look at a beautiful girl?"

I snorted. "Oh my God, please." Hattie's ideas for charring him spun in my head. But I couldn't remember anything except the word *herpes*. Not helpful.

"Let's do it," he said, his mouth brushing my ear.

I backed into a pyramid of hay bales. He followed. "Yeah, I don't think so," I said.

His arms wrapped around my waist. "You know you're good to go," he murmured, kissing my neck. I couldn't move. "You're a hot secret."

Posey and I exchanged looks of disgust.

"Secret?" I snapped, pushing his shoulders with both hands. He was too big. I heard Hattie. *It's all about the power.* I hid my panic by standing taller. "That's what you call pretending you didn't see me after the prom in the cafeteria? A hot secret?" Just *asking* it gave him the edge, goddammit.

"What?" he laughed softly. "That's bullshit." He traced my cheek with his fingers. I wanted to bite them. Hard. His breath swept my eyelashes. "Come on," he whispered in my ear. He kissed my hair and then my mouth, running his hand up my thigh, under my skirt. I squeezed my lips tight. Scream? *Keep your power.* Kick? I didn't want to show weakness and my brain scrambled. I felt his disgusting boner against my hip. He moaned, sounding helpless. Was this power?

I tried to maneuver us past the hay bales so I could wind up and shove my kneecap into his balls, tolerating him only to get the payoff of dropping him to the floor.

Just then, the barn door opened. Over Jay's shoulder, I saw someone enter the room and stop short. Jay did his jump-away-from-me-like-I'm-toxic thing, but he was too late. Noah.

Noah saw us kissing.

Noah saw Jay jump away from me.

The three of us were stuck in an agonizing freeze-frame until Jay turned toward the horse. Noah raised his chin slightly, his brows tugged together the tiniest bit. I wished I knew what that meant. I dropped my eyes and saw my skirt caught in the waistband of my underwear. I yanked it out and my breath shook, tears filling my eyes.

Goddamn you, Jay Seavers. All the blood in me sucked backward into my heart. Captain Dickhead just branded me an embarrassment.

"No worries, bro, nothing happening here," Jay said.

Nothing? My eyes shot up. I spun toward Posey, wanting to hop on her and ride away forever.

And then I remembered.

That night of the Headless Horseman, when I hid in the woods and Jay came to find Ichabod Crane.

Jay Seavers wasn't so tough.

He started for the door. Noah raised one eyebrow at me. "He's lying," I said, pushing my voice strong before the moment escaped.

Noah stepped in Jay's path without saying anything.

"That wasn't nothing. That was Jay not wanting you to catch him with me," I said loudly. That was it. "I'm only good enough for him if nobody knows."

"This is crap," Jay said, trying to push past Noah. Noah didn't budge. I wished he would say something!

"We had sex once," I blurted, pointing back and forth

between Jay and me. "At the prom? At school the next Monday he pretended he didn't know me. Couldn't even *see* me when I was standing six feet from him."

"I didn't see her," Jay said, palms open.

"Liar. You saw me. You *always* see me, especially from *here*"—I put one hand above my boobs and one below, like a sandwich—"to here."

Noah looked like he might laugh. At me or at Jay? His shoulders shifted.

"Dude," Jay said quietly. "She's batshit. Come on, I'll get you a drink."

"I don't think so," Noah said, staring Jay down. "I think we stay here and listen to Reid."

"He, uh . . ." *Own yourself.* "He didn't care about consent until you came in," I said, steadying my voice. "But that's just Jay Seavers being Jay Seavers." I was sort of rabid. Jay's face contorted into a sneer, then his eyes darted to Noah. There he was! Scared boy in the woods. Time for me to punch.

"When's the last time you heard from Hattie?" I said, panting in the most controlled way.

He squinted. Vulnerable still.

"She's playing you like a puppet." It didn't quite make sense, but I kept going. "Did you think I wouldn't find out, or did you just not care if I did?"

He stared somewhere to my left. A calmness rose in me. I was right. I was strong. I think I was alpha. Maybe. "She's not going to risk our friendship for you. She chose me. We're bigger than that. Than *you*." He still wouldn't look. I took two steps closer to him and lifted his chin with my finger. Who was I? "So do *not* fuck with me or my friend ever again."

I pushed past him. Noah opened the door. I stepped into the darkness without looking back.

Stepping through the boundary of tiki torches, back into the party, I was giddy. I took out my phone and texted Hattie.

Me: I took down Jay Fucking Seavers! And it was amazing!

This was what it felt like, I thought, striding through the beautiful people, to be an alpha. Of course, there are alpha wolves, and alpha sea turtles. I definitely fell into the latter group.

Still, what you really need at a moment like that is your best friend to celebrate with, so you can dance like fools in the middle of a party where you know only a handful of people. I missed Hattie and couldn't wait to recount that scene in the barn to her. I might just get in the car and drive to The Thimble myself.

I spied Gib, also alone, a satellite to the action. I made my way to him and I plunked into an empty chair beside him.

"Hey," I said.

His slouch into the crux of the seat and the way his hair cast a shadow over his eyes seemed unfriendly. I readjusted myself in the chair, trying to shake the creeping self-doubt I knew so well. This was Gib. Gib was my bud. He loved my girl.

"You having a good night?" I asked, cool conversationalist that I was.

"Yup," he said. He seemed oddly focused on making holes in his empty Solo cup with the corkscrew tool on his Swiss army knife. "Thanks for warning me," he said, casting his bloodshot eyes my way for a half second.

"What warning?" *He's hammered*, I realized. "About what?" I noticed two cups riddled with holes near his feet. He didn't say anything. "You mean about Hattie?" Nothing. You know what? I wasn't going to let his mood infect this night. "Okay," I said, standing up. "See you."

I set out to find Max and Hammy. Tons of people danced on the grass near the stage and I let myself move to the beat as I scanned the crowds. The band jammed and I picked out Noah's bass line, which meant a) he had not lingered with Dickhead and b) *I could pick out Noah's bass line*. I found Hammy and grabbed his hand.

"I'm a badass baby sea turtle." I beamed as we danced, my voice lost somewhat in the music.

"What?" he asked, amused and bewildered.

I just smiled and twirled, loving the feel of my skirt fanning around me. Who knew how I got invited to PR VI, but it was my best Scofield night this summer.

NOW

September 1

The house phone rang. My mother answered. She came to my bedroom door moments later. I pawed for a pillow to cover my eyes.

"Reid?"

I didn't budge.

"Reid?" A little louder. The floor creaked and she set something on my bedside table. I felt her sit on the bed. She jiggled my legs. "Can you hear me? The high school is opening this morning for students to gather. I have your breakfast."

I couldn't make sense of what she meant.

"Can you look at me?" She moved the pillow. I blinked in the light. She swept hair from my eyes. "Grief counselors will be there. It starts in a half hour."

I rolled away. A gathering with grief counselors?

"It will be good for you to talk to peers. And professionals."

She exhausted me.

"Why don't you go, honey? Sam said he'll pick you up."

I thought of all the kids who would be there, most barely knowing Hattie, but sad and mystified and trying to make sense of it. And Charlie, Alesha, Max, and everyone who did know her better. They'd think I had answers—because I was the sidekick. I was the closest. And I really didn't know a single fucking thing.

I thought of Hammy. I'd avoided him without realizing it fully. Now that we'd had the funeral, he and I both teetered on the edge of this black canyon of sad unknown that dropped into forever. Imagining our combined sadness made my heart squeeze into a small, hard rock. No.

"I can't go to the high school."

She shifted on the mattress, probably deciding whether she should force it. I waited, now smelling eggs and toast. My stomach rolled. She did her reverse sigh. "Well, Dr. Dankin suggested some counselors for you to see on your own. And Ms. Beiderman would come here."

Beiderman? The school guidance counselor? I shook my head.

Her tone sharpened. "I don't know why Uncle Baxter felt *you* needed to know the cause of death. If the family isn't releasing that." The words were shards of glass and I hardened myself. "It's too much."

"She didn't do that. He's wrong," I said.

Her breath shook. She squeezed my hand. "Please try to eat, honey." She left.

Apparently, I exhausted her, too.

I let my vision go fuzzy, looking at the leaves.

"Reid? What are you doing here?" Faye blinked behind the hostess stand.

I honestly had no idea where she came from. Without moving my face, I searched the surroundings. *Shining* carpet. Tomblike air. Oh yes. I'd come to work. To get away from my mother.

Faye came toward me. "You didn't need to come to work today—the day after the funeral. I told your mom that!"

Jasper backed through the kitchen doors, pulling the coffee cart. He stopped short. "Hey, Reid," he said, like I'd just come out of a coma. Had I?

We stood dangling in awkwardness for a moment. Then Faye remembered herself, rounded the hostess stand, and hugged me. She smelled of cigarettes and cheap hair product. "I'm so sorry." She kept her hands on my shoulders. "What a fucking shit-hook deal." She welled up. "When Ricky passed," she said, like I'd known him, "I was in a haze for three months." She grasped my hands. "The shock." She pressed her mouth tight. "Give yourself time," she whispered. "You'll come around."

"I'm okay," I said, struggling to recall dressing for work and driving here. Had Scott brought me?

Her eyes darted back and forth, reading mine. "Okay, I get it. Sometimes you just need to keep moving." She kept nodding. "But little Sarah over there has finally learned how to move her ass in this place, so if you change your mind . . ."

We looked at Sarah, counting programs. She glanced up, shifted uncomfortably, and returned to her task.

I followed Jasper into the dining room.

He hugged me, rocking me side to side. "How *are* you?" My emotions were frozen. "I thought you'd go to the high school thing."

"You went?" I asked. I felt him nod into my shoulder.

"I've thought about you constantly," he said. "You didn't answer my messages."

I hadn't touched my phone in days. It made me think of texting Hattie, and also it felt too normal. Like picking it up meant life just . . . resumed.

"Seriously, why are you here?"

I shrugged. "I couldn't stay home. My mother is a nightmare. She's threatening a Beiderman visit."

"Guidance counselor Beiderman?" He retrieved the vacuum from a closet. "That wouldn't be bad."

I grimaced. "One on one? In your *house*?"

He shrugged and dragged the vacuum to Section A.

I started in B, filling salt shakers and rolling napkins. As I filled water glasses, my vision blurred. How must Hattie have felt when she knew she had to suck in lungfuls of water? I couldn't breathe thinking of it. And she was such a good swimmer. I knocked a glass and it bounced on the gross carpet.

I moved close to Jasper until he turned off the vacuum. "It's more than Beiderman," I said, tapping my fingers on a chair. His expression was blank, waiting. My cheeks heated up. "Faye's right. I have to start moving. I'm afraid if I don't, I'll . . . just . . . be swallowed away. But, if I do start moving, she's really . . . gone."

Jasper studied my face. "I can't believe I'm saying that Faye's right, but I think it will get better."

I dropped my head. "I'm not sure I want it to get better, Jasper."

Three actors burst on the stage behind us, rehearsing a sword fight. Don Q dodged a swipe of the sword and did a pratfall. Sancho moved in, pushing back the enemy with slashes of his blade. I saw Hattie with an eye-penciled, curlicue mustache and beard, lying on the stage, playing dead, stifling her laughter. I blinked.

Hattie sat up high on her horse Lyra, giggling. I'd done a pretty good job on her Don Quixote mustache. "You look awesome," she said. I rubbed my fake Sancho Panza beard thoughtfully. We'd stuffed a pillow in my shirt for Sancho's gut, and even though I had about an inch on Hattie at this point, my sidekick horse Barnaby and I were comically shorter than our counterparts.

Mrs. Darrow, our video crew, directed us, pretty much unable to stop laughing the entire time. "Ride down to the apple tree and come up the hill."

"To La Mancha," Hattie said, spinning Lyra into a loping canter into the field.

"Wait for me!" I called, puttering behind.

I shook my head and she was gone, the stage empty.

"I'm Hattie's Sancho Panza," I told Jasper. "I don't know how to be anyone else."

Jasper squinted and tilted his head.

"No, I'm serious." I said. "I was nobody before her." My hands shook and I felt myself starting to cry.

"Chang!" Mike, the cook, bellowed into the theater from the kitchen.

"One sec!" Jasper called, rolling his eyes. He took my hands, steadying them. Holding my gaze, he said, "Sancho Panza outlasts Don Quixote, Reid." Then he hauled the vacuum up the steps.

I watched the circular window on the kitchen door swing back and forth. Yes, Sancho Panza *does* outlast Don Quixote, but nobody cares. Don Quixote dies, and the curtain drops.

I had no story without her.

I grabbed on to the stair railing. I thought I might go antigravity—float right through the theater ceiling. Faye had my arm and led me up the steps to the lobby doors. "Are you up to seating guests, Reid?" She said it in the same chipper voice she used with old people.

I forced myself to stand straighter. "I'll be fine."

She handed me a stack of programs. "I know you will," she said, but as she walked away, she whispered to Sarah at the Section C doors. Sarah looked at me and nodded.

I pasted on a smile, guiding guests to their seats, helping with sweaters until we shut the doors for Act One. I'd never cared that the waitstaff had to do prep work during the actual show. "No freebies," Faye said. Like we wanted to watch. But this time I found myself peeking through the kitchen window as Don Quixote swashbuckled and Sancho scurried behind him. When we opened the doors at intermission, I smiled my way through, pouring decaf. With strangers, faking it was effortless. And I was moving. For the final scene, when Don Quixote dies, I hid in a bathroom stall and cried a little, thinking of Hattie in her mustache.

Finally the theater emptied of guests. I wiped down the Bunn coffee maker. The wall sconce behind it buzzed. What *was* Hattie doing when it happened? Their explanation was obviously utter bullshit. There was so much I hadn't asked, so much I hadn't been clear enough to wonder. My fog was safer.

"That is one clean coffee maker," Jasper said. He held the laundry bag toward me and I dropped in the cloth.

"You okay to drive home?"

"Yeah," I said, listening to the wall sconce.

"You sure?"

"Yep."

Lying was so much easier.

I left the dinner theater. Hattie sat in the back seat of the car, but still, she was there as we drove the twisty roads to my house. I saw her curlicue mustache in the rearview. She sang the play's theme in her atrocious caterwauling:

To dream, the impossible dream . . . to right, the unrightable wrong! She mimicked Mr. Darrow's opera voice, chuckling to herself. *To reach the unreachable staaa—aaa—aaarrrrr!*

But it was like I wasn't there. Our bond was breaking.

What if I just drifted off the road?

I glued my eyes to the white line marking the shoulder. If I swerved just a few feet, I'd hit a tree. I'd hit a tree and escape this unbearable reality and be with her again. Above the clouds maybe. My pulse thrilled. I let the car stray right, only a little over the white at first, then more. Both passenger-side tires rode the shoulder, grinding loose gravel. I loosened my fingers. The perfect curve to let the rest go lay just out of the headlights' reach.

"*Don't!*" she barked, staring me down. "Do *not* be a dumbass." Next to her in the back seat, the fawn huddled against her, blinking her wise eyes.

I jerked the car left, my breath labored. In the back, I saw only Hattie's hoodie, which had been there since my horrible encounter with Helen.

Rolling up our driveway felt like rolling out of a dream. Did I almost drive off the road? I turned the engine off, closed my eyes, and took a deep breath. Then I grabbed the hoodie and stuffed it in my bag.

My parents perched at the bay window in the kitchen, watching. But when I walked inside, they were reading in the family room.

"Oh, hi," Mom said.

"How did it go?" Dad asked.

Fakers, I almost said. But it seemed cruel, so I lied some more. "Fine."

"Sam called again," Dad said. "He really wants to see you."

"Yeah, okay. Maybe tomorrow." Lie.

"Ms. Beiderman *is* coming tomorrow. Around eleven." She said it softly but matter-of-factly.

I stopped halfway up the stairs and groaned.

"Don't be like that, Reid. She can help you."

I stared at her. Beiderman was *that* guidance counselor, the one who liked to be right in the middle of everything. Like she was one of us. "Help me what?"

Her eyes flickered away and she brushed imaginary lint off her sleeve. "Keep going."

I turned so she didn't see my eyes well. I caught the scent of Hattie's perfume on the hoodie. I pulled my bag closer to my nose and inhaled.

Hattie, I need you, I said in my head. *I need you I need you I need you.*

NOW

September 2

“What a lovely home,” Ms. Beiderman said, following my mom into our living room, now a regular hub of activity. I was busy trying to look like I had my head together, trailing them with a coffee tray. In a small but significant way, I felt more alert today. Okay, I hadn’t showered. But my thinking seemed a little clearer, my headache gentler. Maybe it was adrenaline from dreading Beiderman.

At school, I’d never paid much attention to Beiderman. She was younger than I realized, and prettier. Her blue sundress matched her flowered Birkenstocks, and her toned shoulders and calves were tan.

"Thank you," Mom said. "We're so grateful you came."

I wanted to say, *Define* we, *Mom.* Furthermore, I noticed the vagueness of my mother's words—was this Beiderman's idea or hers?

Mom poured the coffee and left us facing one another in the wingback chairs by the fireplace, like a PBS talk show.

Beiderman watched me with a small, sympathetic smile. She had the kind of wildly curly hair that always looked messy and she wore it twisted into a bun with those chopstick things sticking out of it. I wondered if she was a rule-breaker in high school, and if so, if it was because she had rule-breaking hair, or if her personality somehow influenced the way her hair came in. Then I rubbed my eyes, pushing my sanity back inside my head.

She spoke first.

"I'm so sorry, Reid. I know this is . . ." She stopped and her eyelids fluttered. "So, so hard."

I mumbled, "Thanks."

After a torturous silence, she said, "You seem tired."

I raised my eyebrows.

She shook her head. "Of course you're tired. Let me try again. Are you able to sleep at all?"

In fact, the nights since August twenty-seventh strung together in a nightmare-laced delirium. Too restless to close my eyes, I'd black out around five a.m. Mom had woken me thirty minutes ago. I wore cropped yoga pants and a purple tank, and I now regretted not looking in a mirror. I pulled a fleur-de-lis pillow across my lap. "Sometimes," I said.

"Shock can do that. Your emotional distress has a life of its own."

I stared at a Matisse art book on the coffee table. A black cutout person with a red hole for a heart hung in a blue, starry background. Me.

And Beiderman thought she knew what this was like.

She leaned in slightly. "I can't say I know how you feel, exactly."

Okay, that was weird.

"I've never been through this kind of trauma," she said. "But please know, you've always got someone to talk to. I want to help you . . ." She trailed off.

My eyes darted to catch hers, daring her to say *move on*. Then I could tell her to fuck off and be done with her.

She raised her cup like it was a shield or something. "I want to help you *be okay*." I eyed her suspiciously, wondering how she knew what I'd said to the fawn on the road the other night, after I'd left Helen in Hattie's room. She welled up, but adroitly covered by digging through her bag. She laid a pamphlet on the Matisse me. A sepia-toned girl on a tree swing amid a sepia-toned field. "When a Friend Dies."

I felt so heavy right then—a big, fat, clay wad sunken into the chair.

"It's normal to be—" Beiderman began.

I opened my mouth.

She waited, eyebrows high in encouragement. "Go ahead."

I paused, deciding. Then, gesturing between us, I said, "There is nothing *normal* here." I rubbed my eyes. "You're a high school guidance counselor I barely know, in my living room—where my family never sits—trying to get me to talk about my best friend dying." I let my words sink in. For us both. "Not. Normal."

"Right. Of course, *this* is far from normal. I'm saying the grieving process—"

I tapped my foot aggressively on the rug. "If you thought you could fit me neatly into some case study on teen grief, you're high."

She straightened. "Look, Reid. Losing Hattie, it's unthinkably horrible. People go their whole lives without this kind of trauma."

"*This kind* of trauma?" I echoed.

She forged on. "Your parents, your friends, your teachers, we all want you to come through the other side."

I snickered. "What friends are you talking about? Hattie is my friend. My only friend."

"I know. That special bond with Hattie is all yours, Reid. But losing loved ones is part of being human, and I want to support you in your recovery."

I studied her perfectly manicured, metallic-blue

toenails and fought the urge to spit on her flowered fucking Birkenstocks. *I don't want to recover.*

She sat silently for a solid thirty seconds. The house phone rang. Mom answered it.

"You can read this, maybe," she said, pushing the pamphlet toward me. "When you're ready."

I made a sound somewhere between a laugh and a sneeze. "When I'm ready," I repeated, shaking my head. *That's me, Reddi MacGregory.*

"I know you may not feel it *now*," she said apologetically.

I liked her apologetic, so I didn't explain the nickname. But my conflict-avoidance policy kept me from actually tearing the pamphlet into bits and blowing them into her face like dandelion down.

"You're my priority, Reid. I'm yours." My self-appointed therapist rose, slinging her bag over her shoulder. She placed a business card next to the pamphlet. "You can call anytime, any day. That's my cell."

She seemed to be waiting for me to dismiss her, so I said, "Okay."

My parents intercepted her at the front door. They talked in hushed voices, and she left.

"Well?" Mom asked, coming back into the room. Her eagerness hurt my ears.

"Meh," I said.

"She seems cool," Dad said.

"The Birkenstocks have you fooled," I said.

He smiled, but Mom started straightening pillows on

the sofa. "She can help you, that's all I'm saying. School starts this week, your senior year."

"School?" I shake my head. "I *cannot* go to school this week." Any concept of school without Hattie would not materialize in my imagination. All I could see was a fuzzy wall poised to swallow me. I barely survived her damn binge skipping last year—and that was only a few days at a time! Just thinking about it turned my lungs to sand. My eyes stung.

Parental glance exchange. Reverse sigh by Mom.

Dad said, "Let's take one day at a time."

"A routine is the best thing, Reid," Mom said, like I was Spencer, who loves routine. "Everyone thinking about college, new classes . . ."

"Cannot," I said.

Dad said, "Why not let her decide when the time comes, Laura?"

There was zero fucking chance I was going no matter what they said, but I didn't bother to spotlight that reality. I knew it, and that was enough.

Mom said, "Oh, Sheila Burnham called. She and Emma Rose would like to visit later."

"Oh my God, am I in *hell*?" I cried.

Mom tossed her head dismissively. "Reid, stop it! They want to cheer you up!" she said.

"And you said *okay*?"

"Well, yes," she said, uncharacteristically hesitant.

"Come on," Dad said. "Emma Rose isn't that bad."

I closed my eyes again. I wished I could fall asleep right that second. "Dad, you're remembering her from softball in fourth grade. She is a drama vampire."

"What are you going to do?" Mom asked, her voice thin and shrill. "Hole up in your room? *Alone?*"

I shot her a dirty look. *Yes!* I wanted to yell. *What of it? What is your goddamned hurry?* "Can you *please* just *back the fuck off*?" I yelled before I could stop myself.

She froze, like I'd pierced her chest with a poison dart. My dad watched her, worry hollowing his cheeks. Her face crumpled. I felt sick. "*No*, I cannot," she sobbed, and rushed from the room. Effectively backing off, but it didn't feel like a victory.

Dad sighed. "Reid."

I stayed quiet.

"Your mom is just . . ." He sighed. "This is all bringing up old stuff," he said. "Like when Spencer got diagnosed. The loss."

"Oh." I felt my back go rigid. "So, she's not worried about *me*? My God, can *anything* ever *not* be about Spencer?" I whisper-yelled.

"She *is* worried about you. *I'm* worried about you! Look at you!"

I pulled the pillow across my chest again. I disgusted myself.

He rubbed his face. "We've already had one baby slip away." He moved behind the chair and rubbed my shoulders. He meant Spencer, of course—the neurotypical version of him anyway, who disappeared from our Spencer at age two. But Hattie slipped away, too. Slipped under the water. A flash of her flailing in the dark, struggling for air, invaded my head. I whimpered and put my hands on top of his.

"We're all doing the best we can. Can you try to remember that?" he said.

Tears streamed down my face. I nodded.

"I love you so much," he said.

I pulled his hand to my cheek, pressing his joints and all the tiny muscles between his finger bones against my skin. I felt the blood swish through his veins, warm and alive, and I ached for its preciousness.

I wished I could fold myself into a tiny square and hide in my dad's pocket forever.

Later, I lay on my bedroom floor, trying to motivate myself to shower. This day was a marathon. My mom hadn't talked to me since Beiderman left, and I still had Emma Rose and her mom to go. Hattie's hoodie spilled out of my bag, on the desk chair above me. I laced the dangling sleeve through my fingers. Would keeping it be wrong? I tugged it and it crumpled onto my face, surrounding me with her smell. I found myself standing to slip into it.

I let my vision go fuzzy and tried to see Hattie in the mirror. She deserved to be here more than me. She *knew* life. I unzipped the pockets and stuck my hands in. My right fingers bumped something.

I looked at my reflection, remembering the hoodie's heaviness as I fled the Darrows' house. Instantly, I knew what I'd found and slid Hattie's cell phone out.

For many seconds, I could only stare at it.

It felt like she'd hand-delivered it to me. I glanced around, like she might be watching. Would she want me to look through it? Or not? I paced my room. What if I discovered something everyone needed to know? That showed she didn't do what her family said she did. I should look, shouldn't I?

Hell yes.

It could have been her who said it. It could have been me.

I pressed the power button, my finger shaking. And nothing happened. I tried tallying the days since it could've been charged, but my brain buzzed and I finally settled on a bunch of days. My own phone lay charging on the bedside, where Dad had left it a few nights back. I plugged in Hattie's and slid it under my pillow so I could think.

Holding my phone brought a sort of muscle memory. I missed Hammy. I scrolled past the many text notifications from everyone—Gib, Charlie, Max, Emma Rose—and texted him.

Me: Hey.

He might not reply. Who could blame him?

Me: I'm sorry I've been so out of it.

I got my robe for the shower. My phone buzzed.

Hammy: Reid! How are you doing?

Me: I don't know. Okay. Maybe? I found something.

I hesitated. Maybe I shouldn't be sharing this.

Hammy: Are you going to tell me what?

Shit. A phone is kind of intimate. I rubbed the hoodie sleeves, feeling the soft fleece on my forearms. I shouldn't have told him.

Hammy: Yoo-hoo.

The charge cord from my pillow resembled a snake. "Fuck it."

Me: Her phone. It was in a hoodie pocket I kind of stole from the Darrows.

Cyberpause.

Me: It's charging. I'm scared to see what's on it. Can you come by?

Hammy: Wow. I'm on till eleven at the gas station.

He worked at Scofield Getty.

Me: ☹

Hammy: I have the damn early morning shift, too. Eleven thirty tomorrow morning at the latest. I'll try to get a sub.

I hid in plumes of steam until the water turned tepid and I couldn't stand it anymore.

Wrapped in a towel, I sat beside my pillow. This time, her phone pinged to life. My stomach lurched. No way I could wait for Hammy. Anyway, maybe I shouldn't.

I tapped her passcode, my jaw tense.

Immediately, her messages updated. My texts rolled in, unread—the ones I sent when I saw her—or not—in Snowcap. Before the world shattered. Avoiding those, I scrolled to the previous exchange, with Helen, from last to first message. These *had* been read, maybe by Hattie. Or possibly Helen or another Darrow. Maybe all of them.

Helen: We're all looking for you. Cut it out. You're scaring Mom.

My heart thumped in my chest. Before that:

Helen: Are you in the boathouse?

Helen: Dad's pissed. You better come back now.

Helen: We're almost back from the party.

A tear slid down my face. I thought of Helen reading her own messages to Hattie, like me now. How hard that would be. Had Helen then hidden the phone, to spare her parents, in the hoodie? Or had Hattie read them and nobody noticed the phone zipped in the hoodie? I started to imagine the chaos of that night, everyone searching room by room and realizing she wasn't anywhere. I imagined them running the footpaths, driving the island, combing the beaches. Calling the police. Bile spun in my stomach. My throat prepared. Swallowing, I straightened my spine. I needed to see this. To feel this. I didn't know why.

I reread Helen's words.

Helen: We're almost back from the party.

Why would she be alerting Hattie like that? Where would Hattie be coming back from? Somewhere Helen thought had Wi-Fi. Somewhere off island? Why had Helen mentioned the boathouse? It annoyed me all at once that I had no concept of what happened August twenty-sixth. Nothing made sense, especially the suicide bullshit. Did the Darrows think I knew all I needed to know? I tried to calm myself. *They're in shock, Reid. Be kind.*

I scrolled to the next exchange.

Gib: Wish we were here. With a photo of the Siwanoy pier.

"Wait," I said aloud. "Gib?" I looked at the time stamp. Aug 17, 11:00 p.m. I rapid scrolled backward. Dozens of texts from him, starting in July. I couldn't even focus to read word by word, but I got his gist.

Miss you.

Love you.

"Love?" Had he turned stalker? I kept reading.

I'm so bored without you.

When can we meet?

On and on. Nothing from her. Just him.

Goose bumps swept my neck. "Creeper," I muttered. I switched to Hattie's photos, auto-arranged by date. August twenty-fifth, the day before her last, had nature pictures: pink sea roses, Pulpit Head, first sunny, and then with a mist, and next shrouded in fog. The damn fog.

The rest were from July. She didn't take one other picture in August. Strange. In July, there were Santi pictures, smoking hot fixing boat riggings. Tennis. Cousins. A fox slinking along the trees.

A video, July nineteenth. I tapped it and recognized the rocky ledge of Pulpit Head. The surf crashed and seethed.

Male voice: *Whoa.*

"*Another* guy?" I said. "Seriously, Hattie?"

Hattie: *I love when it's wild.*

A few seconds of toiling waves. She directs the camera out to sea.

Hattie: *I saw a pod of humpbacks out there last week.* Her pointing finger enters the screen. *Six.*

The guy doesn't respond, and she shoves his hip. *Are you listening?* she laugh-asks. A corner of my heart pinched. The faceless guy moves closer. The phone skims his shorts and her hand and muffle muffle—end clip. I guess they started making out.

I played it over and over, trying desperately to recognize him. Santi wouldn't need an introduction to Pulpit Head. Besides, he'd left by July nineteenth. I couldn't identify the voice, no matter how closely I listened to *Whoa*. Only the leg of his shorts and a scrap of leg. I rolled it again.

Madras shorts. Hairy leg. My face tickled. Reroll. Madras shorts, hairy leg. Madras shorts, hairy leg. I'd seen those things—together—on my front steps the day Hattie left for Maine. Gib. Gib was on The Thimble. In July.

The towel around me fell apart and I sat there on my bed, naked and numb, staring at the phone, afraid to touch it and find out more about what I didn't know.

Later, our phones sat side by side, friends giving each other the silent treatment.

Could there be a worse time to have to deal with Emma fucking Rose? I needed stiff resolve if I wanted to keep breathing through this day. I put on cropped khakis and a sleeveless blue blouse. Very Scofield conservative. Very much molding me into the proper shape of sane.

If she were not . . . gone, how mad would I be at Hattie right now? I raked a brush through my hair, waving the hair dryer. How could she not tell me Gib came to the island? He didn't tell me either, and I'd seen him a bunch of times. He was so weird at the Pig Roast. What's with the secrets, I wondered as I blushed my colorless cheeks. The doorbell rang.

"Shit."

"You poor girl," Mrs. Burnham said, handing my dad two bags from Red Carpet Catering and hugging me. "We can't imagine." She studied my face. Her lipstick matched the splashy scarlet flowers on her pants.

"Devastating." She moved to Mom, who grabbed my hand. "Laura," Mrs. Burnham whispered, choked up. Clearly Emma Rose had an excellent drama vampire role model in her mother. Really, the Burnhams barely knew my parents outside of country club parties.

Emma Rose held a bouquet of white lilies. I imagined her, later at the beach: "I brought Reid MacGregory flowers. She looked *awful.* I feel *so* sorry for her." But actually, her eyes had a glassy sadness that unnerved me. The rich scent of the flowers put me in the church vestry, looking at the big picture of Hattie. I cleared my throat. "They're beautiful."

Dad led the moms to the patio.

"They're from Mimi, Greta, and me," Emma Rose said.

I winced inside but attempted a smile. "I'll put them in water," I said, going into the kitchen. I hoped she'd stay put, but the heels of her flats clicked behind me.

"How *are* you? I am so, so sorry." I laid the bouquet on the counter and bumbled through cabinets looking for a vase. "You never think this could happen to someone you know. Especially Hattie."

I found a vase but kept my back to her. *Breathe*, I thought. *In and out.*

"I'll cut the stems." She found scissors. I filled the vase at the sink and turned to find her waiting to place the flowers in it. She fluffed them this way and that.

"There," she said. "I thought they might make you feel . . . brighter. Kinda stupid, I guess." The flowers hid me from her.

"No," I said. "It's really thoughtful." I leaned against the counter, unable to think of anything to say. But then, I didn't need to; she was Emma Rose.

"Let's put them in your room, so they feel like just yours."

I nodded. She *click-clicked* behind me. I willed my stomach still.

"Everyone is worried about you, Reid. You can't believe how many people have asked me how you're doing."

I wondered why people would ask Emma Rose about me. Just because she's in everyone's business?

"Poor Hammy. I didn't know he was crushing on her." Of course, she'd talked with him. "I thought he only had eyes for Reid MacGregory," she added coyly.

I tossed a half-hearted "as if" face over my shoulder as we entered my room.

"I did! Wow, I haven't been in here since fourth grade." She moved around my room like it was a museum. "Where's your Groovy Girls collection?"

I set the flowers on my dresser and sat on the bed, glad I'd neatened it.

"I was always jealous of your Groovy Vespa." She wore a sea-green sundress with little white starfish embroidered on it. Her blond hair moved like a satin curtain across her tan shoulder blades. The air around her seemed so weightless and pain free, I wanted to suck it in with some sort of breathing tube.

Her eyes caught on my bedside. "Two phones?"

"Oh." *Crap.* I stumbled for words. "That one's mine," I said, pointing.

"And the other one . . . ?"

I had nothing. "Hattie's."

She stared at it, then at me.

"I—I have it by accident," I said.

Emma Rose, a social networking junkie, pinched her brows like knitting needles. "By accident."

I nodded.

"How?"

My mind hurtled through possible replies. I could lie. I could tell the truth. I could confide in her. Her expression—frozen, patient—seemed sincere. Maybe I needed Emma Rose.

"I—" I traced a circle on my khakis. "I thought she might be pranking and hiding at her house here. It sounds so stupid now. I was in shock, I guess. I went to the Darrows' to catch her, but—" I closed my eyes, seeing Helen's face. "When I realized it was real, I ran out of their house."

She blinked, sitting alongside me. "With Hattie's phone."

"Well, it was in her hoodie, which I"—I shrugged—"stole."

Emma Rose made a surprised face.

"By accident," I repeated. "I just"—I pushed my hair behind my ear and looked at the carpet—"ran out with it in my hands. I didn't find the phone until just today."

"Wow."

"I don't think they know I have it," I said.

She nodded. "I'm sure the phone is the least of their worries." I wanted to reject her sympathy, but found her words comforted me. "Does it work?"

A flash of the hairy leg and madras lit up in my head. My stomach clenched.

Emma Rose put her hand on my forearm. "Sorry. I'm being nosy."

Yep. I wasn't sharing the secrets I'd only just learned myself. Hattie was *my* friend. She had never liked like Emma Rose.

Sensing my discomfort, she began to explore again. "A Ouija board?" She was next to my pile of Hattie's care package loot.

"It was a joke."

"Ouija boards scare me," she said.

"Me too. That's why she sent it."

Emma Rose laughed.

"Ever the prankster."

"What's in the smaller box?" she said.

"Another joke. You can look," I said.

She opened the box. "Ew!" She laughed, lifting the eyeball bracelet like she had a mouse by the tail. "Seriously?"

An alien feeling rolled up my throat and I realized that was me, laughing. "She said ancient Egyptians believed it would ward off evil. She got it from a psychic."

Emma Rose read the sticker on the box. "The Dancing Newt, Damariscotta, Maine. Well." She surveyed the pile in its entirety. "Those are kind of freaky gifts." She tapped her chin with her index finger.

"I guess, in context of now," I said, suddenly uneasy.

Buzzzz.

We startled, our heads spinning toward the phones. Hattie's shimmied. Emma Rose's kitten eyes opened wide. "Did she just get a text?"

If Emma Rose wasn't there, I might not have found the courage to check. As it was, my hand reached for it, like a disconnected body part.

New text message.

I tapped her passcode. Emma Rose sat beside me again. I couldn't help but tilt it from her view.

From: 877655

The automated refill for your prescription #453323670 is ready for pickup at your preferred RiteRex location 122 Route 1, Scofield, Connecticut.

Relief lapped at my edges. "Just a prescription refill."

"Huh," she said, all John Watson–like. She tapped her chin again.

"What?"

"I don't know." Her foot jiggled. "What's it for?"

I shrugged. "Probably a summer cold or something."

"Refill?" Emma Rose said. "You don't get refills on antibiotics." Her dad was a doctor. "Birth control, I guess," she concluded nonchalantly.

"No," I said, but the walls rippled.

"Why not?"

"She would have told me," I said, a lie that stabbed my heart.

Emma Rose paced. "We could call the pharmacy and find out. Pretend you're Hattie. Or better yet, use the drive-through and pick it up."

I yanked my bedside drawer, put in the phone, and shut it loudly.

Emma Rose squeezed her eyes shut. "God, I'm such an idiot! That was so inappropriate. I forget she's really gone." She shook her head hard. "Ehhh! I can't stand to think of her afraid. In the water."

Why was it so easy for her to say things I felt?

"I don't think of it," I said quietly. That was mostly true. I bit my thumb cuticle.

She nodded. "Right. Good plan." She stopped at my desk. "I'd get that Ouija board the hell out of here if I were you. Those things are evil. Want me to take it? I totally will."

I shifted, unsure why taking a Ouija board felt overly familiar. "No, I might want it."

She raised her eyebrows.

"Maybe."

"Emma Rose!" Mrs. Burnham called.

"Coming!" She paused. "Listen." She lowered her voice. "You should hear this from a friend."

"What?" My mouth felt dry.

"There's a rumor going around that—" Her doe gaze flickered away, then returned. She took both my hands. My stomach bottomed out. "That it was suicide," she whispered, eyes welling.

I tried to respond, but only made a series of weird vowel sounds. I pulled my hands away.

"I know! It's ridiculous. Any time it comes up, I set people straight. Not Hattie Darrow, folks. She's a rock star." Emma Rose was up, pacing in a little circle. "*You* know it's stupid, I know it's stupid, so forget it. I'm sorry to even tell you. I just don't want some insensitive jerk to take you off guard at school." She hugged me. "Just focus on feeling better."

"Em, come on!" her mom called.

She rolled her eyes. "I'll check on you tomorrow," she said, and left.

I was stupefied. Immobile. I didn't really care about the rumors. I knew the truth. Well, not really, but I knew Hattie. Uncle Baxter's call tugged, but I pushed it off. Instead, I thought of Emma Rose. It took guts for her to tell me that. And she was so . . . kind. I looked at the drawer with Hattie's phone. "Could we have been wrong about her, Hattie?" The reality of Hattie's forever silence made me fold over on the bed and cry.

NOW

September 3

I don't know why I slept in Scott's room last night. He'd left for Colgate after the funeral, so it was empty and felt untarnished, I guess. Mine was riddled with memories. But I lay in his bed for seven hours, perseverating on the fact that Gib knew more than me. So *slept* isn't the correct word.

I resisted texting Gib until 5:40 a.m.

Me: Can we talk? About Hattie.

I knew I'd have to wait for a response. In a sleep shirt and shorts, I stuffed my feet in my running shoes. I crept past Boomer and left the house, heading for the pond trail. I'd barely made it into the woods when he called. "Shit!" I said. Why the fuck was he calling? I didn't like not having time to edit my thinking. What was I going to say? I took a deep breath of morning air and answered it.

"Hey, Reid."

"Hey, so . . ." Already awkward. I took another breath and tried to picture him walking beside me, like that day in June when everything seemed possible. "I was looking through the pictures on her phone—"

He interrupted. "You have her phone?"

"I stole it. By accident." His tone made me defensive.

Quiet.

"I know." Breathlessly, I explained, watching my sneakers snap sticks. I said, "You're on her phone a lot, actually."

There was a sound like he was shifting the phone to his other hand and exhaling at the same time. "Nobody told me you went to Maine in July," I said, like a suspicious mom.

If we were walking together, we'd have gone twenty paces without speaking. "Maybe we should meet," he said.

"I'd like that," I said, my voice cracking.

"Yeah, yeah," he said, softening. "I'm really sorry, Reid. I know how close you were."

I gazed up at the canopy of dewy leaves.

"Can you come by? My mom and Kate leave at seven ten for the train," he said. I nodded, wiping my nose with my wrist. "Reid?"

"I'll be there."

* * *

I sat across from Gibson Soule at a picnic table in his backyard, under a huge pine tree. The yard was small and tidy, like most in town. Thick air threatened rain. I brought Hattie's phone, just in case, and held it in my lap.

Gib looked changed. It was like someone had buffed him to a dull matte.

"After that night in June, when Hattie and I . . . I couldn't—" His heel tapped rapidly. "When you told me she was gone for the summer, I just really wanted to see her again. I thought if she saw me, maybe—"

Of course. He'd never been flat-out rejected by anyone. Even Priya dated him for six months.

"So I went to Maine with a guy from lacrosse camp whose family has a house near The Thimble. I was only like four miles from her, and I called and texted, but she wouldn't get back to me."

I knew the culprit was the cell service, but I didn't stop him.

"My third day in Maine, she finally called me."

I shook my head. "She can't get her voicemail, though. No service."

"She told me she'd found a spot in the loft of her boathouse where her phone worked. I mean, the connection wasn't great, but we talked."

I slouched. Over Gib's shoulder I watched Hattie sitting in the bottom of one of the old rowboats, leaned against a life jacket, chatting away. Why had she never called or texted me?

"She had me meet her at this lobster shack," he said.

"Sister's Cove?" I asked.

He smiled. "Yeah."

I had my first lobster roll there.

"She invited me to The Thimble and showed me around."

He stopped.

I shifted on the bench. "What did you see?"

"We took out a little Whaler and motored around the bay. And she showed me this cliff."

"Pulpit Head," I said. My chest pinched up as I connected the video to his story.

"Then she took me to her house and tried to freak me out with the player piano. She said it hadn't worked for years and left me in the living room—"

"And it mysteriously started playing?" I grinned and hurt at once. "'When the Saints Come Marching In'?"

He nodded, smiling, then looked away.

"That's it?" I asked quietly, after a moment.

His eyes were on me, but he wasn't seeing me. It creeped me out for a second. "Gib?"

He blinked. "Yeah, that's it," he said with vague annoyance. Then, embarrassed, he stood. "I'll be back in a second."

Alone, I massaged my forehead. Hattie tried to blow off Gib at first, but gave in and was going to meet him for a lobster roll, then . . . what? She saw him and got sucked in? Certainly understandable for the rest of us mortals. But Hattie didn't need anyone, she told me that. And oh my God, I dreaded having to tell Hammy *any* of this.

Gib returned with a towering bowl of Cheerios. "Want some? I gotta eat before soccer."

I shook my head. "I guess I was wrong, Gib, when I told you not to pursue her." I looked at the gray sky. "I'm happy it started working out."

His confused expression didn't match my words, like we were a poorly dubbed foreign movie.

He finished chewing and swallowed. "She really didn't tell you any of this?" His eyes were the blue of a cold sea and it made me sad.

"No."

Gib raked his fingers through his hair. "After Maine, I never talked to her again. She didn't return a single call or text. Nothing."

"Nothing?" I wasn't sure I believed him. "That doesn't make sense."

"Nothing."

"Would you ever have told me this?" I asked.

"I thought you knew!" He threw his arms wide.

I traced the wood patterns on the table.

He twisted his spoon. "I shouldn't have left her."

"I can promise you *that* wouldn't have worked," I said. But what did I know, really? Lava gurgled in my stomach. I took a slow breath.

"If I stayed," he went on, "it wouldn't have happened. I would have been with her."

I almost said, *What, like, from July until August?* He wasn't making sense. We weren't that different; we were just two grief-stricken people trying to make sense of what the hell happened to Hattie. "She'd still be here," he said. His voice wobbled.

I pulled words from some reserve in my head. "Nobody's to blame for an accident." It sounded like one of my mother's phony platitudes, but it was all I had. I could barely keep from collapsing.

"You believe that?" Gib stared at me. Rain started to sprinkle us, but we didn't move.

"I don't know," I whispered.

His laugh lacked any joy. Abruptly, he thumped the table with his palms. "I have soccer." He swung his long legs over the bench.

I stood, suddenly awkward.

The screen door clattered shut and rather than follow him like a duckling, I called, "See you, Gib." I hurried to my car.

I'd driven halfway home before realizing I'd left my bag on the picnic bench. I turned around, hoping his car, and he, would be gone. They weren't. Steady rain fell as I rounded the house. A loud crash sounded inside. I stopped.

Another loud crash with a sickening cry. I thought maybe he'd hurt himself and was torn between running away and checking on him.

I peered in a dining room window but saw nothing, then noticed lights in the basement window near my feet. I squatted. Gib's back was to me as he swept a shelf load of books with his forearm, hurling them against a brick fireplace. They slammed to the floor, splayed like dead soldiers. Grunting, he rammed the sofa like a linebacker, his face bloodred, veins bulging on his neck. The sofa flipped on end and he charged at an easy chair. His gaping frown stretched his face into a scary mask. I think he was sobbing.

Horrified, I backed away. The rain came harder, soaking my shoulders. I was desperate to escape unseen, desperate to unsee, partly because he scared me, and partly because I knew I had the same rage brewing in me.

At home, I couldn't shake the uneasiness that started at Gib's house. I had so much to process, and I still felt half in the fog. My mother kept hovering around me. I used to want her to do this, when I was little. When Spencer got diagnosed, she drifted away from me, embarking on her doomed crusade to save him. I tried not to be mad at her for this. But now, staring at my haunted self in the bathroom mirror, I realized my friendship with Hattie let me forget that I came second. They were kind of alike, Hattie and Mom. Laura MacGregory is alpha, for sure. Maybe that's how Hattie became so important to me—she was my friend, but she also filled an emptiness in me where my mother's attention used to be. But now,

I didn't want my mom in my space. I needed to figure things out myself.

It was hard to fall asleep and I put in one earbud and listened to the most boring podcast I could find, letting the voices of total strangers usher me into unconsciousness.

Stroke by stroke she swims, even and strong. I am so heavy. I grab at the waves. She glows against the black water and I confuse her with the tufts of fog skidding across the surface. She waits. "Hurry," she whispers, eyes vigilant and darting. Her feet churn like a propeller, growing the distance between us. The fog thickens and I lose her. Slurping waves echo off the mist. I tread water. "Hattie?"

I hear the splashes of a swimmer.

"Is that you?"

"Swim!" she yells from another direction, panicked. "Swim like hell!"

I dive. Her blond hair radiates around her face. Her mouth opens, bubbles escaping. Fear in her eyes. Something pulls her—I see it wrapped around her ankle. A rope? The tentacles of an octopus? A hand? It shape-shifts in the gurgling dark. I stretch to reach Hattie. Her face is frozen in a scream.

"Noooooooo!" I cry.

I stared into the nebulous darkness of my room, patting the mattress, short of breath. "Momma?" I called, like I was four and she hadn't floated away from me. Slowly, shadows took form in my room: desk, dresser, lamp. I was back in my new reality, which was hell.

A ringing started up in my ears. I listened with my eyes closed. I took ibuprofen and left on the light, too hot and too cold to be comfortable. I'm not sure all of me was in my body anymore. I was leaking out, like steam from a kettle. Maybe that was the ringing in my ears: me, evaporating, and a teapot whistling.

Tomorrow, Hammy would come. I would have to tell him about Gib and Hattie. *Goddammit, Hattie.* I turned the volume low on my phone and restarted the boring podcast, trying to get back to sleep, but too exhausted to let it happen.

Hammy arrived at 11:11, which I thought was Hattie's idea of a joke. The funeral, when I'd seen him last, seemed like a very long time ago, but it had barely been a week. We drove to Siwanoy in the rain. The farther we got from my house, the sicker I felt about having to tell Hammy about Gib and Hattie. We rolled to a stop in a parking spot facing the woods. My palms were clammy and I rubbed them on my thighs.

"I ended up looking," I began, "on her phone." I was a skydiver in free fall.

He tipped his head in acknowledgment. "And?"

"It's not what I expected," I said, stalling.

"What were you expecting?" He picked up the phone.

I put my hand on it, touching his fingers. "Wait." I felt like I was about to punch him in the heart. "There's a video of Gib and Hattie on The Thimble. Together."

"Together?"

"Yes."

"*Together* together?"

"Well, not like porn or anything. But they were together. Without telling anyone."

He looked at the phone blankly. "Gib?"

I squeezed my lips and nodded.

He exhaled loudly and thunked his head against the driver's seat headrest. He stayed like that with his eyes closed. "She was never going to go for me."

I thought about saying, "I don't know," but I decided I needed to work on my honesty policies. "Probably not," I said softly. I knew the feeling. Mac. Noah.

I reached for the phone, but he clutched it. "Not so fast. What's the passcode?"

"You sure?"

"Yep." I tapped her code. "I thought girls told each other all the hookup shit," he said as the video loaded.

I remembered how long I kept Jay secret. "We don't always, it turns out."

The familiar windy sound came from her phone. "Are you sure that's him?"

"It's him. The shorts," I said flatly.

"Wait a minute," Hammy said. "They must have been seeing each other before she left. He wouldn't show up in Maine out of the blue, would he? God, that guy's got balls if he did."

"Actually . . ." I looked at him apologetically.

His eyebrows pointed up sharply, like those military guards with the fuzzy hats in front of Buckingham Palace. "Did you know all along?"

"Not about Maine!" I said, grateful for something I could feel un-guilty about.

He waited.

I sucked in air for strength. "They hooked up Hattie's last night home. At Sabrina Bradley's."

Disbelief swept his features. "Jesus, Reid! I thought you were on my side!"

"I'm sorry!" I said. "She didn't even care about him."

He stared at me.

My mouth had gone completely dry. I tried to swallow. "If I told you, it would have been mean. Wouldn't it have been mean?" I sounded desperate. "She swore she didn't want to date him."

"Based on what I know," he said, "*no* girl hooks up with Gib and doesn't want to go out with him for, like, fucking, ever and ever."

To say *I know!* would've been excessively honest, so I said, "I would have loved it if you two were a couple." It sounded hollow, but I meant it. Didn't I?

He flinched, his expression inscrutable. His lips moved like he was going to say something, but he reached for the keys.

I squeezed my eyes shut. "Maybe I should have told you. But would you have made the pact of Hammy and Reid if I did?" He didn't respond, so I opened my eyes.

He squinted, confused.

"I mean, if we're being honest—really honest—here?" I said. "Our summer was based on the promise of you and Hattie." My chest fluttered.

"No," he said icily. "It was based on the idea that *we* would have fun without her," he said, pointing back and forth at us. "Did you have fun, or not?"

I sniffled. Now I'd insulted him on top of everything else.

"Did you?" I felt his glare. "Because I thought we were having fun." His calm stung me.

I nodded, wiping my nose with my wrist, unable to look at him.

"You should have been honest."

"I know," I said, but he'd flipped on the radio. Maybe that was okay, because really, I didn't know anything at all. What was the truth of the Summer of Hammy and Reid? Had I been honest with myself about it? Did I even know how to be honest about it? My feelings were so simple: I loved Hammy. My feelings were so complicated: I might *love* love Hammy. How could I tell him that? I dared to look at his face, but he kept his eyes glued on the trees in front of us. His dark lashes were long in profile, his jaw muscles grinding under his boyishly rosy cheek. A shadow of razor stubble grazed only the tip of his chin. Hattie had managed to bring me this amazing friend, and I still managed to fuck it up.

He sighed, and backed out of the parking spot. I needed to say something. I couldn't lose him, too. We left the beach, and he turned left instead of toward my home, which gave me hope. He was giving me a chance.

I waited for the song to end and turned down the volume.

His eyes followed my hand, but he still didn't look at me.

"Hammy?" I said.

"Mm," he said, unwilling to even move his lips.

"This was the best summer of my life." As soon as I said them, I realized how true my words were, but I had to qualify them. "Until it turned into the worst summer of my life." A tear plopped onto my shorts. "What if I didn't have you now?"

He stayed quiet, but his face softened. The windshield wipers squeaked once. Twice.

At a stoplight, finally he looked at me, his dark blue eyes so tired and sad.

"I'm so sorry," I said.

He watched my face for a few seconds, maybe debating whether or not to accept my apology. The light changed. He looked at the road and resumed driving. "Let's forget it," he said. "What does it matter now, anyway?"

It seemed skimpy, but I was the one who needed to be forgiven, so I didn't ask for more. The wipers counted off several suffocating moments of silence.

"For what it's worth," I ventured a few stoplights later, "she blew him off right after he left Maine. Never talked with him again."

"Well." Hammy snickered. "There's that."

"Yeah," I said.

He took a right onto White Birch Avenue, a road that went all the way to Westchester County, New York.

"Are we going somewhere in particular?" I asked.

"Nope. I just need to drive. Don't you?"

I shrugged, unsure how to react. I didn't want to be anywhere else on earth but with him, even like this, but it felt like he simply didn't feel like going all the way to my house to drop me off.

We rode for miles and miles. Around five thirty, we passed a sign welcoming us to South Salem, New York. I glanced at Hammy. He kept driving.

Not talking became spellbinding. Hypnotizing, almost. It stopped raining and sunlight twinkled sideways through the foliage, at its deepest green of the summer. Cool, damp air swirled through the windows, tossing the radio songs with our unspoken thoughts, and eventually the tension between us seemed to blow away, too.

Being nowhere in particular let my mind wander with a freedom I couldn't find at home. There, I had to be Reid, who could be counted on to stay out of any real trouble, keep a respectable GPA, and wear panty hose and gross loafers to earn extra college money if she couldn't pull in a lacrosse scholarship like Scott did. Reid: who was neurotypical, took Spencer to OT every Saturday without asking questions. My lack of demands, I realized, defined me—fit me into a neat little box that my mom could put aside or pull out as needed. But now, the box was obliterated, and I kept expanding, like a gas or a vapor, without Hattie to stop me. I imagined myself stretching thinner and thinner until I disappeared altogether and became part of the sky. Or maybe a cloud, to float with her again. I breathed deeply, fighting tears.

We rounded a long curve in the road and the trees opened to a field that sloped to a brook. Without a word, Hammy parked on the shoulder, got out, and hauled two beach chairs from the hatchback. "My sister," he said by way of explanation. He arranged them overlooking the field and sat. He didn't invite me, but after a moment, I joined him.

Somehow, outside of the car our silence felt claustrophobic again.

"Pretty," I said, taking a seat beside him.

"It is."

I couldn't stand it. "Hammy, I'm so sorry."

"I know, Reid."

"Okay, but . . ." I paused, trying to rid my voice of annoyance. "But do you forgive me?"

He stared out at the landscape. "I forgive you, of course," he said, like that was obvious. I'd been expecting something more exonerating, but it brought some relief. He went on. "I'm mad at myself for being . . . so chicken-shit."

"What are you talking about?" I asked.

"I skulked around hoping, secretly wishing . . ." He said it in a voice that self-mocked. "Look at Gib Soule. He just drove to Maine. He knew he wanted Hattie and he went for it." His head dropped, and he rubbed his forehead with two fingers. "I wasted my chance worrying about rejection."

His expression was so pained it broke my heart. "Hammy, how could you have known you wouldn't have this year? And you wrote her, right? And asked her to prom," I added, trying to remember something else to add to the list.

"No." He shook his head stubbornly. "I didn't put myself out there, really. I hid behind the idea of being *just friends*."

I blinked, feeling his words resonate in my chest. My cheeks flamed and I looked at my lap.

"And you know what?" He stood, picked up a rock, and threw it. "That was the stupidest fucking thing I could have done, because a girl like Hattie—Hattie of all people"—he closed his eyes and shook his head—"isn't going to be interested in a guy who won't even take a risk to win her over."

I hated to think he had a point there, but he probably did. Hattie was only attracted to the bold. Maybe this was the *why not* I'd always tried to pry from her regarding Hammy. I couldn't say that, though, and it wasn't really the point. "Hammy, what were you supposed to do? Be a person you aren't just to get her attention?" I said.

The brows slid together. "Yes," he said. A momentary smile played on his lips, then fell slack.

I rolled my eyes, smiling myself. "No," I scolded. "And let me tell you," I continued, "she didn't want a boyfriend! *Any* boyfriend. We discussed it at length when I was up there in July. And PS, Gib didn't win her over for long, either." I hadn't planned on divulging this part, but I added, "Jay Seavers was all over her business too, and she played him like—"

His eyes darted to me. "Seavers?"

"Don't get me started on that *dickhead*," I said, unable to mask my loathing now that I was on an honesty roll. "He was less than nothing to her, anyway."

He plunked back into the chair and for a while we watched the sun sparkle on the still-wet leaves, and the brook, glittering amber in the distance. When he leaned forward suddenly, I started. He looked at the ground, lacing his fingers behind his neck. "I feel like the shock is wearing off and now all I have are a million questions that will never be answered. And all these fucking dark feelings that completely suck."

"I know," I said. "I know." I almost told him about

hearing her voice then. About seeing her on the Post Road that day, but it kind of scared me and also made me feel like I still had a thread of connection to Hattie somehow. "I think she took part of me with her, Hammy. I don't think I'm ever going to get it back." I whimpered, and he pulled me out of the chair and into his arms so I could cry on his shoulder.

A breeze rippled the grass. It reminded me of ocean waves, and my nightmare of the octopus pulling her under flashed through my mind. I pinched my eyelids. "I don't know how long I can stand these feelings, to be honest." My voice went soft.

He drummed his fingers against his thigh. Like a mind reader he said, "What do you think happened to her? Really?"

"I don't know." I had to stand up. "It terrifies me. She *did not—*" I couldn't say the words aloud. "Emma Rose said there's a rumor."

"Oh," he said. "I don't even listen to that bullshit." And I was so relieved to hear him sound definite, too, that I didn't tell him about what Uncle Baxter said. Still, the holes left us grasping for answers with almost nothing to go on. "But," Hammy said, "why would she swim at night like that? Was she drunk?"

"Who would she have gotten drunk with? Her friend Santi was in Alaska. Other than him, she hung out with family."

"Helen?"

"No, I saw Helen's texts to Hattie from the night it happened." I forced out the words, so he would know what I knew. "Helen was with her parents and when they came home, Hattie was gone. Helen kept texting Hattie to get home, that Mr. Darrow was pissed. Hattie didn't respond."

"There's no one else she could have been with?"

I shook my head, trying to remember clues from the phone. I sucked in a breath.

"What?"

"Gib."

He looked at me sideways.

I brought my hand to my mouth. "He could have been there. He could have been with her."

"What are you talking about?"

"He went there in July, why not in August?"

"I thought you said she blackballed him."

"Oh my God," I said. "What if he went up there and they got in a fight and something happened . . ."

Hammy made a face. "What?"

"He could have tried to confront her. He could have gotten mad, really mad." I thought of him in his basement, veins bulging.

"Are you trying to say it wasn't an accident?" Hammy said.

"Hammy! What if he did something to her?"

"Reid." He stood and put a hand on my shoulder. "Slow down."

I shook him off. "It's the oldest story in history. Possessive guy can't have the girl, so nobody else will." I saw the sofa roll over.

"So, you're accusing Gib of murder now?" We stared at each other. "Seriously?"

"It explains so much." I was Sherlock illuminating the facts for Watson. It was like a surreal play. "First of all, Hattie Darrow is too smart to go swimming"—I raised one finger—"*in the fog*"—I raised a second finger—"*at night*"—third finger—"*when the riptide was strong. And* it explains why Helen didn't know where she was."

"No, it doesn't," Hammy said, jaw clenched. "She snuck out."

"Yeah, but she wouldn't sneak out to swim alone!" I said.

"She snuck out all the time!" he said.

"I *know* her," I said, ignoring the piles of evidence to the contrary. "Oh my God!" I grabbed his arm. "The Eye of Horus bracelet! That's why she sent it," I whispered, my words unable to keep up with the racing thoughts. "She was trying to tell me!"

"Ow," he said, and I realized I'd grabbed his arm. "Tell you what?"

"She wanted me to know she was afraid of him!" I pictured Gib, veins bulging in his neck. "He has a temper!" I couldn't slow down to explain now. We had to get home so I could see when she sent me the bracelet. I folded my chair and opened the hatchback. Then I got scared.

What if Gib knew I knew? Was that why he agreed to meet today?

Hammy shook his head again. "Reid," he said. I grabbed his chair, barely getting it folded before shoving it into the car. My mind spun in dizzying circles, my headache swept into the whirl.

"We need to go look at what she sent me," I said from the passenger seat. "At every clue we can find on the phone."

Hammy puffed his cheeks, hands on his hips, then rested his forearms on top of the door. He leaned in, his body blocking the sunlight like a big fat rain cloud. "Reid." His voice was patient. "Gib's a nice guy."

I reached for the keys in the ignition and turned over the engine. "We need to go."

The ride back to my house started in a new kind of silence. Hammy: annoyed but maintaining his Zen. Me: combustible, hurtling through possibilities. Maybe I *had* been seeing her ghost. Hattie wanted me to bring Gib to justice. I didn't dare tell that part to Hammy. His skepticism already felt like an invisible passenger in the back seat.

When his headlights led us around the familiar corner of my driveway, the sky glowed amethyst and the trees loomed in blobby shadows. My mother's silhouette at the kitchen window disappeared as we got closer to the house.

I got out of the car. "Why aren't you turning it off?" I asked when I'd rounded the hood.

Hammy looked at his dashboard clock, then at his knees.

"Hammy. I can't—" My chin quivered. "Won't you help?"

He closed his eyes. "I need dinner," he said.

"You can eat here. Please?"

"My mom . . ." he started. Another sigh. The engine clicked off. When he stood, I hugged him. He rested his chin on top of my head. He felt solid. Grounded.

"Thank you," I said. "I wish you could spend the night."

He stiffened and laughed. "Your dad would kick my ass."

"Not like that!" I stumbled backward. God, did I really just invite him to sleep over?

He blushed but turned toward the door. "Let's see if Emma Rose is around," he said quickly.

"Emma Rose?" Now I stiffened.

"You guys had a good visit yesterday, right? She thought so."

"You talked to Emma Rose about her visit here?" I didn't have a right to be jealous, but it felt a little like a betrayal.

"Yeah" was the only word that came out of his mouth, but within it was the question, *What's the problem with that?*

"I don't know. I wasn't aware you two had that kind of relationship."

"I know she's not your favorite—"

"Hattie can't stand her," I said. Then, "Couldn't."

"Right, I get that. FYI, Emma Rose doesn't know that and she is sad about Hattie, too. But she and I go back, and when you wouldn't return my texts or anything after I got the news, I just—" He shrugged.

"Oh God, I'm such a shit," I said, but he waved his hands.

"I don't mean that—Jesus, it's so enormous for you. I knew you needed time. But I needed a friend. And she's been—" He searched for a word and gave up. "Reid, I think you're going to need a friend. I think you need one right now."

"I—" *Have you*, was what I wanted to say. But then it occurred to me. He needed a buffer person between us. "Okay." I nodded, making peace with it on the spot. Emma Rose might believe me about Gib. She had been a comfort yesterday, truth be told. But I couldn't bring myself to think of her as a friend.

"Reid?" my mom called from the front door.

I sighed. "Coming!"

I hadn't had a meal at the table since it happened. My parents welcomed Hammy joining us. The novelty of Hammy-as-dinner-guest gave my parents a perfect shot at regaining normalcy. Once we were seated in the dining room, my dad said, "I wouldn't feel right if we didn't say grace tonight." My eyes popped to his. We were grace-at-holiday-meals kind of people. He smiled a sad smile at me. "For Hattie," he said. My heart got a little bigger. I nodded and everyone joined hands and we all tipped our heads.

"Dear Lord, we thank you for this bountiful meal before us and ask you to please take special care of the Darrow family as they grieve their beautiful Hattie." He paused and cleared his throat. I stole a glance at Hammy, who watched my dad respectfully. "Bless Hattie as she joins you in heaven, and please remind us to keep a little piece of her wonderful spirit in our hearts always. Amen."

We echoed him, even Spencer, who loved to know what to say. Dad and I shared another smile, as my mom said, "Bon appétit, everyone."

With the acknowledgment of our loss aside, my parents seemed bent on avoiding the topic of Hattie, and for once I was glad for their formal sense of dinner guest etiquette. Laura and Rob MacGregory skipped through small talk the way kids splash through puddles, from summer jobs to college to college football. While they ate and blabbed with poor Hammy, I stole peeks at Hattie's phone under the table, in full-blown investigation mode. If Hammy noticed, he didn't let on.

I scrolled and re-scrolled. I checked different apps that had photos. I had this unshakable feeling I had missed something, something that would help me understand. It was odd she didn't keep any pictures of Gib. And not one pic from August. On a whim, I opened a folder called "Recently Deleted Photos" while the conversation turned to hopes for the Yankees in October. *Sixty-three photos recently deleted.*

My stomach flipped. I tapped. Gib's blue marbles stared at me, his perfect smile beaming in shot after shot. Hattie, hanging on him in selfies. Gib, no shirt, in the Bat Cave, tangled in the thin white sheets I'd slept in myself. A selfie of the two of them, somehow posing in front of Hattie's bedroom mirror in bathing suits. She smiled at the camera straight on, her arm around his shoulders. He had his arms wrapped around her waist, pulling her toward him, his gaze so mesmerized, so guileless, so adoring, I could feel it through time and space. Gib was in and he was in deep. "Jesus!" I blurted, finding the end of the photos at last—two shots of Gib alone in the driveway.

"Reid," my mother said.

My face got hot. Hammy looked at me, questioning.

"Jesus!" said Spencer. Everyone laughed, but I caught my mother's worried expression. I tucked the phone under my thigh and pretended to eat, annoyed I couldn't ditch them and focus on what the hell happened to Hattie.

I'd never have thought I'd be excited to hear Emma Rose's voice in our family room. So many, many things

I'd never have thought. She inspired a full evacuation of the dining room. Her tan set off the white of her eyes and teeth, so she looked like a shimmering goddess. After a lightning round of polite talk from my parents, they generously said good night and went upstairs.

Hammy took his usual island in the family room, and Emma Rose sat beside me on mine.

"So," I said. "Did Hammy tell you?"

She and Hammy exchanged glances and he said, "I thought I'd leave that to you."

Emma Rose squinted. "What?"

I took a long breath. "Did I mention Hattie had a fling with Gib Soule?"

She blinked like someone had pegged her with a spitball. "I knew he wasn't telling me something!"

I paused. Of course, Emma Rose talked to everyone, about everything. Where Hattie found gossip boring and trivial, Emma Rose found it fascinating. Hattie barely went on her phone, Emma Rose was a social media addict. I realized her skill set fit the situation perfectly.

"When?" she asked.

Clearly still stinging from the revelation himself, Hammy's heel bounced aggressively against his flip-flop. I stayed the course. "It started at that party Sabrina Bradley and her sister had in June. Hattie left for Maine the next day."

"I was at that party," Emma Rose said. She looked

into some space above our heads, remembering. "Define *fling*," she said. "Did you know this, Hammy?"

I tried to make eye contact with him, but he stared out the window. "No." He packed a lot of bitterness into such a small word.

A pang of guilt made me twitch. "I'm sorry, Hammy, I don't want to rub it in, but it's important. If we go to the police—"

"Police?" Emma Rose said.

"It's fine," he said. "Tell her your"—air quotes—"'theory.'"

"You're killing me, people," Emma Rose said.

After showing her the video, I opened the deleted photos folder and handed it to her. "Look, Hammy, I found these during dinner." Reluctantly, he rose and peered over her shoulder.

She scrolled through, her eyes giraffe-sized. I told her how Gib surprised Hattie in Maine; how at first she wouldn't see him. "And then, this!"

Emma Rose stopped short at Gib tangled in bedding. "Whoa. Boxer-less?" She lingered on the one in Hattie's bedroom. "That's a fling, all right. And she didn't tell you this? Why?"

I shrugged, though I'd started to wonder if Hattie wanted to forget she *could* get hooked, after all. Despite all her talk of games and power. *I don't want a damn boyfriend, Reid! Why is this so hard for you to comprehend?*

she'd told me—with no shortage of sass. It followed that that's why she shook Gib once he left Maine. Like she'd come back to her senses.

"They would've been the biggest power couple ever," Emma Rose mused. "Way bigger than him and Priya." Then, before I could change my mind about her yet again, she added, "As if *that's* worth one frigging thing." She looked at the ceiling and shook her head. "Sorry, I don't know what I'm thinking. Keep talking."

"She dumped him after he left Maine," Hammy said.

"Why?"

"Small junk," Hammy said. "Duh."

"Unnecessary," I said at the same time as Emma Rose said, "Hammy!"

"The truth hurts. Reid, those pictures don't prove anything. Gib already told you they hooked up." He stood. "Anyone want ice cream?"

"I'm not getting the police part," Emma Rose said, ignoring him.

I looked at Hammy for backup, but he raised his hands and turned toward the kitchen.

"I think he turned stalker." I folded my arms.

"Gibson Soule?" Emma Rose said. "No way."

"Exactly," Hammy called from the kitchen, rummaging through the freezer.

"I think he became obsessed with her when she shut him down." I felt reenergized saying it aloud. "We don't know what a jilted Gib Soule is capable of."

"Well, we do, because of Priya," Emma Rose pointed out. "He was just bummed. Not creepy. Or, you know, *physical.* I would have heard about anything like that."

I pictured Gib in his basement. A part of me felt scummy exposing it, because that was obviously a private moment I wasn't meant to see. But my idea that he had something to do with her death was gaining momentum, and what looked at first like an outburst of rage and grief now proved Gib's dark side. "I have to tell you what I saw this morning," I said, spinning the Eye of Horus bracelet on my wrist.

Hammy returned, managing half an ice cream sandwich in one bite. "Reid, what are you talking about?"

I told them how I'd gone to talk with him after finding the first video on the phone of him in Maine. And how he told me she was reluctant to see him but gave in. And the pictures on her phone told *that* story. He also said he never saw her again after that, and that she never returned his calls or texts.

"That is so sad," Emma Rose said. "Imagine how awful for him . . ."

Hammy exhaled sharply.

"That's not all," I said. "I forgot my bag and had to turn around to drive back and get it. When I did, I saw him in the basement in a complete meltdown. He threw books and plowed furniture into walls—big! A sofa and chair. His veins were popping out of his neck and his face was dark red—he looked like the Hulk." I shivered and pulled a sofa pillow in front of my chest. Armor. "He was really . . . violent."

"Maybe he's sad," Hammy said with a shrug. "I mean, sometimes guys have a hard time telling sad from mad."

Emma Rose dropped her eyes, rubbing her forearms. She saw the possibilities, I could tell. I loved her then.

"I'm not saying he planned it," I said. "It could have been a crime of passion. He could have shown up and tried to win her back, she would have nothing of it, and his temper spiked. They argued . . ." I let my voice trail off.

"They argued and what? She decides it's a swell time for a swim? Come on, Reid, it doesn't add up," Hammy said, popping the other half of the ice cream sandwich into his mouth.

"How do we know she didn't fall in?" I asked.

"You can't *fall in* from the shore," Hammy argued. He unwrapped a second ice cream sandwich.

"He could have chased her into the water and she got caught in the riptide." They watched me pace the room. "Or, *or*"—I stabbed the air with my finger—"she could have been pushed from Pulpit Head." I waited to let it sink in. "He didn't even have to push her. Listen, I've been on those cliffs when it's foggy. You can't see the water. One stumble while running and she's over the side."

"But then the cause of death would have been head

trauma from hitting the rocks or something like that," Emma Rose said. "The papers said she drowned." Doctor's daughter.

"It might have *looked* like an accident—especially if nobody knew he was there." My hands were all over the place. "Hattie Darrow would not accidentally drown. And she sure as shit wouldn't drown *on purpose*."

Hammy lifted two fingers. "*That* part is true."

"Maybe the Darrows don't even know," Emma Rose said. Her shoulders shivered. "This is scary."

Hammy groaned, pulling his cheeks down so his eyes bugged. "Reid, you have to stop. You're upset. We are all. But don't you think you may be getting *carried away*? This isn't an episode of *CSI*!" He rubbed eyes. "Pardon me, *Sherlock*. There's no proof he was even there when it happened."

I ignored him. Foul play had to be involved in the destruction of Hattie. Foul play was the only thing big enough to take her down. "How can we find out if he went up there?" I said, pacing the room. "Who would know?" I tried to remember the name of Gib's friend with the house in Maine.

Emma Rose snapped her fingers. "Instagram. What was the date again?"

"The twenty-sixth," Hammy said.

She tapped away. "He may be lying about the blackballing to cover his tracks."

I considered this idea.

Smack.

"Oh, Christ." Hammy had his hand on his forehead. I thought he'd killed a mosquito. "Gib was at the preseason soccer cookout on August twenty-sixth. We both were."

I crinkled my forehead. "Are you sure?"

A flicker of delay. "Yeah."

"Really sure?" Emma Rose asked. "Did you drive together?"

He squinted. "No . . . I rode with Charlie."

"Did you *see* him?" I asked.

"You need to be definite," Emma Rose said.

"I'm sure. Besides—" He cupped both hands around his mouth. "*Gib Soule is a nice guy.*"

"Lots of assholes act like nice guys," Emma Rose said. I imagined she was no stranger to aggressive guys. "There was that thing about Gib and the Braeburn hockey player with the broken nose last spring. I wonder now."

"I thought it was a rumor," I said, looking back and forth at them.

"He did it," Hammy said.

"What?!" Emma Rose and I exclaimed at once. I threw my hands wide. "For crying out loud, he beat that guy up? And broke into his car?"

Hammy deflated a little in his chair and examined his thumbnail. "He was upset that Priya slept with the dude," he said, barely audibly. "His moms had to pay fifty thousand in damages in return for the story never getting out."

I stood up, looking at Emma Rose. "That's insane! I can't believe I didn't know that—my God, he is a good liar."

"What?!" I said again. "Oh my God, he really did it. He did something to Hattie." I paced around the room. "I knew she was trying to tell me something, with this." I shook the bracelet. "I knew it! It didn't make sense." I felt victorious and terrified.

Hammy shifted to pull his phone from his back pocket. "Okay, even if he broke that kid's nose, it doesn't mean he'd *murder* someone. Jesus!" he said. "I'm calling Charlie. He'll tell you. Gib was at the soccer dinner!"

"That's good," Emma Rose said, shaken.

We waited.

Hammy said, "Charlie, call me. ASAP." He dropped his phone on the cushion. "He's probably with Alesha. What I really want is a joint right now, but I'd settle for a beer."

"I'd love some wine," said Emma Rose.

I checked the grandfather clock: 11:50. I hadn't heard any sounds from upstairs in a long time. "Screw it," I said. "If ever I'd get a pass for bad behavior, it's right now."

"Damn straight," said Hammy.

I tapped Hattie's passcode and handed her phone to Hammy. "Read Gib's texts to her." I didn't wait for his response. My limbs were lighter than they'd felt in days.

We had a wet bar off the dining room with a mini fridge. Hattie and I stole vodka from it in ninth grade and put it in an empty Gatorade bottle to take to a football game. I'd puked. My dad blamed my brother Scott, who didn't turn me in but blackmailed me to do stupid crap for him for weeks. I hadn't dipped into their reserves since.

The bar had a dark wooden counter and four stools, mirrors behind, and a few family photos on display. I picked the wine bottle from the mini fridge with the best label (Puss in Boots, in a boat, one boot on the bow, toasting the moon)—and opened it. I took a Heineken for Hammy. After pouring two glasses of wine, I paused to admire Puss in Boots, his eyes cast to the night sky. "Cheers," I said, taking a drink from my glass.

The chandelier flickered, which it does when someone is walking over it upstairs. In the hall, outside my room. Which meant Dad. Like I was nine and it was flashlight tag, I ducked. The lights blinked again. *Shit!* I waited, pressing myself against the mini fridge door. Nothing happened. I peered over the counter.

A voice came from behind me. "You're a pirate now, Reddi-Wip."

Hattie!

"Kicking ass and taking names."

I jumped to my feet. Crystal glasses chimed together. The chandelier flickered again. I searched the half-darkness of the room. A bubble of her laughter tickled my ear. I faced myself in the mirror.

Cold heat prickled my arms. Hattie's face appeared

over my shoulder. She laced her fingers and held them next to her cheek. "All growed up!"

I spun, but she wasn't there. I checked the mirror again. I saw myself. My skin glowed.

That was her. Whether she was inside my head or floating somewhere between what's real and not real, who knew? But Hattie visited me then. And I knew why. We were on the right track with this Gib thing. *Taking names.*

I balanced the two wine stems between my fingers, grabbed the beer in my other hand, and hurried back to Hammy and Emma Rose.

"To Hattie," Hammy said quietly, and we clinked our drinks.

"To Hattie," Emma Rose said.

I couldn't say it, but I nodded and let the wine spread through my mouth, sweet and bitter. I forced myself to swallow.

Hattie's phone sat on the coffee table. "Did you read all the texts?" I asked.

Hammy stared out the window. Emma Rose nodded, her eyes rimmed in red. "God, it's awful. Her poor family."

"And doesn't Gib sound stalker-ish?"

Hammy didn't say no.

Emma Rose looked alert again. "Mind if I get that stuff she sent from your room?" She was halfway up the back stairs by the time I answered.

"She's getting the stuff Hattie sent me this summer," I told Hammy.

He pinched his caterpillar brows. "What stuff?"

"I told you about the care packages," I said. "The bracelet?" I rattled the eyeballs at him.

"You didn't say there was more," he said, but we both knew it was fake. I could practically see him rifling through his brain's memory files.

"Yes, I did! You didn't listen. She sends me stuff every summer." There would be no more care packages, and I realized with renewed sadness that every day for a long time would bring another realization of some tiny but huge loss.

I'd almost finished my wine when Emma Rose returned with her arms full. "I took the liberty," she said, waving a mug of rainbow Sharpies and the Roz Chast wall calendar my grandma had given me. "If we reconstruct the timing of these mailings, we may figure something out."

She arranged my suspicious loot on the coffee table as I read the postmark dates off the envelopes for the Don Quixote print, the Ouija board, the bracelet, and the fishnets, which cracked Hammy up. Emma Rose copied the dates on the calendar in turquoise. Hammy slipped into the dining room and returned with a fresh Heineken and Puss in Boots. I knew I was woozy and welcomed his refill of my glass.

Next, we checked the time stamps on the photos of Gib in Maine. Emma Rose switched to green and added *G on Thimble* on Wednesday, July eighteenth, and drew an arrow to Friday, July twentieth.

"Anything else we should add?" Emma Rose asked.

"Hattie first got there on June nineteenth," Hammy suggested.

Emma Rose flipped the calendar to June and scrawled in turquoise, *H to Thimble.*

"And she was supposed to come home . . . ?" Her pen hovered.

"Gus twenny-eight," I said, sinking lower in my chair.

Emma Rose reached her hand onto my forearm. She was such a toucher. "We don't have to do this," she said.

"No," I said. "It's important. Santi left for his Alaska NOLS trip on July fifteenth and was due home sometime at the end of August, I think. They do—did—everything together on The Thimble." I wondered now whether he'd been home when it happened, and made a mental note to call him when I felt strong enough. I was stunned by all the details I'd neglected to consider.

"We should add the final . . ." Hammy stared at the calendar. "Her last day."

"August twenty-sixth," I said, my voice thin. I took a long sip of wine.

Emma Rose looked at both of us, then down at the calendar. "God, what do I write?"

Hammy and I looked at each other. I wished I was curled into him on the chair.

"Write *H ad astra*," he said.

"Add what?" I asked.

"*Ad—A-D—astra.* It's Latin for *to the stars,*" he said, and I remembered his Latin classes. *Hattie to the stars.* That sounded so beautiful it stung my eyes. I silently toasted her again and drank more. It was smooth to my mouth now.

Emma Rose took a long breath. She pushed the pen in sure lines and curves. The felt tip scraped the paper with the tiniest skritching sounds.

"To the stars, above the clouds," I said in barely more than a whisper. Georgia O'Keeffe's painting.

Emma Rose stood back. "It's a start," she said. I closed my eyes. My brain spun.

"You look exhausted," I heard Emma Rose say. "Hammy, we should go."

I tried to protest, but my head felt like my grandmother's curling stone. Emma Rose pulled my hand upstairs. "We'll talk in the morning," she said.

She turned the lights out. I marveled, and was appropriately grateful, that Emma Rose Burnham was tucking me into bed. I slipped into the black fuzziness of my room, so happy to be relieved of thinking, of feeling, one more thing.

I awoke with a start just past three a.m. I was unsure why, which was better than a nightmare, but anxiety tightened my muscles.

Hattie's phone balanced on the edge of my nightstand. Impulsively, I took it and scrolled through the photos from the deleted folder. I stopped at the one in Hattie's Thimble bedroom on July nineteenth. Gib's intense gaze at Hattie turned my stomach. My vision blurred and I saw his neck bulged with veins. I turned off the phone and, heavy lidded, watched the blurry shadow of the pear tree outside my window. I felt ashamed for letting Emma Rose into my world so fast. I wished I had Hattie. "But you're not here," I said to the tree. "And I don't know what else to do."

Shifting slightly, I looked up to the sky. A thin veil of clouds stretched across the universe, a smattering of stars stubbornly shining through. *Ad astra*, I thought. To the stars.

NOW

September 4

The next day, when I said Emma Rose would be over again, my mother was ecstatic. “You may be ready for school Thursday, Reid,” she said to me in the kitchen. “Really.” I poured myself coffee and didn’t argue. She was trying to put me back in her box, but I knew I wouldn’t go.

Emma Rose and I sat in patio chairs in the shade. I searched Hattie’s phone again, but my eyes glazed and I possibly drifted to sleep a couple of times. When I’d notice myself again, a jittery anxiousness spurred me along.

Gib's texts, I verified, went 100 percent unanswered by Hattie. *I know you aren't sure and that's why you don't respond. It's okay. I can wait.* That sounded possessive. Controlling. It made me sick to my stomach and sweaty.

Emma Rose combed Instagram for pictures of Gib on August twenty-fifth, twenty-sixth, or twenty-seventh. She'd made a list of all the soccer players and any of Gib's friends she could think of and checked them off one by one.

"Guys never tag people in their pictures," she was saying. "It's *super* frigging annoying."

"Mmm."

I studied the pictures of Gib alone in Hattie's drive-way, which before I'd dismissed for their lack of . . . Gib's flesh. I noticed they were taken from Hattie's bedroom window as opposed to up close and personal. He looked up toward her, squinting into the sun. In the second one, his back was to her. I zoomed in on his face in the first one. He may have looked annoyed, his eyes narrowed to slits, shoulders slumped.

These shots were different.

"Doesn't Gib look weird in those last two pictures?" I asked Emma Rose.

She shaded the screen with her hand. "He looks sad. Or mad, maybe? That one looks like a Bigfoot photo."

I shot her a look.

"That didn't come out right," she said apologetically. "He looks creepy."

I silently reviewed what he'd told me two days ago. He never mentioned being sad when he was there. Supposedly they were in la-la land at that point. "Maybe it's when he's leaving for home."

She scratched her ear, puzzling. "So why isn't she next to him eating his face?"

She was right. I checked the stamps for exact times.

I gasped.

"What?!" Emma Rose said, hand to her throat.

I shook the phone, unable to speak.

"Hold still!" She leaned in. "August twenty-sixth. *August twenty-sixth?* Oh my God. That's the day she died." She covered her mouth. "He was there the day she died! How did I miss that?"

I didn't answer. I missed it, too. "He really did it," I whispered.

"What do we do?"

"I don't know. Call the police?" I said, wrapping my hands around and around each other. "I'm scared."

"Maybe we can leave an anonymous tip," she said.

"I'll have to give them the phone. It's evidence."

She waved her hands like she had spiderwebs stuck to them. "Does it actually prove anything?"

"He was there!" I said. "And he lied!" Or did he? "At the very least he didn't tell me he was in Maine the day . . . *that* day! Why would he leave that out if he was innocent?"

Emma Rose double-checked the picture. She tapped her chin, walking in a circle. "My God, Reid."

My tears rolled unfettered.

"Here's the thing," she said, sitting on the edge of the chair. "Once we tell, they'll arrest Gib."

"They should," I whispered through my tears. I remembered Gib's twisted expression as he threw those books. "What if he knows I know?"

She put her hand on my arm. I clasped my own together to stop their shaking. "I need to think," I said.

If he did it, I was bringing justice. If he didn't, I was bringing more trauma. I pictured Helen's puffed, tearstained face in Hattie's closet. I walked to the rosebushes, like I could escape it. "We have to be sure. We have to find out more."

"You say her friend was away?"

"Santi? I'm pretty positive." I brushed the rose petals with my palm. I dreaded calling him. "I wish I could ask Helen. *Why* did I just run away from her like that? I should've stayed and asked questions."

"Reid, cut yourself some slack. Besides, if you hadn't run with the hoodie, we wouldn't know any of this." Her voice perked. "You could call her now. Or Mrs. Darrow."

I shook my head. My brain sloshed against my skull, making my stomach billow. I steadied myself. "I'm too afraid."

She waited for more. I walked in a loop, watching my

feet land. "I'll make them sadder," I said. "Because I'll lose it crying and then they'll feel sorry about me. On top of their own horribleness. I can't do it." I was evaporating again. I squeezed my eyes shut. "Their sadness is so much bigger than mine."

I opened my eyes. Emma Rose was at my side. "Reid. Nobody's sadness is bigger than anyone else's. It might help you to talk with them." Her voice was hoarse and I saw she'd begun to cry.

"She's their baby," I said. "I can't."

"Okay," she said, hands on my shoulders, holding bits of me in. "We'll do something else."

I nodded.

She wiped a tear from her cheek and sat on the chair. "I could," she said, her voice stronger, "call Ben."

I crinkled my brow. "Ben, as in Ben Darrow?"

"Of course; what other Ben would I call?" she said with a quick laugh.

The sun burned my shoulders and I moved back to the chair. "Why would you call Ben Darrow?"

"I know him," she said. "Very well."

"Wait a minute. Ben is, like . . ." I counted on my fingers. "Twenty-three. How do you know him?"

"Well," she said slowly. "We used to hook up."

"Emma Rose, what the hell are you talking about?" I sounded condescending. I was okay with that. Ben Darrow wouldn't hook up with someone our age. Just the thought made me mad for Hattie. Why was I with Emma Rose, anyway?

"I went to a party in Greenwich with my sister a long time ago," she said. "He was there—a friend of a friend, prep school, la-di-da, you know how that goes."

I stared. Hard.

"He thought I was older." She shrugged, examining her knee. "It was pretty straightforward. He was hot, and we fooled around."

My mouth fell open.

"Come on, would you have said no? I was in eighth grade."

"You slept with *Ben Darrow* in *eighth grade*?" I counted again. "He would have been a senior?!"

"I didn't sleep with him! Well, eventually. . ." A smile snuck onto her lips, but she squelched it fast.

"I do *not* want to know this," I said, circling behind the chairs. "Is this why you and Hattie never got along?"

Her eyes went giraffe-wide. "No! Hattie didn't know. We got along fine." I elected not to call out her inaccuracies. "I didn't realize he was a Darrow until a couple years ago."

"So, you were hooking up with a guy named Ben *Darrow* and you didn't know his sister was Hattie *Darrow*?"

"It was out of context. Reid, jeez." She frowned. "I didn't have to tell you. I'm trying to help." She shook her head. "It's been over a year, maybe two." She sounded like she was exaggerating. "But I could call him."

"How do you know he didn't share this with Hattie?"

"He wouldn't," she said. And she believed it, I could tell. I thought of my recent discovery: when people want to believe something, they play along.

Well, he may not have—he hopefully has some shame—but I can promise you Hattie figured it out. I smiled, having unraveled one of the great Hattie mysteries: why she couldn't stand Emma Rose.

"Call him," I said.

She watched me, like I might change my mind. I set my jaw.

"Okay," she said.

"I can't listen," I said, waving a hand. "I need to get ready for my shift." I stood. "*Don't* mention Gib. Just in case."

"Right." She slung her purse onto her shoulder. "I'll text you."

I slid the screen door closed, grateful to be alone. Although her company relieved me, Emma Rose was still Emma Rose. "And I am still Sancho Panza," I told Boomer softly. Boomer's tail thumped. I missed Hattie. My eyes stung from it; my bones ached. Hammy was right; I did need a friend. But how could I befriend the one person Hattie couldn't stand? I slid to the floor and hugged Boomer.

When I came back downstairs from changing my clothes, Emma Rose was gone. I drove to the dinner theater and called Faye from the parking lot to say I wouldn't make my shift. "Take your time, Reid," she said. Like a bad parody of Clark Kent, I ducked behind the dumpster, hidden by trees, and changed into shorts and a tee. I forgot sandals and wore my gross hostess loafers, which in my very recent past would have meant a trip home. Not today. I wasn't fully in my body, and wingmen don't care about shoes anyway.

The sky was high and the same peacock-feather blue it was on August twenty-seventh, when I saw her. It couldn't have been her, I knew now, but was it some echo of her soul? I mean, it could have been Helen. But Hattie's car? I shook my head. I'd give anything to see her again. I realized I was near Gib's house and headed for the back roads. I turned on the Dissidents so loud it hurt my ears and sang at the top of my lungs. I would roam. I couldn't go home anyway, and nobody would find me.

I tried to remember happy times, like learning to jitterbug in our socks so we slid around her dining room floor, and teasing her for the way she emphasized the *T* instead of the *V* in *TV*, or for the way she tried to laugh without letting her braces show for all of seventh grade. Hattie sang with me as I drove, seated beside me. Her voice cracked, which made her laugh. I loved every awful note. "Padiddle!" she said when a one-eyed pickup came toward us, and whopped my shoulder, and I laughed and cried all at once. Then she was gone.

* * *

Near the New York border, my phone vibrated on the passenger seat. Scott was calling from Colgate. I listened to the voicemail over the car speakers. He filled the air around me.

"Hey, I hope you're okay. Mom appointed me to find out if you're going to start school on time. She thinks it will help your recovery. Come visit me. Get your mind off things. Call me. Love you. Bye."

And all of a sudden I think I started suffocating. Like a mouse in a laundry basket full of clothes. I opened all the windows and pulled over. Black dots swirled in my eyes. I might be dying. Or having a seizure. I heard myself rasping and fumbled to recline the seat. I closed my eyes or fainted. Gib's distorted face floated across my eyelids. I squeezed them, making him vanish. But he kept coming back.

Please.

I heard rushing water and remembered I'd parked by a bridge. I listened to the chorus of splashes, sending Gib away.

Out of nowhere I remembered a long-ago day of kindergarten when I didn't hear Mrs. Nettles's recess whistle. Maybe I'd fallen asleep in the red plastic tunnel; I couldn't remember. But when I popped out onto the deserted playground, I realized I'd been forgotten. I panicked and ran to the classroom door. It was locked. I peered through the window at everyone circled up on the rug, singing to Mrs. Nettles's piano.

I cried, and finally the distractible kid, Christopher, tugged on Mrs. Nettles's skirt and pointed. Mrs. Nettles blanched and hurried to let me in. She hugged me on her lap, but it was too late. I knew not a single person noticed me missing. They went on without me.

Hattie was the first person who ever noticed me. She got other people to notice me, too. Her death ripped away layers and layers of me that she helped build. I was raw and alone. Everyone else would go on; they'd forget. And forget me.

I lay still in the reclined seat, fighting the panic, for a long time. A bird trilled near the car window, and suddenly I could breathe. I opened my eyes. I could see.

I discovered I'd parked beside a picturesque stone bridge over a wide stream. It seemed not by accident. I got out, allowing my muscles to unfold, and stood at the bridge railing. The water rushed over rocks on the streambed, swirling at the edges, pulling in leaves and twigs, on an urgent, relentless journey somewhere while I stood perfectly still. I wasn't sure why it seemed tragic.

A pair of chickadees swooped over my shoulder, landing on an overhanging branch. For reasons I didn't have the energy to fathom, I peeled off my hideous hostess loafers. I took two steps back from the railing and heaved them, one after another, as hard as I could, startling the chickadees into flight. The loafers arced overhead in a clumsy spiral and plunked into the current. One. Two. I leaned on the metal bar, my shoulder muscles tingling from the sudden exertion, and watched them hurry off without me. I stayed like that until they disappeared around a bend. I think that was the old me leaving once and for all.

Barefoot, I got into the Fiesta. I was ready to go home.

At twilight, I was back in familiar Scofield territory. I heard a bunch of texts come in and I left them unanswered. Hammy called. My shift would be over by now, so I put it on speaker. "What did Charlie say?" I asked, my voice thin. I was so afraid to know Gib didn't have an alibi and I was so afraid he did.

"He doesn't remember Gib *not* being at the dinner . . ." My heart kicked up a notch. "But he *does* remember Coach Lewis took a team picture. So, I emailed Lewis and asked him to send it to me. He gets back to players pretty fast."

I was silent.

"Heads up," he said. "Your mom invited me and Emma Rose to dinner tonight."

I squished up my face. "She did?"

"She's worried about you," he said.

"Um-hmm," I said bitterly. *She's not used to having to worry about me*, I thought.

"Especially when you're alone," he added.

"Jesus! And what does she think I'm going to do?" But secretly I remembered almost swerving into a tree after work the other night. Maybe she paid closer attention to me than I thought. "Frigging Uncle Baxter!"

"Who's Uncle Baxter?"

I turned onto our road and into our driveway. Hammy leaned against his Subaru near our garage. He waved. The sweetness of it made me smile.

"You're already here?" I said, glad I didn't have to explain. Emma Rose got out of his car.

I smelled the grill as soon as I got out. "BBQ and everything," I said.

"Where are your shoes?" Emma Rose said with a quick hug.

I shrugged. She looked me over.

"Did you change out of your uniform? Or skip work?" she asked.

I put my finger to my lips. She and Hammy exchanged glances.

"Did Ben call?" I asked her quietly, swinging the gate open.

She shook her head apologetically. I wasn't surprised.

We made our way to the backyard. My dad sat at the patio table, newspaper open, cocktail in hand. "There she is," he said, rising to kiss me. "I made kabobs. Your favorite," he said into my hair. I let my cheek rest on his chest and fought the urge curl myself into his arms like a puppy. He went inside and Emma Rose followed, eager to be helpful.

I retrieved Hattie's phone from my bag. "Did Emma

Rose show you the driveway pictures?" I whispered, holding a picture toward Hammy. He nodded without looking. "He *was* on The Thimble August twenty-sixth," I said.

"I know you think I'm full of shit," he said quietly. "But we were in the Woods' kitchen, talking about the freshman players."

Emma Rose returned with seltzers for us, seating herself.

"I'm ready for the cops," I whispered.

"Wait till we see this team picture," Emma Rose said.

"You gotta wait," Hammy whispered. "It will devastate so many people. The Darrows, Gib and his family . . ."

"Stop protecting him, Hammy!" I hissed.

"Reid," he said evenly. He startled and grabbed his phone from his shorts. "Lewis! Finally!"

We scanned the photo, face by face. My hair prickled. Emma Rose clutched my hand.

"What the hell?" Hammy said. "Where is he?" He stretched the photo larger.

The black dots came back. The voices turned to mush. Gib wasn't in the picture. Gib really did something terrible on August twenty-sixth.

"I swear I saw him," Hammy said. "I swear."

Emma Rose looked nauseous. "Wait, let's think."

"Police," I said, unable to say more.

"No!" Hammy said. "I remember him there. I swear it on my mom's life."

Emma Rose stood. "Okay, maybe he just missed the picture. Could he be . . ." She waved a hand. "In the bathroom?"

Hammy stared at the table. "I'm calling Charlie." He walked to the roses. Emma Rose paced, not looking at me. I felt the earth tilt. I'd lost her, too. They were deserting me.

I floated above the patio, watching Spencer step outside with Boomer. Dad brought out a tray of raw kabobs. Spencer and Emma Rose's chatter sounded like squirrels. Spencer jiggled on his toes. Something tugged at me—pulled me back to earth.

His shirt wasn't red. His shorts weren't either. His shirt was green. The shorts were green plaid. He held his green dinosaur.

"Spencer!" I said, interrupting. Their eyes clapped on me. I fished through my bag. "Want this?"

He stopped moving, gazing at the green tube of lip balm in my hand. He beamed and snapped it up. I knew it! It was her sign to me. I'd figured it out. Green means go! Hattie was telling me I was right about Gib.

"He's on a green kick." Emma Rose and Hammy stared at me.

Turning in Gib Soule was my job. I wouldn't let anything stand in the way.

"I might have something green," Emma Rose said. While she searched her bag, I casually tucked Hattie's phone in my pocket and waited for my moment to escape.

* * *

Through the passing of kebabs, the pings of silverware on plates, and the MacGregory small talk, I was patient.

I excused myself when people were three-quarters deep in their meal. Boomer eyed me, suspicious. I gave him a stare and his ears twitched. He resettled at Spencer's feet.

In my bathroom, I flipped the light on, knowing they'd see it from the patio. I snatched Hattie's hoodie from my bedroom. Her scent was disappearing, but I didn't linger in sadness. I snaked through the shadows down to the family room, grabbed my bag from the chair—where I'd planted it on a trip in for napkins. I eased open the front door and slipped out.

Still barefoot, I scampered to the Fiesta, climbed in, and pulled the door until the latch clicked. I left the stick shift in neutral, released the hand brake, and held down the clutch. The car rolled backward, gaining speed. I slung my arm over the passenger seat and strained to see in the near darkness. Relying on muscle memory for timing, I turned the car onto the road. I started the engine, praying nobody noticed, and gunned it for the Scofield PD.

Two minutes into the ride, my mouth dried out. Hattie's phone poked my butt; I tossed it on the wadded hoodie next to me. My mom would worry. I eased my guilt knowing I couldn't have risked telling them. They would've stopped me.

"I'm fucking Sancho Panza."

A car like Gib's waited at a four-way stop, perpendicular to me. What if he knew I knew?

"Sancho Fucking Panza," I told myself, edging through the intersection. Did Gib sneak up on Hattie in her room? Did he look like a perversion of himself, purple and sweaty? Did he plow her over Pulpit Head like he plowed the sofa?

My palms were wet. For sure I'd been discovered missing by now. Hammy would know. They'd come after me. My heart thumped in the middle of my throat. Two stoplights until the police station.

At the first one, I pulled the hoodie on, assuming her power, tucking her phone in the pocket so I could demonstrate how I'd come to have it in the first place. My own phone vibrated in my bag. I shoved it aside.

I parked near the Scofield Police Department sign. My eyes darted over the cars on the road as I hopped across the blacktop. I winced, catching my toe on the steps.

The lobby was all marble and dark wood. A blocky Johnny Law perched behind the counter. He trained his eyes on me the minute I entered, noting the lack of shoes. We regarded each other for a moment without speaking. His eyes were such a pale green they were almost yellow. A bird of prey.

"You okay, miss?"

I nodded. Fluorescent lights buzzed. I tried to begin. "I—are you familiar—" Words caught in my throat like fat frogs.

He cocked his head, expressionless, assessing. They were fact-finding eyes. My heart pushed against my lungs. I stared at his badge and name tag. Detective Anthony D'Andrea.

My stinging bare feet wanted to run away—without me, like the loafers in the stream. I inhaled deeply. "Hattie Darrow?" These were the words I could say. I fished Hattie's phone out of the hoodie.

He looked away momentarily, surely rifling through the files in his mind. "Yes," he said heavily.

I woke up the phone. "I have—"

His bird eyes shot to the door behind me. Hammy and Emma Rose tumbled in.

"Reid, wait!" Hammy said.

I turned my back on them and tapped in Hattie's passcode. I bumbled it and the phone shook its screen at me.

Hammy put his hands on my shoulders. "Pardon us, Officer. Our friend is—she's not herself," he said with his best Scofield polish. "Reid," he said, spinning me toward him. "Come see what Charlie found." Emma Rose nodded at me. "Can you come outside?" Hammy said. His voice shook like I held a grenade. Which I kind of did.

"You *need* to, Reid," Emma Rose whispered. Her eyes reached a new level of glossy enormity. My stomach began to roil.

I turned to Detective D'Andrea. I didn't say anything, but he nodded, and I followed them. Outside, the cement pricked the soles of my feet. Hammy's car idled with the lights off, and next to it, so did my dad's. *Crap.*

Hammy showed me a photo of a thumb holding a greeting card. I couldn't read it.

"I forgot that, at the end of the party, the seniors signed welcome cards for the new freshman players," Hammy said. "Charlie asked a couple freshmen to text him photos of their cards. Look: Gib's signature *there.*" He switched to a new picture. "And there."

My eyelid twitched. *Gib Soule*, on both cards, in pathetic cursive.

"But he was in Maine," I said.

"He was in Maine that *day*," said Emma Rose. "At two forty-seven."

I blinked.

"He must have driven home right after those pictures at Hattie's, because he was at the party before it ended—just after ten. He had to have been in Scofield to sign these cards."

I shook my head.

"It's a six-hour drive. Two forty-seven," Hammy said, and counted on his fingers. "Three forty-seven, four forty-seven, five forty-seven, six forty-seven, seven forty-seven, eight forty-seven." Fingers wiggling. "Six hours. *That's* when I saw him in the Woods' kitchen," Hammy said. "He missed the team photo but made it to the party. I *knew* he was there . . ."

A small cry left my mouth. My skin, mind, and body came together for a second, and then my vertebrae melted into one another. I slumped against the side of Hammy's car. *She just plain died.* How could it be? Had I, all this time, made a lie out of Hattie? For my own selfish, needy purposes, had I made her into something she wasn't? Something nobody could be? So I could believe she saved me? Hattie was just a person, who was mortal and fallible. And human.

Emma Rose touched my arm, her hand warm and soft. "Really, this is good, right? Nobody was violent. It was an accident. Just like the newspapers said."

She just plain died, like anybody else.

At home, my mother folded my bed down, all fresh linens. She handed me a shopping bag. My face muscles were too tired to react. "I got you a present while you were at work today."

Work. An arrow of guilt struck my throat. Pushing tissue paper aside, I slid out a pair of pale blue summer pajamas. They had pink velvet trim and the fabric was light and soft. Confused, I looked at her.

"You need something pretty," she said, nodding toward the floor and the ratty shorts and tee I'd been lolling around in lately. She drew me into a hug. "I know you were just being a true friend to Hattie," she whispered into my hair. "I'm going to be a better mother to you, Reid. You deserve the best."

Her words, so unexpected, brought relief somehow. I nodded into her shoulder.

After she left, I began to undress. Before putting Hattie's hoodie into the laundry, I pressed it to my face and inhaled deeply. A hint of her remained, but it was only a matter of time.

I slipped into the blue pajamas, then let myself disappear into the tender and wordless sympathy of sleep.

NOW

September 5–6

I sat at the picture window in the living room, watching birds like I had the first few days after I got the news. I felt more myself than I did then, and I was unsure if that was good or bad. Any distractions from the truth evaporated at the police department. Hattie was gone. I wasn't. It hardened me and left me raw.

Dad brought me a lunch tray and handed me my phone. "There are a ton of messages for you on here, Reid," he said, kissing me on the cheek. "Maybe it's time to open yourself up a little."

He left and I watched a fir tree waving in the wind,

silenced by the glass of the windows.

Eventually, I ate the sandwich. Another hour passed before I touched the phone.

I'd avoided social media since it happened. My Instagram showed sixty-six notifications, roughly sixty-five more than usual. When I tapped the icon, I found fifty-five direct messages and eleven friend requests, dating from August twenty-eighth.

Emma Rose: Call if I can bring you a treat.

Alesha: Sending you hugs!

Charlie: Hang tough, Reid. She loved you.

Mimi: Thinking of you, Reid.

Matt Stedman: Peace.

Max: This completely fucking blows, Reid.

Your friends are here.

And on and on. Dozens of Scofield High kids having *me* on their minds. If they'd posted publicly, I could have dismissed all of it as an attempt to be part of the spectacle. That Hattie's death brought me any attention at all sickened me, but I found comfort in people caring.

Jasper texted me instead of using social media.

Jasper: Hope you are feeling okay today. Thought you'd like this.

I tapped the link, which led me to a series of cats-on-glass-top-tables photographs, taken from under the tables. I laughed out loud, and maybe, fleetingly, I heard Hattie laughing with me. I texted Jasper a heart.

My mother didn't ask what I'd decided about school tomorrow, the first day of my senior year. Instead, she artfully laid my backpack on my desk and watched me from the doorway as I brushed my teeth before bed.

"Maybe you want to call Ms. Beiderman tonight," she said.

I stopped scrubbing.

"For a little pep talk," she added.

"No fucking way," I said, knowing she wouldn't understand me with my mouth full of bubbles.

She got the gist. "Just a thought."

I'd barely slid into the sheets when Hattie's phone buzzed with a text. I jumped.

From: 877655

The automated refill for your prescription #453323670 is ready for pickup at your preferred RiteRex location 122 Route 1, Scofield, Connecticut. This is your second reminder. Please contact your RiteRex pharmacist if this message is in error.

I remembered Emma Rose's words. *You don't get refills for an antibiotic.* "Ughh," I growled. "It. Doesn't. Matter. Reid." I shut the phone down and tried to read a book.

Tap tap tap.

The sound tugged at the edge of my dream.

Tap tap tap.

My eyes shot open. My back was to the window.

"*Reid, it's me. Open up.*"

I held my breath.

Tap tap tap.

"*Wake up, Reddi.*"

I couldn't turn.

"*I need to tell you something.*"

My skin prickled.

Tap tap tap.

Her voice sounded farther away.

"*Okay, meet me at Pulpit Head, Reid. I have to stop at the pharmacy, but I'll be there soon. Do not wimp out!*"

I was tangled in my bedding. I thrashed free and rolled to the window. She wasn't there. I opened my eyes again, and I lay in my bed, sweating—the light on and my book collapsed on my chest. My eyes darted to all corners of the room.

I couldn't turn out the light. Instead, I pulled my pillow over my eyes and tried to empty my head.

I woke to my mom at the foot of my bed, patting my legs. "First day of school, Reid."

I didn't respond.

"You got this," she said.

I definitely did not have this.

"Routines are good, Reid. They keep you moving."

I thought about asking her what was routine about

going to school without picking up Hattie first, without walking in with her, but didn't have the energy.

Finally, she reverse sighed and left. I kind of wanted her to stay and keep telling me I could do it. But more, I wanted her not to.

I rolled toward the pear tree window and blinked at the light twisting through the tangled branches. Hattie sat there, in shadow with the sun at her back, watching me through the screen, all Cheshire Cat. The familiar pulse of my headache started up.

You don't get a refill on antibiotics.

"It's not an antibiotic," I said to Hattie.

She swung her foot back and forth in a slow rhythm, the way a cat swings its tail: gracefully and inattentively. Her flip-flop barely hung on to her toe. "Nope, not an antibiotic," she said patiently, like she was coaching me in a game of Twenty Questions.

I stared at her metronomic flip-flop, a swirl of anxiety in my throat. "What the hell is it, then?"

She was gone.

Over breakfast, which I didn't actually eat, the angry thrum in my head drowned out my parents' conversation. Mom flitted about the kitchen like a happy bee, soaking in the normalcy. I moved my spoon around the milk and wondered: How much of our lives is plain bullshit? I pushed my Cheerio under the milk with my spoon, then had a compulsion to save it.

* * *

I did not go to school. Obviously. I faked it convincingly enough, though.

Really, I drove straight to RiteRex, repeating Hattie's date of birth over and over the whole way so I didn't say mine by mistake.

As I idled in the drive-through line, my eyes rested on the car in front of me. A Jaguar. I thought back to the one I saw in traffic August twenty-seventh. I caught eyes with the driver through her rearview mirror. Gray puffy bangs! It was Jaguar Lady! She began to look away and then lowered her eyebrows. I could practically hear her trying to place me. She broke our stare when the pharmacist greeted her over the microphone. Chipper conversation ensued. The drawer opened and closed, thank-yous, and Jaguar Lady drove off.

I rolled up to the window. The pharmacist's name tag said "Sally." Sally looked mid-forty-ish and not in love with her job.

"Name?"

"Harriet Darrow."

"Just a moment." No chirpy patter for me.

She turned to the racks of bags, rifling through a bunch in the *D* section.

I chewed my thumb. I'd picked up plenty of medications for Spencer at Greenway's Pharmacy, but what if RiteRex made you show ID? Or if it came up that Hattie was deceased on Sally's computer?

"Date of birth?" She barely looked at me, her hands hovered over her keyboard.

I rattled it off like I lied for a living.

She tapped. Receipts spewed from the computer.

"That's fifteen dollars," said Sally.

The drawer opened and I dropped in a twenty. The drawer retracted like a mouth swallowing a pill. It stuck its tongue back out at me. A mini clipboard with a pen attached. Oh God, I forgot I'd have to sign. Should I forge? No, it had to be a worse offense to forge a dead person's name than to sign my own. I scribbled as messily as I could without risking some other issue and shoved the clipboard back in the mouth. It swallowed, then spat out the white bag.

"Have a nice day," Sally said, not very convincingly.

"Thanks." I rolled away from the window casually, then gunned it out of the lot in case Sally realized her mistake and came after me. I drove a couple blocks and pulled off on a shady street.

The bag crinkled as I fished out an orange plastic vial. I expected one of those blister packs, but I was no expert on birth control. I scanned the label. *Lamotrigine.* Three refills remaining. Prescribed July of last year. "Were you sleeping with someone a *year ago*?" I asked the air. Dr. Sulyman, Gretchen. *Do not take this product if you are pregnant or plan to become pregnant.* "Duh," I muttered. *Contact your prescribing doctor immediately if you experience suicidal thinking.* I'd never heard of that side effect to the pill. I opened the bottle and looked at the contents. Little yellow hexagons. I pulled reams of informational literature from the bag.

Lamotrigine is used as an anticonvulsant to treat seizure disorder or epilepsy, and as a mood stabilizer to treat bipolar and mood disorders.

Seizure disorder? Bipolar? I held the bottle up in the light, as if that would help me figure out what the hell was going on. I reread the warning. Not a word about birth control. *Consumption of alcohol while taking lamotrigine can result in increased drowsiness. Do not stop taking lamotrigine without consulting with your doctor.*

The tiny fear I'd hammered into a thin piece of nothing at the kitchen table with my mom on the twenty-seventh grabbed both my lungs and pulled like hell. I rolled down all the windows in the car, then dropped my forehead to the steering wheel and let my hair fall like a canopy around my face.

Inhale.

Exhale.

Who could I talk to who would know the truth?

Inhale.

Exhale.

I stared absently at a Lycra-clad woman pushing a toddler in a stroller. She eyed me suspiciously. Me: clearly a teen, clearly not in school, clearly looking like I'd been struck by lightning.

I broke our gaze. The dashboard clock read 8:35. By

now, Beiderman had been alerted to my absence. Soon she'd call Mom. I fumbled to turn on the engine, like that would help. The transmission screeched, metal against metal. I'd never turned the car off. The lady jumped. She bent to comfort her baby. I drove, hands shaky, praying she didn't use that phone to report me.

Inhale. Exhale.

I pulled onto the Post Road and kept driving, rifling through names of who to call, besides a Darrow.

"Try Santi," Hattie said from somewhere above the car. It probably wasn't Hattie, I told myself, but Santi might know.

I didn't have Santi's number, so at the Pickle Barrel stoplight, I instructed Hattie's phone to call Santi, and set it to speaker.

"Calling Santi," Siri responded. I'd drifted across the yellow line. I yanked the wheel back, turned into the Presbyterian church parking lot—our church on Christmas and Easter—and made my way to a far corner, away from preschoolers on the playground.

"Hello?" He sounded cautious.

My voice stuck for a moment. "Santi?" I managed.

"Who is this?" he demanded. I realized his caller ID would have shown Hattie's number.

"Shit! Santi, it's me. Reid. Hattie's Reid."

I waited.

"Why do you have Hattie's phone?"

"I . . . it . . . It's a long story. I'm sorry if I scared you."

"You did."

I wiped my palms on my jeans. "Sorry."

He exhaled in drawn-out fashion. I tried to formulate my question.

"How are you doing?" he asked. It startled me.

"Okay," I said. Lying. "Sort of okay." Still lying. "Actually, like shit."

"Me too."

"Are you at school?" I asked, watching two preschoolers chase each other down a red plastic slide.

"I'm supposed to go the tenth."

"Supposed to?"

"Yep."

He didn't say anything else, so I said, "I'm *supposed to* be at school right now." God, it felt great to say this.

"Yeah, I can't deal with *that* bullshit."

He sounded like Hattie.

"My parents keep saying, 'Routines are good. Eventually you'll be okay.'"

"Yup."

"I need the world to stop," I said.

Quiet.

I thought about asking if he ever heard her or saw her, but it sounded flipping insane even to me.

"Listen, Santi. Can I ask you some things? About Hattie?"

"Ye-ah." He stretched it into two syllables. "Like what? I was in Alaska when it happened, Reid." Why did he sound defensive?

I ventured on. "Hattie's phone got this text reminder to pick up her prescription at RiteRex and I was curious. It made me, I don't know, sad, to think of this prescription sitting in the pharmacy, waiting for pickup." I couldn't think how to ask the next part.

He said, "And?"

"Did Hattie have"—a preschooler pushed her friend down the slide—"seizures?"

"No." Definitive.

I waited for him to say more, but he didn't. "Right," I said. "I mean, I would know that, obviously." I chewed my thumbnail. "So, the prescription says it's for seizures or to treat bipolar disorder, but she didn't have those things . . ." My voice trailed off. I rubbed the top of my chest. It hurt.

He still didn't speak, but I heard muffled noises. Finally: "Fuck," he whispered.

I closed my eyes. Inhale. Exhale. "What?" I said, hardly loud enough to hear it myself.

"Do you know how she died?"

"She drowned." I heard my blood slowing its path through my veins. Ink leaked over the trees and the pavement and the playground and the children.

He moaned quietly. "She died by suicide, Reid. She

jumped off Pulpit Head in the fog." He took a breath. "Riptides."

A whimper spilled into the air around me. Uncle Baxter had told the truth. The pieces didn't make sense from the beginning, but I buried it all.

"I'm . . ." He stopped. "I'm sorry you didn't know. Jesus. I thought they'd tell you, at least."

They did, I wanted to explain, but my tears were like bats fleeing the cave.

"It turns out," he said. I heard thickness in his throat. "It turns out," he repeated, "that she had big ups and big downs. Big manic episodes and big bouts of depression. Her bouts—" He stopped again. "She had them for at least two years, when I guess she'd barely leave her room for days on end. She was diagnosed with bipolar two. It's milder than bipolar one."

"What bouts?" I was on a thirty-second delay.

"Are you alone right now?"

"Bouts?" The word was repulsive in my mouth, like a dead spider. I leaned and spat out the window.

"You shouldn't be hearing this over the phone. She didn't tell me either. But our mothers—"

"*What fucking bouts?*" I demanded. Now I was up, out of the car, storming around the hood, yelling at the phone. "What the hell are you talking about?"

"Do you want to meet?"

"No, I don't want to meet." I gritted my teeth. "I want

you to tell me what the hell the goddamn motherfucking *bouts* are!"

"How about FaceTime? Or I could be in Scofield in a few hours."

"TELL ME!"

Two preschool teachers eyed me. One of them let herself out of the penned yard and took a few steps toward my end of the parking lot. "Can we help you?" she called.

I threw the phone onto the passenger seat through the window, turned toward the teacher, and flipped her off with both hands. *Fuck you and your stupid fucking swing set bullshit*, I wanted to scream.

She took a step back, hand to her chest, and for a second I thought maybe I did say it out loud. The other one blew a whistle and all the kids ran to her. I got back in my car.

"Goddammit!" I growled, slamming the door behind me. "Is there no place in this stupid-ass town where a person can just *be*?" I put it in reverse and got myself back on the Post Road. A cop perched by the elementary school driveway.

"Of course, Johnny Fucking Law!"

"Reid?" Santi's voice came through the Bluetooth. "Take it easy. Seriously. Are you driving?"

"Yes!"

"You need to stop driving. Give yourself a minute."

He was right. "Sorry," I said. I whacked the steering wheel. "I'm so—"

I couldn't finish my sentence. "Are you sure it's not a mistake?" My voice quavered.

"I'm sure. Someone should have told you," Santi said.

"They did. I didn't believe it."

"Shit. I should have told you. I'm so sorry, Reid."

My voice broke and I coughed back two quick sobs. "She did it *on purpose*? How do they know that?"

"Can you go home? I really don't want to have this conversation while you're behind the wheel."

I most definitely could not go home. I wouldn't have thought he was the patient sort, but his voice was calm and warm. "I'll—I'll call you back."

When the call disconnected, I started to shiver—like I'd been left in a meat locker. My hands, my legs, my teeth, all trembled in a macabre dance. I guess it was shock. Because my task at that point became simply keeping the car on the road in spite of my shaking. I picked my destination, and I just kept driving.

THREE YEARS AGO

July ~ The Thimble

"See that stripe of purple out there?" Hattie asked.

We lounged in folding beach chairs we'd carried to the grassy part of Pulpit Head. The sky was the kind of blue that reminds you we are, indeed, on a planet floating in a galaxy. If I cupped my hands around my eyes, it looked like the grass dropped off the edge of the world. But stands of pointed firs curved on either side of us and, closer by, rocks baked in the sun. I knew, from my previous jumping experiences, the grass dropped off to the ocean. Or at low tide, the rocks.

"No, but do you see those seagulls?" I said. "How do they stay in the same place like that?" A group of three white gulls hung suspended above the rocks, wings outstretched. "Shouldn't they glide somewhere when they do that?" One of them dipped a wing and disappeared over the cliff.

"I don't know. This is much cooler. Look at that stripe, out on the horizon. Do you see it?"

I squinted. A thin, purply-pink ribbon rested on the top of the water's navy-blue horizon line, beyond Shelf Island and its lighthouse. "What is it?"

"Fog bank. The big ones are unreal." She leaned forward in her chair, studying it. "I hope it's a big one."

"What's a fog bank?"

"It's what it sounds like: a bank of fog. A wall of fog. A *tsunami* of fog."

"That sounds not so great to me." Another seagull tilted slightly right, disappearing below the grassy gangplank of Pulpit Head.

"Please" was all she said, without looking at me. "I give it twenty minutes tops until we can't see those trees. Or the house."

"What?" I scoffed. "It's a perfectly clear day."

"Twenty minutes. Nineteen now." Hattie settled back with a smug grin.

I distracted myself with my magazine, stealing glances every few minutes. The purple ribbon grew taller and less crisp each time I checked—ragged at the top. A shiver of fear spread over me, as if it were an approaching sandstorm and we were in the desert, soon to be suffocated—a scene I'd seen in some blockbuster movie. "Should we go inside?"

"No way! A good fog bank is mystical. Look."

She nodded to our left, where bits of cloud rolled over the tops of fir trees like phantom tumbleweeds.

Over the water, the horizon line had dissolved into the gray mist, which stretched high into the sky. But if I looked the opposite way, toward the house, the sky was still electric blue.

"For a couple of minutes, it's like two totally different days at the same time," Hattie said, standing. She closed her eyes and faced the ocean, arms outstretched, until the fog slipped over us, blotting out the sun. I couldn't see the water at all, and the landforms around us were dark masses. I grabbed my towel and pulled it over my shoulders as a cool film seeped into my skin. The house was gone—everything was draped in heavy gauze.

"This is crazy!" I laughed.

"See? It's a Maine thing—cold water and hot air or something," she said.

"I can totally imagine zombies coming out of the woods right now," I said.

"Nah," she said, her voice quiet. "It's mystical, like a space between reality and something else. Everything you see, everything you think you *know*, is suddenly nothing." She took a few steps toward the cliff. "It's like if you stepped off the ledge, you wouldn't fall, you'd step into . . . some netherworld."

I made my skeptical face, even though she wasn't looking at me. "Did you steal your brother's bong?"

"I'm serious. What if you could walk into a time portal right now?" she said. "Into the future. Into the past. Or into the afterlife or something."

She kept walking forward. Where did the ground stop? Earth and mist were one. "It's surreal," I said.

She looked down, past her feet, and I knew she had her toes curled over the edge of the cliff. "Could you back up?" I said. "You're going to fall, for shit's sake!"

She turned and sidled toward me, all mischief and grins. She grabbed my shoulders, looking into my eyes. "If I twirled you around right now, you would have no idea which way you were facing when I stopped."

"Ha ha," I said flatly. "I'd hear the waves." I plunked into my chair, though, in case she decided to try.

"No. Sound bounces around in the fog." She plopped down next to me. "*You'd* end up in some other world." She drummed her fingers on the arm of her lawn chair. "Hmm. Where would Reid go? I'm seeing you in ancient Egypt."

"What? No way. I'd get sunburned."

"Okay, okay . . . I know! You'd be in Scotland, on the moors. Hanging out with some bearded dude in a kilt. Like that character in *Brave*."

We cracked up because of the resemblance we'd discovered long ago. "I'd need to learn to play the penny whistle," I said.

"And become a master archer," Hattie replied.

"And the kilt dude would definitely be hot," I said.

"Naturally," she said. "A Dude of Dudes."

"His name would be Angus. Or Hamish."

"Wow, you've clearly thought about this before now," she said.

"I'm going with Hamish."

We laughed, and I started humming the tune to "Touch the Sky," the only song from *Brave* I could think of. Hattie joined in, warbling. When we finished, she sighed in that happy way she always did after a good laugh.

I closed my eyes and leaned back in the chair, letting the mist roll over me. For a while I imagined the Netherworld Reid with Hamish, galloping on our Clydesdales over the moody moors, hunting ermine and elk and villainous British lords. This made me laugh out loud and I opened my eyes so I could tell her. Her chair was empty.

She sat on the rocks, leaning back on her hands, knees drawn up, a zigzag of a girl staring over the cliff. The fog had thinned in uneven patches, and parts of the water were invisible while others glittered with sunshine. Shelf Island remained shrouded. The top of the lighthouse appeared to float on clouds. I understood how the magic of this island so captivated Hattie. With its ancient, craggy cliffs and pounding surf, its huge night skies sheathed in stars, this place would always be bigger than her, and she loved it.

"Hey," I called to her. "You never said what your netherworld would be."

She looked over her shoulder at me, thinking. "I don't know," she said finally, turning toward the sea. "I guess I want it to be something I haven't imagined yet."

What Hattie wanted, I realized with a sense of wonder, was the unknown.

PART THREE

September 6

I'd managed to keep the shaking under control enough to drive to the Darrows'. Rolling onto their quiet dead-end street, I passed the barn, the fields and apple trees. The house was dark and shut-up and sad. The horses didn't appear to be in the barn. I wondered where the family might be now, but also, I was scared to see them. I had no power over my own grief, and combining it with the only sadness bigger than my own—theirs—was unthinkable. The empty house emboldened me.

I inched past the Caldwells' house, also dark, and I saw the moonflower ghost, dancing a wide circle by the apple trees, braid over her shoulder. Or maybe I didn't. The road dead-ended after the Caldwells'. I pulled onto the grass, behind a wall of hedges, and parked under a weeping willow tree. Aside from one corner of the roof, I'd done a pretty good job camouflaging an ugly blue car in broad daylight.

"Ninja in training," Hattie said.

"Don't talk to me," I replied. And I slunk to our place.

Popcorn clouds floated over me. I lay in tall prickly grass that poked through my shirt, on the cloud-watching hill that sloped into the Darrows' fields. The sun was behind me somewhere, and it heated the top of my head. I reminded myself to call Santi. In a minute.

Jumped. Didn't just drown. Jumped.

I wanted to deny it, but I was so tired of lies. Lies I'd told myself. Lies I'd told Hattie. And the lies she'd told me.

If you lined up a hundred kids I knew from Scofield High School, put them right up against the brick wall in the café courtyard, and asked me to order them from most likely to die by suicide to least likely, I'd have put Hattie absolutely last. As in, I'd stand her at the Pickle Barrel across town.

"You don't know depression," she said.

I turned my face to her voice, squinting as the sun came through the side of my glasses. She lay next to me, a silhouette in golden summer light.

"You're the strongest person I've ever known," I said.

She didn't move and for a flash I feared I was looking at her dead body. Then she stuck a long piece of grass in her mouth. "There's some pretty compelling evidence to the contrary, Reddi."

I shook my head. "You had to be. You're Don Quixote. I'm Sancho Panza."

"Look at that one," she said, pointing up to the sky. "It's a sperm."

I followed her finger, squinting.

"Don Quixote was nuts, you know," she said.

I turned to her again, but she was gone.

I stayed there for hours. The clouds migrated in a massive unquestioning herd to something just beyond the horizon. My tears were like that, rolling out of my eyes on their way somewhere. Every now and then I'd touch my cheek to check if they were still coming.

Questions rolled around my mind like stray marbles. Why hadn't she confided in me? How could I be so blind? Didn't she realize how many people loved her? Why wasn't I enough to make her want to stay?

The clouds looked like things. A horse galloping. A turtle stretching its neck. Hands almost touching. The spray of waves crashing over rocks. On approach, they're one thing. When they're closer, they're completely different. By the time they pass you by, they may look like nothing at all.

* * *

The sun dangled in front of me now. When the clouds threw me into shadow, I felt a chill I knew signaled sunburn. I flipped onto my stomach and put my hands behind my head. My mouth pressed against the grass and a little dirt touched my lips. An ant crawled along a dead blade of grass, sticking its feelers into the air when it reached the end.

The tiny sound of approaching feet crackled into my consciousness. I didn't look.

"Reid?"

I was not ready. I pressed my lips shut, grass between them.

"Reid!"

I wanted to refuse to answer. But I probably looked dead, so I moved an arm.

"Yeah?" I said eventually. It took effort from this position. My lungs pressed against the hard ground with every breath I took.

"You okay?"

The white rubberized toes of Converse sneakers stopped near my nose.

Hammy knelt down, lifting his sunglasses. "Hey," he said. "You okay?"

I shrugged as best I could.

He sat next to me. "People wondered where you went today."

I didn't respond.

"Your mom and dad, they wondered. And worried."

I could only see the side pocket of his Polo shorts, but I could tell he was jiggling his foot. "And Beiderman. Emma Rose. That kid Jasper."

I stayed quiet.

"And me. *I* wondered. *I* worried."

A pebble of guilt pelted me. My face twitched. I wasn't trying to be dramatic. Drama is a funny thing, though. When you're by yourself, lying facedown in the grass, drooling a little on yourself while you try to figure out how this horrible, horrible thing could have possibly happened, it isn't dramatic. But as soon as you add a witness, it becomes absurdly dramatic. I guess the audience makes the difference.

I rolled onto my back, wiping my cheek and plucking grass off my forearms.

"Your mom," he said haltingly as he texted, "was actually crying." His thumbs stopped moving and he waited. I heard a buzz. "She knows you're okay but would like you to call." He held his phone toward me. When I didn't respond, he texted something else. "I told her you'll call soon."

He examined the instep of his shoe. "I had to hack your Find My iPhone app to find you." His eyes flickered in my direction.

"You know my password?"

Now he turned toward me. "I guessed. It's the same as your Netflix account."

"Not bad, Watson."

He ignored that. "I get not telling your parents, but me?" Hammy said. "I could have told them not to worry without telling them where you were."

"I'm sorry. I . . . forgot. I meant to go to school late."

He exhaled. I realized, right then, how easily Hattie could have forgotten how much people loved her and needed her. I remembered I needed to call Santi back, too.

I sat up. Hammy watched my face, and I let it crumple. I'd have to tell him. I buried myself in his shoulder.

"Okay," he whispered, wrapping me in his arms. "We'll be okay."

"Please be right," I said, wiping my face on my shoulder. He took my chin and turned me to him. His breath smelled like honey.

"I'm right," he said.

My tears stung my sunburn. He brushed them away with his thumb, and suddenly his eyes were so intense and blue and near. His face came closer and a powerful urge to lose myself in him overcame me.

I'm not sure who initiated the kiss, but his soft mouth felt so perfect I let myself dissolve. I closed my eyes and lay back on the prickly grass and he followed me, and we kissed and kissed. It seemed like forever. Doubt and worry floated around us, so I kissed him harder.

He moaned in such a delirious way that, *snap.* My eyes popped open. Hammy shot upright.

"Shit, Reid. I shouldn't have done that." He smoothed his shirt. "I—" His cheeks blazed.

"It's—I—" I stammered.

"That was not cool." His eyebrows bunched together in their caterpillar way. "My sister warned me."

"It's okay. Don't—"

His eyes looked deadly serious.

"What do you mean, your sister warned you?" I said.

He floundered. "I shouldn't have done that. When you're feeling so sad."

A little part of my stomach buckled. "It's okay. I, uh—" I swept my hair into a ponytail. I could have said, *I think I did it, not you.* "You made me forget for a minute."

He blinked and looked toward the apple trees.

"In a good way," I added. It felt strange to have no filter on my words, to think and speak at the same time. I noticed how light the words were leaving my mouth. And how two basically nice kids kissing in a field seemed so harmless compared to all the bad things that can happen.

His jaw muscles knotted and loosened. He wanted to change the subject, but he didn't know what was coming. I had to tell him that the real love of his life, the true object of his affection, took her own life. He deserved to know almost as much as me. He was trustworthy. When he knew, he was bound to realize the terrible fact that he wasn't enough to make Hattie want to stay, either.

And he would fall into the same dark hole as me.

I stood, pulling his hand. "Let's go," I said. Oddly, mobilizing for him allowed me to think more clearly than I had in days. He didn't protest, and we left the

Fiesta under the willow and drove his car toward town. "I'm hungry. Can we go to the Pickle Barrel?" I said, procrastinating.

"Sure. I could use some food." As he signaled to turn into the parking lot, I tried to imagine telling him, there, sitting at a cramped wooden table elbow to elbow with other sandwich eaters. What if he cried? It was too public.

"You know," I said. "Come to think of it, I feel like going to the beach first."

He gave me a look, but kept driving. His tolerance was so endearing it hurt me to think about. Then, as we approached St. Paul's, where the Darrows held Hattie's funeral, I blurted, "Turn here!"

"Into the church?"

"Yes." I am not a religious person and I was pretty sure he wasn't either. But this was the place.

He pulled into the same spot we'd had the day of the funeral and turned off the car. He cocked his head. "What are we doing?"

I tried to remember Santi's words. "Let's get out," I said, opening my door. He followed me to the bench in the courtyard, dotted with well-tended hydrangea trees. Their puffy, periwinkle-blue flowers struck me as so beautiful, and I suddenly knew this place was designed to bring comfort in moments of intense pain.

We sat. "I feel like we're ninety," Hammy said. "All we need are ducks to feed."

His eyes met mine. My heart thumped mercilessly

against my ribs. With a bone-deep certainty I'd never felt before, I knew I was the right person to tell Hammy, even as I dreaded it. "I have to tell you something," I said. "It's really horrible."

"What?" He drew back the slightest bit, fear clouding his face.

I drew a slow breath.

"*What?*" he said sharply.

"It was suicide," I said. The words were precise and I watched them hit him like sniper bullets.

He blinked, and I thought he might argue it, as I had, but then he began to absorb the shots and looked away. I could see he was searching his memory, seeing her and trying to make the information stick to the buoyant, irrepressible girl we loved.

When his eyes returned to mine, I started from the beginning, from the prescription to my conversation with Santi. I said it all while staring at my hands folded on my lap, which I hoped gave him privacy. Really, I was afraid to see him cry. He stood and walked in an aimless way for quite some time. The sun was lowering, and it was getting buggy in the shady garden. I went and touched his arm.

"So the rumors were right," he said.

I shrugged. "I guess they were."

"How could we be the last ones to believe it?"

Goose bumps rose on my sunburned arms and I tried to smooth them. "I don't know. Maybe," I offered, "we were so close to her, we just couldn't see."

He shook his head, still lost in his memories.

"The Darrows want it kept private." I waited, but I didn't think he heard me. I was left wondering what the hell good it did to keep her suicide secret. That choice might not be up to me. But I knew better than the Darrows which friends deserved to know. Hammy did.

He squeezed his eyes like he was punishing them. "Why would she do that?"

"I don't know." This fact embarrassed me.

"Why wouldn't she let us help her?"

I hugged him and he finally cried. The sound of it tore my soul into tiny gray pieces. A fuzzy, malformed anger at Hattie rose in me. *Look what you're doing to people!* I held him tightly, cheek on his shoulder.

"I would have helped her," he said.

"I know." My tears had finally, finally dried up. "Me too."

Eventually, I drove us back to my car, under the willow.

Hammy didn't move.

"You all right?"

He stared at the hedges. "This is the most effed-up day of my life."

"Yep." His eyes held mine and I remembered our kiss. I looked away.

"I think I should tell Gib," he said.

Guilt rolled through my chest. I thought of the

picture in Hattie's Thimble bedroom again, and of his adoring gaze on her. "Of course. Gib should know."

"I think it might help me to tell him, in a weird way."

I nodded, knowing just what he meant.

"Are you going to be okay tonight?" he asked. "Because I can stay with you . . ." I heard fear in his voice.

"I'll be okay." I shook my head. "That's a lie. I'll be the opposite of okay, but I'm . . ." I didn't know how to finish. "What about you?"

He shrugged. "Maybe we check in?"

I nodded. "That's good." I started to open my car door when he reached for my arm.

"Reid," he said, choked up again. "Let's be there for each other."

I felt the familiar heat sweep my face, all the behind-the-scenes machinations of my body bringing tears to my eyes. *I'm alive*, I thought. *It's so obvious I don't even notice.* And seeing a tear roll down his cheek, I thought, *We're both alive.* I squeezed Hammy's warm hand. "That's the best idea I've heard in a really long time," I said.

As I drove home, I wondered why being strong for someone else is easier than being strong for yourself. Maybe Hattie had been trying to be strong all by herself, and it was just more than she could do. "I could have been strong for you, Hattie," I said, my voice heavy in my throat.

Her answer startled me. "You already were," she said.

* * *

Hammy spared me from having to tell my parents I'd finally come to understand the truth. I was so relieved I didn't have to say it myself. I felt stupid and so, so sad.

Mom stood by the door as I came in, her eyes spooked, her hair messy. "I love you so much," she said in a choked whisper, over and over, hugging me. Her rawness frightened me, but I clung to her, and I felt something between us, something deep and sleeping and ineffable, latch together.

Mom let go and Dad took over. "You're brave" was all he said, quietly, into the top of my head. "So brave."

They'd gotten the chicken pho I love from the Vietnamese place in town, and I brought a bowl up to my room. I plugged in the two phones, setting them side by side on the dresser, and dropped onto my bed. Mom had made it up neatly, in her never-ending quest for the perfect household. She only wanted everything to be all right, and that didn't seem like such a bad thing today.

While I ate, I thought about how wrong I'd been about Gib. I felt foolish for even thinking it now. Still, I wanted to know about his August visit to The Thimble. The thought of asking him exhausted me. Step one: make peace with him in my own mind. I didn't have the energy to send all those photos to my phone and then send them to Gib, so I picked up Hattie's phone and wrote him a text, quickly identifying myself so I didn't scare him.

I'll be sending this phone back to the Darrows and I thought you'd want these pictures of you and Hattie. xo I forwarded all the pictures except for those last two, which my gut told me would upset him. I had barely set the phone down when it rang. I jumped. I expected Gib.

"You didn't call me back," Santi said.

"Oh. I'm sorry."

"It's okay. I wanted to make sure that you're . . ."

"Home?" I offered.

"Yeah." He paused. "And okay."

"I'm not okay," I said. "But I'm here."

"That's actually key, I've discovered," he said.

I propped myself on my pillows. "I have a lot of questions."

"Such as . . ." he said.

I looked out at the pear tree. I'm not sure why, but I drew the shade. "For one thing," I said, "why don't the Darrows want anyone to know?"

"Two theories," he said right away. "Either they can't face it themselves, or they think they're protecting her privacy. She obviously wanted it a secret."

I rubbed my temples, feeling another headache. A thought struck me. "Maybe they don't feel like they owe anyone an explanation."

"They don't. It's hard enough for them," he said.

"Yes," I said. "Was there a note?"

"No. But she knew what she was doing out there. She'd been having a hard time for a while. She barely left her room for almost three weeks in August."

He was describing a person I'd never met. "And they left her alone?" The words barely squeezed through my throat. I didn't want to blame anyone. But it didn't make sense.

"I asked that, too. Apparently, she got out and went sailing with Mr. Darrow two days before," Santi said. "I don't know much more. But it sounds like they thought she was improving. Hattie can be convincing as hell."

I made a tortured grunt in agreement. "I can't imagine a worse mistake," I whispered. "To have to live with it . . ." My chest throbbed. I closed my eyes.

I remembered thinking she was extra animated when I visited. The wildness in her eyes when we "summoned" Ponytail with the Ouija board. Our doomed sail to Shelf Island. I said, "Do you think she was manic when we sailed into the fog bank?"

There was a sound like he switched ears. "I wondered the same thing. She didn't like the way she felt on her medication, according to my mother. But it kept her from big mood highs. And lows. I read up on bipolar. It seems like people can love their highs and miss them when they're on the meds."

"I would have made her stay on her medication," I said. Like I could have.

"She didn't do it to piss anyone off. You know that, right?"

My eyes misted.

"She was sick, Reid," he said.

Of course Santi was right. Hattie was sick. A couple of hot tears rolled down my skin, which felt about five hundred degrees from the sunburn. I sniffed. "I'm so tired." I pressed my cheek into the cool pillowcase.

"I know."

We stayed quiet.

"Hey, Reid." My eyes popped open. "We should meet," he said. "On The Thimble. We can stay at my house."

I cocked my head. "What?"

"That funeral was bullshit," he said. "Wasn't it?"

"It *was* bullshit!" I said. "It was so un-Hattie."

"We need our own memorial. On The Thimble. No bullshit. We'll be in this weird limbo forever if we don't do something real."

My mind stumbled around. She loved that place. "When?" I asked.

"Tomorrow's Friday," he said. "We can go for the weekend."

"Tomorrow," I said. A school day. I calculated the drive. "I can be there by the afternoon." I thought. "Can I bring a couple friends?"

September 7

“You made out with Hammy.”

She woke me. Bluish light crept around the window shade. The clock read 2:47. If she was in the pear tree, I didn’t want to see her.

“You kinda went at it, actually,” she added.

“You watched?” I said. “Creeper.”

“You were in my yard,” she said defensively. “Anyway, that’s not the point.”

I tried to ignore her and go back to sleep.

“The Sandwich likes you,” she said. I reopened my eyes.

I growled. "Hammy loves *you*. *We* are just emotionally *fucked up* right now, thank *you* very much." That felt mean and true and devastating. I didn't stop. "He always loved you," I said. "You knew he loved you, too. You let him love you without ever loving him back."

"I loved him as a friend. And let's focus here. *You made out with Sam Stanwich. Yesterday.* Let it be about you for once, Reid. Jeez."

"About me? About me. Ha. That's a good one, coming from you." My face tingled. "My whole life is built around being in your shadow."

Silence.

I waited. She was gone.

"Perfect," I said.

I punched down my pillow. My skin tingled hot against it. I was mad at her. Hattie and I didn't fight in real life. Maybe not even once.

I texted Hammy.

Come with me to meet Santi on The Thimble tomorrow. We'll have a memorial for her. A real one.

No response. He was undoubtedly asleep, like a normal person. I pictured him, the color high on his cheeks, the bushy brows, the way one tooth crossed the tiniest bit over the other. The hair that pointed in all directions at once like it was staging a revolution he himself wasn't quite ready to stage.

My phone buzzed, as if I'd conjured him.

Hammy: What time do we leave? I'll drive.

I smiled.

Me: I usually leave for school around 7:15. We have to be stealthy.

Hammy: I can do that. I think. I'm like James Bond.

Bubbles bounced as he composed another text.

Hammy: I went to Gib's and told him the truth.

My nose crinkled.

Me: Thank you. How is he?

Hammy: Like us. We should sleep so we're ready.

Me: Right. 😴

Hammy: Good night.

Of course, there were practical details to contend with. My parents. Hammy's parents. School administrators. What to pack and how to smuggle it out. Should we bring Gib? (Yes.) Emma Rose? (No; it's for Hattie, but we agreed to tell her the truth.) It was the easiest day for me to get up since I'd found out. I had purpose: to understand.

Hammy would pick me up at 7:25, as if we were going to school. I had about twenty minutes. I jetted around my room, packing my duffel. In the bathroom, gathering toiletries, I stopped to face myself in the mirror.

"You can be mad at me. But you're the one still here," Hattie said.

I flinched.

Her athletic grace, her comic timing, her long limbs and the face that had turned so beautiful. She was gone, and I was here, all fading sunburn and Oscar the Grouch–green eyes.

"Reid the Scottish warrior," she said. I couldn't bring myself to hum the *Brave* song. Hattie did it for me. Like so many other things, Hattie did it for me.

She warbled out the chorus when I heard talking downstairs. My mother's "company" voice—slightly louder and higher-pitched than normal. And, no, not Hammy . . . a woman. I knew the voice. Younger than a parent's. A little raspy. Serious yet somehow lacking gravity. Mom said something, and the reply traveled up to my bathroom. "I'm glad you called. I've been thinking about Reid nonstop."

"You've got to be kidding me," I said to the mirror.

Beiderman.

"Reid?" Mom called. "We have a breakfast guest. Come on down!"

Oh, Mom. Sneaky, sneaky Mom.

She knew better than to say to my face that she'd called the guidance counselor. I'd spent half of last night convincing my parents that, in spite of it all, I was fine enough and would go to school today.

Of course, I *would* go downstairs and greet her, and my mom knew I would, because to refuse would require a reality TV–level confrontation, which we all knew—including Beiderman—was not going to happen in the MacGregory household.

"Good morning, Reid! It's me, Ms. Beiderman!"

I dropped the f-bomb to myself in the mirror, my mind racing to think of a way to smuggle the duffel past them. The upside of having a distracted mother is being able to slip your damn secret-escape-for-the-weekend duffel bag past her. But she was acting decidedly undistracted of late.

"Almost ready!" I called, buying seconds.

I hurried into my room and pulled my school backpack from the closet and crammed everything from the duffel into it. I could barely zip it and it looked like I'd inflated it with helium. Beiderman would sniff that out in a heartbeat. I wriggled out of my shorts and swapped them for the jeans in the backpack. I replaced a thick sweatshirt with a binder from my desk to make it look like there were just books in there. I stood back and studied it with a keen eye for trouble. Satisfied, I hauled it onto my shoulder.

I quickly texted Hammy.

Help. Beiderman is in my house.

Not waiting for a reply, I shoved both phones into the backpack and marched downstairs, all business. I had no idea how I'd bluff my way through this, but I was not ready for a new school year. I needed to complete my quest: to understand. I tucked the backpack behind a chair by the front door.

My mother and Beiderman sat at ten and two o'clock around the kitchen table, which was set with place mats and featured a steaming bowl of oatmeal and a big fruit salad at the center. On a weekday morning. Mom's eyes cast my way and Beiderman pivoted toward me.

"Here she is," Mom said, her tone fit for a game of peekaboo.

I smiled primly.

Beiderman stood with her arms awkwardly open, like she might hug me. She second-guessed herself, wisely, and clasped her hands together. "Hi, Reid."

"What's going on?" I asked my mother, who was doing an awesome job of not looking at me.

"Ms. Beiderman thought it would be easier if you walked into the school *with* someone."

I raised my eyebrows.

"So you're not alone," she added quickly.

"As in . . ." I said.

"If you're with me," Beiderman offered, "you can head straight to your first-period class. Skip right over homeroom! Mr. Slowinski's fine with it."

"How big of him," I said.

"Reid," Mom said.

I shifted my weight. "Hammy's picking me up in ten minutes."

"Sam will understand," Mom said. "Ms. Beiderman can support you."

"I have someone, Mom."

She and Beiderman exchanged glances, then Mom pushed in her chair. "You two have breakfast. I need to wake Spencer."

She left the room and I could feel Beiderman's unsureness settle over us. While it would have been much cooler to deny this breakfast, I'd have to live off $47 of birthday money left in my silver piggy bank for the entire weekend. This was free.

I served myself and handed the spoon to Beiderman. The mechanics of this distracted from the awkwardness of our proximity. She smelled very clean and botanical, kind of like the beauty aisle at Whole Foods. Her silver ring with the sun stamped into it hung loose, revealing a tan line. I pictured her at the beach all summer, reading school counselor theory books in a floppy sun hat, her crazy curls escaping in the breeze. Or maybe she surfed. Or did hippie yoga on surfboards. I sipped my orange juice.

She took a breath like she had something to say. I stirred milk into my oatmeal to resist my etiquette-born reflex to look at her. I waited, but she only blew out a big puff of air.

After another minute of nothing but silverware tapping ceramics, she said, "Your mom told me."

My mom could have told her a whole lot of things, but I didn't ask for clarification. I examined a spoonful of berries clumped with mush.

"That it wasn't an accident," she added.

In spite of myself, her words stopped my muscles from moving. I wanted to be mad my mom told, but the secret felt so flimsy.

"I'm so sorry," she continued. She was trying hard to be a good counselor. Addressing divorcing parents, plagiarism, and pot smoking in locker rooms couldn't have prepared her for this. I forced another bite, repressing the urge to spray it all over the kitchen windows.

"It's especially shocking and harrowing for *you*," she said, reaching her hand toward mine. I let her touch me for a second before sliding my hand into my lap. "I have a friend from graduate school who works at the Suicide Prevention Center."

"It's a little late for that." I attempted to sound bitter, but I sounded anemic. I drank my juice like it contained my secret superpower.

"Yes, well," Beiderman said. "Her name is Grace Eliopolis and she would like to meet you."

"Oh, my God," I said, under my breath, but we were right next to each other. I sighed.

"This feels like a Hallmark Channel movie, all right? I don't want to talk to Grace Eliopolis. Hattie wasn't like other people. Hattie was different. We were different."

She put her hands out in front of her. "Of course, Reid. It's your call, totally. There's no rush. Your parents, they're just worried about you. Suicide loss survivors have a unique set of challenges."

I almost said, *Hello, Hattie didn't* survive *the suicide, you moron*, but then I realized she meant me. I was the survivor. Like Hattie told me upstairs. There was an actual name for it. *Suicide loss survivor*.

I focused on the raspberries popping in my mouth as I chewed. I needed to seem reasonably collected so she'd let me go with Hammy. I *would* go to The Thimble. Avoiding a Bonnie and Clyde escape scene would probably work in my favor, though.

I put down my spoon. "I need space," I said, which couldn't have been truer.

"That is *absolutely* understandable," she said, nodding and shaking her head in one spastic movement that telegraphed: *Yes! No! Whatever you say, Reid!* I felt my power returning.

Our eyes connected for the first time. She wanted to read my mind. I felt it. I had trouble breaking the gaze until Spencer's voice tumbled down the stairs. "All done getting dressed! Good job getting dressed! You are such a good boy!"

My eyelids fluttered. "He likes to congratulate himself," I said. She waved her hand while nod-shaking *and* making a dismissive sneezy sound. "How fantastic. We should all have that self-esteem." Clearly back in her comfort zone, she looked at my nearly empty bowl. "Shall we go?"

I checked the wall clock and glanced out the window to the driveway. "I think I'm going to stick with my plan of riding with Hammy—you know, Sam," I said.

She stared at me, so I carried my dishes in the sink.

"Maybe you should reconsider, for your mom . . ." Beiderman ventured. She probably didn't want to answer to my mom. I don't when I can avoid it.

"I feel like . . ." I stretched for words that would work. "I can do this if I go with Sam." Not exactly a lie.

"Sam's a good kid," she said, half to herself. "Friendships *are* healing," she added, preparing for my mother, obviously.

The rumpus of Spencer descending the stairs, followed closely by Mom, stole Beiderman's attention just as Hammy's Subaru appeared in the driveway. Spencer swirled into the kitchen, filling it instantly.

"Hi!" he exclaimed as I slipped into the family room and scooped up my backpack. "I am good how are you?"

"Hello, I'm very well, thank you," said Beiderman. "Are you Spencer?"

"Yes!"

"Easy, Spencer," Mom said, which I knew meant Spencer was invading Beiderman's bubble.

"Do not touch people!" Spencer said gleefully. God, I loved that kid right then. Maybe Hattie put him up to it.

"It's okay," said the counselor. "High five?"

I opened the door. "My ride's here," I said, volume low. "See you at school, Ms. Beiderman. Bye, Mom. Bye, Spence."

I shut the door and took off for the green Subaru. Hammy's eyes were wide, and I rolled mine. He looked away suddenly.

"*Reid!*" Mom's voice cut the air.

I winced, then faced her. We stood, ten paces apart,

a Wild West shoot-out in which Mom was the sheriff. She looked so tired in her perfectly pressed outfit with her neat hair. My heart clutched itself for her, it did. But I was the outlaw.

"Mom, it's okay. I need to do this."

I saw her chin tremble. She sniffed and straightened. "I love you, baby." She turned and went inside.

September 7, Continued

Hammy's Subaru rumbled in the Soules' driveway, humbly cushioning our silence. We watched the front door like we were on a stakeout. "He took it pretty hard," Hammy said after five minutes had passed.

"I don't know how you did it," I said. "Telling you took everything."

"Just keep moving," he said.

The door opened. Gib's mom hugged him, then his stepmom. He slunk to the car, no bright eyes, electric teeth, or easy stride. Gib was a watercolor version of himself.

I wondered suddenly if he wished—even for a moment—that he'd never played pool with Hattie that night at Sabrina Bradley's party. His life would forever be shaped by the suicide of a girl he'd only just started to fall in love with the summer of his junior year, someone who could easily have remained a school acquaintance if, for instance, he'd not been restlessly seeking distraction from his ex-girlfriend. If Gib did wish that, I would never hold it against him.

Without greeting us, he opened the hatchback and threw in his duffel. I contemplated whether or not to get out and hug him, but couldn't decide before he climbed into the back seat. It's possible his eyes were swollen. I didn't want to stare.

"Hey." He rubbed my shoulder and settled back, all six feet of him sprawled across the seat. I felt guilty anew for suspecting him. "Thanks for those pictures," he said. The bill of the cap curled down and all I could see was his chin.

"I'm glad you're coming," I said. I wanted to ask him so much, but I couldn't yet.

Hammy backed out of the drive and turned toward the parkway—the opposite direction of Scofield High School.

"What's the plan when they call us?" said Gib. "Because Beiderman's gonna freak."

"Do you think they'll come and get us?" I asked. I thought of my mom's face this morning. When

Beiderman called and said I didn't make it to homeroom, she'd send out a SWAT team. "Should we tell them where we are?"

"Let's wait until the last possible moment. The farther away we are, the less likely they'd follow," Gib said. At 8:05, Mr. Slowinski would log attendance. It was 7:41.

Hammy gunned it up the Merritt Parkway on-ramp, but as soon as we rounded a curve, he hit the brakes. A sea of cars packed the lanes.

"Crap," said Hammy. "Rush hour."

"What if we don't get out?" I said, biting my thumbnail.

"Oh, we'll get out," Hammy said. He revved the engine and nosed up on the next car, wedged us into the slow lane, then cut into the fast lane.

"Nicely done," said Gib.

"Not how I'd describe it," I said, one hand clenched around the door handle and the other on the center console.

"We just need to put fifteen miles behind us and we're golden," Hammy said.

"And not get arrested," I said.

"Seriously, how could they get to us in this traffic?" Gib said.

"Have you met my mom?" I asked.

Hammy continued the zigzagging hell ride, twice using the shoulder as a third lane.

My cell rang a little before eight fifteen. "Shit," I said,

wiping my hand on my jean shorts. "It's the school."

"You better answer it."

"We might be okay," Hammy said. "Ms. Beiderman can be cool."

I made a face like he was crazy and tapped the speaker button.

"Hello?" I said.

"Where are you, Reid?" Ms. Beiderman asked, un-chipper as hell.

"I—"

"We had an agreement," she said, interrupting.

"Sam Stanwich here, Ms. Beiderman. Don't blame Reid. It was my idea."

I glanced at Hammy. He wagged his eyebrows.

"What, exactly?" she said flatly. "What was your idea?"

"We're going to—"

Gib shoved Hammy's arm. We swerved a bit and I dropped the phone. I glared, scrambling to retrieve it.

"Massachusetts," Hammy said. "To Hattie's friend's." He sounded unsure, but Gib gave a thumbs-up.

"Where *are* you?"

Hammy winced. "New Haven." (Untrue; we were at least fifteen minutes from reaching New Haven.)

The sound of Beiderman blowing a big puff of air came through the phone; surely she was raking her fingers through her hair.

"Let me explain, Ms. Beiderman," I said.

"I can't wait," she said dryly.

"We need our own memorial service for Hattie." I looked at Gib. "At her friend's. Now that we know the truth, the funeral last week seems pretty meaningless."

"Uh-huh," she said, clearly unimpressed. "Do your parents know about this?"

"Not yet, but I'll tell them once we get there. Ms. Beiderman, I need to honor Hattie in my own way. So do Hammy and Gib." I sounded so fake, but it was actually true.

"Gibson Soule?" she said. "He's with you?" (Keyboard clacking.) "He is marked absent."

"Hey, Ms. B.," Gib said.

In the pause, we looked at each other.

"Okay, look," Beiderman said. "I can get in a lot of trouble for this, but here goes. You should have your memorial. It's a major step. I don't know why you have to go to Massachusetts to do it, but I'm going to take your word for it that it's important. I will explain this to Dr. Higgins and we can allow you the excused absence today. Not next Monday. Today, only."

Silent cheering around the Subaru.

"Provided, and I'm serious, people," she said, "provided your parents report your absence to the school in the next ten minutes. Gib, you're set, but Reid and Sam, YOU need to tell your parents yourselves. NOW. You're lucky Dr. Higgins didn't call the police."

We thanked her and hung up.

“Fuck yeah!” Gib said.

“I did not see that coming,” I said, smiling in a way I hadn’t in forever.

“I told you!” Hammy said. He pulled into a service station so we could make our calls. I dragged myself to a shady corner of the parking lot, pulled out my phone. Mom answered during the first ring. “Hi, Mom,” I said, and began. And Laura MacGregory actually listened.

Several hours later, Gib said, “I recognize this!” He pointed to the six-foot fiberglass ice cream cone in front of Carousel Dairy Barn, a landmark that normally served as my cue to get super excited for Thimble-ness. We’d lost dependable cell reception on and off for the last forty-five miles, so I served as the GPS.

“We went there,” Gib said.

“Carousel,” I said. “Hattie and I used to ride bikes there every day in middle school.”

The boys wanted to stop, so we waited in a short line on the barn porch, placing our orders through a screen, as if ice cream were the most serious business around. Once we all had our cones, Gib said, “To Hattie.” And we clinked them. His lip quivered and he turned away.

I leaned toward Hammy. “God, I feel like such a dumbass about him,” I whispered.

He tipped his head toward my ear. “You were just doing what you thought was right by Hattie,” he whispered.

I looked at him dubiously, but he raised his eyebrows and nodded. We let Gib be and got in the car, and after a moment, he joined us. "Okay, let's do it," he said. Hammy turned over the engine.

"Turn here," I said moments later, pointing to Montsweag Road. It led to the Thimble causeway. A vague nausea billowed through me. I considered pitching my ice cream out the window, but I'd toasted Hattie with it.

We rounded a bend near the brown house Hattie called the gingerbread cottage. Hearts and birds were carved into its woodwork, and she claimed the witch from Hansel and Gretel lived there. A little German woman, she told me. I always pedaled like hell past that house.

Then the causeway came into view, and behind it, The Thimble, rugged and green. Our tires left the pavement. *Thud-duh-dunt, thud-duh-dunt, thud-duh-dunt.* I remembered how I used to hear that sound as a circus drumroll. Today all I heard was a car rolling over wood.

The boys were quiet, hearing their own sounds and thinking their own thoughts. To me, the chop of the waves on either side of us made the water seem alive and hungry. I had to shake away the image of it swallowing Hattie, her blond hair fanned around her face like the glow of the moon. What if she changed her mind at the last second?

Hammy rolled down the windows, and the car filled with smells so linked to Hattie for me: briny seaweed;

balsam heated by the sun. Thimble air was cool and never still. The sensory memory of it squeezed my heart.

By then we'd made it to the gravel. It split around a towering stand of pines, and I directed Hammy left, toward the Herreras' side. Santi's house had a similar style as Hattie's—weathered shingles and green trim, a rambling jumble of triangular roofs, unexpected outcrops, and lots of windows. I counted three terraces on the second floor, none of which matched the other, and two fat stone chimneys. It was like Mr. Darrow and Mr. Herrera challenged each other to a friendly game of Draw Your Ideal House, and each kept adding to his design to outwit the other. I contrasted it to architecture at home, where houses clamored for symmetry and grandeur. These were much more interested in being clever than opulent.

I couldn't see the house as just a house anymore, and I realized part of me had always thought this place would be Hattie and Santi's someday.

We brought our bags to the front steps. The door stood ajar. Hammy knocked. We waited.

"Hello?" I called.

We glanced at each other. I shrugged and the others followed me into the dark, airy entryway. You could see to the back of the house, where the bright ocean view lit up like a movie screen. I picked up a note from a table and read aloud. "'We're at the Sandy Beach firepit.'"

"Know where that is?" Gib asked me. I nodded. We

bobbed along the path that sloped toward the beach. I ran my hands along the top of the seagrass on either side of me, inhaling the tangy air.

We spotted Santi and Mac in Adirondack chairs facing the water, an impressive fire blazing. The waves were noisy and foamy.

"I could scare the crap out of them right now," I said, a surge of Hattie coursing through me. Both boys responded with dismissive chuckles. "I think I will." I bounded ahead of them.

Creeping up on people is so satisfying. It must tap into some primal instinct we have. They rested beer bottles on the chair arms. I could tell Santi was talking by the tiny movements of his head. Mac sipped from his beer.

I jumped from the grassy dune onto the sand and sidled toward them. At two feet I yelled, "Boo!"

Santi sprang to his feet, spun toward me, and took off his Ray-Bans in one stealth maneuver, while Mac simply yelled, "What the hell!" and bounced from his seat like a cartoon mouse.

I doubled over and Hammy and Gib cracked up behind me. "Jesus," muttered Mac, picking up his Holderness baseball cap.

Santi grinned. "Nicely done, Reid." We hugged.

"Hattie wouldn't have been able to resist," I said, then inhaled deep, for strength. Since it would have been strange not to, I hugged Mac.

Gib and Hammy approached, and I made introductions. They all shook hands in that way guys trying to impress each other do. Hattie and I would have made fun of it later, in our twin beds before we went to sleep. I missed Hattie. I missed her, I missed her, I missed her.

They made small talk, about schools, grunting mostly monosyllabic answers to each other. Mac chucked a piece of driftwood onto the fire and we sat in the chairs, facing each other around the crackling pit.

"Now what?" asked Gib.

"You're the girl," Mac said. "Girls always know."

"That is so sexist I cannot believe you said it out loud," I said. "You're the one who invited us, Santi."

"Let's drink beer," Santi said. Hearty agreement.

I thought they were joking. Wrong. He passed each of us a bottle from the cooler.

"Seriously, Santi?" I said, only a little under my breath. We were here for a reason. A big, important reason.

He either didn't hear me or ignored me, lifting his bottle as Mac stood and proclaimed, "To Hattie!" The rest stood, me last. I clenched my jaw as the bottles clanked together. When they chugged, I didn't.

They resettled in their seats, stupidly quiet for a solid three minutes. Their utter lack of imagination was infuriating. "Is this the best we can come up with?" I said, waving my bottle. "*Really?*" I tacked on a forced laugh, an attempt to soften my hostility.

“We could go for a sail,” Santi said. “And drink beer.” Chuckles all around.

I held back a smirk. When did they morph into clueless meatheads? We were *not* going to drink all weekend as our way to say goodbye to Hattie. I wasn’t. I couldn’t. Hattie didn’t even like drinking that much. “We owe her more,” I said, unable to look anyone in the eye. This was an awful idea.

They started babbling again and I tried to put my thoughts in line. What did I expect? They hardly knew each other. *I* didn’t even know what we were supposed to do. Why had I thought we could do this?

I picked up the bottle and took a long, bitter, mouth-stinging drink.

An hour or maybe two passed. I walked the beach alone, unable to listen to vacuous guy talk any longer. The thin swirls of white in the sky seemed like they didn’t have their shit together enough to form clouds. The surf pitched and rolled, unsettled and strong. Even though early September is technically still summer, the lowering afternoon sun and the new tilt of the earth gave the beach grass, the sand, the water itself an autumnal shimmer.

At a bend in the beach, the Darrows’ house appeared over the dunes, tucked into the landscape. Something about the faded cedar shingles and the green shutters that matched the spruce trees made it seem like an integral part of the landscape. The Darrows belonged here. Hattie belonged here. My chest lurched. Each step I took brought more of her: the dock, the rocky beach, the Bat Cave. Way off I saw the rise of Pulpit Head. It all pulled at me—an undertow, willing me toward it. But I was afraid, and turned back toward the safety of the boys.

On the way, I focused on how we could do the memorial. She meant something different to each of us; it was hard to think of a single way that would work for everyone.

A band of round, speckled birds raced the frothy waves, sticking their needle beaks into the sand. They moved like a team, back and forth, back and forth. I lost myself in their game.

The closer I got to the campfire, the clearer it became that the boys were not planning a memorial. They roasted hot dogs on sticks. I didn't think they noticed when I rejoined them, but Santi promptly handed me a stuffed hot dog roll. "Have a cheese brat," he said. "Good for the soul."

Two bites in I realized I was famished. They bantered on about some soccer player from Chile who Santi somehow knew. I settled into a chair to watch the sun set for good, still thinking of what we could do.

Gib sat on the arm of my chair. Maybe it was the cast of the shadows right then, but he looked like he might cry.

"You okay?" I asked.

He nodded, watching the fire.

"I can feel her here," Gib said. "You know?"

I nodded, but truthfully, I'd felt oddly disconnected from her since our arrival. The finality of it made my bones ache.

I glanced around. Now would be a good time to ask.

"Gib, I found two pictures of you up here on the day of the accident," I said.

I sensed him stiffening. "What?" he said quietly.

I told him about the pictures, that looked like they were taken from her bedroom window. "You were here on August twenty-sixth," I said, my pulse tapping my neck. "I know in a way it's none of my business, but in a bigger way it's absolutely my business," I said. "Can you tell me?"

"I did tell you," he said. "She wouldn't return my messages and I just wanted—" He stopped, then in a lower voice said, "I needed to know why. I drove up on August twenty-sixth, and when I got here, she still wouldn't see me. Her sister Helen told me she wasn't home. But I saw her in the window of her room." He stopped, remembering. "It didn't matter, I realized. She wouldn't see me. So, I left."

He wiped his nose and pressed his eyes. "The single stupidest thing I've done in my life."

I listened, horrified at how devastating the timing must seem to him. Suddenly, his rage made sense. If he had stayed . . . Well, in his mind he may have saved her life—and that was *before* he knew the real truth. My heart crinkled and a cry escaped my mouth. I stood and put my hand on his shoulder. "She was sick," I whispered. I hugged him. He pulled away and looked into my eyes. "She was sick," I said again. He nodded.

Gib rubbed his fingers to his chin, resting his elbow on his knee. "Here's the thing that's the most fucked up for me." His voice was loud. I realized he was drunk. "Hattie loved life," he said. He'd caught the attention of the others. "I never met anyone like her. She didn't want to stop. Ever, really." He straightened his back and turned to me, studying my face for a reaction. "You know?" I nodded again. He looked to the fire. "It's the most fucked up thing," he said.

"I'm pretty sure I learned *how* to live from her," I said. Then I felt embarrassed. But when I dared look around, I saw four guys lost in their own thoughts.

"Maybe life here wasn't big enough for her," Mac said.

"Maybe she loved life the way she did because she was afraid to lose it," Hammy said.

"Maybe she was afraid to stand still," I said.

The fire hissed and sent embers into the darkening sky, tiny SOS flares.

"Why did she need it to be so secret?" blurted Hammy. Also crocked. "How shallow did she think we are?" His mouth was pinched and sour.

"I wish she gave us more credit," Santi said, flipping

a bottle cap into the fire. "So we could have done something."

"You know," Mac said, "there is a stigma to mental illness—stupid, but true. Maybe she was plain embarrassed for us to know she had this thing that she saw as a weakness." Nobody responded and he looked around to read our reaction. "The Hattie I knew didn't even like losing at Scrabble."

Santi stared at the sky with a half smile. "We were playing Scrabble once with her grandfather and she spelled *tofu*. Grampy wasn't buying that it was a real word, but she was not going to give in to him. He was about a hundred and ten and mostly deaf, but she wasn't going to lose those twenty-four points."

"That's my girl," I said.

"She was like, 'Grampy, *tofu* is so a word. It's bean curd. Vegetarians eat it.' And he was like, 'Who ever heard of people eating bean curd? I don't believe it.'" Santi did a great imitation of Grampy, who had terrified me on more than one visit, once laughing at me when he found out I'd never seen a salt cod.

Mac poked the fire with a hot dog stick and said, "So what makes you think someone like Hattie would tell you she had bipolar?"

"Bipolar *two*," Santi corrected him. "It's milder."

I flinched. I didn't want to associate bipolar one or two or sixteen with Hattie. And then I realized she was right in a way—my first reaction was shallow. Guilt rushed me. "I just wish she could have trusted me. We could have figured it out together." I felt like screaming it to the stars.

"I wish she gave us one chance," Santi said.

"*That* part is exactly like her." Hammy threw a stick on the fire. "Keeping the power to herself."

I eyeballed him, stuck between agreeing with him and hating him for saying it. Hattie was all about the power, really. It wasn't a bad thing. I wanted desperately to feel powerful, like her. She owned herself. Hattie owned herself from the first day I met her. I thought of the photograph her parents displayed at the funeral—an element in and of herself, like fire and water and thunder. I raked my toes through the sand. "I hate that she didn't think I would be there."

"It's a betrayal, right?" Santi said, his voice pitched so it could sound like he was joking. We all knew he wasn't.

"I feel that. But I keep reminding myself: She was *ill*, Santi. Really not in her head."

Hammy tipped his head, jabbing at the ground with his stick. "It's probably bad karma to talk like this, when we're all here—"

"And *breathing*?" Gib interrupted. "We're breathing, assholes. Remember?"

"Take it easy," Mac said. He patted Gib's shoulder, but Gib shook him off.

I dug my toes deep, feeling a smooth rock under the sand. I flung it off my foot as hard as I could, sending it all of six feet before its unsatisfying thud.

"We'll never know what she was thinking, really," Santi said.

But I knew. I knew.

It took shape for me, like a spruce tree in a thinning fog. Hattie couldn't stand her illness because it beat her. She couldn't outrun it, out-swim it, out-joke it, or out-Scrabble it. In her illness she was *vulnerable*. And that was something Hattie never allowed herself to be.

"I don't think it had anything to do with us," I said, convinced. They stared at me. "Hattie was at war with herself."

"What, like we didn't matter?" Hammy asked.

"No." It was all wrong out loud. My thoughts folded in on each other. "That's not what I meant. Maybe she thought she was protecting us by keeping it a secret. Look at us. Who are we kidding? We all *needed* her to be who we thought she was!" She was more than that, or maybe less than that.

Nobody said anything.

"I didn't need her to be anything," Gib said, standing. "And I didn't come all the way to Maine to trash talk her." He brushed past me and hopped onto the footpath. "Later," he called. The darkness and seagrass swallowed him.

Santi rolled his eyes at Mac, who shook his head dismissively. Hammy looked at me. "Nice job," he muttered.

"I wasn't trash talking her," I said. "I was . . ." But I didn't know anymore. I was forgiving her?

The fire popped.

Waves broke.

We were flatlining.

"Who's ready?" asked Santi, opening the cooler.

"No, thank you," I said, not caring about the edge in my voice.

"Is that guy always such a d-bag?" asked Mac. He flicked his beer cap between his thumb and finger. It landed in the embers.

Hammy said, "He doesn't know her the same way we do."

"Then what's he doing here?" Santi asked.

"They kind of . . ." I struggled. "Had a thing. Right before she left Scofield this summer." That more or less summed it up. "He came up here and surprised her after we left." I left off the rest.

Santi forgot himself. "Hattie had a *boyfriend*? I thought she was immune to testosterone."

I shrugged. But the way he said it, staring into the flames, made me curious as to what else I didn't know.

"Yeah, no shit," said Hammy.

Santi and Hammy locked eyes, and I knew they recognized themselves in each other. Santi looked away and snickered.

"Jesus," said Mac with a shake of his head. "I'm the only one here who wasn't in love with her."

"I wasn't in *love* with her," Santi said.

"Right," Mac said.

"Me neither, for the record," I said. They laughed. But in a way, I was lying again. Is there a way to be in love with someone in a nonsexual way? "I'll take a beer, I guess."

Eventually I ended up in one of the bedrooms in Santi's summerhouse. I managed to brush my teeth before tumbling into a pink canopy bed. I felt like My Little Pony. The drunk edition.

I'd been asleep for an hour or so when a blinding light woke me. A figure stood silhouetted in the doorway.

"Reid?"

"Hammy?" I managed.

"Can I come in?"

"Yeah." He shut the door behind him and only the moon lit the room.

My swimming thoughts tried to coalesce as one. Hammy. Darkness. Bedroom. Our mosh session in the grass, which neither of us had brought up since. I was simply too overwhelmed to deal with it. I needed it to go away. I didn't want to hear him tell me again how it was a mistake.

He walked right past me, though, and that's when I discovered there was a second bed in the room. My

Little Pony II. "I'll be over here, okay?" he said. I heard the subtle but unmistakable muffle-y sounds of undressing. He kicked off his shoes. There went his shirt over his head. I heard the zip of his shorts.

I rolled toward the door. "Seriously, Hammy?"

He hopped, probably losing his balance while pulling off his socks. Then I heard his long body slide into sheets. He sighed, "Can you call me Sam once in a while?" His words sounded slurry and sweet. "Please?"

"What?" I squinted into the dark.

"My name is Sam. You know that, right? Can you just call me by my name?"

I thought of the loafers I'd chucked into the stream. They were more than loafers. And Hammy wanting to be Sam might be like that. Maybe he wanted to be done with Hammy. "Okay," I said, and added, "Of course," so he felt understood.

"I need to talk to you," he said.

I moaned. "I'm asleep." This became less true by the second. "What is it?"

"I have things to tell you," he muttered, his consonants soft.

I was intrigued. "What do you need to tell me?" Then I started to worry that it was going to have to do with the kissing, and I wasn't prepared. But I didn't have to worry. The next thing I heard from Hammy was a nasally snore. I was relieved and disappointed at the same time.

I was used to Hattie's breathing sounds as my

sleepover buddy. Hammy was all around louder. I could smell him, too, laundry soap and wood smoke and boy. I remembered his honey breath and the soft feel of his mouth. Had it really happened? Because I'd gotten really good at pretending it hadn't. I let myself keep pretending and drifted back to sleep.

September 8

"Reid?"

My teeth had been replaced by mossy pebbles.

"Reid, come on. Let's go to Hattie's house."

I groaned. Hammy stood over me. I pulled a pillow over my face, trying to remember what I was wearing. "Hammy. A little space, please?"

"You talked in your sleep," he said. "About some guy . . ."

I bolted upright. "What?"

He laughed. "Gotcha."

I picked up a unicorn stuffy and beaned him with it.

We sat in silence for a moment. "Can you take me to Hattie's?"

"Is *that* what you wanted to talk to me about last night?" I said. Disappointed. Relieved. I'd gotten pretty carried away in thinking he'd bring up the mosh.

He looked puzzled, though. "Um, yeah?" he said, scratching his arm.

"You were tanked," I said with a laugh.

"Yeah. Anyway, can we go to her house?" he said.

I remembered seeing the Darrows' side of the island from the beach yesterday, the house filled with memories and haunting new truths. I dreaded it, I realized.

"We can drive or walk." He moved to the window. "It's nice outside."

"How do you not feel like dirt?" My head pounded. I rubbed my cheek and felt a little dried spittle.

"I smell breakfast meats," he said. "Come on. You're young and healthy."

"Arrrrgh," I said. "All right! Shoo."

As I dressed, I thought of an idea I'd had in the night for making one celebration out of many friendships. I might need coffee to articulate it.

Mac, Gib, and Santi sat around the table, freshly showered and hunkered over steaming plates of eggs and bacon. How was I the only one feeling hungover here? I wasn't cut out for drinking.

"This is civilized," I said, helping myself to the coffee.

Mac raised his hand while slugging back some orange juice. "Yellow Front Grocer on Route One, ayuh," he said in an Old Man Maine accent.

"Grab a plate," Santi said, pointing with his elbow toward the counter.

Hammy sat next to Gib. "Where'd you get to last night, bro?"

"I don't know. Around," Gib answered, which sounded overly dramatic until I realized he meant it literally. The footpath was a nonintuitive labyrinth, probably designed to intimidate the newcomer, knowing Mr. Darrow. You could end up anywhere, especially in the dark. It was a wonder Gib made it back at all.

We ate quietly, aside from the occasional request for the butter or salt. If the tension from last night carried over, I couldn't find a sign of it. Boys don't really need to talk much, I decided. The eating thing maxes out their brain space.

"So," I ventured. "I thought of what we could do. As a memorial. For Hattie." I sounded like I was giving an oral report for history or something, but they waited patiently. I put my fork down. "Okay, she hid it from us. She underestimated us, maybe," I said. "But I think we should show Hattie"—I swallowed—"we would have loved her anyway. That we *do* love her anyway." I tried to read their expressions but couldn't. "I don't want disappointments and regrets to be what's left. Do you?"

"No," Santi said. "I don't at all."

"I want the opposite of that," Hammy said.

That hung above the table for a while. Then Gib said, "I'm not mad at Hattie. I'm here to send her off."

I smiled. For the first time since we'd arrived, I felt hopeful. We talked a little more, and I got them to agree that each of us should create our own way to send her off. We'd meet, here, at five o'clock.

Hammy thought he'd convinced me to go to Hattie's, but I already knew I'd go in spite of all my apprehensions. It was all part of the quest to understand.

As the more seasoned Thimble visitor, I drove us through the dark woods until they opened to a sunny field. We passed the tennis court and Hattie's house came into view. A blue Jeep was parked by the porch. "Is someone here?" Hammy asked.

"Maybe a caretaker?"

The screen door opened and Ben Darrow jogged down the steps with a cardboard box in his arms. He shaded his eyes, trying to see who we were.

"Shit," I said. The first thing that popped into my head was that he slept with Emma Rose when she was fifteen or something, and then much more vividly: Why the *fuck* hadn't I thought to ask Santi if anyone was here?

He had tawny hair and dark eyes, like Mr. Darrow, and was built like an Olympic swimmer. But as he got closer, I saw the gray under his eyes and the paleness of his skin.

"Who's he?" Hammy said. "Wait, I recognize him from the funeral."

"It's Ben Darrow, her next-to-oldest brother," I said. I waved to him, stupidly. "Fuck! I am so not ready for this!"

"Are we not supposed to be here?"

"I don't know. I mean, no?"

Ben walked toward us.

"Hi, Ben," I said, stepping out of the car.

He froze. "Reid?" he said. "Wow, I—"

"I'm so sorry. I should have called—" I said, looking anywhere—the porch, Hattie's window, the sea roses—anywhere but at his eyes. I heard Hammy close his car door. He stood beside me.

"Um, no," Ben said. "Of course, you're always welcome. I, uh . . ." His voice got tortured with emotion and trailed off. He seemed to notice Hammy for the first time. Remembering himself, Ben set the box on the hood of the Jeep and hugged me. He stuck his hand out to Hammy. "Ben Darrow. And you are?"

"Sam Stanwich," he said, like he had his own law firm or something. "We're staying with the—" He waved over his shoulder.

"The Herreras," I said. "We're having . . ." I stumbled for words. God, this was awful. "Our own memorial weekend for Hattie. My own manners kicked in. "Ben, I'm so, so sorry." And there went my composure. My chin wobbled. Ben stepped toward me and we shared an awkward embrace. I'd probably met him six times over all my years with Hattie. He was always off at boarding school, then college, or on some far-off surfing safari or something.

"Thank you," he said into my hair. He pulled away. "She was my girl, my little Hattie Bean. And your girl, too. I know that." I nodded, unable to speak.

Hammy said, "She was definitely the most unique individual I ever knew." He looked Ben squarely in the eyes. "I'm so sorry for the loss." I felt Hammy sending me strength through the space between us. "We miss her."

"It's been a really, really rough few weeks," Ben said, turning toward the house.

Worry flooded me. "Is your family here? Helen?"

"She went back to Providence." He pulled his phone from his pocket and checked it. "An hour ago." He tipped his chin toward the box on his Jeep's hood. "I'm packing Hattie's room. Helen thought she was up to it, but . . ." He shook his head.

"What about your folks?" I asked.

"Dad's in Montana at Uncle Baxter's. Mom's at Aunt Lu's in—"

"Oregon? They're not together?" I blurted, regretting it immediately.

He cocked his head, face hardening. "Not right now," he said.

I couldn't stop myself. "What about Helen's fellowship? In England?"

"She's not going this year," he said.

My blood darted from limb to limb. The mighty Darrows were falling apart. I stepped backward from the impact of it.

"Can I help you guys with something?" Ben asked. A polite way of saying, *Why are you here?*

Hammy touched my arm. "We wanted to come by for memory's sake. We didn't mean to intrude."

"Come on in," he said.

Hammy followed Ben toward the porch stairs. I forgot to move, I guess, and he wrapped his fingers around mine. Startled, I looked at him. If eyes can comfort you, that's what his were doing.

"Can we help you out?" Hammy said over his shoulder.

Ben paused for a moment. "Sure." Then he added, "There's a lot."

This was how I found myself in Hattie's Thimble bedroom, where she spent the final days of her life.

"I've got a few boxes going. The heavy-duty ones go to Goodwill, the tub is for storage," said Ben. He led us upstairs. The smells of the Darrows' house—aging wood, slightly damp upholstery, and some foody smell I'd never been able to identify (grains? dried herbs?)—flooded me with a yearning to see Hattie pop out of one of the bedroom doors, along with the fear that she might.

"Helen wants clothes and shoes to go to Goodwill," Ben said. He stopped on the landing and turned to us. His gaze settled on me and I tried to breathe.

"Are you sure you're up to this?"

I looked at my feet.

No.

Yes.

Lifting my eyes, I nodded. Damn the chin wobble.

"For me, I just have to keep moving," he said. His candor surprised me, and I wiped a tear away. He proceeded down the hallway.

Her bedroom doorway loomed ahead of us, spilling sunlight across the hallway floor. I braced myself for Hattie's room smell—the scents from her favorite body butter mixed with shampoo and the botanical perfume from Telluride—and I felt light-headed in the final steps to the door.

My face twitched. Only the dimmest hint of her remained, and judging by the unmade bed and scattered clothes, the room had been untouched since August twenty-sixth. Her blue striped sailor shirt stuck out from the dresser drawer. Her Chuck Taylors sat next to the open closet, like she stepped out of them moments ago. The Stephen King novel she'd been reading when I visited sat on the bedside, a second one stacked atop it.

"Where do we start?" asked Hammy, examining a picture frame he'd taken off the bookshelf. I didn't have to look to know it was the prom group shot Mrs. Darrow had taken. He set it down, slow to pull his eyes away.

"This is so great of you to help me," Ben said. I realized that maybe this was a good thing after all. Maybe we were lifting his spirits a little just by being there. Plus, we were helping with the terrible job of laying the memories of Hattie's life here to rest. "I'll make trips to Goodwill if you load the boxes," he continued. "You can start in the closet. I'm thinking we wash the bedding and remake her bed. So, you know, my mom can come in and it will be . . ." His voice roughened. "Yeah, you know what I mean."

"Yes," I said with Hammy.

"If we take out the more recent reminders but keep the timeless stuff, like this—" Ben held up a frame from her dresser.

I sucked a breath, almost reaching for it. It was a copy of the Don Quixote and Sancho Panza pen-and-ink by Picasso she'd sent me. I put my hand on the bedpost.

"She sent me the same print a few weeks ago," I said.

An awkward silence followed. "I can start in the closet."

"Good, good," Ben said. "I'll get a laundry basket."

Hammy moved toward the bed. "Want to help me strip the bed?"

"In a minute," I said, heart thumping. I stood facing a solid row of Hattie clothes.

"Right," he said.

I pulled a blue cotton button-down shirt off its hanger. She wore it with leggings, usually. I folded it, carefully laying it in the bottom of a box. Next was a floral tank we bought together at Collective Eye. Again I folded, neatly laying it next to the blue shirt. Jeans, the ones she said gave her a camel toe. I smiled, gingerly stacking it on the shirts. Then I came to the white strappy top I'd seen her in (or dreamed I'd seen her in, or hallucinated I'd seen her in, or seen her ghost in) on the Post Road the day I found out she had died. I saw her all over again, bopping to music, zipping effortlessly through traffic in her convertible. Weighed down by nothing. Disappearing into her ephemeral O'Keeffe clouds.

"I'm not sure I should be doing this," Hammy said, startling me. He stood in front of her open underwear drawer. "It feels wrong." His expression was drawn and embarrassed.

I smirked. "It's underwear, dude."

"It's not okay," he said, "for me to be in there." He waved his hand toward the open drawer.

"I'll do it," I said. *Hammy's a prude!* I wanted to tell her. I half expected to hear Hattie's raspy, squeaky laugh, but I didn't. Still, she was with us then, I knew it. Reminding me how funny things can be, silently challenging me to pick up a pair of her Victoria's Secrets and chase him around the room with it. *Not the time*, I told her.

"Can we strip the bed now?"

I nodded.

We pulled the bedspread and blanket off the bed, piling them on the floor. I tugged the pillows out of their cases, catching a hint of her shampoo, while Hammy yanked the fitted sheet corners out from under the mattress. When he did, tiny objects scattered to the floor.

"What was that?" he said, kneeling.

"Holy shit," I said, recognizing the yellow hexagons. "Her meds."

Our eyes met. "Well, that explains a lot," he said softly in a non-question question.

I stared at the pills, a galaxy of them spread across the hardwood.

Each one provided touchable, undeniable evidence of Hattie's condition. "Oh my God," I breathed. Hammy reached under the mattress and pulled out a couple more. I imagined her, lying in bed, waiting until Helen or her mom left, stuffing the pills away, refusing to need them but needing them more and more every time she did it.

"We would have helped," Hammy said. "If we knew, we would have helped."

We heard Ben on the stairs.

"I don't think we should talk about this," I whispered. "It's too upsetting."

Hammy nodded. We scrambled to gather the pills and toss them in the trash, silently agreeing to protect her privacy. We were shaking out the pillows when Ben returned with fresh linens.

The three of us worked in quiet, focused unison. I stuck to the dresser, piling her underwear in the trash, conveniently covering the pills, then progressing to socks, T-shirts, and shorts for Goodwill. Hammy moved to the closet and busily put shoes in a new box. Ben remade the bed.

Each time I took something from a drawer, laying it atop the other clothes and smoothing it with my palm, I knew I was putting a little piece of Hattie away. And even though I noiselessly cried tears the boys didn't see, this was a sacred task I needed to do. For Mrs. Darrow. For Helen, and Camilla. For myself.

When they left to load the Jeep, I found it.

A poem.

It was in the drawer of her bedside table, under a bunch of old crap: bookmarks, tide charts, hair ties, a deck of cards. She'd glued it to the back of a photo of Pulpit Head in a light fog. Some of the letters, written in blue felt tip, were smudged, but the sight of her familiar handwriting wrapped around me like a blanket. I read.

Sheep in Fog

by Sylvia Plath

The hills step off into whiteness . . .

A chill swept my scalp and I slumped to the floor, leaning against the bed. I reread it three times. The imagery—blackening mornings, rust-colored horses, disappointments and still bones—so sad. I flipped from the words to the photo, fingers trembling. She meant Pulpit Head stepped off into whiteness. She stepped into whiteness. How could Hattie think she was the sheep? And the end compared heaven to dark, cold water.

The guys talking outside reminded me where I was. I pawed at a book on the bedside table above my head, pulling it onto my lap. *Calvin and Hobbes.* I shoved the photograph between the pages.

I closed my eyes and thought about disappointment and people and stars. People *were* disappointed. I was. God, how I hated to admit that, even if it was only a tiny part of me. Had that been fair of me? Her secrets killed her and she hid them from me. Me, her best friend. Is there a bigger deceit than that? But I lied too, about Jay, and I lied so I wouldn't disappoint her. But was it really Hattie I wanted to protect from my weakness? Or myself? Couldn't she have felt that way, too? I knew one thing for certain: the stars? The stars do know Hattie by name. I know they do. And the only disappointment is the length of her light on earth.

Using the wall for leverage, I stood to check the status on Jeep packing. They were strapping boxes onto the back seat with rope. I had more time.

Moving to the bookshelf, I picked up the Picasso pen-and-ink. I sat on the corner of the neatly made twin bed, the one I'd slept in so many times, and stared at Picasso's pen strokes. I wondered for the first time if Don Quixote was supposed to look not victorious, but defeated and sad. Sancho Panza looked like he could be consoling Don Quixote instead of gazing in admiration. You could interpret it either way.

I wished I could see it through her eyes.

"How's it going?" Hammy said from the doorway.

I didn't answer but replaced the frame in its spot. Tucking the book under my arm, I nodded to him.

"I think we may be done," he said.

"Yeah," I said, backing toward the door. It was too hard to imagine never seeing this room again, so I closed the thought out of my head, and tried to memorize everything, from the white pom-pom curtains to the braided rug to the creak of the floorboards and the ceramic Cheshire cat. *Bye*, I thought. My fingers fluttered a butterfly breath of a wave near my hip.

Bye.

We thumped along the causeway toward town in silence. While I was glad I'd come up with a memorial plan that everyone liked, I hadn't thought of my own contribution yet. The Dancing Newt—the store that brought me the Eye of Horus bracelet—might have that certain something I hadn't thought of. Hammy drove. I stared out the window.

The tide was out, exposing rank mud, rocks the color of rust, and other unseemly secrets of the ocean. My mind was lost in a maze of memories and poetry.

I imagined Hattie shoving those pills under her mattress, and I thought of Santi's words. *Big highs and big lows.*

Starting freshman year, Hattie would be absent from school without warning. When I called her on it, she'd vaguely reference stomach cramps. "Eat some Tums and get over it," I'd teased. I didn't want her to be absent in the first place, and I didn't like that she felt utterly unaccountable to me.

Now I realized my belief in Hattie's strength was turning out to be what our English teacher, Mrs. Langhouser, would call an "ultimate irony." When Shakespeare has Romeo kill himself upon discovering Juliet killed herself? Not ironic yet, but (spoiler alert) Juliet was only faking it, and does herself in for real because her true love Romeo is dead. That's an ultimate irony.

This heaviness overwhelmed me, so I said, "Low tide smells." Not much forethought and out of left field, but Hammy rolled with it.

"Indeed," he said with a forced smile, his eyes on the road. We were quiet the rest of the way.

The air in the Dancing Newt was thick with patchouli perfume and crowded with merchandise. Brightly painted elephants and laughing buddha statues lined shelves. Batik maxi dresses and general Sherpa fashion loaded the racks.

Hammy pointed to a blackboard. It read, "The Psychic Medium is IN. Walk-ins welcome. Meet your Spirit Guides!"

We exchanged amused glances, but I didn't mention I'd been having a bumper crop of spiritual encounters this season. It didn't matter. He wasn't serious, and anyway, he got sucked into the used vinyl collection.

My eye caught a case full of evil eye bracelets. I gazed at the dozens of mini glass eyes gazing back.

"Aren't they awesome?" a man asked. "Awesome," he repeated. I couldn't locate him at first, then saw a wiry middle-aged guy emerge from a mountainous soy candle display. He wore a rainbow swirl tie-dyed jumpsuit and had one of those unfortunate pube-resembling beards. *Dude*, I heard Hattie say. I swallowed a laugh. "Turkish glass," he said, sidling up next to me so we could admire together. "Exactly like the charms used to ward off evil from 3000 BC."

"I know," I said, trying to be affable. "My friend sent me one from here a few weeks ago."

"Cool friend. She cares about you," he said, pointing at my collarbone. He had Siberian husky–blue eyes that bore a discomforting likeness to the beads. They darted about the store. "She here?"

I flinched. "No." I worked to keep up the retaining wall holding back all I didn't say. He squinted at me like he was doing some kind of laser scan of my chakras. "Now you're safe for life, my friend," he added, all business. "But I get that vibe from you anyhow!" He chuckled. I couldn't tell if he was flirting or weird or just really baked, and settled on all of the above. He leaned in close enough for me to catch his earthy-but-not-awful, anti-commercial-body-products smell. I tipped backward, smiling awkwardly. He flapped his eyebrows, lowered his voice, and didn't blink once. "You're a survivah!"

He winked and spun toward Hammy. "Hello, sah! How's about old Bert helps you find some music to *blow. Your. Mind?!*" He spread his fingers wide and waved his hands around his head, chuckling again as he bobbed over to unsuspecting Hammy.

I couldn't budge. Someone else calling me a survivor. Me. Now *there's* your ultimate irony. I watched Bert chat up Hammy. He had a ponytail I hadn't noticed from the front view. I remembered Ponytail, our friendly ghost. Looking up to the rafters, I wondered if Hattie set this up.

I shook my head and resumed scanning the merchandise. Next to the candle mountain, to the right of the crystals, an eight-by-twelve cardboard display said, "Eco-friendly Sky Lantern! Ancient Tradition! Celebration! Good luck! Wishes! Wedding! Biodegrading!"

Admittedly a little wanting in the grammar department, but still, the photo had me: hundreds of candlelit paper balloons sailing into the night sky.

Bert appeared by my side. "That's the shit, right there, sweetheart," he whispered, nodding. He leveled his husky-dog eyes on me. "Mystical."

"Perfect," I said.

Back at Santi's house, I retreated to my appointed bedroom. There was something weird about a pile of teenage boy clothes next to the My Little Pony bed, especially in broad daylight. It made me smile.

I flopped onto the bed I'd slept in, stretching my legs out. I wanted to look at the poem again in peace, so I retrieved it from the *Calvin and Hobbes* book. On my seventeenth reading of Sylvia Plath's words, I said out loud, "Hattie, this is the most goddamned depressing poem I've ever read."

I lay back and propped the cool pillow over my eyes, but I was too restless to nap. If I'd had any Wi-Fi or cell service to speak of, I'd have Googled the poem and Sylvia Plath. Instead, I pulled Hattie's phone from my backpack, searching through her photos from August. Boredom and angst led me on an exhaustive tour of her apps, the ones nobody uses. Apple Books: empty; Wallet: empty; Notes: nothing; but when I opened Voice Memos, there were two files labeled simply, *August 18* and *August 19.*

I sat up, tucking my hair behind my ears. I tapped *August 18*. The cursor raced across a thirteen-second timeline muffled with nothingness, like a butt dial. *August 19*'s timeline went from zero to three minutes, eight seconds. I tapped to hear muffled nothing again a few seconds and then, loudly:

I've been awake since five, but I—

My stomach lurched. Her voice! I clumsily tapped to stop it. Glancing at the door, I turned the volume low and tapped again.

—don't let on when I see my mom's slippers through the crack under the door.

I stopped it again. She sounded tired and secretive. My protective instinct kicked in. Santi's house felt closed-in and like the wrong place for me to hear what Hattie had to say. I rooted around my things for my running clothes and the earbuds. I plugged them into Hattie's phone and laced up my shoes, thankful I'd decided to mash them in my overstuffed backpack.

Quietly, I descended the stairs. Nobody inside. Through the screen door, I saw Santi and Mac in the driveway. I put in the earbuds and nonchalantly bounded by them. "Going for a run," I called without making eye contact. I loped to the footpath, knowing just where I'd go.

The air was crisp and damp, like the forces of ocean and autumn had joint custody over it. I ran too fast and got winded, but I didn't stop. By the time I reached the bench swing I loved, my left side had cramped.

I plopped onto the swing, sending it swaying, and touched the phone screen to bring it to life. I pulled in a breath, exhaled slowly, and tapped play.

I've been awake since five. I'm not going to lie, Dr. Sulyman, this feels stupid. But you said explaining it might take away its control over me, so here you go.

I see my mother's slippers through the crack under the door. It's Mom's third pass by my bedroom and this time she stops. I roll to face the closet. Sunshine creeps around the edges of my window shade, which bounces in an annoyingly perky way.

Another perfect day in Maine. I can tell it's a bad one for me.

On the bad ones, morning's not like morning. It's like an extension of last night and I haven't slept at all. My limbs are sandbags. My shoulder muscles are tight and achy, from trying to stretch down and protect my heart, I think. Because my heart is replaced by something dark—I think it's some kind of octopus locked in a jail cell made by my ribs.

Octopuses are smart. They can climb ladders, open jars, and be sneaky. I saw a show about this octopus at an aquarium in Australia who climbed in and out of his tank every night to eat lumpfish in the tank next door. Finally, the scientists caught him on camera. My octopus won't leave me. He just sits in my chest, spewing blackness into every corner of me, until I'm nothing at all.

Mom calls my name, softly. She doesn't open the door. I scare her. "You still have an hour to make it," she says. The hope in her voice is painful to listen to. "Dad's down at the boat."

My octopus is a slippery one. Most people don't even know he's there. Most people would be shocked. Even Reid. Even my dad. My dad, who is down at the docks, in our sailboat, thinking, "Where the hell is Hattie? We can win this thing." He's right, too. I'm really good at winning. I get that from him. I know how to make it happen when it needs to happen. Maybe that's the upside of the octopus: the Darrow Competitive Spirit, which is really a cover for an intense hatred of losing. Dad's version extends to hating losers, too, but we're definitely different people. I only hate the loser in me.

Mom repeats my name.

"Yeah?" I say. I don't say, "Leave me the fuck alone," because even now I know that's plain mean. It's not her fault I'm like this.

"Can you do it?"

"Sure," I say. We both know I'm lying. She knows I'll stay like this for most of the day, like I have for a week or two or three. She'll cover for me, again. Probably say I'm PMSing or something. The tears are so hot in the corners of my eyes. I can't stop myself from disappointing her.

It doesn't make perfect sense as an analogy, I know. Like, if my English teacher heard me she'd say I can't be *the octopus and* be trapped by *the octopus, but she never knows what the fuck she's talking about. Depression traps me, but I am trapping myself. I'm some kind of mutant zombie that eats herself instead of other people. Deal with it, Langhouser.*

"Great!" says Mom, and it's so fake. I know, because I can hear her tears as they crinkle the sides of her beautiful soft cheek. I wish I could put my cheek against hers and feel the warm happiness pumping through it, but I am so toxic with black ink I want to disappear from the sound of me burning her tenderness away. I can't burn her. I can't burn Santi or Gib or Reid or anyone.

That's how it feels, Dr. Sulyman, and no, I don't feel better for naming it.

The cursor stopped at 3:08. I stared out at the ocean, unable to produce a single thought or emotional reaction. Popping the earbuds out, I wrapped the cord around her phone like a neat little mummy and set it at the edge of the swing, away from me.

A bird's song echoed through the trees, beautiful and eerie and earnest. On and on the bird sang. I closed my eyes and leaned back, letting the swing press into the base of my skull.

Her despair scared me. How could a creation of someone's own mind be so destructive? I wished I could reach through time and help her. If she had taken her medication, she could have bounced back. Couldn't she? Why would she choose not to do that?

Leaves crunched in the pattern of footfall. I tried to ignore it.

"Reid?"

Hammy. I opened my eyes and stared up at the canopy of leaves and patches of blue sky. He sat next to me. I hoped he wouldn't notice the phone was Hattie's, because I wasn't sure if I could share what I heard.

I felt for his hand on the swing seat and rested mine inside.

Somehow Hammy knew not to speak. I was lucky to have him. Hattie gave me Hammy, really. If it hadn't been for her, there would be no Summer of Hammy and Reid, and the hole of loneliness would be excruciatingly black.

The bird sang some more. "I love that sound," I said.

"Yeah," he said.

small part of me was glad I had been ignorant of all this. I couldn't imagine coming back from it.

"It's killing my parents. We shouldn't have ever left her." The quiet sound of her crying grew clearer. I waited, wanting to be there for her. "They can't even be with each other," she said.

"Helen, I'm making you sadder," I managed, about to sob myself.

"No!" she said, sniffing. "No, it's good for me to talk like this. Nobody knows her like you."

My heart squeezed. "I've wanted to call your parents so many times, but all I can do is cry and I don't want to do that to them," I said.

"Don't worry. They're not taking calls yet, but my mom would always welcome a call from you, Reid. We all adore you."

I pulled the phone away, my nose stinging. I snuffled and sat tall. Maybe I was helping Helen. Who could she talk to?

"I have another question," I said. "I don't want to make you think about it—"

"It's fine," she said, sounding stronger.

"On her phone, there were these two pictures of Gib on The Thimble. It looked like she took them from her bedroom window—they're from August twenty-sixth," I said.

"Oh. I took those pictures," she said simply.

He rocked the swing slowly for a while by pushing the ground with his feet. I could have stayed suspended there forever.

"Can I tell you something?" he asked.

I didn't really want him to, but I nodded. When I finally turned toward him, I smiled. "Yes, *Sam*?"

He smiled, too, his eyes on the ocean. Then he got all serious again and looked me in the eye in a way that made me stop breathing. "I'm in love with you."

I moved my head a little like a chicken. "What?"

The corner of his mouth turned up. He brushed a strand of hair from my face and tucked it behind my ear. "You're amazing," he whispered. His hands slid to the small of my back. He leaned in and we kissed and everything from the other day returned: the honey, the softness, the shyness.

I kissed him back. I did love him, I knew I did. I might have from the beginning. I'd been waiting for this exact feeling for so long.

His hand touched the front of my ribs and I melted into it. The bird sang on. We were so alive.

I stopped and pulled back.

"What?" he asked, his eyes glassy.

I cleared my throat softly. "I'm not her."

"I know."

"You love Hattie." He'd never made a move on her. But I was safer, and now she was gone anyway. I was the second choice.

He sat back, dropping his head. "I thought I did, but it was a crush. I was a dumbass."

"That's not . . ." I said, barely hearing myself.

"You knew, Reid. All along you knew she wasn't ever going to be into me."

I opened my mouth to deny it, but he was pretty spot-on. "Okay. That might be true," I said. I chose my words carefully. "But I thought she was really, really stupid."

He started kissing me again and at first, I thought, *Okay*, and then I thought again. He realized he couldn't have Hattie. Even if she was still here, he couldn't have had Hattie and I was his reconciliation with reality. "I can't," I said. I touched his chin, felt stubble I couldn't see, then let my hand fall to my lap. "I can't be the consolation prize."

"It's not like that," he said. "I wasted all my time—all the time we could've been together—stuck on an idea of something that would never be real. My sister was right. She told me I stayed stuck to keep myself from getting hurt. I hid too long and I wasted time for us to be happy together."

"We couldn't have been anything close to happy," I said flatly, even though I knew he didn't mean it that way.

"Apart from what happened," he said. "Obviously. Jesus."

"There's no apart."

We sat there, quiet.

He tried again. "She's gone, and it's awful. For all of us. But I've learned—"

"Learned what, that the runner-up is okay, now that you thought about it?" He looked confused, and I tried to shift my tone. "Hammy," I said. "*Sam.*" He stared at the ground. "One day soon, maybe in a week or a month or two months, you're going to wake up and say, 'Damn, she reminds me a lot of Hattie. But she's not Hattie.' And I'll be alone."

"No, I won't," he said, defensive. "Aren't you listening to me?"

"I can't take it," I said. It was worse than Seavers. At least I didn't care a bit about him. "Please. Can we just be best friends for a while? I don't have a best friend anymore." He looked at me for a long time, like I might crack. "I'm not what you really want," I said. *I deserve to be first choice.*

He stood, his eyes dark. "I may be stupid in a million ways, but I don't think you get to tell me what I want, Reid." He walked a few paces, then turned. "Who do you think sent you that Pig Roast invite?"

I stared, speechless. I tried to recall how the Pig Roast unfolded, but it was so distant now I could think of nothing.

He shook his head. "My feelings for you started to change a long time ago, but I, I was stuck on the idea of her, the promise of something that deep down I knew couldn't happen. But it was safer, to love an idea, than—"

"Ham—" I closed my eyes. "Sam, I just can't right now. I'm a freaking mess."

"We both are," he said. "So what? Why can't we just let ourselves be happy?"

"I can't be alone," I said, crying. He shook his head again, and left.

The swing swayed, off-kilter. I looked at Hattie's phone next to me, wrapped up tight.

Maybe I'd been alone all along, anyway.

Shifting splotches of sunlight scattered the path ahead of me. Everything fell in stride, creating the rhythm I'd come to know so well this summer. Before. My rhythm.

Breathe in, foot foot, breathe out, foot foot.

For a while I had no destination. My legs carried me across the tangled trails that split the island, allowing my mind the freedom to navigate the new landscape of my friendship. Nearly all my truths about Hattie had morphed into untruths. The tectonic plates on which I formed my concept of us shifted with each revelation. And yet, I ached thinking Hattie didn't trust me enough to know I would have stood by her, would have adjusted my footing. I *was* adjusting, but it was wasted. We couldn't grow and change, because she was gone.

Breathe in, foot foot, breathe out, foot foot.

The songbird's brave voice trilled through birches

and evergreens, the notes amplified by the woods' damp acoustics. All at once I remembered its name: the wood thrush.

The trail led to a clearing and I saw a tall shingled building I recognized as the Darrows' boathouse. And just like that, as with remembering the bird, I knew where I'd meant to go all along.

Slowing, I emerged to full sunlight. I was hot, my muscles wobbly, and I padded down the beach to the lapping surf to quickly splash my arms and legs with the bracing water. Goose pimply, I strode to the boat-house's huge door. It hung from an overhead track and to slide it open, I had to put my shoulder into it and dig my sneakers into the ground. Dried pine needles made the going slippery, but the metal wheels creaked along until I stood looking into the dark confines of the boathouse. My few unremarkable visits here provided enough impression for me to recall its smell of warmed cedar, wood polish, and a faint hint of gasoline. Orange life jackets hung on pegs along the back wall, on either side of a window, and the skeleton limbs of mechanical boat lifts and cinches stretched in all directions. To the right of me, the *Aria* slept, raised on a complex metal frame, prematurely put to rest this sailing season. Her sails, rolled tight, hung secured to the wall beside her. On my left, a dinghy and the Boston Whaler reposed, along with two long rowing shells, all arranged as if in bunk beds. A ladder led to the loft, where the crafts of Darrow yesteryear languished.

I knew wolf spiders enjoyed the still shadows of this place, but I wrapped my fingers around the rough wooden rungs and climbed until I could swing my legs onto the loft floor. Dirt and grit stuck to my thighs. I dusted them off, crossing to the large window, where I imagined the cell reception must be best. Sure enough, a small rowboat served as her seat, looking out to the ocean.

Settling into it, I dug Hattie's phone out of my pocket. The service was three bars strong. Scrolling through the texts, I found Helen's frantic messages to Hattie from August twenty-sixth. Without allowing my eyes to focus on those, I started my own message to Helen.

Helen—it's Reid. I accidentally took Hattie's phone from your house when we saw each other. I'm so sorry. I want to return it. If you are up to it, I would love to talk to you.

I sent it and my muscles unclenched from a tightness I realized I'd been holding for days. The text showed as delivered and I waited, knowing Helen's response could come anytime from now to never. I looked out the windows to the quiet, pensive waves. Hattie's phone buzzing in my hand startled me.

"Hello?" I said.

"Hi, Reid." Her voice was welcoming but soft and trembly.

I jiggled my foot. "Hi, Helen." I sat taller in the rowboat. "Helen, I am so, so sorry for the way I acted in Hattie's room the other night." I watched a cobweb sway from the ceiling. "I don't know what I was thinking. Or doing, really."

The line was quiet and I shifted, turning toward the ocean again. Finally, she spoke.

"Oh, please don't worry about that, Reid. I barely remember it—it feels like years ago." Her grace gave me such relief I nearly wept for just that. "You have Hattie's phone?" she asked.

I explained how I came to have it, and how I found out about Gib through the photos and how I worried he might have done something bad but now knew that was absurd. I told her about getting the meds and Santi explaining the truth—or what he knew of the truth about Hattie's mental illness. I told her about coming here and our plan for a memorial and seeing Ben.

"We made her room perfect," I said. "I hope that helps."

"I couldn't do it," she said heavily. "I wanted to."

With each sentence we spoke, I felt my cells decompress, until finally I felt ready to say the really big things to her. I breathed deep, rubbing the wood of the boat with my fingers. "I'm so sad I didn't know."

She made a sound I thought might be crying.

I continued. "I am deeply, deeply sorry that I didn't do more. I'd have done anything—"

"Reid, everyone feels that way. Hattie begged our mother to keep it secret and Mom honored that. I only really saw it this summer. None of us knew how bad it was. The medication had worked so well, but she didn't like it. We think she stopped taking it." Helen paused. "The coroner found no traces of it in her blood."

I told her about the yellow hexagons scattered across her bedroom floor. Who knew when she'd quit taking it? Maybe that's what started her mission to lose her virginity back in June. I felt foolish I didn't notice the pattern of behavior that looked so obvious now. But I didn't want this to be about me, forcing Helen to comfort me. And Helen kept talking anyway.

"She had finally gotten out of bed two days before. She went sailing with Dad. They won, and Dad said it was because of 'her magical competitive spirit.'" She imitated Mr. Darrow.

I could almost touch the pain in her words.

"She did have a magical competitive spirit," I said, sympathetic to Hattie's poor father.

"I know," she said. She sighed. "Dr. Sulyman warned them about leaving her alone. And that once a suicidal person has decided to end her life—has a specific plan—they often come out of their depression because they see a way out. But we were so happy to see her upbeat; she was so normal." She sniffed in a long breath.

"My God, Helen, it's so horrible. I'm so sorry," I said. I knew it was true I would do anything for Hattie, but a

I leaned my elbows on my knees. "You?" I couldn't believe it.

"Yep," she said. "The first time Gib came up, Hattie had a blast with him. I honestly think she fell in love with him and I think that scared her. She didn't like feeling vulnerable."

I thought of Hammy's words today, on the swing. Was I cheating myself of being happy for the same reason?

"No, she definitely didn't like being vulnerable," I said.

"Right. And when you fall in love, there's always the risk of being left—it makes you open. Vulnerable." I thought of the softness of his kiss, and shook it out of my head. But I couldn't stop drawing comparisons. "Hattie didn't *say* this, of course," Helen was saying. "It's just what I think. When Gib left in July, she cycled into a depression, no meds to save her . . ."

That hung there for a bit. In the distance, the wood thrush sang.

"Anyway, the pictures," she said. "I took them of Gib because she wouldn't even go downstairs to greet him that day. He'd driven all the way from Connecticut, for God's sake! And I had to tell him she wasn't home. I thought it was stubbornness. Or they'd had some fight." The pause was long and I took a deep breath, waiting. At last she said, "I took her phone from her bedside and snapped the pics to show her, in case I could change her mind."

"Stubborn," I said.

"Yep. It simply didn't matter."

We talked a little longer, and after we said goodbye, I felt like I was in a state of suspended metamorphosis. Somewhere between hollow and full, between unmoored and anchored. Stiff-legged from the long sit on the wooden boat seat, I climbed down the loft ladder and dug my shoulder into the boathouse door. It slid shut with an incontrovertible, resounding *clank*. Maine's cool, blue balsam air circulated around me, coaxing my blood to life. I drew in a sustaining breath and began the jog back to Santi's.

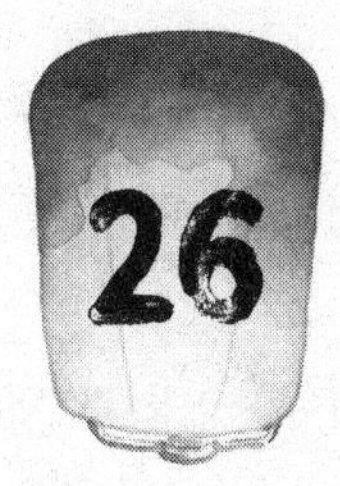

Sky above Clouds

Back at Santi's house, I wriggled into the paisley dress I'd worn to the Pig Roast. I'd wanted to show it to Hattie from the day I purchased it, and this seemed like my best chance. Also, it was bright—sea green and orange—unlike the navy dress my mom put me in for the funeral. I didn't care if I was overdressed. a) The guys probably wouldn't notice. b) *This is our time, Hattie.*

I met my own eyes in the mirror. "Reddi," I whispered, smiling at the irony. I smoothed the dress across my stomach and left the room.

I'll admit I got teary when I stood on the landing and saw the boys in the entry hall below, each in a blazer and tie. They turned toward me at once, and instead of seeing four untouchably hot guys, I saw four friends who, like me, were humbled by the enormity of it all. Somehow, in our covert packing efforts yesterday morning, we each thought to bring clothes fitting the occasion.

We were doing this.

Our lives are millions of moments strung together. Some are louder or bigger, happier or sadder, simply more demanding of our attention when we look back over the sea of moments that make a life. We don't remember the events of our own timeline sequentially, from start to finish—not even the funeral for one we love fiercely. Instead, we remember with aching clarity the smell of wooden pews baked by August heat in an airless church. The strangled cough of a grown man pushing away tears. And the slump of a mother's shoulders. It's these moments, soldered into our souls, that shape who we become.

I knew this was one of those moments, and descending the steps, an eerie feeling that both Hattie and I watched through my eyes washed over me. As the wave receded, I knew I was feeling her regret.

When we were on the same level, standing on the flowered rug in the center of the hall, Santi said, "You clean up nice, Reid," with his smile-frown. He touched my elbow. "Let's take this show on the road." We filed outside. Hammy caught my eye for a blink. I couldn't tell if he was mad, but I couldn't worry.

"So, how does this work?" Santi said in the driveway. "Mac and I know what we're doing. Do you?"

"I do," I said. "Doesn't everyone?"

Gib and Hammy nodded.

Something like pride filled my chest. "Well?" I prodded.

"Hold on," said Hammy. "We should do this Hattie-style. Only tell what we need to know. Like, where you want it to happen."

"Ooh," I said. "The element of surprise." I looked toward Hammy's car, where I'd left my bag of lanterns. He looked at me playfully and we were comrades again. "Mine needs to happen after sunset at Pulpit Head."

"Okay. Mine's all about the boat," Santi said. "Mac's contribution is dinner."

Mac tipped his chin. "I set up the Darrows' firepit already. All I need is this." He kicked a giant Coleman cooler.

"I'm covered," Hammy said.

I shot him a puzzled look. He shrugged. "Gib and I took a ride a while ago."

"So you're set, Gib?" Santi asked.

"Yep." He squinted in the afternoon sun. "If we can stop for a bit out on the water around sunset, that works."

Santi counted on his fingers. "Sail, my thing, sunset interlude, dock at the Darrows', eat dinner, then Pulpit

Head. Sunset's about seven," he said, checking his watch. "Let's do it."

We dispersed, retrieved our provisions, and began our procession toward the Herreras' dock. Gib carried a canvas tote in one hand and a big shopping bag in the other, the contents of which was hidden by tissue paper. Hammy had a Yellow Front Grocery bag that I judged to carry something very light. My curiosity was unexpectedly energizing.

The Herreras' boat was blue on the sides with a polished wood deck. It was as long as the *Aria* but narrower, and instead of being open from bow to stern, it had a single sunken seating area in the middle that doubled as the cockpit. Written across the back in gold cursive letters: *Eidothea*. Even I could tell the thing was a nautical masterpiece.

"Incredible," Hammy said, running his hand along the glossy edge.

Santi hoisted the cooler up with Mac, and his voice strained when he said, "My dad cried when she arrived. No lie."

"What's *Eidothea*?" asked Gib.

"A sea nymph," Santi said. "Greek mythology. Poseidon had a kid with her."

The group considered this, silently admiring the boat.

"Your dad lets you take her out?" Hammy asked.

"Not a fucking chance," he said with a shrug.

"Perfect," I said, and we climbed aboard.

Santi disappeared below deck with my bag. "Wind's pretty good," he said, reemerging. The wild chop from yesterday had calmed, but the water was still spirited.

Mac untied us and Santi motored a ways before they unfurled the sails. The sound of sailcloth catching wind stirred something in me I couldn't describe.

The sky was huge and spotless. A September ocean breeze is brisk in Maine, but I resisted my sweatshirt and let the sun warm my skin. I leaned back and closed my eyes, listening to the bow cutting through waves. Did sailing make Hattie brave, I wondered, or did being brave make her a great sailor?

"Almost there," said Mac, jostling me with his elbow.

I opened my eyes. Shelf Island loomed ahead. I sat up. "Wait, almost where?"

"Ask Santi."

Santi said, "For Hattie, we're each going to touch the Shelf Island Lighthouse."

"Please say you're kidding," I said.

"To let her know, wherever she is, that she left some of her daring in each of us," he continued, enjoying himself. "Five fingers, both hands, on the front door of the keeper's house."

"What's so hard about touching a lighthouse?" Gib asked.

"It's haunted!" I said. "By a lady in a black dress and the lighthouse keeper. And possibly a couple of shipwrecked cannibals. Plus a baby," I added, shuddering.

"*That* is awesome," said Hammy, giggling. He lifted his sunglasses for a better look at our destination.

"Isn't this, I don't know, in bad taste?" Gib asked, gazing toward the horizon. "Given the circumstances?"

"If she can see us, she's loving it," I said.

"She can see us," Santi said to me, and we shared sad smiles.

Santi fired commands at Mac and Hammy, skippering us to Shelf Island's deceptively quaint dock. Meanwhile, I regaled Gib and Hammy with the ghost story. A batch of seagulls scattered into the air as we tied up.

"You know that's probably bullshit, right?" Gib asked me.

"I'd love to agree right now," I replied, eyeing the tower above the pointed fir trees. "But there's a historical record. She sent it to me, obviously."

Mac offered his hand and I jumped onto the dock.

"The bugs are ruthless," Santi said, swatting the air around his face.

I slapped a mosquito on my arm, realizing the air was teeming with more.

"Jesus, they're like helicopters," Hammy said, smacking his calf.

"But we are prepared," Santi said, tossing me bug spray.

I doused myself from head to toe and we passed the spray bottle around.

The dock led to a gravel path, which disappeared into

the woods. If we went fast, it might not be too bad, I told myself.

"Before we go," Santi said, "I want to read this." He pulled a folded paper out of his pocket. "I memorized this poem for English last year. Edna St. Vincent Millay grew up in Maine, and she and Hattie are kindred spirits." We gathered around him. He shifted his weight and cleared his throat. "'My candle burns at both ends; / It will not last the night; / But ah, my foes, and oh, my friends— / It gives a lovely light!'" He stopped and worked to keep his composure. We waited quietly.

Given he'd memorized it for a class, I thought there'd be more than two lines, but Santi said no more. He nodded to none of us in particular. Mac patted his shoulder. Santi bowed his head for a couple of seconds. A twinkle returned to his eye. "Five fingers, both hands." He wiggled his in front of him. "Who's ready?"

I puffed my chest. "We love you, Lady in Black! And your baby, too!" I called into the woods. "Please protect us!"

We trod the pebble path through a meadow, Santi and I in the lead. "Pick up the pace, people," I said, jogging. The path ducked into the cool cover of woods. I told myself the sounds were merely squirrels foraging through the leaves.

From a distance, the Shelf Island Light may look picturesque, but up close it was a monument to sun-dried curls of paint and ragged woodwork. I quickly counted five broken windows, their glass abandoned in sharp wedges on the ground. Curtains inside the house moved. I skidded to a halt, gravel pushing between my toes.

"I am not a fan of this idea," I said.

"It's worth it," Santi whispered. He looked at the sky and back at me.

My heart lurched with energy. "Go!"

We sprang for the red door, smacking it at the same time. I shrieked as we spun back toward the path, nearly crashing into the others.

"Sweet mother of Jesus," Hammy huffed, racing past me toward the door. "Those fucking curtains are moving!" I laughed. The soles of my feet stung from running in sandals, but I didn't stop until the dock. The boys didn't either.

"That wasn't so bad," Gib said, flushed.

"The curtains moved," Hammy said, hands on his knees. "A lot."

Mac leaned backward on a dock post. "That's what made it worthwhile."

"That was her, I bet," Santi said. He pulled a Leatherman from his pocket and began carving into a post. I stepped closer as he brushed away the wood dust. *HMD*, enclosed in a heart. He stepped back and cocked his head, then closed his knife. "To the boat."

"Wait," Hammy said. He passed Santi on the dock to get to the brown grocery bag he'd left near the boat.

He pulled out a stack of green beach buckets and handed one to each of us. We looked at each other. "We're making a cairn once we're back on The Thimble," he said. "Using Shelf Island rocks will make it even better. Like our pirate loot from the dare."

"And a cairn is . . . ?" said Mac.

"It's a pyramid of rocks, marking a special place. Usually in the wild," Hammy said.

"Yeah," said Santi. "Hikers add to a cairn on a mountaintop—different hikers over a span of months or years. It's like a communal monument to ballsiness."

Something about their nods of approval rubbed me wrong. "You know," I said, "Hattie didn't have *balls*. She wasn't *ballsy*." Santi squinted at me. "You need to come up with a better way to describe her," I continued. "You're giving boys credit for Hattie's gutsiness—like somehow she derived her bravery from boys. She did not," I said. "You derived yours from her. We all did. That's the whole point here, right?"

Glances shot among them.

"Okay," said Hammy, stretching out the word. It bothered me that he cast this as some kind of concession. "How's *badassery*?"

I mulled it over. "Fine," I sighed, annoyed that there wasn't a single word I could think of that meant female, well, ballsiness.

"Good," Hammy said, already scanning the sand.

We scrambled around on the awkward shoreline,

the sound of the surf and gull cries punctuated by the thunks of rocks in our buckets. I gathered eight, in varying shades of gray and black and one speckled pink. The bucket pulled my arm slack as I made my way back to the dock. Silently, we piled into the *Eidothea*.

Mac untied us from the dock. We drifted away from Shelf Island until Santi swung the boom. The sail rippled as the wind caught it, carrying us over the waves.

The sky glowed yellow in the setting sun, the sails pink instead of white and the wood a deep rose. We'd been underway a short while and had passed the tip of Shelf Island, now heading back toward The Thimble, which appeared in purple silhouette in the middle distance. Behind it, the mainland stretched low and long.

"Gib, how's this?" Santi asked.

Gib nodded, surveying the water around us. "Yeah, this is good."

Santi and Mac pulled at lines and then Santi let out the anchor. Gib stepped below deck and returned with a massive bunch of red roses and an old-fashioned boom box.

He handed each of us a bouquet. I raised mine to my nose and inhaled and rubbed the soft petals against my cheek. Hattie was more of a wild rose kind of girl, I thought, but then, I didn't know the same Hattie that Gib knew. It was kind of like the sails in the setting sun. If you only saw the sails now, you'd describe them as pink. But if you saw them three hours sooner, you'd know they were white. Maybe later they'd be the blue of night. Gib and I saw Hattie in different lights, which made me a little jealous of him; I thought I knew all Hattie's colors.

"Can I go on the bow?" Gib asked Santi. "Sure," Santi said. Gib handed Hammy the boom box.

The skinny boat was sensitive, and we rocked as he made his way up there. I gripped the railing for balance. Gib turned to face us, eyes downcast until he spoke. "My dad died when I was eleven. Every year on his birthday my mom plays this Van Morrison song called 'Into the Mystic.' If I could play the guitar or sing for shit, I would. Anyway, Hammy?"

Hammy pushed a button. A gentle guitar intro began. Gib turned toward the setting sun. "When he sings the line, 'Let your soul and spirit fly into the mystic,' you can throw your roses into the water. If you want." Hammy stood and it seemed the right thing to do, so the rest of us did.

Listening to the lyrics, I watched the waves. "We were born before the wind . . . Smell the sea and feel the sky . . ." The romance of it was so perfect, it stung my eyes. When the line about the spirit flying came, I leaned toward the edge of the boat and flung the roses with all my might. I let a silent cry go. Hammy's and my hands brushed as we tossed our flowers. Our eyes caught; his were damp, too.

The song ended. Gib returned to the cockpit, sitting next to me, and Santi pulled up the anchor. Without a word, he and Mac hauled the sails back up and we turned toward Pulpit Head, a brilliant trail of red roses in our wake.

When we tied up at the Darrows', the sun hung low and the water glowed lavender. Our shadows stretched long across the rosy sand as we approached the firepit. We put our bags by the picnic table, aged silver. While Mac got a blaze going, Gib and I sat on one side of the picnic table. Santi sat across from us, and Hammy reached for his bag. He handed each of us a large flattish rock, rounded at the edges, and a Sharpie.

"I thought we were using the rocks in our buckets," Santi said.

"These are prettier than the Shelf Island ones," I said. Mine had three concentric white lines around it.

"What's the pen for?" Gib asked.

Hammy stood at the head of the table. His shorts were hidden and he looked like a CEO in his blue blazer. This amused me. "We're using these for the base layer, so the cairn will be sturdy," he said. He held up a Sharpie. "You're going to write on your rock. A word, a few words, whatever. Write something you think of when you remember meeting Hattie for the first time."

We were quiet.

"That's too hard," I said after a moment.

"Don't overthink it, MacGregory," Hammy said,

pointing the tip of the pen at me. "That's not the idea."

Mac joined us at the picnic table.

I thought back to the first day of gym class in sixth grade, to the scrawny, scrappy girl playing scooter board basketball. "Look, I'm a squid!" I remembered her saying before propelling herself backward. I uncapped my Sharpie. *I'm a squid!* I wrote. I drew a little squid. I went to thank Hattie for the millionth time in my head for saving me from joining Emma Rose and the Bobbleheads, but then I thought of my role in that moment.

I chose Hattie. I saved myself. I blinked, stunned, wanting to tell someone. The guys were writing. Gib stuck his tongue out the side of his mouth in concentration.

I saved myself and somehow here I am. Here we are. Survivors.

One at a time, they recapped their markers, smiling to themselves.

"Do we share?" I asked. I was so curious how they'd all remember their first Hattie encounter.

"Not yet," Hammy said. "We need to finish it." He wore the biggest grin, obviously proud of his contribution to the weekend.

"Well done, Sam," I said. "What a cool idea."

He nodded humbly as the others agreed. Next he herded us over to a huge boulder that stuck out from the seagrasses and rosebushes onto the beach.

Santi said, "The walrus."

"Huh?" Gib said.

"She always said this rock was a giant walrus belly-up," Santi said. We considered its round shape, flipper-like outcrops, and creases that shaped a face.

"She did?" I asked quietly.

"It definitely looks like a walrus," Hammy said.

"Yup," Gib said.

Hammy hopped on top of it. "Let's build it here," he said, pointing. "Like he's holding it on his belly."

He directed us to place our rocks, words down, so they formed a circle. "This is very Zen," said Santi. The fire burned orange, the sun had disappeared, and the sky faded to a pearled blue. I hugged my arms. It all felt right.

Hammy handed us our pails. "Do the same on these—any memories, things you want to tell her—and keep building the cairn."

Gib played the Van Morrison CD and we got to work. Mac tended an enormous lobster pot. Meanwhile, the cairn grew.

I'd written *You, on our pear tree*, and *Thunderstorms in the Bat Cave while Red Sox-Yankees on the radio*, and *T-bar fail*, for when she took me on an ancient T-bar ski lift and I'd panicked, trying to exit too early. I face-planted, stuck in the deep snow. We laughed so hard I couldn't get up for a good five minutes. Writing it made me giggle again. *Scaring Hammy at 2:30 a.m.*, and *Flim-flam on the jim-jam (from Scott)* and *Otter's Island (from Spencer)*. For a while I was on such a roll I could have built a mountain.

Adding rocks to our sculpture evolved into a wordless game—a reverse Jenga. Two or three or all of us would be standing around it, pondering the perfect placement. Gib and I waited patiently while Santi tried three spots and finally balanced his so it looked right. I found a cranny for mine, and by then Hammy had come along, and so on. I was putting mine in chronological order and I adored the symbolism of transforming the foundational moments of our friendship into the strong base of our cairn. We were making a spiritually uncrushable monument to Hattie.

When I got down to my last rock, a knot of anxiety tightened in my chest. Hammy had one left too, but the others were finished and used long sticks to poke the fire.

"Hmm," Hammy said, rolling a Sharpie between his fingers.

"I don't want to waste my last rock on something dumb," I said.

"You're overthinking," he said.

"And what are you doing?"

He paused. "Overthinking."

"Busted."

"Yeah. Oh well." He sat up, stretching. He didn't smile, like maybe he remembered he was supposed to be irritated with me.

"Thank you," I said. "For the Pig Roast."

Our eyes locked. He nodded.

"You're my favorite person, Hammy." I hugged him. He was still at first, then finally hugged me back.

After a moment, he uncapped his marker and wrote something on his rock. "What did you write?" I asked.

"I wrote *The Summer of Sam and Reid.*" He left me at the picnic table.

Right then a gull landed on the table, startling me. It stood so close I could see a purple scar across its scaly yellow leg. "Aren't you brave," I whispered.

Unblinking, it leaned in and cocked its head, assessing me with one golden eye. We stared. I barely breathed. It dipped its head three times, then swooped off, ghostly in the twilit sky.

I stared at my rock, the same pale gray and white as the gull, a perfect oval. Something about the way it fit into the palm of my hand, cool and ancient, made me strong.

I wrote, *I am Netherworld Reid of the Scottish moors. You made me Brave.* Gripping the rock, I rose to crown the cairn.

Over dinner, we told stories. Water balloon wars. Driving around the island before anyone had a license. Mr. Tomten. A ten-year tennis rivalry. Pool hopping. Portrait paintings that she swore had moving eyes. Sailing races. Stealing pot from her brothers. Dares from when she was eight, ten, twelve, and a few weeks ago.

"We're at this little tourist grocery in town, and she's

all, 'Gib, I dare you to ask the lady behind the counter where they keep the sexual lubricants.'"

"She did not," I said, my hand shooting to my mouth.

He nodded.

"Did you?" asked Mac.

He nodded again, breaking into an embarrassed smile.

I cackled.

Dinner involved plastic bibs and smashing lobster claws with rocks. I resisted sharing the topper of all stories: how Hattie set out to lose her virginity one night and ended up with Gib Soule falling in love with her. It didn't seem funny anymore. She never wanted to fall in love, and that's what was most confounding. Helen was onto something there. Maybe you can't let down your guard too much when you're already wrestling an octopus.

When we had nothing but piles of broken red shells and bald corncobs, we took an unplanned moment of silence. Night had arrived completely, rippling with stars. I caught myself sighing in the satisfied way Hattie did after a huge laugh.

Mac left the picnic table for the cooler and came back with a bottle of champagne, skillfully holding five plastic flute stems between his fingers. "Reid, kindly do the honors." He handed me the bottle. I hadn't opened champagne before, but if ever there was an occasion to learn, this was it. For light, I turned toward the fire, unwinding the wire that held the cork.

"Point it away from your face!" Santi said, so I did.

I pulled the cork, but it stuck tight.

"Twist it a little," said Mac.

I did, turning toward them without thinking. *Pwump!*

They ducked, pivoting simultaneously toward the seagrass behind them. Mist rose off the bottle in my hands.

"Jesus," said Santi.

"That felt pretty badass."

I poured, misjudging how quickly the bubbles overflowed. There's exactly five flutes in a bottle, turns out, allowing for spillage.

Hammy stood. "To the memories."

We clinked the plastic flutes together, and the fizz of champagne prickled my tongue. I'm not gonna lie. I liked it.

After bagging up the trash, Mac opened another bottle and we stood around the fire. The orange glow of it caught the bubbles in my cup, racing each other to the top.

"My turn," I whispered.

Beside the fire, the night seemed too dark to see the *Alice in Wonderland* path I knew cut through the dense shrubs toward Pulpit Head. But away from the fire, the moon hung low and big, and the ocean amplified its light enough to reveal the way. I carried my bag of secret sky lanterns in one hand and my champagne flute in the other. Santi carried another two bottles, telling us his mom bought it by the case because it's all she drinks.

"I like your mom," Gib said.

"Cheers, Mrs. Herrera," said Hammy.

The path climbed, curving through foliage. My heart beat loud. Bats darted over the bushes, but instead of fear, I felt a shiver of witchery.

The trail opened up to the field of Pulpit Head. A thin, quiet cry pushed its way out of me. I was here. Her stepping off place.

The boys walked past me, except Santi, who put his hand on my shoulder. I thought he'd say something, but he pressed his lips together and nodded. He took a few steps forward, then turned around. He nodded again, his hands out wide, face pained but smiling.

"She loved it here," I said.

"She did."

He waited, and put his arm around me. We fell in step together.

All of us, then, stood at the edge, watching the waves pitch and rush against the rocks below. It was so powerful and beautiful and wild.

"It's ironic," I whispered, "how alive it makes you feel."

Santi squeezed me closer. "Maybe that's the point," he said.

We hugged.

I squared my shoulders and breathed evenly. Mac poured a round of champagne. I rested mine in a tuft of grass. "Sam?" I said.

He pulled his attention from the waves and looked at me for a second before replying. "Yeah."

He helped me spread the lanterns on the ground. They came out of the package flat and looked like the white paper bags you'd get at a takeout place—the big size. Crazy Bert back at the Dancing Newt assured me that if we released a bunch of them simultaneously, it would blow our EVER-LOVING MINDS. He said, "My advice is this: release one. Get a feel for how it works. Have the rest lined up and ready. Then let 'em go! Like a fleet!" He swept his arm through his imaginary scene, apparently watching them fly. Then his eyes clapped on mine, twinkling. "Oh, that will kick SO. MUCH. ASS!" Bert also set me up with a bunch of Bic lighters, thank God. I could've blown my entire plan.

Hammy and I crouched side by side, laying the lanterns in rows.

"Is that good?" he asked, straightening them and standing to admire his work. I glanced at the other boys, chatting back near the path.

"Sam," I whispered.

He looked up.

"I love you, too." And I pulled his face in for a soft kiss.

I'd stunned him speechless, and I smiled. "Help me pass out the Bics," I said, handing him some.

He laughed, and shouted to the boys.

They filed in line, and I showed how to shake air into the lantern and light the fuel cube. "Hold it like this," I said, demonstrating, "until it feels like it wants to fly."

"We better take off our ties," Mac said. "Fire hazard."

I tried to take a photograph in my mind, the four blazer-clad boys standing poised in the moonlight, floppy lanterns in one hand and lighters in the other.

"Light 'em," I said.

I held my Bic to the cube. It flared. The balloon part drooped close to the flame. "Oh, shit!"

"Where'd you get these things?" Santi asked. "If they catch fire, jump on them."

Don't fail me, Bert! I eyeballed the space around me, so I could drop and jump, but the balloon took shape.

I glanced at the line of us. All the lanterns stood aglow. "Okay." I took a shaky breath and steadied my heart. In a loud, clear voice I said, "Hattie, you belong with the stars, above the clouds." Just like our Georgia O'Keeffe painting. Tears ran down my cheeks, but I couldn't wipe them away. I sniffed, and smiled, feeling my arms rising. "Let go."

The balloons ascended, spirits lifted by the deep blue night.

We let them go again and again, stirring champagne bubbles into the starry sky. The boys hooted, but I was quiet. I was correcting her mistake. Her mistake of stepping off to fall. I was defying gravity, sending her up to the immense, unknowable somewhere that waited to catch her.

"I'll always love you, Hattie," I whispered, launching

another lantern. On my last one, I think I said out loud, "Be happy up there, friend," but I'll never know for sure.

The lights drifted out, over the ocean, the first ones now just small fireflies, valiant little sailors crossing the boundless vastness of forever.

Acknowledgments

They say writing is a solitary business. Bringing a book to life, however, is anything but. I'm so thankful for the talented women who ushered this one into being. Thank you to my agents, Allie Levick and Bri Johnson. You are the *perfect* chaperones for Hattie and Reid's incredible journey, and for mine, too. I'm so lucky! To my wonderful, patient editor, Karen Chaplin: knowing how much better this book is because of you makes me humble and forever grateful. I wish I could paint a sky full of O'Keeffe clouds over Manhattan for all three of you. Heart-shaped thanks to the rest of the team at HarperCollins: Alexandra Rakaczki and Jessica White, Catherine San Juan, Jacquelynn Burke, Ebony LaDelle, and Audrey Diestelkamp. Thank you, Michaela Goade, for the gorgeous cover! And Aless Birch and Cecilia de la Campa of Writers House, I love that Reid and Hattie are seeing the world because of you.

My writing friends are a bona fide superpower collective. Julie True Kingsley! My critique partner, my retreat codirector, my riotous, rollicking, semi-psychic friend. Your instincts are unparalleled, and I'm so fortunate you share them with me. Lynda Mullaly Hunt, you had me at the platypus analogy. Your heart is generous, your insight remarkable, your sense of humor ridiculous, and my life is better for knowing you. Kim Savage, you are a crazy, evil genius and I'll haunt a writing retreat with you any time! Jenny Bagdigian, your clearheadedness during my plotting woes delivered me from the abyss. The way you connect with my characters combined with your attachment to 80s music makes me certain we would have com*plete*ly rocked high school. Good thing there's time to make up for it. To the other Knights of the Long Table: Janet Costa Bates, Liz Goulet Dubois, Jen Thermes, Laurie Smith Murphy, Carlyn Beccia, Mary Pierce, Brook Gideon: I kneel before you!

I couldn't possibly forget my nonwriting friends, so generous with their time and expertise. To Faith Barnes, thank you for lending your keen professionalism by reading multiple drafts to vet my handling of the sensitive topics of teen grief, suicide, and mental illnesses. And Trisha Brink, I so valued your professional input and enthusiasm for the project. Tracy Greenwood, your editing eye remains peerless, and your nautical know-how priceless, but it's your steady friendship I love the most. Maryjane Johnston, you're the kind of friend everyone should have but very few do. Shelly Haffenreffer, you always know when to prod a girl and are the world's best tea buddy. Also, to my favorite high school critique squad, Helen Vaughan, Vivian Sullivan, and Olivia Emory, you are so honest and brave—the best kind of early readers a writer can have.

Thank you to the earth angels who help us care for Jack, especially Dave Crockett, Kayla Brant, Hope Duncanson, Hannah Bynam, and Katie Taylor. *You* made this book possible and make my heart bigger.

I appreciate my family beyond the stars. To my parents, Jim and Betsy Kelly, nothing means more than sharing this milestone with you. Pat Lewis, I hit the mother-in-law lottery. I cherish your wisdom about writing and all else. Kim Chapdelaine, you taught me to laugh from my first breath, and your intuitive heart helped shape this book from the beginning. Torey Chapdelaine, who else can I text the question: "What's a good synonym for badass?" Jimmy Kelly, we are creative twins born five years apart. It's all ahead of us, Captain Howdy! To my beautiful babies, Betsy and Jack, you bring me so much joy—everything is for you. And, Paul. You have cheered me, critiqued me, and given me endless hours to pursue my dream, always, always, always with love in your heart. We are the best kind of team.

Author's Note

Dear Reader,

I care deeply about the mental health issues raised in this book. Still, I never imagined I would write a novel centered around them. I hope you have not been touched by suicide in your life, seen the devastation it can have on families and loved ones, felt the ripple effect it can have on communities for years. Few things challenge the human spirit like losing someone you love or care about to suicide. I know this personally, and I wish I didn't.

I wrote *The Stepping Off Place* to help myself process the suicide of a lifelong friend. She was hilarious, independent, athletic, and confident. We were so close, I think we actually leaked into each other's very beings as we progressed through high school, and we kept each other laughing well into adulthood. Writing this book was a way for me to grieve and to confront what scared me to my core: that a person can at once be so funny and fun and beautiful, have all manner of creature comforts, *can be loved by many*, but also can secretly be suffering a sadness so immense, it's unimaginable to those who have never experienced major depression. To the person inside depression, it can seem like an unstoppable fog bank—distorting and disorienting, a suffocating, endless gray despair.

The Stepping Off Place started as a rallying cry to *myself.* I wanted to explore how we who are left trying to make sense of a shattering and seemingly senseless loss, can come out the other side of that fog bank with our human spirit intact. Because I believe that we can—maybe not as the same person, but as someone who can carry on with the messy business of living a life, with all its joys and heartaches, loves and losses. Maybe, we are someone with a new eye for recognizing when someone's sadness—even our own—is getting too big to handle without help.

Because, there is help.

There is hope.

While researching, I discovered that "Depression is among the most treatable of mental disorders. Between 80 percent and 90 percent of people with depression eventually respond well to treatment. Almost all patients gain some relief from their symptoms." (Source: *psychiatry.org*) I hope *The Stepping Off Place* promotes constructive discussion around mental health and suicide so we can normalize the conversation. We so need to normalize the conversation! It will lead more people to seek treatment.

I am inspired by these two organizations leading the charge to diminish the stigma. Not surprisingly, they involve teens taking action.

The Yellow Tulip Project (www.theyellowtulipproject.org) in my home state of Maine has a "Smash the Stigma!" campaign, featuring teens sharing their own stories about coming through depression. The Yellow Tulip Project invites teens to open chapters of the organization in their schools.

Project Helping (www.projecthelping.org) in Colorado used scientific findings around the mental wellness benefits of volunteerism to launch a program that links teens with meaningful local volunteer opportunities. A project board of opportunities makes signing up to help as easy as tapping your screen, and you can contact the "Volunteer Concierge" to add opportunities for people in your community. (This is when I love the internet.)

Maybe the next organization will be led by you. You are a precious, precious gift, and have much to share with the world.

With love,
Cameron Kelly Rosenblum

If you are struggling, or know someone who is, please call the National Suicide Prevention Lifeline for free, confidential help, 24/7, at 1-800-273-8255, or find the chat lifeline at www.suicidepreventionlifeline.org. You can also text HOME to 741741, the Crisis Textline (www.crisistextline.org).